The
Bartender's Secret:
A Cruise of Deception

Other Bella Books by Jody Valley

A Venomous Cocktail
Twisted Minds

About the Author

Jody Valley's first two novels in the Kera Van Brocklin mystery series, *A Venomous Cocktail* and *Twisted Minds*, take place in Michigan. This novel of her trilogy, *The Bartender's Secret: A Cruise of Deception*, takes place in Alaska. Its setting comes from an adventure cruise that Jody and her wife took on a small ship that followed the inside passages of Alaska. Shortly after being aboard, Jody told her wife, "This ship would be an excellent place for a murder." Not exactly a settling thought for her wife, but that thought did give birth to *The Bartenders Secret: A Cruise of Deception*.

Jody loves Michigan, the state in which she grew up. After college, she moved around to various parts of the United States and finally returned to Michigan and has lived there for the past thirty years. She and her wife have a small cottage in northern Michigan on a scenic quiet lake where Jody does much of her writing, and her wife does her art work. They have two Cavapoo dogs, Daisy and Lucy.

Recently, Jody celebrated her thirtieth year of commitment to her best friend and wife, Elaine. They were able to legally marry five years ago. Together, she and Elaine have four adult children, three daughters and one son, along with one daughter-in-law and two sons-in-law. And to their delight, they have three wonderful granddaughters, Layla, Ella and Eowyn. The author says, "All our kids are great and wonderful adults. Our three amazing granddaughters add so much flavor and texture to our lives."

Jody spent twelve years as a clinical social worker, working at a mental health center and in private practice. She has worked with the LGBTQ community, both as a counselor and a workshop leader in the areas of coming out, self-esteem, and relationship issues.

All her life, Jody has been an activist, being upset early on by seeing the inequalities of life. She has been standing up and fighting for equal rights starting with the Viet Nam war, for women's and LGBTQ rights, as well as racial equality. In the past few years, she's been active and passionate about protecting the planet and an active leader in the Resistance against the Trump regime.

The
Bartender's Secret:
A Cruise of Deception

JODY VALLEY

BELLA
BOOKS
2019

Bella Books, Inc.
P.O. Box 10543
Tallahassee, FL 32302

Printed in the United States of America on acid-free paper.

First Bella Books Edition 2019

Editor: Chris Paynter
Cover Designer: Kayla Mancuso

ISBN: 978-1-64247-080-2

Acknowledgments

I want to thank my wife for going with me on our adventure cruise to Alaska where I got the idea for this book as well as a great time. Not only that, she was a huge help to me as an initial reader and editor. I also wish to thank Jane Chemacki for being a beta reader. And for my editor, Chris Paynter, for her editing prowess, and to the staff of Bella Books.

Last, I couldn't give life and expression to the characters that roam inside my head if I didn't have the internal peace that I derive from having such a loving and supportive family.

Dedication

To my loving wife, Elaine.

PROLOGUE

The ocean's waves rocked the small ship as it headed out into the night. The storm resounded through her, intensifying her distress, escalating her anxiety. The open window above her bed—a few yards off the ocean's surface—invited the mixture of briny water and rain, sprinkling her face.

She licked the salt from her lips.

Lightning stung the night sky, allowing momentary glimpses of the cramped lodging, in disarray, unkempt...

Like her mind...

Like her life.

Wherever you go, there you are.

Those words echoed in her head and reverberated in ripples. She'd offered that platitude to many a client. Now, it stuck in her craw.

She'd left her job, her home, her twin sister, her best friend, and her girlfriend. Left them all back in Michigan to take a job on a small adventure cruise ship in Alaska. She left because if she hadn't, she would've burst out of her skin and splattered.

Her life was too tight, pinching her. She needed to breathe and figure things out.

At the beginning of the cruise season, her past had moved over, made room for her to focus and learn the ropes. But with competence came space, a vacuum that allowed self-doubts and confusion to suck back in, jangling her nerves, preying on her spirit, and dumping her into depression: a self-absorption that blinds.

Is that why she hadn't seen it? Hadn't questioned?

Was it even true?

A spear of ice pierced the base of her spine and released chilling needles that pricked her core.

She pulled out her diary from the wall-side of the bed where she kept it hidden. Her entries from the last weeks recorded her day-by-day slip back down into the emptiness and sadness that she'd climbed out of through the new challenges of her job.

And now this.

Did she even dare record her anguish, her fears, her anxiety?

With fatigue trumping anxiety, her eyelids grew heavy, and she tucked the diary back in her hiding spot. She rolled on her side, balled up like a fetus, and surrendered to the tossing and rocking of the waves.

Her eyes closed and sealed as she drifted off.

Until a scream ripped through the dark.

She sprang up.

It seemed to come from the deck above her, toward the bow.

She poked her head out the window just as something fell from above and smacked the water's surface, and watched as the waves quickly gulped the foreign object. She only caught a brief glimpse and couldn't be certain, but the shape of the falling object appeared to be a human form...

My God!

She ripped her body out of bed and tore up to the ship's bridge.

CHAPTER ONE

Kera

"It's your break, Kera."

Vinny's voice pops me out of my trance. I was deep in thought but whatever it was is gone, now—nothing new about that. This is the second game I've won tonight against Vinny, my partner in crime, literally. He's the only employee in my business, Kera Van Brocklin Detective Agency, but he's also my good friend and pool partner. I'm aware that multiple kinds of relationships with one person are not advised, but it works for us.

Vinny digs into his pocket and pulls out quarters. Our agreement is, whoever loses has to pay for the next game, so it's on him to feed the table.

"You're going to send me to the poor house, boss."

I rack up the balls, let loose on the cue ball, and send a packed triangle of stripped and solid colored balls scattering over the green felt surface, smacking into each other. A solid sinks.

"Why is it that when you break, you almost always get the solids?" Vinny takes a swig of his beer and sits down on a chair.

"I never noticed." I wonder how he keeps track of such things or why it even matters. I study the lay of the balls on the table and calculate my best shot.

Vinny and I play pool at least two or three times a week, right here at the Out and About Bar, Lakeside City, Michigan. Given the size of our town, we're lucky to have a gay bar, although a college here does help raise our queer population. We agreed this morning to come early so we could warm up for our regular Thursday night tournament that we've played in ever since I returned from Iraq.

"I have a mind for detail," he replies to my not noticing that I tend to get the solids on a break. He sits there tapping the handle of his cue stick on the floor in rhythm to the music of the Zac Brown Band blasting throughout the bar. He reaches down with his free hand to give some love to Lakota, my Rottweiler/German Shepherd service dog.

"That's right, you do." I appreciate Vinny's ability to remember minutiae because I'm not all that good at it, and in my line of work details are important. My notepad serves as my memory, that is if I think to write it down. Along with a minutiae-gathering deficit, I have a mild case of ADHD, recently diagnosed by the VA. My twin sister, Deidre—her friends and I call her Dee—says it's a bit more than mild and that everyone who's ever known me is aware of it.

Whatever.

I sink two more balls but muff the third shot. So, I plop down in a chair on the other side of Lakota and run my fingers through her fur. It's part of my therapy. Petting Lakota calms me down. In response, my furry buddy rubs her muzzle against my leg. It might be weird, but I love it when she does that. I got Vinny to thank for my pooch. He's the one who trained Lakota to help me deal with my post-traumatic stress disorder (PTSD), one of the *perks* I'd acquired from the war. Training service dogs for vets is just one of Vinny's talents that I appreciate. He also gives me big discounts at his store, Vinny's Gun and Knife Shop, not that I'm into lots of guns. I'm not. I'm mostly just a looky-loo and visit his shop to shoot the shit.

"Okay Vinny, get to it, let's see you run the table. You need to up your game for the tournament. Didn't you get your beauty sleep last night?"

"As a matter of fact, I didn't," he snickers.

"So, I take it your date went well."

"Indeed, it did." His smile is filled with satisfaction. "But as you've pointed out, I'm paying the price tonight." Before I can get him to say more, he asks, "Have you heard anything from Dee lately?"

"No, not a lot, but that's by design. I'm trying to give her space."

"Space? Does she want that?"

"It seems so, and it's good for her to have some time to be by herself, figure things out. She told me she's never digested all that's gone on in her life. Being a social worker, I think she took on everyone else's problems and ignored her own—'stuffed them' is the way she put it to me." I take a swig of my IPA, Bell's Two Hearted Ale. They have it on tap, here, thanks to me.

"Yeah, like not knowing whether or not she wants to be with women or men," Vinny says. He hits the cue ball and sinks a difficult shot.

"That's more like it."

"What's Dee's tally now, men versus women?"

"I'd hardly say some of them were really relationships, more like brief encounters, but I haven't kept count. If I did, I might accidentally mention the number and it would piss her off. She's aware that the amount of relationships she's had is a problem but doesn't see her gender flipping as an issue. She says it's not about which gender but about the person. At least that's what she says, but you know my thinking on that one."

"Everyone knows your way of thinking. You've said it a thousand times, many different ways: Since you two are identical twins and you're lesbian, that's what she must be too." He slammed another ball into the corner pocket.

"Yup, you'd think she'd get it, wouldn't you?" I'm laughing but I seriously believe, no, I'm convinced that Dee is lesbian, full blown, and not bisexual. Period. She just can't face it, not for very long at a time anyway. When she's with a woman for so long, she bails. Up next, a man. Then she's not happy with a man. Nope. So back she trots to a woman. It'd be funny if it weren't sick, and if it weren't my sister. She's seriously got issues in that respect.

Vinny's smiling his I'm-humoring-her smile.

I ignore it and take a swig of my ale and add, "But I do understand her need to get away. Hope it's working for her."

"So, what are her issues, if she thinks it's not her sexuality?"

"Dee told me, when she was applying for the Alaskan job, that she's never dealt with our parents' deaths. Mom died when we were not even teens yet. As you know, our dad died way too early in his life, and unexpectedly. Then her husband's betrayal and death. Losing her unborn child. Jesus!

Vinny stops his play. "Yeah, when you add it all up, she's been though the shitter all right."

Besides that, I know she's spent years worrying about me, even before I went into the army. "After Mom died, she took on trying to keep me from getting into trouble, not easy for a twelve-year-old kid taking over a mother's role—and at that, she was only minimally successful."

Vinny nods in agreement, along with a snicker.

I ignore that and move on. "I've often wondered if she went into social work to try and be successful in changing somebody." The poor kid was trying to deal with me. It kind of makes me sad, though sad is not a well-developed emotion in me. It's too painful to face…so says my therapist.

Vinny lines up his next shot.

I don't think he's listening anymore to my mental health musings, but I continue, nevertheless.

"Anyway, when the army sent me to Iraq, I think that episode did her in. She'll never forgive me for that one." I see that Vinny has finally fucked up and sunk the cue ball after an impressive run, so I set down my mug.

"By the way," Vinny grabs his beer, sits, and slaps his feet onto a chair, "I have an appointment to get inked tomorrow."

"Where the hell are you going to put it?" I poke Vinny in his chest with my cue stick and let it slip down his arm, "You have tattoos all over your chest and back, as well as running up and down your arms." I laugh. "I honestly wonder where you're going to squeeze another one in."

Though short, Vinny is a burly, strong guy, about three inches shorter than I am, which makes him about five-seven. And he's more body than legs, proportionally speaking. His dark hair extends to his shoulders, falls in his face, so he's constantly brushing the mop back in order to see what he's doing. I've told him he should clip it back, a bit, at least get it out of his eyes. Frankly, he's a good-looking guy under it all, though I don't tell him that.

He's staring at me, now, waiting for my punch line, so I hand it to him, "I suppose you could start on your legs, although there's limited space when it comes to them." Vinny laughs, but he shakes a shaming finger at me. Insulting each other is how we show our love.

"My legs are bare canvases, needing some artwork, and there's more room than you'd think."

"Yeah, just enough length in those stumps to keep you off the ground," I say, "but not much room for pictures."

He cocks his lips up to one side, like he's considering the next insult he's going to lay on me.

"Hey," Ally Davis, the bartender, yells over to us, "Do either of you need another brew?"

"Yup," Vinny answers, "both mugs empty, and we can't have that, now can we?"

I nod in agreement but know I should probably wait on another drink. I'm trying to watch how much I have before the tournament starts. I don't want to get blitzed and not be at my best, but come to think of it, this would only be my second brew. So, I'll be okay. I've developed a formula to get me to the right state of relaxation—as I like to call it—on pool nights. It turns out that weed—PRN—and a couple of drinks before the game, then no more than two an hour while playing works best for me. It'd taken a while and a few bad calls before I perfected my recipe for a successful game night, and I won't have a hangover the next day when I have to teach my Friday taekwondo class. There's nothing worse than kicking and punching with what feels like rocks bouncing around in my head. I was hungover when I went for my fourth degree in black belt. It about killed me.

I hear someone behind me. I turn to see Ally with two frosty mugs. "Special service tonight, at least before the crowd shows up," she says.

Ally's been the bartender here for years. She's a priestess for her Wiccan coven, dresses alternative with spiked hair, piercings, and peppered with tattoos. She's a walking billboard for counterculture. I love her look.

Ally and I go way back. She gives me office space here—that is, any available table or stool at the bar. I can indulge in weed in the backroom, sometimes she joins me. It couldn't be any more comfortable, convenient, or cost-effective for me—unless she provided me free beer. I meet my clients here, never bring them back to my lighthouse residence. My sister and close friends are the only ones who are welcomed into my home space—and of course my sweetie, Mandy, who has logged a lot of time there. Mandy and I don't live together because I have a need for mucho alone time, a retreat where I can hole up, block out the world. She understands that but would definitely like to cohabitate. That's my goal, to someday live with her. She's a wonderful, beautiful woman. Vinny says I don't deserve her. He's right.

"Hey Kera, are you going to shoot or not? My hot stick is cooling off, waiting for you." Vinny takes his mug from Ally, glugs down half of it, and wipes his mouth with the back of his hand.

"Cool your heels, Vinny." I concentrate on how I'm going to sink two balls with one shot, so I will have the eight ball in a doable spot.

A few years back, Vinny started working part-time with me when I needed extra help for some jobs. Now he's full-time. As far as his shop is concerned, he's hired another person to tend the store so he can work for me. He enjoys sleuthing and I needed more help because my business has picked up. Vinny's a natural at snooping, which is the bread and butter of my cases: wayward husbands, wives, lovers, blackmailing, and insurance companies that want me to spy on folks they believe are pretending to be disabled. Only occasionally do I get an interesting meaty case that I can sink my teeth into. But it's a living and I don't have to answer to a boss.

I can see the bar trade has picked up, along with pool players toting their cue cases as they come through the door.

"Let's finish up," I say to Vinny, "it's almost time for the games to begin."

* * *

I step into my house, set my cue case down on the floor by the coatrack. Lakota heads toward the little room that connects the residence to the lighthouse. Hearing her claws click up the steel steps, I know my huge pup is on her way up to the lantern room in the tower. Lakota loves going up there. Most often it's the first thing she does when she comes home. From that vantage point, she's able to see out over Lake Michigan and watch the vessels' comings and goings—at least that's what I think she's doing. Even in the night, movement can be tracked by the ships' lights. Come to think of it, she's probably more interested in the air dance of the gulls.

I plop down on the sofa, spread out lengthwise, barely able to keep my eyes open. The lantern light overhead bothers me, so I click it off. I converted that old lamp to an electric one when I first moved here. I've been determined to retain the original 1800s nautical decor of the lighthouse keepers that have come before me. To be clear, I'm not a lighthouse keeper of old. Really not a keeper at all, since the tower is automated now. My job is to keep an eye on the place, try to prevent vandalism, do any minor repairs. For that, I receive free rent.

I look at the time on my phone and realize my sweetie must be in Juneau by now. Our plan is that Mandy will call me tomorrow when Dee's ship docks there from its first leg of the cruise. At that time, I will be able to talk to them both because they'll have cell phone coverage. Mandy has been so excited to be able to hop on the second half of the voyage, the return trip that goes from Juneau to Ketchikan via the inland passages. My sister was able to arrange it, though it's too bad that she'll still have to work the cruise. But she assured Mandy they will still have plenty of time together, and there are lots of activities for Mandy to participate in when Dee's working. Damn, I wish I could have gone along but I've already taken a lot of time off this past summer, camping and hiking. It would be unfair to Vinny to cover for me when he hasn't had any time off all this year, especially since he'd like to travel around Michigan so he can vendor at some of the gun and knife shows this September.

I miss Mandy already, but I'm glad she could go. I'm anxious to know how Dee is doing. At first my sister seemed to like her job on the ship, but the last time I talked to her, underneath her fake—I believe—cheerful tone, I could hear something else, like she was depressed, or something was wrong. I remember telling her that it sounded like something was not right, but she denied it, then her tone perked up a bit more. She should know better, neither she nor I can keep things from each other, not for long anyway. The good thing is, if anyone other than me can pry something out of Dee, it's Mandy. Mandy's a lawyer who possesses those kinds of skills. And besides, Mandy and Dee are close friends and share things. As a matter of fact, Dee considers Mandy her best friend—other than me, of course.

I hear my cell sing out. Digging it out of my pants' pocket, I notice Mandy's name on the screen. Hmm, it's a little early for her to be calling me. Maybe she's missing me too.

"Kera, honey," her voice sounds grave, "Dee was airlifted to the Juneau hospital, yesterday. I haven't seen the doctor yet, so I don't know her condition. But I'm here with Dee in her room right now."

"She's okay, right?" My heart is thumping so hard, it could fly out of my chest. I couldn't stand to lose my twin sister. It'd be like half of me died—more than half.

"Yes, yes. She's in and out of consciousness but not lucid when she's awake."

"What the hell happened to her?" My gut churns like I'd swallowed a box of nails.

"Oh honey, I'm so sorry. They're saying she tried to kill herself."

CHAPTER TWO

Mandy

The door to the hospital room cracked open, widening slowly. Mandy watched as a face with aviator sunglasses peeked around the door. Kera stepped in with Lakota by her side, followed by an elderly woman she didn't immediately recognize. Soon she realized who it was by the woman's hippy dress style, long gray hair, and ever-present Detroit Tiger's baseball cap. Moran Brady was somewhere in her late eighties. She was Kera's shaman friend and, most importantly, her mother figure. Mandy had no idea that Moran would be joining Kera but was glad to see her and, frankly, relieved by the elderly woman's presence. Moran was a stabilizing figure in Kera's life, which Kera certainly needed, especially when she was under stress. Like now. Mandy didn't put it past Moran to have insisted on coming with Kera.

Mandy got up from the bedside chair and hugged Kera then embraced Moran and whispered in her ear, "I'm so glad you're here. Kera didn't mention you were coming too." She turned to Kera. "My God. I didn't believe you when you said you'd get here by today."

Kera removed her sunglasses and ran her fingers through her short auburn-brown hair. "Private plane, private pilot. A vet friend of mine flew us. It was the only way I could get here fast enough and bring Lakota with me."

The dog raised her head with the mention of her name.

"Not someone from your PTSD group, I hope." Reading Kera's expression, Mandy knew she was right about the pilot. She flashed Kera a disapproving glance.

Kera ignored her and slipped over beside Dee's bed. "I'll tell you later. First, I need to know how my sister is doing."

Meaning that Kera didn't want to talk about it so was telling her to drop it. She figured it was Rob Crandall who'd flown them to Alaska. He owned a small charter airline company. She knew Rob, or more like heard of him, from Kera. He was in her PTSD group, and they'd become friends. Rob was even more unpredictable and reckless than Kera could be. Just two months ago, on a planned personal trip, he'd crashed a plane on take-off. Luckily, Rob sustained only minor injuries, but the plane didn't fare as well. At the time, Rob was experiencing a flashback from his days in Iraq and reacted as if he were in his army helicopter, instead of a small jet passenger plane in Michigan.

Mandy realized she needed to let go of how Kera got there. Everything turned out okay. Kera was here safe and there were more important things to concern herself with now. She watched as Kera leaned over and kissed her sister on the cheek, while Moran scooted her chair up to the other side of the bed.

"Have you been able to speak to a doctor?" Kera gently rubbed her sister's shoulder.

Mandy lowered her voice to almost a whisper. "She has a head injury from her fall, but they don't know the extent of it."

"Jesus." Kera shook her head. "It's a wonder she can sleep. Beeps and other noises coming from the machines connected to her. And all the goddamned tubes going in and out, everywhere..."

"She's in a medically induced coma. The doctors decided to place her in it after I talked to you. They're worried about brain swelling from the blow to her head."

"For how long?" Kera blurted out, obviously rattled.

"They don't know exactly." Mandy put her hand on Kera's shoulder. "It depends on how long it takes for the swelling to go down."

"Jesus," Kera repeated. "Anything else?" She took a deep breath and blew it out.

"Incredibly no, not that they know of anyway. Well, her left ankle is badly sprained." Mandy lifted the sheet to expose Dee's lower leg. "The X-ray showed no break. That's pretty much it except for the scrapes and bruises you can see on her legs, arms, and face."

"Were you able to talk to her before she was placed into the coma?"

"Yes and no. She was pretty much out of it when I got here. She muttered some things but wasn't coherent."

"Did she say anything about what happened?" Kera put her hand on Dee's chest, as though she needed to confirm for herself that her sister was breathing.

"I talked to the EMT who was part of the rescue crew. He said he was told that she left the ship by skiff with a group for a scheduled hiking trip on land. Sometime on the hike, Dee stopped at a place near a cliff overlooking the inlet and said she wanted to meditate there. According to what was relayed to the EMT, Dee told the rest of them to go on with the hike and she'd rejoin them on their way back. But when they'd returned to where they'd left her, they didn't see her until someone looked over and saw her lying on a small ledge that caught her fall." Mandy shook her head. "I guess if that ledge hadn't been there, she'd have gone down all the way. No chance she'd have survived."

"Holy shit." Kera swiped her forehead with her hand. "I don't get it. Why in hell do they think she tried to kill herself?"

"Apparently, members of the crew were concerned that she'd been depressed and isolating herself. In the last couple of weeks, she barely came out of her cabin except to eat and work. And when tending bar, they said she wasn't herself, friendly and joking with people, as she usually did. So, they figured she probably hadn't really gone there to meditate as she'd claimed, but to kill herself."

"Jesus, Mandy, we both knew she was down. I could hear it in her voice on the phone. And I thought that maybe she was upset about something, but she kept denying it." Kera began pacing then stopped and looked at her and Moran. "But that depressed? That upset? Enough to want to kill herself? I don't buy that. Then, maybe I don't want to believe it. Jesus, why wouldn't she tell me? God damn it, why wasn't I more persistent with Dee and insist that she let me know what was going on?"

"I know, honey. We both missed it, at least the severity of it, if indeed that's what happened. It's still just speculation, still an unknown."

"Isn't that why you were coming to see her, Mandy?" Moran interjected.

"Yes. Kera and I both agreed it would be a good idea for me to spend some time with her, and Kera didn't feel like she could get away, so—"

"Still, kill herself?" Kera shook her head.

"I know," Moran mused, "it doesn't seem like something Dee would do."

Mandy could tell that Kera had disconnected from the conversation when she started pacing again. She watched Kera for a moment, trying to decide whether or not to lay more on her right now. She figured she might just as well get it all out on the table.

"The EMT mentioned hallucinations too."

That stopped Kera in her tracks. She turned around and stared at Mandy like Mandy was making that part up.

"The hiking guide from the ship told the EMT that she'd been hallucinating about something, not on the hike, but sometime earlier." Mandy said. "The EMT didn't know when or what they were talking about but did ask me if she happened to be on any meds or been taking any kind of drugs. The hiking guide from the ship didn't know."

"Mandy, they can't be talking about my sister. This shit about Dee is getting worse by the minute." Kera sat down and put her elbows on her knees. She cradled her head in her hands as she stared at the floor.

Lakota rubbed alongside Kera's leg then settled down next to her.

"I know. All this sounds like they're talking about someone else." Mandy shook her head. "It just doesn't sound right. Good god. We both knew she was feeling down. That's why we thought it important I come—"

"I know, I know. She was really glad you were coming. Making plans for things you two could do. So why would she do something like try to kill herself?"

"I agree. She was excited when the captain told her he'd let me come aboard for the second half of the cruise, and I could stay in her cabin with her. Hmm, maybe it was because he knew she was depressed and was grateful to have someone who might help her get out of it."

"Is this a cruise for gay people?" Moran asked. "I mean, I'm wondering if she got involved with someone, and it went bad for her. I know she was upset about all the relationships she's had."

"No, it's not just gay people," Mandy said. "Well, mostly it is, but straight folks can come on if they're relatives, allies, or gay friendly. But to the second part of your question, Dee would've told me if she were involved with someone else, I'm sure, given I'd be coming on the ship with her. At least I think she would have."

"She's going to come out of this, right?" Kera asked. "Dee's the stable one. If anyone is supposed to do something stupid or nuts, it's me."

Mandy almost laughed at the unlikely self-revelation that had escaped from Kera's lips. Kera nailed it. She and her sister had inadvertently changed the nature of their respective roles. It was usually Kera who was in trouble or hurt, and Dee was the one stuck with worry. Now, Kera was getting a dose of what Dee had to endure most all their life.

Moran got up, went over to Kera, and pulled her into a hug. "Dee will be all right. She'll get through this. She has a strong will. And we're all here for her now."

Mandy thought she could see Kera's shoulders drop and relax a little. Then Moran led Kera over to a chair and gently sat her down.

Mandy joined them, rubbing Kera's back. "Dee's doctor said she should be okay, and they'd be bringing her out of the coma as soon as possible, maybe in the next day or two…three, at most, I think she said." The doctor hadn't really said that, but what good would it do to tell Kera that the doctor hadn't been particularly reassuring.

"My mind is racing, flitting around." Kera put her hand on her forehead. "When it stops for a second, I get stuck on the *why*. It isn't like Dee to do this sort of thing, no matter what. If for no other reason, Dee wouldn't do that to me. I know she wouldn't. Dee's the responsible one, the one who holds things together, not blasts them apart. She can be counted on, always. As our Mom would say to her friends, "Deidre's the reliable twin." Kera looked up at Moran, then to Mandy, her eyes intense. "Dee's the one who always does things right, even when life goes wrong for her. So, no. I can't believe Dee tried to kill herself. Something's wrong here."

"I agree, honey. It's hard for me to believe Dee would do that." Mandy kept moving her hand gently over Kera's back. "I believe her intent was to sit and meditate, not kill herself. She copes with things that way, always has. But I do keep wondering if it could be that she got too close to the edge, maybe slipped and fell off."

"But Dee wouldn't go that close to the edge, at least not on her own accord, I assure you," Kera said. "She's scared of heights. Terrified really. She was so fearful that on a few occasions when we were together at places with big drop offs, she would have a fit, even if I'd go to the edge to look over. It scared the shit out of her just to have me close. Her comfort level wouldn't let her go—or me either—more than ten feet from the edge, maybe not even that close."

Moran glanced at Mandy and said softly, "Do you know of a place—somewhere else in the hospital—that's private so we can talk? People in comas can often hear what's being said, and if Dee can, we don't want to upset her."

Mandy nodded. "You're right. There's a little room across the hall, one that Dee's doctor used when telling me about her condition."

"Good. I'm sure it's more comfortable, too. My old back doesn't appreciate the chairs they have in here."

Mandy pulled on Kera's arm and encouraged her to get up. She felt her resistance to move. "Don't worry, honey. She'll be okay. We'll be close by and will come right back here after we're done talking."

* * *

Returning to the consultation room with bottles of water in hand, Mandy overheard Kera speaking to Moran, "…maybe, maybe not, but I need to get on that ship before everyone disembarks in Ketchikan. I need to find out what happened up there on that cliff. They have five days left of the cruise. They'll be pulling out of port tomorrow."

After Mandy passed out the drinks, she sat down on a worn overstuffed multi-colored chair with a faded-out design situated across from an equally worn matching sofa where Moran and Kera sat.

"Honey, what were you saying to Moran?"

"I'm going to get on board my sister's ship and find the asshole who did this to her. No one gets to do this to Dee. No one!"

"Don't you think that's the job for the police?" Moran patted Kera's thigh to try to calm her down.

"Yeah, it should be, but it's not been reported as a possible attempted murder. So, there's no reason for them to get involved." Kera turned to Mandy for conformation. "Right?"

"Right, and more to your point, just before you both arrived, I talked to the captain after he'd spoken to her doctor here at the hospital. The captain said that he was sure it was a slip and fall accident. He never mentioned to the police that there are others who believe it was a suicide attempt."

"That settles it. I have got to get on that ship."

"Why do you think," Mandy asked, "the captain will allow you on board to pry around and try to find a possible killer in their midst? Like I said, the captain is treating it as a slip and fall. It's obvious he doesn't want to give any credence to others who believe it was an attempted suicide. I'm sure he doesn't want to believe it could be foul play. I mean, why would he?"

"Because it could be." Kera expression indicated either she didn't understand Mandy's point, or she did accept that explanation.

Mandy spoke as softly as possible as she attempted to keep Kera's rising voice from getting any louder. "It would be bad press for his company and also not good for him, not to mention causing fear and ruining the cruise for his passengers."

"Okay, okay, I get that." Kera hesitated then said, "I have an idea, so hear me out. First, I have a few questions." She stood up and started her pacing again. "Do you have any idea what the crew and passengers know about Dee's condition?"

Mandy considered the question. "Nothing really. Hospitals have privacy rules about revealing information about patients. When I talked to the ship's captain, I met him in the lobby, not in Dee's room. Oh yeah, before I forget to tell you, the captain and the hospital are under the impression that I'm Dee's sister. At the time, I didn't know the extent of her condition and didn't want to put her job in jeopardy, so I told the captain that she suffered a concussion and I had no idea how serious it was. I also said she'd undergo more tests later."

"Do you think they want her back on the job?" Kera asked.

"I think so, he—by the way, his name is Captain James—seemed genuinely concerned for her. At one point, he mentioned that they had some guy to stand in when Dee took breaks, but they didn't have another trained bartender. They'd only be serving wine and beer without one, if she couldn't return. Apparently, there's some company rule about what you can serve without a bartender. It might be a union thing. I don't know."

Kera's stared at the floor and shook her head. "I wonder what everyone else on the ship knows about all this."

"As far as what the passengers know about what occurred, Captain James said he informed them before he come to the hospital that she'd gotten too close to the edge and slipped and fell. He said he would talk to the passengers and crew, alike, and warn them about that kind of danger. He did mention that most of the crew believed she tried to commit suicide, but he was certain they were wrong and advised them against spreading a hurtful rumor like that about Dee. And I can't help but believe he thought that having one of his crew try to commit suicide would be more unsettling to both the crew and passengers than the slip and fall scenario."

"You're sure that the captain didn't get any information about the severity of Dee's head injury?"

"Dee was getting an MRI when he was here," Mandy said. "But he couldn't wait any longer and needed to get back to his ship before the results came in. The short answer to your question is no one really knows her condition other than it's a concussion and she might be able to come back to work."

"Good." Kera lips turned up, ever so slightly, in a partial smile. "For starters, Dee hasn't told anyone in Alaska that she has an identical twin. She apologized when she told me that but explained to me that it was because she needed time to be on her own. She didn't feel required to talk about her life and, in our case, what it's like being an identical twin. People really get into that shit."

Mandy and Moran nodded.

"She just wanted to be herself, not part of something else, like one of 'a set of twins.' That's how she put it. I get that, I really do." Kera turned to and addressed Mandy, "And I'm sure they've heard from Dee that you are joining her on the cruise. So, when I step onboard that ship with you, they'll believe I'm Dee."

When it finally settled in what Kera meant, Mandy felt her jaw drop. She glanced over to see the same shock on Moran's face. Finally, she was able to utter, "My god, Kera, how do you think you'd be able to pull that off? That you're Dee? Sure, you have the physical identical thing happening, but you don't know anyone on the ship, or Dee's job, or your way around, or really, anything? Besides, you look fine. Dee doesn't look so great right now and no one will expect her to be able—"

"But Mandy, no one has seen Dee since her fall, so no one knows the extent of her condition except the hospital staff and us. As far as the captain is concerned—thanks to what you told him and the fact that he didn't see her—she might well come back to her job. Right?"

Mandy hesitated. "Well, right, if she were able, but—

"Okay, with a little theatrical first aid work here and there, I could take her place. They have no idea what to expect when she returns or how she'll look or be."

"Kera, Dee wears her hair long and yours is so short. It's not like you can grow it out in—" She stopped then said, "I suppose they could have cut it in order to deal with your—Dee's—head injury."

"Right, no problem about that. Also, you told me that after they'd spotted Dee, on the ledge, they hustled everyone back to the ship except the guide who led the hike, and he only waited until the EMTs and rescue unit got down to her, right?"

Mandy nodded.

"He didn't see her when they brought her up and doesn't know the extent of her injuries. He left before they got her off the ledge." Kera looked to her for confirmation on that point, and when she got it, moved on. "The ship was ready to continue on to Juneau to make it on schedule. Isn't that what you said?"

"Uh-huh." Mandy hesitated to make sure Kera had gotten all the facts right and in order. "Other than what I just told you, I didn't mention anything to the captain about her injuries…Wait, I did tell him she'd sprained her ankle."

Kera squinted then said, "No problem, I can handle that. The important thing is that, having been airlifted she arrived in Juneau before everyone else on-ship. Therefore, only the EMTs and rescue squad saw her up close. Just the hospital staff is aware of her condition, and none of them can legally say anything, even if the captain would ask."

"You're right, but it wouldn't be easy to fake being Dee, and—"

"Nothing much in life is easy, honey."

Mandy could see that Kera's plans were building and heading out on a runaway trajectory, leaping over any objections or concerns.

"I'll add crutches for my sprained ankle, and I bartended in college like Dee did. I'm familiar with the work. Even if it takes me a bit to figure out their set-up, I'm confident that I can pull this off and—"

Mandy shook her head. "You don't know the ship or where things are or the people she's met or where her cabin is…well, so many things that Dee would be familiar with, and you're not. They'll start thinking something is off."

"I haven't had time to work out every last detail. I'm glad that you're questioning and playing devil's advocate." Kera put her hand on her chin as she thought. "It'll be challenging, for sure, but how else would I be able to get aboard to figure out who did this to my sister? I need to know what really happened to her."

"Oh my." Mandy was horrified that she was viewed as playing the devil's advocate, when what she was trying to do was dissuade Kera and come up with another option or plan. "What if you just tell everyone that you're her sister and you're able to take her place while she's recovering. Like you said, it would make sense being you have bartending experience, too. Then you wouldn't have all the stress of trying to fake being her."

"It'll be better if I pretend I'm Dee, not her twin sister. Dee had a relationship with people—good or bad or mixed. But whatever was going on, it was something that led her to being almost killed. For me to figure out who might want to hurt her, I need people to believe and treat me as though I am Dee."

"Kera," Moran broke in, "if this was an attempt to kill Dee, she probably knows who pushed her, and whoever tried to do this to her knows she's in the hospital, wouldn't this person leave the ship and skedaddle, knowing she'd report it to the police?"

"Well, if I find out that someone has suddenly left after Dee's so-called accident, then I'll know who to go looking for, won't I? The only way I'm going to get answers is if I can get aboard and start asking questions."

"Or," Mandy broke in, "Dee might have been taken by surprise from behind and didn't see her assailant, so maybe that person isn't worried about being seen by Dee and is still aboard. That would be so dangerous for you—"

"But—" Kera blurted.

"And another thing," Moran continued, not allowing Kera to cut her off, "if she had been pushed off, would it not seem strange that Dee or the hospital hasn't reported the incident to the police?"

"Maybe, probably, but I think I can cover that." Kera gave them a thin smile.

"And how's that?" Mandy's words came out full of sarcasm and doubt, but she couldn't help herself. She was terrified as she envisioned Kera running off doing something really dumb, when what they should be focused on was getting Dee well enough to take her back home to Michigan and getting on with their lives.

But Kera was undaunted. "Dee has a head injury, right? I'll let people know that, if they don't already. I'll say I don't remember what happened to me—whether it's from the injury itself or the trauma of the fall, it doesn't matter. I'll let everyone know I believe what people are saying about me, either I tried to kill myself or maybe I slipped and fell. Either way, I'll appear unsuspecting of anything else. So, I wouldn't have any reason to get the police involved."

Mandy was beginning to realize that no matter what she or Moran said to try and poke holes in this crazy plan, Kera was determined to do it and nothing would bring her to her senses.

"I think it'll work." Kera glanced back and forth, waiting for a reaction from Mandy or Moran.

The old woman looked as stupefied by Kera's single-mindedness and determination as Mandy did. But Mandy realized once Kera was determined to do something, that to dissuade her, it had always been like stopping a runaway train heading down a mountain.

"I got to do this." Kera turned to Moran. "But I need you to stay with Dee and watch out for her. You and Mandy are the only ones I trust to be with my sister at a time like this."

Kera looked Mandy's way. "You can let the hospital staff know that Moran will take your place," Kera added with a smile, "'since you're her sister.' Hell, you can tell them that Moran is Dee's aunt. They'll probably prefer a relative."

Mandy figured Moran was still in as much shock over Kera's plan as she was, since she didn't say no. "If you go through with this, uh, plan, I could still be here with Dee. Moran could go home, if she wanted to, but Kera—"

"Mandy, I need you to come with me. Remember, you came here to get onboard and be with Dee. It's important we stick with what Dee and you were planning. It helps validate that I'm Dee."

Oh god, Mandy felt like she'd just climbed aboard Kera's runaway express. Then a horrible thought occurred to her. "Posing as Dee will make you a sitting duck, honey. If someone did try to kill Dee, and if I were that someone, I'd be really worried about Dee's remembering what happened to her. Memory sometimes comes back, you know. I'm sure a killer would be aware of that fact. And having the person who tried to kill Dee worried about her memory returning will put Dee's life in danger. Well, in this case, I should say *your* life."

"I understand and will definitely be on my guard but having the asshole who did this to Dee worried would actually be a good thing. Hopefully, they'll give themselves away."

By the expression on Kera's face, Mandy could tell that Kera understood that she'd gone too far in scaring the shit out of both her and Moran, because Kera rephrased it. "Don't worry about that. I can handle myself. That's why I'm going to be there, to see who is disturbed about me being back."

Mandy could barely breathe. Kera's attempt at reassuring them hadn't done the job.

Oh god!

"Moran, would you watch after Lakota, too?" Kera asked. "I'd rather not kennel her, and she knows and loves you. I couldn't suddenly show up at my job with a dog. It shouldn't be that long. Hopefully, I'll find something out before the end of the cruise." Kera stopped, took a breath and added, "At worst, it would only be a couple days longer than we'd initially intended on being here. The desk clerk at the rental cabin said it would be available if we wanted to extend our stay. When Dee is better, you'll be able to take her home to her place in Ketchikan, and we'll meet you there."

That seemed to jolt Moran out of her shock. "But, Kera, how do you think you'll do not having Lakota with you? She's a stabilizing presence for you. You need your dog, dear."

"I know, but I can do it. I have to do it. Besides, I've got my weed with me. That'll have to get me through."

Moran appeared to be mulling things over in her head. Finally, she replied with a sigh, "I guess I could do that, if you're so determined and we can't stop you."

Mandy took a deep breath and let it out slowly. She knew she wasn't going to get Kera to scrap this crazy idea. If Kera was set on doing this, Mandy would have to go along and get on the boat. At least she wouldn't be back here on land worrying about what was happening to Kera. She almost laughed at that thought...

No, she'd be there on the ship worried to death about her.

"Honey." Kera cupped Mandy's face and looked into her eyes. "I just know I need to get on that damn ship and find out, one way or another. And I could certainly use you being there too, observing, being my second pair of eyes, helping me find things out. If nothing else, just by your presence there, you'll be validating who I am and my story. After all, you came to be with Dee, and I'm sure just about everyone on board—at least the crew—knows that."

Mandy thought about what she'd told the hospital staff so she could get in to see her. "I'm her sister according to the hospital, but everyone on-ship will know me as her friend. How do I—?"

"No problem. No one from the hospital staff will be on-ship... Wait, did you tell the captain you're her sister?"

"No, but I think someone here at the hospital did because a nurse came and told me he wanted to speak to me. They undoubtedly told him I was her sister."

Kera scratched her head. "Okay, then if it comes up, we'll have to tell him you lied so you could get in to see her—me. Like you did." Kera smiled. "It will be one truth in our magic bag of lies." Kera squatted down in front of her. "Honey, I'm sure Dee didn't do this to herself, and you don't believe it, either. I need to find out what happened, but I can't if I don't get on the ship."

Mandy thought of one more objection, a way to possibly put the brakes on the out-of-control train. "But the medical staff could pull her out of the coma anytime now. Can't we wait a little longer? Just to see if Dee remembers?"

"We don't know how fast the swelling will go down, and I can't wait to talk to her to find out. I don't have the luxury of time. The cruise from here lasts for only a few more days, starting tomorrow. On the last day, everyone will get off and will be on their way to other places. Even the crew will probably be off for a few days before the next cruise departs. We can't be sure it will even be all the same crew."

Mandy shook her head, feeling defeated.

"I can sell this package, I'm sure. Telling stories is all in the acting, looking convincing, not flinching under pressure. I'm good at it, honey. Believe me, I do it all the time."

Mandy frowned. "I don't know whether to be happy about that little piece of information."

Kera held up her hand as though she were taking an oath. "Only in my line of work, honey. I've always told you the truth about things, I promise. Scout's honor." Kera smiled meekly and added, "To the best of my ability, counselor."

"I just bet you have," Moran mumbled, rolling her eyes. Her face turned serious. "You need to take your spirit guides to be with you, my dear, or I guess I need to say, dears."

Mandy wasn't into shamanism like Kera was. But at that moment, she knew she needed some kind of guide to get her through what she'd just signed onto.

CHAPTER THREE

Mandy

Mandy opened the door to Dee's cabin on the ship and stumbled over the lip of the raised threshold. From behind, Kera's hands grabbed her before she crashed to the floor.

"Steady there, girl." Kera abandoned one of her crutches to catch her.

"Wow, I wonder how many passengers kill themselves this way before the trip even begins." Mandy pulled back her long blond hair that had spilled into her face and tucked it behind her ears.

"Holy shit! Small quarters for one person, let alone two." Kera picked up the crutch from the floor and took off her backpack that contained a few changes of clothes and whatever else she'd quickly cobbled together before she left Michigan. "I hope no one who spotted us coming in wonders where I got this backpack, since it's not Dee's. She wouldn't have one coming from the hospital."

"You could have bought it in Juneau before boarding," Mandy said.

Kera unzipped her backpack and ruffled though it. "I know my wallet has to be in here somewhere." In the process, she grabbed her wadded clothes, one by one, tossing them on the bed. "God, these things are really wrinkled. Dee wouldn't wear anything like this. I wish I had a dryer to—"

"Really, Kera, there's no reason you'll need your own clothes, anyway. You'll have to wear Dee's things since you are, as of now, her. Your bodies are the same size, but your wardrobe certainly is different." Mandy dropped her duffel bag by the bed. Dee had told her about the limited room in her cabin, so she'd packed accordingly.

"I know, I need to be femming it up a bit." Kera looked around. "I wonder where her clothes are." She glanced around and then under the bed. "Here they are." Kera pulled out a plastic storage unit containing Dee's clothes. "She doesn't have a lot of shore clothes anyway, mostly work uniforms in here." She held up navy blue shorts, long pants and polo shirts with turquoise trim, all sporting the Alaskan Venture Cruises' logo—a ship with a whale breaching close by.

"Yup, that will be your outfit for now." Mandy shoved her bag under the bed as well. There wasn't any extra room anywhere that she could see. It was a double bed, as advertised, but *double* was stretching it. The bed looked more like a single.

Kera checked out the bathroom. "Wow, you can pee and shower at the same time. Good thing I can multitask." She snickered.

Mandy couldn't help but crack a smile. Since returning from Iraq, Kera was lucky to stay on one task, let alone tackle another at the same time. According to Dee, Kera had attention deficit issues before her war experience. But they'd gotten decidedly worse except when Kera was focused on something of great interest to her, like her pool game or her investigative work. Then she hyperfocused. Luckily, their time on this ship should fall into the category of investigation.

Mandy was grateful that the only acknowledgement anyone paid to their boarding was a smile or a nod. She'd easily found their cabin, thanks to earlier in the morning. She'd met with the captain, lied to him, and told him that "Dee" couldn't make it, as she was dealing with some last-minute details. So, Dee had sent her. At that time, he'd shown her around the ship and questioned her about Dee's physical and mental abilities to perform her job. He was relieved that she was returning to her position but had lots of questions. Mandy explained the nature of Dee's amnesia. She told him it encompassed her whole time in Alaska, that she'd be unfamiliar with the ship and anyone she'd met, and that the doctor said that Dee may or may not regain the memories she'd lost.

"Well," Kera interrupted her thoughts. "So far so good. We are on-ship. I'm glad the captain talked to the crew about my lack of memory and need for space."

"For sure. People let us come through without bombarding us with questions or whatever, but did you notice that weird looking man staring at us as we walked through the dining room? He didn't take his eyes off us."

"You mean that skinny weird dude with huge glasses?"

"Yes, he reminded me of Pee-wee Herman but with bone-rimmed glasses. You know, the guy who had that kid's program on TV."

"Oh yeah, I remember him. Bizarre dude." Kera started changing into the ship's uniform.

"I'll tell you what, that guy couldn't keep his eyes off us. And that peculiar smile plastered on his face. Creepy." Mandy speculated that it probably seemed he was staring at them with a strange smile because she felt guilty, being part of a plan to try to pull one over on the entire ship's crew and passengers.

"How come Dee has a cabin on the deck with the passengers?" Kera asked as she pulled up Dee's uniform pants and fastened them. "On the printout diagram the captain gave you of the ship, it showed the crew quarters down below."

"She won the crew's lottery, of sorts."

"Lottery?"

"Some guests didn't show or cancelled," Mandy explained. "Apparently, when that happens, the captain lets the crew draw straws to see who gets to have the missing passenger's cabin—kind of a morale booster, I suppose. Anyway, Dee won this time. That's why I was able come this trip and share the cabin." Mandy pointed to the double bed. "Otherwise, there wouldn't have been a place for a second person to sleep if she were in the crew's quarters."

"She never mentioned that." Kera pushed Dee's storage unit back under the bed.

"Dee told me about it. By the way, the captain said that the doors only lock from the inside, so if we're both out of the room, the door is not locked."

"I don't like that at all." Kera's frowned. "Shit, I'll have to walk into this room not knowing who might be in here. I guess passengers are on the honor system, but can't say as I trust that arrangement, especially since we're looking for someone who's tried to kill my sister. I wonder why they only make it a one-sided lock. Hmm, maybe it has something to do with emergencies. Well, I'd better make sure that anything that would identify me as *Kera* is well hidden, like my wallet. Good thing I brought my leg holster gun. Glad these pant legs have wide legs, they're like sailor pants." Kera scanned the room. "Doesn't look like there are many places to hide things."

Mandy's stomach churned. She wasn't used to being deceptive as apparently Kera was or as Kera claimed. Good god, how could she remember to even call Kera, *Dee*? She took a deep breath. If they weren't both tossed overboard for being impostors by the end of this day, they'd still have the rest of the trip that would be undoubtedly one challenge after another.

My god, I don't know if I'm up for this.

"Can you help me with this stuff?" Kera held out the bag of first aid supplies. "I think the bandaging is coming loose right here." She pointed to the top of her head.

"Sure, let's put some new tape on it."

When they'd left the hospital, the plan was for Kera and Lakota to hightail it to the rental cabin that she and Moran had secured when they first got there. Kera wore sunglasses and Moran's baseball cap so that the crew and passengers that might be on land wouldn't spot her. In the meantime, Mandy and Moran searched the city until they'd found supplies to help give Kera the physical appearance of having fallen off a cliff.

When they joined Kera at the cabin, Moran's theater make-up skills she'd gained at a local theatrical company, came in handy. They'd done an excellent job of making Kera look like she'd taken a nasty fall, decorating Kera in a similar bandaging job the hospital staff had done on Dee. Even though no one on the ship had seen Dee, Kera had insisted on it, saying something about keeping as close to the truth of things as possible. However, Dee only had part of her head shaved—around the huge wound. But between the three of them, they couldn't think up a good reason why the hospital staff would shave part of her head, then cut the rest of

Dee's hair short like Kera's. So, they decided to shave Kera's head completely. If asked, the story would be that they sheared all her hair due to the blood and matting, as well as the need to search for any more possible bruises and open wounds.

"Stop that," Mandy said. Kera had put her arms around her as she worked to repair the head bandage. "How can I concentrate on fixing this if you're going to be doing that?" Mandy loved the feel of Kera's hands gently caressing her. It definitely had a calming effect. The problem was that it led to other feelings, ones that weren't appropriate right then, probably not until they got off the ship—if they were lucky to get off alive and in one piece...

Anxiety crept back in.

"Well, maybe you have to be my friend when we're out there," Kera nodded her head toward the door, "but when we're in here, you're back to being my sweetie."

"I don't know if I can handle that. It could seriously mess up my different feelings I have for you and your sister, one a lover, one a friend. Just think about it. I need to see and think of you as Dee during the day and Kera at night. Being you're identical twins, it could pose a big problem for me. I might inadvertently transfer my romantic love for you to your sister and—"

Kera put a hand over Mandy's mouth. "You're way overthinking it. And you better not!" Kera snickered. "Or I will have to send my sister away, far, far away, way farther than Alaska."

Mandy finished her first aid work and placed the tape back in the bag. "There, that should stay. But seriously, honey, it does feel weird. Maybe we shouldn't even think about making love while—"

Kera took hold of Mandy's shoulders and looked into her eyes. "What, you have a problem with my shaved head? Have I lost my looks with no hair?" Kera mocked.

"Well," Mandy patted Kera's bandaged head, careful not to disturb the wrapping. "I have to say, you certainly have a nicely shaped head, but it's not your best hairdo." She giggled.

"No, it's my hairless do. But I could wear Moran's baseball cap to bed, brim backwards if that would help." Kera grinned and kissed Mandy's forehead. "How do you expect me to resist your beautiful green eyes and luscious body next to me. Do you think I'm made of steel, no feelings, a robot?"

"No, but I wish I were." Mandy felt the stress she'd lost in the moments of their playful banter return.

"Huh?"

"I wish I had nerves of steel, then I would have a lot more confidence in pulling off this crazy plan of yours." Her body tensed, and her nerves rattled inside of her. Surely anyone will be able to notice it. Kera might be used to this kind of stuff, but she wasn't. Not that she would mention it to Kera, but how could she ever even think of making love under all this stress? This must be like stage fright, but the stakes were so much higher.

"You can do this, baby. I know you can."

A knock on the door was quickly followed by a male voice. "Deidre, you're needed out at the bar."

Mandy felt her heart pound, fast and hard. She searched Kera's face for a sign of worry. Although Kera's lips turned up slightly in a faint smile, Mandy thought she detected a hint of apprehension in her eyes.

"Fuck, I got to go. I'd hoped to have a little more time to get my bearings, check some things out. Oh well, I'll—"

"Another thing, Kera, you need to clean up your language. Dee hardly ever swears, and then only under extreme stress. She doesn't have your sailor's vocabulary."

"Shit...I mean, damn...darn it." A naughty little-girl smile crossed Kera's face, then she got serious. "I was about to say that it's not really necessary for you to come out just yet, so why don't you hang in here, get yourself settled in, and rest until it's time for dinner."

"Not on your life. I'm going with you." As scared as she was, she wasn't about to leave Kera out there by herself. Besides, the sooner she faced it, the better, she supposed. Or at least, that seemed the right thing for her to do. Her Aunt Margaret, who'd raised her from the time she was in grade school, would have told her that.

"Okay, then. The show's on, baby. It's happy hour."

CHAPTER FOUR

Dee's Journal

Most of my training has been on board the ship, which I like. I had a precious week in Ketchikan before my job began. Gave me a chance to get established in my place and to become familiar with the city. Darling little city. Since I'll be on-ship most of the time, I decided to take a room in a boarding house. It's cheaper than having my own place, and it gives me opportunity to get to know some other people who live at the house. Met two women already who work on ocean cruises, though not on mine. From what they've told me about their jobs, I don't think I would like to be on those mammoth ships, either as part of a crew or a passenger. I'm so glad I chose this small adventure cruise line.

It's not been that long, but so far, I like everyone I work with. Captain James has been very nice and helpful and has understood what it's like to be thrown into a job without much time for training.

I've worked the bar two shifts now and am grateful for my college bar experience. I'll also be learning other jobs, which I'm sure I'll enjoy because much of it will take me outside. Yeah!

Though I don't miss hospital social work, I really miss my friends and Kera. But still, I'm glad I'm here in Alaska and on this ship. I think I'll be so busy with work and have some great experiences, so I shouldn't get too homesick, hopefully. All my life I've been known as the conservative twin. I admit that's true, so this is a big move for me. But I can do it! I can do it! Kera has always been the adventurous one. Our mom said I'd probably grow up and live next door to her. Had she lived, I probably would have done just that. Even so, I did take the traditional path and got married. Looking back in my rearview mirror, it was a big mistake in my life. But I guess, that's what rearview mirrors are for—looking back, which is what I need to do more of. If I were my own therapist, I might ask myself how all the deaths in my life have affected my relationships. Sometimes it feels like all too much to deal with.

I've promised myself not to get involved with anyone while I'm here. I won't, I won't, I won't. I mean it this time! I want to break my pattern of short-term partners, as well as deal with my grief issues. I have to get my head on straight before I'll ever get involved again—even though I haven't completely given up on my former girlfriend, Casey. I guess she's former. At least we agreed to think about our relationship, put it on hold, maybe take it back up in the future sometime. Or not. She's a good person, but I need to sort my life out, get healthy, before I share it with anyone. I think if I can do that, I'll feel better about myself.

Getting tired, so signing off for tonight. Big day tomorrow.

CHAPTER FIVE

Kera

My plan hurts for details, vital ones. It's as though I'm in a play without a script, without a character list, without prompts, without knowing what's behind the final curtain. I wish Mandy would've stayed in our cabin and rested for a while. It would've done her some good...maybe. But no, she insisted on coming with me on my first bar shift. I glance at her as she walks beside me toward the lounge. She's tense, rigid, like a tin soldier. I know she's trying not to let everyone notice that she's scared to death. I hate putting her through this. I really do. But I had to bring her along on the cruise, not only because it'd been Dee's plan all along and there are people on-ship who would find it fishy if she weren't here. But also because I can use—*need* is a better word—the extra pair of ears and eyes, especially Mandy's. She should be good at that. It's second nature to her. Because she's a lawyer, she has to listen to and evaluate clients, witnesses, and jurors. Of course, the stress of this situation may make it an entirely different ballgame for her.

Mandy warned me not to swear *unless I'm under extreme stress*. Holy fuck. How could I be under anything other than extreme stress being here on this ship, worrying about my sister in the hospital, pretending to be my sister and needing to respond to her name, having to watch my language, trying to femme up my personality. And top that off with trying to be more gracious, more deliberate, all so I'll appear to be Dee. I know that I also must slow down my speech pattern. Jesus, slow down everything. Dee moves five miles per hour below the speed limit. If all that weren't enough to make me grind my teeth at night, there's someone here who tried to kill her.

Now I'm Dee, the target. As of yet, I don't have a goddamned fucking clue as to who that person is. It causes the back of my neck to tingle.

Okay, I need to focus. *Focus. Focus!*

I've got to clean up my mouth, right now, and to do that, I gotta stop even thinking the curse words that are at my ready and waiting to help me express myself. Otherwise, those so-called nasty words of my thoughts will come flying out of my mouth before I can snag them and stuff them back down. God damn it, communication is going to be difficult. I should have brought a fucking thesaurus.

Breathe in, breathe out, breathe in, breathe out... Let me feel my feet connecting with the floor, smell the ocean air...

Focus...

Okay, I'm better. Somewhat.

At least while on the job I'll be wearing the uniform, not femmy things. Don't know if I'll need to wear anything else Dee brought. At least I didn't see anything too outlandishly girly when I checked out her clothes. She mostly brought hiking-type attire. So, I'll be okay on that front.

Then, there's the problem of my gait. As we were leaving the hospital, Mandy tried to change my way of walking. To be exact, she said, "carry yourself more feminine." It's not like I don't know what she means. But me wriggling or swaying my ass or hips without thinking? That will not just tax my focusing abilities but also my feminine mimicking talents. Mandy thinks I overplayed it, exaggerated Dee's walk, like I was making fun of her. To be truthful, I have made fun of my sister, more than once. Like my whole life. I wasn't trying to do that this time. I was sincerely attempting to put Dee's body into mine and let it take over. Luckily, in the middle of our walking practice—which was going miserably—I realized I didn't have to conquer that piece because Dee has a sprained ankle.

I'd be hobbling around and not having to worry about a girly gait. The crutches hinder me, but I got that covered. I'll ditch them after a while, use the cane Moran and Mandy purchased, and then walk with a limp—which I can't believe is ever feminine, no matter who's doing it.

As far as slowing down, my crutches are helping on that front. The cane will too. Maybe the bang to my head made my speech faster. That's what I'll say if it comes up, because I won't be able to remember to slow it down. I speak fast and I'm not sure I could decelerate it for more than five minutes before the unfiltered, backed-up words in my head would shoot out like a bad case of diarrhea.

The last of Mandy's plan for me to appear more like my sister is to be *graceful* and *deliberate*.

I don't even know how to go there.

* * *

There are four or five people waiting in the lounge, watching me make my appearance, or maybe they're always the first to the well for happy hour. At least they're making an effort not to stare at me, but they glance my way, now and then, pretending, I'm sure, that they're not looking at me.

Let's see. What would Dee do? A WWDD bracelet would be helpful. I know, she'd put a big smile on her face and pretend all is well with her. I smile, but my lips can't seem to hold it long enough for me to get to my station to start serving.

Two women approach the bar. Not exactly arm and arm but it's obvious they've got something going on. Their eyes for each other give them away. The tall blonde struts as if those gathered have been waiting for her arrival. The shorter one, brunette with more than ample breasts, swings and sways to the music as she and the blonde move up to the bar. Then the hip swinger glances back, her smile fades into annoyance as she moves to the dish of nuts I've just set out on the bar and starts nibbling on them. The blonde catches the signal and bellies up on the opposite side. Then I see their problem. A gray-haired woman, considerably older, probably in her mid-sixties and stylish, bulldozes through the gathering crowd. She makes her way to the bar and puts her arm around the tall blonde, as if in possession, not friendship. I check back at the bar's nut dish. Mission accomplished. The brunette has moved on.

The bar's setup is standard. The open shelves behind me are where the hard stuff and wines served at room temperature are located. Glasses, straws, mixing sticks, blah, blah, blah. All looks well-stocked. I open the refrigerator to see what brands of beers, sodas, mixes, and chilled wines are in there. Ah, I find a laminated card with the beverages that are available, along with their prices. Oh good. There's a second card with recipes for the mixed drinks. I planned on claiming memory loss for mixing drinks since it'd been a long time since I bartended, but with this cheat sheet I'll be okay.

"Do you need any help, Dee?" Mandy says. She's now perched on a stool at the bar, watching me. By asking me that, I'm sure her intention is to remind me who I am—I know her, and she knows me.

"No, hon…uh, Mandy. I think I got it." Shit, even with her cueing me, I fucked up, but at least no one is close enough to hear my slip. I comfort myself with knowing women often call their friends "honey" or "hon." Don't they? But still, I need to get myself into being Dee. All the way in.

Jesus!

Looking around, I don't know a soul, of course, so it's no time like the present to start to make some acquaintances. I pour Mandy a glass of pinot noir and ask her to go mingle. Learn names, get backgrounds. She gives me her OMG look but then peels herself off the bar stool and starts walking towards a sturdy butchy woman who must be over six feet tall. She has short brown hair with enough product to form it into what looks like a mountain range running down the middle of her head. Dressed in the crew uniform, she stands alone and gives me a look. Surely, it's not that she's attracted to me. Butch women don't hit on me. Then I realize that to her, I'm Dee, and they sure as hell are attracted to her and her sashay. Good thing I've set myself up to hobble around on crutches. That makes me think of another difference between my sister and me. A subtle difference—at least I hope it's not blaring. Mandy says that even though we both have hazel eyes, Dee's eyes have a softness to them. Mine are more intense. I don't see it… Okay, now I start to worry about how the fuck I can soften my eyes. Then I figure the concussion and lack of memory could cause me to look more intense.

Whew!

I check under the bar for some napkins and find them. As I look up, I see some customers approaching. It's past four o'clock, and they're ready to soften their perception of life, probably anxious to see what *she* is going to be like, now that *she'd* either fallen off a cliff or tried to kill herself.

Morbid curiosity, like staring at a car wreck.

I'm hot, sweat oozing out of my body. A small fan I put on the bar is blowing air at me, but it's hard to suck in. It seems like there's a lack of oxygen in the room. I tell myself to breath slow, measured, or I'll sail into a panic attack. Bad form. And besides, it would freak Mandy out, and she's looking to me to be the calm one and in control. After all, I'm the confident one and this is my "crazy-ass" plan, as she's taken to calling it.

Before I can even take my first order, I hear a deep baritone voice enter the area then see that it's the captain coming from the dining room. I know who he is because Mandy described him to me. She was surprised that he wore the same clothes as the rest of the crew, unlike the fancy impressive uniforms sported by the captains on the big ships. He's a large guy, more like huge without being fat, other than a bit of a potbelly. He's well-kept with salt and pepper beard and mustache. His large eyes match the blue that's in his camouflaged Australian outback hat that has one side snapped up and tie cords dangling down from either side. He's one cool-looking dude.

He spots me and is on his way over. He says loud enough for all to hear, "Deidre, we're all so glad to have you back." He flips on a big smile. "Especially those of us who aren't into beer or wine and need the hard stuff to keep our wits about us." He winks at me.

He and everyone within earshot laugh, which loosens the atmosphere. More people are coming up to the bar now, ordering, being patient with the speed of my service. I hobble around behind the bar, my pained facial expression meant to clue them into the fact that I'm hurting. I'm relieved that no one is asking me questions. It's all just news, weather, and sports chitchat. I owe that to the captain since he kept his promise to Mandy and briefed them on that courtesy.

After I've gotten through the first wave of orders, the captain comes over and says in a hushed voice, "How's it going for you?"

"A bit rough," I tell him, "but I'll get through it. Thanks." I figure that says nothing, really, other than what he'd expect me to say and yet leaves things open for all the people and things I don't know.

His smile is one of those you give to a kid who's getting back up on her bicycle after a nasty fall. He reaches over, gives me an encouraging pat on my shoulder. His eyes glued on mine he says, "It'll get better with time." Then, "I'll take my usual."

I panic because I should know what he drinks. Then I realize that of course I don't know. I have amnesia. Relieved and breathing again, I give him a look and shrug my shoulders. Now I'm concerned, paranoid: Was he testing me? Or did he momentarily forget, like people trying to turn on a light switch when they're aware the electricity has gone out. Is he reacting out of habit? Before I can decide, a guy comes up, slaps the captain on the back and says to him, "I bet you're happy to give up that nasty beer and get back to your good ole whiskey and water."

The captain glances toward me to see if I heard the guy and smiles when I say, "One whiskey and water coming up."

"You got that right, Mick," the captain says to the guy.

I give Mick a once-over. He's short, scraggly bearded, head shaved, and almost perfectly formed half-circle ears that jut out ninety degrees from the side of his head. Unfortunately for him, his eyes are planted too close together, barely separating the beginning of a straight nose that follows a narrow path to his lips. He looks like a mouse. I'll remember his name by thinking of Mickey Mouse. Then I decide to think of him as Mick the Mouse so I don't call him Mickey.

Mick doesn't assume I know what he wants, or maybe he changes off on drinks. He glances my way and says, "Hey Deidre, glad you're back." He beams at me and I immediately take to him. He has one of those smiles. "I'll have a draft, Alaskan Lager." His attention returns to the captain. "I fixed the dripping water in cabin ten. It was the air-conditioning."

I hand Mick his mug. Okay, so the mouse repairs stuff. I put a wrench in the hand of my mental Mick the Mouse image and add Bob the Builder's hat.

"Thanks, Mick. You're a genius. I swear there's nothing you can't fix." The captain reaches for the dish of bar nuts that I've just refilled.

I check out Mandy. She's still talking to the butch. They seem deep in conversation. *Come on, Mandy. Move around, gather names and short blurbs, not a fucking life story.* On second thought, I got to believe Mandy is hanging there for a reason. Besides, this woman could easily push someone off a cliff without any problem. As I look around the room, I evaluate each person: Could they or couldn't they? It's certainly not my only criteria for suspicion, but it's clearly going to be one of them. For instance, Mandy's Mr. Peewee doesn't appear to have the body mass or strength to do the deed, so I place him low on my list in this particular category.

A picture of my sister sneaks into my brain, in a coma, lying there in a hospital bed. Someone tried to kill her. Rage harpoons my gut. I feel blood rush to my face and threaten to blow my anger out through the top of my head. I know I need to block that image, fast. My mind is wired in a way that instantly connects with other past scenes of anger and distress and piles on top of it, like the experiences of war in Iraq. And when that happens, my PTSD charges into action, full speed. This is no time for one of my flashbacks. My hand drops to my side as I search for my Lakota. She's not there. I concentrate hard to remember how it feels when I run my fingers along Lakota's back. My fingers burrow into her fur. She's beside me. I tell myself:

Be calm...

She's here with me...

Breathe, breathe, breathe...

I have to deal with my stress by using all my "coping skills." Those are my therapist's words. She's not aware that one of the ways I cope is with weed. That's not something she approves of. I don't care, but I don't tell her.

People who know me think I have no fear, but that's not true. Not anymore. Before Iraq, I was fearless, more like stupidly reckless. Since then, my wiring is fucked up, I run on frayed nerves. Bad fuel. The thing is, I still do stupid stuff, making me appear as though I'm undaunted, but I'm not. It's just that I don't know how to function differently.

I glance around and catch sight of Mandy. She's on the move now, mingling. I wonder how I ever landed such a beautiful woman. Smart, loving, curvy, feminine, perfect in my eyes—and, I've noticed, in others' eyes as well. She doesn't share my opinion. According to her, she has dozens of flaws. But that's not true. When she walks into a room, eyes turn. I love how she moves, more like flows. It's hard even now to keep my eyes off her, but that's okay. Watching her is a distraction that helps quell my nervous energy and takes it somewhere else, although it's inappropriate for my task at hand. How can I do that and worry about my sister and my predicament here on-ship? Faulting wiring, I guess.

"Hi, Deidre." I'm jolted by a voice. "In honor of your return, the chef is making your fave meal. I saw to it myself," the woman says.

"That's real nice of—" I stop, not knowing which pronoun to use—her or him. I try not to appear puzzled about my "fave meal." I try to think of what Dee's favorite meal is, but under pressure, come up short. Besides, her favorite meal here on the ship might not be the one I might remember. Oh well, I'll have to blame it on my head injury, like other things I'll screw up. I assume the late twenty-something, curly strawberry red-haired woman must have some authority. Maybe she heads the kitchen. Cute, like the all-American tomboy girl. Someone you could bring home to mom. That is, if mom's okay with bringing home a female.

"The chef is a she." The redhead has a great toothy smile and the kind of teeth that could bring in a major contract for a toothpaste company.

I tap my head and make a little spin with my finger. "Thanks for understanding my memory problems. I hope it gets better, but the doctors aren't sure." I want the possibility of my memory returning to get around. Let's see who gets edgy with that information.

"I'm Britt." She slips up on a bar stool and holds her hand out. "I head the kitchen staff. I asked the chef to cook your shrimp dish as a welcome back meal for you. We're all so happy you're doing well, but I'm not supposed to be bothering you about all that. So, how about fixing me up a Manhattan."

I shake her hand. Her lips move into a smile, showing off her gleaming white teeth. I think, I'll remember her as Bright Teeth Britt.

"If you need anything or want to know something," she continues, "please feel free to ask me."

We small talk and I ask her stuff about where things are and other questions I have about what-the-fuck tasks I'm supposed to be doing. I look up and see Mandy as she sidles up to the bar next to Britt and asks for another glass of pinot. I introduce Britt to Mandy, remembering she's my *friend* who has come to be on the cruise with me. Of course, she wouldn't know Britt, and it would be natural of me to introduce her around. Britt flashes her glowing smile and tells Mandy she'll be more than glad to help either of us. They start chatting away, hitting all the topics of the getting-to-know you stuff.

In the back of the lounge, I spot Pee-wee. I expect that's how I'll always think of him, even when I find out his real name. Close by Pee-wee, there's the butch who sports the mountain range of hair on top of her head. Pee-wee looks my way, seems like he's saying something about me, because the dyke looks at me too. I quickly drop my gaze to the glasses I'm washing then glance back up again. They're still staring. I can't figure out the meaning behind either one of their expressions, other than it doesn't make me feel comfortable. Beads of sweat form on my upper lip, and I feel my polo shirt sticking to my back.

A lie is one thing. Living in a lie is another.

Makes me paranoid.

CHAPTER SIX

Mandy

Mandy dropped down on the bed, feeling exhausted. It was midnight. Kera was still in the lounge finishing up at the bar. Mandy scooted all the way back as she pulled her feet onto the mattress and kicked off her shoes. She couldn't remember the last time she felt so completely drained. The past few days had done her in—the long flight to Alaska, the emotional stress of finding out about Dee, having to let Kera know about her sister, and then, for the sour cherry on top of it all, agreeing to Kera's crazy plan. Well, she didn't really sign on to it. It felt more like forced to go along. So here she was aboard ship, playing detective, and scared shitless. Already Mandy wondered if this cruise would ever end and, unfortunately, it had just started. She took in a deep breath and let it slowly out.

She'd talked to a fair amount of people in the bar but didn't think she'd gained much in the way of helpful information, nothing that would point a finger at anyone or even cast a shadow of suspicion. Maybe that was all she could expect of the first night—getting to know some folks and gain their trust enough that at some point, someone might say something helpful to her. It was strange, in the elephant-in-the-room kind of strange. People didn't mention anything at all about what happened or even how Dee—or Deidre, as they call her—was doing, physically or mentally. Twice, she almost blew it and referred to Dee as Kera. *Good god, I need to hammer Dee's name into my brain when I'm talking about her or talking to Kera around other people.* She appreciated the captain for keeping his word about talking to folks and preventing them from bombarding *Dee* with it all. It gave Kera a chance to get used to her new role. But Mandy certainly expected that at least someone on this ship—given she is Dee's friend who had just come aboard—would say something to her about Dee's condition, but no one did.

When she'd glanced over to check on Kera, it looked as though she was handling things pretty well, maybe too well when it came to the red-headed woman, Britt. Mandy was certain she was hitting on Kera. That's why Mandy had downed her wine and gone up to the bar for another. She'd cleverly—if she had to say so, herself—gotten an introduction to Britt, then redirected Britt's attention to herself, so that Kera finally moved on to filling orders. She hoped she hadn't been obvious.

There was a gentle knock on the door.

Thinking it was Kera, she called out, "The door's unlocked, come on in, Ker—" *Good god!* Her heart pounded. She'd almost said *Kera. Again.* Whoever was at the door didn't respond, so she went to open it.

"Hi, I thought I'd stop by for just a moment and see how you're doing." Britt stood there, her head slightly tilted to one side, a concerned expression on her face. "I know the situation with Deidre must be almost as hard on you as it is on her."

It certainly was and though Britt had no idea of the all-of-it, the woman's sympathetic words flew under Mandy's emotional radar. They yanked on the strain and anxiety she felt and sent tears down her cheeks. She quickly wiped them away.

"Oh dear, I'm so sorry." Britt stepped in. "Mandy, I know we hardly know each other, but Deidre and I have become friends in the last couple months, not that she remembers, obviously." Britt's lower lip protruded, slightly. She finally said, "It's so hard. She just looks at me like I mean nothing to her, just another person to serve a drink to." She took a deep breath, "I'm guessing you experienced the same thing the first time she saw you, right?"

Mandy nodded. "Yes, I certainly did." That was true. When she'd initially seen Dee in the hospital, she'd had her eyes open, but when she'd taken Dee's hand and tried to talk to her, she had not gotten any more recognition from her than if she'd been one of Dee's nurses. She could relate to Britt's reaction, all right.

"Yeah, it's hard." Britt shook her head. "I knew you'd understand."

"But fortunately for me, after Dee fully emerged from unconsciousness, she did recognize me." Mandy needed to make this real clear. "She has only lost memory around the incident. Well, more than that, pretty much all her time in Alaska. But it was horrible for the time that she didn't know who I was. Still, her situation is very disturbing to me."

"I completely understand and want you to know that if you need a listening ear, I'll be glad to lend mine. I guess I could use someone to talk to myself." Britt quickly added, "but I'm sure you're tired and need to get some sleep so I'll—"

"No, no, stay for a moment. Dee won't be back here for a half hour or so. Maybe you could help me understand what happened to her. No one seemed to want to talk about it."

"Well, I think the captain's admonition against talking to Deidre about what happened has extended to you."

"That would explain it."

"To be honest, the whole thing around Deidre is more than that she can't remember now. Weird stuff was going on before she got hurt that day." Britt rubbed the side of her neck. "Uh, I'm sticking my head out a bit here, I'm not sure I should—"

"If you're worried, I promise I won't tell anyone what you tell me be about Dee or say anything to her, really. I promise." Mandy smiled internally. She really could keep that promise since she'd be telling Kera, not Dee, what Britt had to say. "At this point, I don't think it would be even good for Dee to get the details. She's having enough of a struggle."

Britt nodded. "I agree. I think we're going to have to trust each other on this, and since we're both her friends, I know we want the best for her. Do you mind if I get off my feet and sit? I've been on them all day, and they're killing me." Britt motioned toward the bed, the only place to sit in the cabin's cramped quarters.

"Sure. Take a seat." Mandy sat down next to her. "Anything you can tell me will be appreciated."

Britt seemed to be contemplating what she should share then asked, "Did you hear that Deidre was having hallucinations?"

"Yes, that was reported to the EMT who took care of her, but nothing was said about what kind of, or how many, or how often. It was very puzzling."

"Let me give you some background first before I tell you what I know. I don't know if you're aware, but Deidre has been quite depressed. No one really knows why."

"She didn't tell you why?"

"Like I said, we've become friends, but apparently she didn't feel comfortable sharing that kind of thing."

Mandy nodded. That made sense to her. "Did she share anything that would give you a clue as to why she was depressed?"

"Not really. We got together when we could, mostly talked about our jobs, other crew members, books, stuff like that. In the beginning, she hung out with me and the crew after hours, but that stopped, I'd say, about two weeks ago."

"Did you ask her why?"

"Yeah, basically she said it was her MO. Like periodically, she needed to escape from the world, but that she'd get over it and be back. I tried to honor that but sure missed being with her."

Mandy thought that description of Dee wasn't at all like the Dee she knew. Dee never had suffered from periods of depression. However, from the conversations with her on the phone, both she and Kera believed Dee was feeling down and it was certainly one reason Mandy had come to see her. She had no clue, though, that she was so severely depressed, as Britt had described. What was most puzzling was why would Dee tell Britt that she was prone to bouts of depression? Maybe to minimize her depression and make Britt think it would get better soon? And as far as Dee not confiding in Britt, it would make sense because their friendship probably wasn't to the point that Dee would feel comfortable disclosing her feelings. But Dee didn't tell her or Kera about it, either. In fact, she denied that anything was wrong.

Britt broke into Mandy's thoughts. "I wish we had been at a place where she would've trusted me enough to talk about what was bothering her. If she had, maybe this wouldn't have happened." She shook her head. "If I'd even been there on the hike that day, I would have stayed with her. But we can be grateful she's alive, can't we?"

"Yes, for sure." Mandy thought that if only she'd been able to get on the ship for the first leg of the trip, Ketchikan to Juneau—as Dee had hoped—things might have been different too. She took a deep breath.

"Well, I guess I'll go. I'd love it if we could talk another time, maybe at dinner, sometime when Deidre is eating with the crew." Britt added, "Most often, crew members eat together."

"I'd like that. Before I forget, I wanted to ask you something. I know the captain believes she slipped and fell. That's the company line being put out there. I'm also aware that many members of the crew think she tried to take her own life. What do you think?"

"I wish I knew." Britt shrugged. "In my mind, it could have gone either way. Even if she didn't intentionally jump, it could be she wasn't paying attention to her surroundings and slipped. I got to thinking about that possibility when I remembered that when my sister suffers from depression, she's really accident-prone. Her psychiatrist told us that depressed people are not as attentive to things around them."

"Hmm." Mandy started doubting Kera's insistence that her sister had been pushed off that cliff. Dee was depressed, and though neither she nor Kera believed Dee would do such a thing, it could have been an accident.

"At some point, if it doesn't look like she's going to get her memory back, I will tell her about our friendship...Well, to be honest with you, it was turning into something more than a friendship, but we kept it on the down low. That's due to company policy. She hadn't mentioned anything about me to you?"

"No." Mandy scratched her head. "She didn't say anything about being involved with anyone."

"Well, like I said, we were just at the beginning stage of our relationship, so I'm not really surprised. I wasn't exactly writing home about it, either." Britt's smiled but looked sad. "I sure hoped—still do—that it would turn into something long term."

Mandy could see what Dee had been attracted too. Britt's sweet smile came not with just super white teeth but also with sparkly blue eyes. Now she understood Britt's flirty behavior at the bar with Kera. Britt thought she was in the company of Deidre. It was very reassuring that Kera passed the identity test with Britt, given their relationship.

Mandy heard Kera's voice coming from the hallway, several doors down from their cabin. "I think that's Dee I'm hearing. I—"

"I should leave," Britt said in a low voice. "For now, anyway, I'd prefer you didn't let her know I told you all this. We're not supposed to be 'gossiping' about Deidre with others. I could lose my job if it gets back to the captain. Let's talk more later, maybe at dinner."

"Of course, I understand. I'll tell Dee that you were telling me about the upcoming ship activities they have going on. I'll give you an update on how Dee's doing at dinner tomorrow, okay?"

"Thanks."

* * *

"I see you had company tonight." Kera managed a tired smile and closed the door. "Britt said hi to me when we passed in the hall but didn't stop to say why she was at our cabin. Did you learn anything from her or anyone else?"

"Nothing much from the happy hour or dinner gig." Mandy hugged her. "Mostly just names and what adventures they're going to sign up for. People aren't talking about the incident or you, at all. Apparently, the captain not only told everyone to not say anything to you. They're not supposed to gossip about you, either."

"As nice as that might be under regular circumstances, it's not helpful to us." Kera stashed her crutches and sat down.

"But there is some good news. I'm becoming friends with Dee's latest."

"Britt?" Kera arched her eyebrows.

"Uh-huh. At first, she said they'd become friends, then later admitted they'd gone beyond that. To her credit, she doesn't want to tell Dee—uh, you—about that yet. She figures you have enough on your plate right now but will tell you when she thinks you're ready."

Kera looked thoughtful as she rubbed her chin. "The nuisances of taking my sister's place just keep popping up."

"What do you mean?"

"When Britt was at the bar, I felt like she was sending me vibes, as in sexual. It confused me for a bit since she's so not my type, and I didn't see her as someone who'd be attracted to me, either—

she's too butch. Then, I realized that she's flirting with Dee." Kera grinned.

"She was attracted all right. That's why I came up to save you." Mandy gave Kera a mock frown.

"I noticed."

"I was hoping you wouldn't."

Kera put her arm around Mandy and kissed her cheek. "Not to worry, my dear. You're all I can handle."

"You got that right."

Kera smiled. "I know what I got with you, my love. But back to Britt. Did you get anything more from her?"

"Yes, she talked about Dee's depression and said Dee told her that was her MO and she often needed time to escape from the world, but that she'd get over it and be back. Even better, since she sees both of us as feeling bad about Dee having forgotten who we are—even though she knows Dee has remembered me—she wants us to be each other's support during this time. We're having dinner together tomorrow night."

"That's great," Kera said. "I'm sure you'll get more than I will since I'll be eating with the crew who won't be mentioning anything about what happened. I plan on asking questions, though not directly. It will be from the standpoint that I don't know the routine of things and need to find out the lay of the land, what goes on and when, and my job duties on the ship."

"Oh yeah. I almost forgot. Britt started to tell me about Dee's 'hallucinations' but felt she had to give me background information first. That's when she got into Dee's depression and their budding relationship. I'll try to dig into what the hallucinations were about tomorrow at dinner."

Kera nodded. "Good work, honey. Let's get some sleep. Oh, I didn't tell you about Captain James. He caught me in the hall coming back here. He wants to meet with me tomorrow morning."

"Did he say about what?"

"No. But it makes me feel uncomfortable."

CHAPTER SEVEN

Kera

I feel like I'm taking the long walk to the principal's office—
like when I was a kid and in trouble. I hobble along with my faux
sprained ankle. Captain James said he'd be up on the bridge so
that's where I'm headed. I wonder if it occurred to him how hard it
is to navigate all the stairs with crutches. He probably didn't think
about it, or maybe he did. I'm leery. I wonder if he sees something
that gives me away. It's my nature to be paranoid, and it should
serve me well while I'm trying to pass myself off as my sister.

I'm trying to prepare my responses for any of his suspicions.
Should I act indignant? Confused? Disbelieving? Insist I am Dee?
Or should I fess up and throw myself on his mercy, ask for his help,
and try to bring him into my investigation? That wouldn't be easy
since he undoubtedly doesn't want the possibility of a criminal act
having been committed aboard his ship. He's already made that
clear. But what could I say to get him to cooperate? Blackmail him?
I'm not above threatening but have no dirt on him for a shakedown.
Hopefully, I'd think of something to get him to help me.

I reach in my pocket and feel my small wolf fetish that I carry
with me. It helps me stay in touch with my strength. Somehow my

owl fetish didn't make it with me, so wisdom, on this trip, will be at risk. Moran gave them to me years ago to help me stay connected to my power animals. I roll the wolf around in my hand and feel the smooth coolness of the solid marble figure, hoping to absorb its qualities and power. It helps. But I so wish I had Lakota hanging close to my side. Reaching down and not feeling her near me is like having my right hand suddenly missing.

I make my way upstairs by sticking both crutches together under one arm. That way, I use my opposite arm and hand next to the rail to hoist me up, step by step. For a split second, it'd occurred to me to check around, see if anyone was near. If not, I could scrap the bad ankle act until I got up there. I tossed that idea out and reminded myself that not paying attention to details has sunk more than one ship—my nautical pun makes me smile to myself and releases a bit of stress.

When I get to the top, there are two people in the wheelhouse. One of them is the big butchy dyke, Roni, that Mandy first talked to last night. Mandy told me she's the second-in-command, otherwise known as the staff captain. From what I've observed, this ship functions on a barebones crew. Just about everyone needs to be multi-useful. So, Roni also conducts several of the tours and oversees the water and boating equipment. The other person in the wheelhouse is the captain who is perched on the pilot's chair. He notices my arrival and comes out and escorts me to several freestanding chairs located on the deck. He holds mine to keep it from sliding while I clumsily sit down. Then he grabs the other chair and scoots it close as he faces me.

"That was quite a trip up." I wipe my brow as I act as though I'm catching my breath. Those stairs didn't give me any grief, cardio-wise, but I need him to believe I'm seriously hurt and in pain and that those steps would be a challenge for someone recovering from a nasty nose-dive off a cliff.

He cringes. "Jesus, I'm sorry. My bad. I don't know why I didn't think about you having to deal with using those crutches and having to climb the stairs." He points at the crutches. "I guess it slipped my mind, because you weren't using them behind the bar last night."

"Too hard trying to deal with these things," I told him as I pat my crutches that are balanced across my lap. "Hopping around on one foot is more efficient, though jarring." I smile like I'm a trooper. "I use the bar to steady myself, so I'll have my hands free for fixing drinks."

"I bet it's painful to bang your body around like that." He furrows his brow. "It must take some getting used to, moving around the ship using those wooden sticks. Sea legs on crutches, a whole other skill." It's as though he'd just realized what I might be going through. "Again, please pardon my insensitivity by asking you up to come up here, but I have to say I'm incredibly impressed you made it."

"It's totally thanks to my pain meds," I quickly let him know.

My retrofitted comment about the medication was my attempt to downgrade my supposed superwoman accomplishment. Shit, just about everything I let out of my mouth, or whatever I do, needs to be pre-approved by my charade filter. I need to think things through more carefully. I wipe the sweat off my brow again.

"By the way, since you've had your head shaved and even though you have it mostly covered with all that bandaging up there, you still have bare spots and will need to be sure to wear a hat. Doesn't take long to burn your head when you're outside in the sun. Mick learned that lesson with his bald head. Water does quite a job of reflecting and intensifying the sun's effects."

"I haven't thought of that. You're right." I was glad he mentioned it. I have Moran's baseball cap but forgot to put it back on this morning.

"I'll see to it that you get a company cap that goes with your uniform, if you don't already have the regulation one."

"Maybe I do. I didn't see one but then I haven't really checked out my clothes stash that well."

"Let me know."

I nod. He looks at me like he's trying to see through my skull. I hope I'm not coming off as paranoid as I feel.

"The reason I wanted to meet with you was to see how your first night went for you."

"Has there been a complaint?" I ask. "I thought everyone seemed okay with their drinks, and I pretty much stayed up with the traffic."

"No, no complaints. I just wanted to find out how it's going for you being back on-ship. This has to be a difficult situation for you."

He pulls out a cigar that's half sticking out of his shirt pocket and leans back in his chair, like he's got all day to sit and jaw with me.

I nod, again, acknowledging with all the sincerity that I can dig up and put on my face that it is a difficult situation for me. Frankly, it's challenging to concentrate on impersonating my sister, which I hope isn't the meaning of his remark. I plan on being as guarded as possible, without appearing like I am. I'll offer up nothing unless directly asked, as Mandy suggested. That's what she tells her defendants when they're testifying. I plan to sit back, see what he has on his mind, and deal with it. As I wait for him to say something more and watch him light up his cigar, I can't help but wonder if he's ever set his beard on fire. My mind works that way. It entertains me during life's pauses and helps loosen the knots in my stomach when things are tense...like now.

"I want to make sure you're doing okay. You know, with your horrible accident and, uh..." He's stumbling around, trying not to say what he wants to say, but finally comes out with, "Your injuries and difficulties." He puts his Bic lighter back in his pants pocket.

His stare seems piercing, like trying to poke through my eyes, though I keep them armored. I note his emphasis on *accident*. I know he wants me to believe I had an accident, not a suicide attempt. He takes a long draw on his cigar and slowly blows out smoke. The wind catches it and sends it into my face. It doesn't really bother me. Lots of guys in my unit in the army smoked those nasty things. I'm sure smoking weed has also helped to condition my lungs to the abuse. He reacts quickly, fans the smoke away from me as he apologizes. Then he says, "So, you don't remember anything around your accident? None of it?"

"No sir," I say, then wonder if I should have used the word *sir*. It's a holdover word from the military. A word that can fly out of me in a pecking-order situation like this, but probably not a word my sister would use. Well, maybe. He's a captain and she'd be—

"What do you recall?" He leans in closer to me.

"Nothing." I try not to let his move in bother me, but my heart pounds. When someone hovers in like that, it makes it tough for me to breathe. Worse yet, it sets off my attack mode. So, I focus on my breathing to try and calm myself. I've been living with PTSD a long time now and have my techniques to help me deal. This morning I smoked a little weed. Unfortunately, I still can lose control. When I do, it's not pretty. Not helpful.

"What's the last thing you remember before all this happened?"

"Getting on a plane headed for Alaska." I figure that covers it. It's pretty much what Mandy told him.

"I see." He leans back and arches his eyebrows. "So, you remember nothing else about the ship or your job or your duties, or anything else?"

"Well, apparently my skills are still in place. At least so far, they seem to be. Although I had to acquaint myself with the setup of the bar. It's people's faces and my experiences and present environment that have fallen through a black hole for me." I'm being very careful not screw myself by saying something that will get in the way of what I do or say in the future. I think I did okay with that.

"Uh-huh." He nods ever so slightly, sucks in on his cigar, and lets it seep out between his lips and swirl around his head.

I don't say anything more. I'm waiting for his next question and focus hard on keeping a neutral expression on my face. All the while his eyes scrutinize me.

What is he thinking?

"I wanted," he finally says, "to make sure everything's going okay for you, and we're not working you too hard. We can always shorten your hours if that would help."

"No, sir. I think I'm okay." Shit, I said *sir* again.

By his deadpan face, I have no idea if my performance has settled any of his concerns with me. I also wonder if he's now convinced that I have no memory of the event and that I completely accept the accident scenario instead of a scenario of a suicidal attempt— or even potentially more damaging for him and his company, someone else's criminal intent.

"I heard you had headaches and," he gestures toward my bandaged ankle, "that must be painful. In fact, your whole body must feel like hell from your fall."

"You're right about that but, as I've said, I have meds to help me through it. So, I'm okay." Then I glance toward the staircase and say, "But if possible, I'd rather not do those stairs again, at least not until I'm feeling better."

"It's a deal." He nods. He looks embarrassed again for having asked me to climb them. "Still, I've instructed the crew to go easy on you and let you determine what jobs you can handle during your recuperation period."

"Other than the bar, what else had I been doing?" Finally, I get an opening to pull out some information as well as assure him I don't remember stuff.

"I guess you wouldn't know that, would you? Let's see, you've been a valuable crew member, a jack-of-all-trades. Mick is impressed with your ability to pick up on things, says you're a fast learner and have helped him out when he's needed an extra hand. And we have certainly been taking advantage of your Great Lakes water-related skills, like your ability to pilot the various skiffs." He takes a drag off his cigar and blows it away from me. "You've been teaching kayaking and paddle boarding to our customers and instructing them on water equipment, snorkeling. Uh, helping with hiking trips." With the mentioning of hiking trips, he stops a moment then leans in and asks, "How much have you been told about what happened to you?"

"That I was on a hiking trip, not officially a guide at the time but on my own, so I was able to stop and meditate. Apparently, I got too close to the edge, lost my footing, tumbled over, and I'm lucky to be alive."

"Yes, you weren't working at the time. You were off duty, on your own time." He emphasized the "off duty" and "on your own time."

"Yes, uh…" I almost said "sir" but caught it. "Yes," I repeat. That answered one question of mine. I didn't really know, one way or another, that my fall occurred on what would be considered "off duty." I can see why he'd want my "accident" to be during my own time, not when I was officially working and therefore not the cruise line's responsibility.

"There are a few folks," he says, "who think you tried to kill yourself." His cigar is now stashed to the side of his mouth, allowing him to speak, but smoke trickles out through his lips as he watches my reaction to what he just said. I make sure I'm stone-faced, giving away nothing. I can play that game too. After a too-long pause, he continues, "I wasn't sure if I should mention this to you or not. I didn't want to upset you." Another pause. Then he asks, "What do you think about that? Do you think you tried to hurt yourself?"

"Like I said, I have no idea what happened, but slipping over the edge certainly seems possible. I don't feel depressed now, like wanting to kill myself. But frankly, how would I know at this point?" I figure I have to say this to stay believable. It would only make since that I wouldn't know how I felt then.

"Well, from what I've seen and know of you and your character, I have no doubt that it was an accident."

Hmm. I never thought of attempted suicide as having anything to do with a person's character, more like a bad case of hopelessness.

"You're not the type to do such a thing." He stopped then added, "I haven't had a chance, till now, to tell you how sorry I'm for what happened to you. All I can think is that there had to be loose stones you didn't notice, or maybe you got dizzy."

"Or maybe I made a clumsy move or wasn't paying attention to where I was," I add to help him out.

He smiles. "Yes. Anyway, that's why I told them at the hospital. That it was an accident. Didn't want them to think that you were a danger to yourself and have you locked up in some psych ward, all because someone thought you were suicidal."

"Thank you, uh, I wouldn't have liked that."

As I thought, he doesn't want this whole event to be anything but a clumsy screwup on Dee's part. At least now he can keep an eye on me and will know if my memory of the event comes back. He probably worries that if I were confined in some psych ward, I might get my memory back through therapy, remember something that wouldn't look good for the company or him, like if I were suicidal. Maybe he's afraid he didn't observe my mental condition well enough before hiring me or hadn't taken me off duty because of my weird "delusions" and depression. Whether or not he noticed Dee's mental state, the crew members certainly knew and no doubt mentioned it to him. And I'm sure he doesn't want to entertain the possibility of the incident having been a crime on his watch. It brings up security issues and is bad for him. Bad for the cruise line.

In a way, I can't blame the guy. He's undoubtedly under the gun by corporate to get this swept under the rug ASAP. Probably fears for his job. He must be in his mid- to late-fifties and getting another position could be difficult for him, likely impossible. He desperately needs my fall over the cliff to be an accident of my awkwardness or lack of attention while being on my own time.

A case of her bad, her clumsiness, her fault in order to minimize any negative publicity and avoid a lawsuit.

He keeps his job.

It also means he won't be of any help to me in trying to find out otherwise. He will be checking in on me, hoping I won't remember anything and continue to believe the fall was something I brought on myself due to my lack of awareness or just plain awkwardness.

* * *

It's almost noon and I'm hungry, since I only had coffee for breakfast. I head to the room behind the galley where the crew eats. The only person at the table is Mick the Mouse. I grab a plate, fix up a couple of tacos, and sit down across from him. Very carefully, I remove my cap, that I'd grabbed on my way here, to keep my bandaging from popping off. What a catastrophe that would be. Jesus.

Mick's eyes track up to Moran and Mandy's clipping handiwork that bares the part of my shaved head that's not bandaged. "I guess we're kinfolks now, minus all the gauze wrapping, of course."

"It looks that way all right." I take a mouthful of my taco, using my hand to wipe off the salsa that drips down my chin. Damn. Dee would have used her napkin. Next time.

"But your hair will grow back," he quips and smiles.

"At least, in your case, you have that cool beard going for you." I return the smile. "I'm as hairless as a cue ball."

"Speaking of that, are you a pool player?"

I nod then quickly realize Dee's not a pool player, and someone on-ship might be aware of that fact. A detail error. If I could have smacked the side of my head without having to explain why, I would have. Instead, with a sheepish smile, I quickly add, "Well, no, not really, but I had a small kid's pool table when I was little. I loved it at the time but never graduated to the big table." I was about to add, *but my sister did.* I caught myself this time. Dee didn't want anyone to know she had a sister so never would've made that comment, and that would have opened a whole other bag of worms.

This con of mine is fucking hard to pull off. Too many loose strings of my façade. I stupidly reach out, go too far and catch a snag, then end up trying to mend it back together again. I need to let my words out at a school zone speed. It would give me more time to catch my errant ramblings, ones that belong under lock and key. I'm quite certain, though, that he didn't catch my slip because he doesn't register any confusion if his grin is any indication.

"I'm sure your skills would transfer if you did start playing," he says. "I've been impressed with what a quick learner you are." He takes in a mouthful of refried beans.

It's an opportune time to try to see what information I might glean from him since I have him here, alone, one-on-one. Like, who went on that hiking trip with Dee? I can't ask him directly, given the almighty directive from the captain not to discuss anything that has to do with Dee's accident.

I bite a big chunk out of my taco as I try to think of a way to get info without seeming to be asking. Finally, I come up with an opening. "Being Mr. Fix-it on the ship, you must not get much leisure time around here like some crew members do."

He swallows and licks his lips. "To be honest, no one around here gets much time to play when we're doing the cruise. It's pretty much 24-7. I can get away, now and then. Remember after you helped me with—" He looks sheepish. "Sorry. I momentarily forgot. I didn't mean to say anything that would upset you."

I wave off his comment, like it's no big deal, and move on. "What do you like to do when you can get away and play a little?"

"I like paddle boarding." A big grin slides across his face. "Before I forgot about your memory problem, I was going to say, remember when you and I went out together on the last cruise, missed dinner, had to scrounge for food when we got back? Anyway, that's really the only thing around here I enjoy in the way of playing."

"Not kayaking?" I pretend to give a shit.

"Nope."

"Land activities?"

He gives me a puzzled look. "No, I'm not a hiker, if that's what you're asking."

Shit! That sounded like probing, asking for something he's been told not to talk about. I need to back away. "I'm interested in the small town—Petersburg, I think it is—the place we'll be docking on our way back to Ketchikan. Wondering if you've been there and if it's worth getting off the ship to wander around. Anything much to do or see? My friend, Mandy, was asking me about it. But if I was ever there, I don't remember the place." I take another chunk out of my taco.

"No, can't say as I've spent much time in Petersburg. Oh, maybe early on, but don't remember much about it. If I need something from land, I usually ask someone to pick it up for me. From what I do know of that little town, let's see, there's a pizza place that has a bar. I hear that lots of the crew like to hang out there. There's also a small café, and the food's just okay. If you're interested, there's a tribal museum that has a few statues. You might ask someone else about it."

Okay, that pretty much convinces me that Mick wasn't on the hiking trip, though I don't cross him off. Actually, I won't cross anyone off, just raise or lower them on my list, depending on what I find out.

Britt comes rushing in, gets two plates, and makes piles of hamburger, cheese, and shredded cabbage. My sister had told me that lettuce is at a premium in Alaska, so they use cabbage instead. Britt adds refried beans then throws on two corn shells per plate. She turns and hands them to a woman chopping onions, who looks to be native Alaskan, and tells her where to take the food. Then Britt leaves.

"Is there room service around here?" I ask Mick.

"Not really. It's probably for a crew member who can't take the time for lunch or is sick."

We go back to our food. After a few minutes, Britt is back, fixes a plate for herself, and sits down. "Good grief. It's only noon, and I'm already behind."

"Well, it looks to me like the kitchen workers are on top of things." Mick licks his fingers.

"It's not about lunch. Today I need to help on the launch platform. It's almost time for the afternoon folks who want to take out the kayaks and paddle boards. I have to be"—she looked at her watch—"there in five minutes or less." She takes several gulps of her soda.

"The captain told me I've been helping out on the launch pad," I say. "Sorry for the extra work I've caused you by me—"

"Hey, no problem." Britt douses her taco with salsa. "You'll be back in no time, and I can handle it till you're ready." She gives me her toothy smile.

"Well, ladies, I got to get back to work." Mick gets up and leaves his dishes on the table. Another female native kitchen worker picks them up. I know there's extreme poverty for most of the Alaskan native population, so getting a job on a ship has to be a really good thing for them. I wonder if the women have opportunities for anything other than the kitchen and cleaning jobs, but I don't mention it. Job opportunities information is not a place I need to explore. I need to stay focused.

Now is my chance to find out what Britt does when she's not working. "It must be hard to be on duty so much, no time to really play and yet have to help others have a good time."

"That's for sure. But you should know about that. Oh, I'm sorry, of course you don't know." Britt put her hand on mine. It sits there a little longer than it should then she quickly removes it as though it just occurred to her that I have amnesia and don't know who I am to her. It must feel weird, having someone you love, or at the beginnings of a relationship, anyway, suddenly not know who in hell you are. I almost feel bad. Then my next thought is to take advantage of her distress. "How often do you get to do something other than work?"

"Not enough time. That's for sure," she mumbles between bites.

"What do you like to do?"

"What do you mean?"

"When you're not working and have some time to play here on the ship."

"Okay, got ya. I'm a water enthusiast. I love kayaking, mostly, not so much paddle boarding. Snorkeling when I can, but it's not that frequently that we are someplace we can do that. As a rule, the passengers usually take all the spots available. There is only so much equipment and so many wet suits."

I nod.

I don't know how long I'll have with her alone, since I assume other members of the crew will be showing up to eat anytime now. She needs to go back to work soon. I jump right in and ask, "I take it you're not one for land activities."

"Not at all," she says, crinkling her face in distaste. "Tromping over land is not my exercise of choice. I end up getting dirty and, more likely than not, cold and wet. Frankly, it can be too much of a workout. I get enough running around here on-ship." Then she looks down at my injury and says, "I guess you won't be doing that yourself very soon, not until your ankle gets better."

I can't believe she just said that. It's too close to the topic of my tumble, a place she's not supposed to go. But I don't waste the opportunity to push her closer. I say, "I think I'll stay away from heights. Apparently, I'm clumsy and need to stay away from the edge of cliffs." I take a deep sigh for effect and shovel in a mouthful of food.

"Well, like I said. I need to get to the launch platform. I'm sure Roni is wondering where I am." She picks up her silverware and plate, puts them on the tray for dirty dishes, and leaves.

I note how quickly she signed off the topic of my injured ankle. The good thing is I've learned she's not a hiker, and she can now assure anyone who's interested that I believe the story about being a klutz.

CHAPTER EIGHT

Dee's Journal

Training goes well. I think I'm going to really like this job. In a week, we'll be taking out our first passengers for the season. Very exciting. My bar skills are rusty but luckily intact. I love that I can do other things, too.

Mick teaches me how to fix stuff, and it should serve me well in life. Minor things, mostly, but things I didn't know before. Seems like a nice guy, and he's eager to help and show me around, probably because he really doesn't have anyone else who is willing or has time to help him.

Roni's second-in-command, and she acts it. She's been showing me the ropes when it comes to the water activities. Where stuff is, procedures. She's been fine with me but has a short fuse when things don't go like she wants. Yesterday, she got upset, red-faced, and yelled at a crew member—everyone on the ship probably heard—for not following protocol while getting a skiff down into the water. From what I understand, the person who'd messed up didn't show proper recognition of her mistake, which made Roni angrier. Then she got in the woman's face about it. Thought Roni was going to punch the poor person. If the captain hadn't been around and stepped in to pull Roni back, not sure what would have happened. Her labile behavior is something I'd put in my hospital notes if I were back at work. But since I'm not serving as a social worker on this ship—yeah!—just a bartender, I don't have too. I don't enjoy feeling like I should tiptoe around her, though. Along with a bad temper, I've heard crew members complain that she cares more about the physical parts of the ship than the passengers—or crew, for that matter. I had a boyfriend like that once, loved his things, especially his car. I felt more like a car accessory than a girlfriend.

Today, the captain told me that one of the reasons he hired me was because I had other skills, like around water activities, so I can help in that capacity when I'm not tending the bar. He was also impressed that I was willing to learn repair skill to help Mick. So far, I like the captain, and he seems pleased with me. He's helpful and quick to answer my questions, complimentary when happy with people's efforts—pretty much the opposite of Roni's command style. The only thing I don't like is his cigar smoking. I hate the smell, and the smoke seems to find its way to me. Ugh. I hope I don't make too much of a fuss about it.

I've been so incredibly busy with my training that I haven't had a chance to get to know the other crew members that well, but so far most everyone is friendly and helpful. People seem to like working on this ship.

Alaska is indescribably beautiful. I can already feel weight lift off my spirit just looking out into the never-ending ocean and at the huge mountains. I feel awestruck by the enormity of it all. It lightens me and makes me feel as though my problems are small or insignificant.

Also, I've always loved being on the water. I'm sure I've made the right decision to come here and experience what it's like on a ship in the ocean, even if my sister was dubious about this choice of mine. I think Kera's concern was more about me being so far away, like I was when she was in Iraq—a problem I'm sure is typical of identical twins. At least Mandy understood and was able to talk to Kera about it. I do so miss them both, but I think the sea breeze will be good for me and help me clear my mind.

Signing off for today. Need my rest.

CHAPTER NINE

Mandy

"Remember to sign out," Roni called out to Mandy. Roni was helping the crew at the launch platform get the passengers into their kayaks and out into the water.

"Oh yes. Sorry I forgot." Mandy made her way over to the in-and-out board, which had the list of all the passengers' names. It had been emphasized how important it was that everyone use it when they left or returned to the ship. That way, everyone could be accounted for at any one time. She had hoped Kera would be able to come with her this morning, but she had a meeting with the captain and didn't know how long it would take.

Mandy watched as a female couple got into a tandem kayak on the deck. She noticed that the small craft sat on rollers embedded on the platform floor. It provided an easy push off by the crew. As she watched the women's smooth departure, she noticed a kayak that was headed back into the ship. The crew grabbed the boat as it nosed onto the platform and yanked it from the ocean and onto the ship's rollers. When Dee had told her on the phone that she could kayak off from the ship, she wondered how she would be able to get into and out of a kayak without getting wet. Now she knew.

"That's a slick operation," Mandy said to Roni as she climbed into a one-person kayak ready for launch. Roni smiled, handed Mandy a paddle, and pushed her out into the water.

"Enjoy." Roni waved to her.

Mandy's kayak eased into the turquoise-blue calm water of the ocean's inlet. She felt the tension in her body begin to melt into the serenity of the surroundings. It felt as though the mountains on either side cupped her, harbored her, and created safety in their arms as she lazily paddled along the shoreline in the silky tranquil waters. Peering into the ocean's depth, she found a jellyfish, expanding and retracting like floating gossamer lace. Soon, she spotted another one, then another, and another. All in a graceful dance. This had to be as close to nirvana as she could ever get. Her breathing slowed and pulled from deep within her. It kept her in the moment and movement of the ocean, it felt caring...or maybe non-caring, non-judging. A state of grace...

But the feeling shattered.

Off in the distance, she spotted fellow passengers who'd decided to take the supervised hike on land this morning. They zigzagged up the mountainside. The sight took her breath away. Dee had fallen from somewhere high like that. It was a place that appeared serene but was a place that betrayed her. Or maybe the betrayer was a someone. Either way, the sense of tranquility melted away. She felt guilty for having enjoyed even a moment. How dare she when Dee lay in a hospital bed, severely injured.

It made Mandy desperately want to hear Dee's voice, to know that she was okay and would recover. She brought her cell phone to take pictures while roaming around the inlet. Maybe she would be able to catch a random tower signal. The crew had said that sometimes that happened if you were at the right spot at the right time. She punched in the number for Moran's cell phone. The elderly woman had not been using anything more modern than a phone connected to a wall, but she'd adapted to the cell they purchased for her—much to her and Kera's relief. Moran was proud of herself for being able to function with it.

Mandy's phone showed no bars, which meant no chance. Didn't matter. She punched in the numbers anyway. What would it hurt to try?

No response. Nothing.

Oh well, it was a long shot. She and Kera would have to wait, maybe hear through the captain on the ship-to-shore communications. They'd known that getting info from Dee would be problematic. Before they had left Juneau, they recognized the lack of ability to communicate privately. She and Kera devised a way for Moran to get news about Dee through the captain via his ship radio. Their plan was that when Dee came out of the coma, if she remembered that she'd accidentally fallen over the cliff or had tried to hurt herself—no foul play—the message would be, "Your aunt had a heart attack but is doing well." But if Dee remembered someone had pushed her off that cliff or she didn't know, the message would be, "Your aunt had a heart attack and is in critical condition in ICU." That still left a problem. If Dee knew who had pushed her, it would be dicey getting that information to them going through the captain. They'd decided that if Dee knew who the person was, Moran would also mention that so-and-so was flying in from Michigan to be with her. That fake person would have the same initials as the person who'd tried to kill her. Hopefully, there wouldn't be two people with the same initials on that ship. That was the best plan they could come up with at the time.

Mandy tried to shake off the unrelenting images her mind rolled out for her, ones of all the horrible scenarios that might have happened to Dee while she was up on the cliff. Then, like a double-header horror extravaganza, her fears projected the various terrorizing situations that could, probably would, occur as she and Kera tried to find out who attempted to murder Dee. Mandy shuddered then shook her head as though she could shake the muck out. It didn't work. She sucked in the ocean's cool air, hoping to return to her prior calmness, or at least something close. No deal. She paddled harder toward a small island and tried to outrun her haunting thoughts.

As she drew closer, she decided to circumnavigate the tiny island. She'd make her return to the ship by paddling over to and hugging close by the mountains and several small coves with narrow waterfalls that snaked down the rocky cliffs. As Mandy circled alongside the heavily treed isle, she heard voices ahead. Women arguing.

She slowed her craft and pulled in close to the shore. As she paddled, she hoped she was going in the opposite direction of the women. Suddenly, the discord got louder. She'd made the wrong choice of direction. She stopped short of a bend, believing that if she proceeded around it, the women would be on the other side. Irritated by another stab to her mental health, she worked to rotate her kayak around so she could get away.

As she struggled to turn around, the voices grew even louder.

"I saw you flirting with her!" A raspy voice shouted in an English accent. "Do not try to refute it, my dear. You need to sort your life out, decide on what's important."

"I was not flirting. You're being paranoid, Bev." This voice was calm, like someone who's trying lower the heat in a dispute.

"Don't you forget, Charlie my dear, your next time is your last time. Then you're out the door for good," the Brit said, leveling out her emotion, but in a markedly cold and threatening tone.

"I haven't done anything, and I don't plan to. Relax, will you? Jesus Christ, let's enjoy the trip."

"So," Bev fired back, "who was that woman at the bar?"

"Nobody, Bev, I swear."

"Just remember what I—"

Before Mandy could get her boat maneuvered completely around, the tandem kayak with the spatting twosome came into view. She recognized them as the couple who'd launched right before she had. Noticing Mandy, the women passed by in silence.

Paradise lost for them, as well.

Mandy paddled on.

* * *

When Mandy had returned from her kayaking, exhausted, she fell asleep. When she woke up, she couldn't believe she'd been asleep for almost three hours. She'd planned on having dinner with Britt and agreed to meet her in the dining room five minutes ago. She quickly changed her blouse, ran a brush through her hair, and left.

Britt sat by a window at a table for two. Her curly red hair made her easy to spot. Mandy hurried over.

"Hey, thought maybe you stood me up." Britt smiled.

"I'm sorry. I fell asleep when I got back today and just woke up." A server came by with a water pitcher. Mandy thanked her. "It's nice to see your company hires native people."

"So far, they've all been good workers. They pretty much only speak their native tongue, at least to each other. They do understand English and have no problems communicating with the passengers but seem reluctant to speak it around the crew. They certainly understand me when I'm training them or asking them to do stuff." Britt stood up. "I'm going to get another drink. Can I get you anything?"

"Ah, sure, why not."

"You were drinking pinot noir last night. The same?"

Mandy nodded and watched Britt head for the bar. Kera was busy waiting on passengers. It appeared that she'd settled into Dee's work quite well as she made drinks like she'd been at it for some time. As Mandy panned the bar area, she spotted the creepy guy who'd stared at her and Kera coming aboard ship. He sat by himself with a drink in his hand on a cushioned bench alongside the lounge area.

"Here you go." Britt handed her the glass of wine.

"Who's that guy?" Mandy pointed.

"Oh, that's Wally."

"He stares at me but really mostly at Dee. It makes us uncomfortable." Mandy sampled her drink.

"Don't worry. Wally is definitely weird, but he seems pretty harmless. That is, except he's a bit of a tattletale. He's taken all our cruises this summer. Crazy, huh?"

"Why?"

"I don't know." Britt shrugged. "I guess he doesn't have anything else to do."

"You said he's a tattletale?"

"Uh-huh. He loves to see someone, crew members or passengers, doing something wrong—or at least something he thinks is wrong—so he can run to Captain James or Roni and report it. I don't know what he gets out of it."

"Can't you just imagine what kids in school thought of him?" Mandy shook her head.

"I'm sure he wasn't popular. He likes Deidre though. She's never been the subject of his complaints. Before the accident, he hung out a lot on a bar stool and watched her work. He'd even talk to her. Frankly, I think he has a crush on her. We always teased her about it."

"He's straight?"

"Yes, he let me know that on his first trip. Maybe he's of the opinion he can convert a woman." Britt laughed.

Mandy decided not to mention that Dee was bisexual. It wouldn't matter. Wally was not in Dee's league.

"Actually," Britt continued, "I feel a little sorry for the guy. He's a loner and doesn't know how to connect with most people."

"That's probably why he focused on Dee when we boarded the ship on Sunday. I thought he stared at to me too, but it's probably because I was with her."

"Yeah, probably. Other than trying to get Deidre's attention and sneaking a candid picture of her, he doesn't do much, mostly reads books, has gone hiking a couple of times—which isn't much given all the cruises he's taken. He keeps saying he wants to kayak but to my knowledge, he hasn't."

"Does Dee know he tries to sneak pictures of her?"

"I don't know. It's probably innocent enough. Maybe sometimes he's targeting something or someone else, and she happens to be in it, too."

"He likes to hike?" Mandy didn't want to let that go by without asking more.

"Not sure if he's all that into it. Both times, the naturalist that lead the group he was in said Wally hung back. It made it hard for them to be sure he was still with the group. He described Wally as being like a cat, almost sneaky-like, choosing his own path." Britt giggled. "But really, that's mostly a problem because there are bears out there. It's important for them to maintain a group that looks as big as possible to intimidate any bear that might approach. Besides that, a straggler could be picked off."

"You have a naturalist on board. That's impressive."

"We have two naturalists. Both are excellent. We rely on them for all the land trips we schedule. It's a lot of work. They take groups by day and do talks and films at night. You should go to their presentations. It's very interesting."

Mandy nodded. Dee had told her the cruise line company was into education and preserving the wilderness environment. She'd planned on a land trip. But bears? She'd have to think about that. Right now, she needed to focus on what she could glean from Britt that might be helpful in finding out what happened to Dee.

"Before you came aboard," Britt said, "when we were heading to Juneau, we had some great bear sightings, along with other wildlife."

"I'm sorry I missed the trip to Juneau." But Mandy wasn't sorry she'd missed the opportunity to meet up with a bear, even if she'd been in a big group.

"Don't worry, there are great opportunities yet to come. On the way back, we'll be stopping at different places than on the first leg, except for Petersburg. We stop there both ways. Anyway, I highly recommend you take part in some of the land trips."

"Nobody new came aboard in Juneau but me?"

"No, we ordinarily don't take on new passengers there. In fact, I've never known the captain to allow that. It's strictly a round-trip cruise. You were lucky he let you come aboard at that time."

"Why do you think he let me on?"

"I don't know." Britt shrugged. "Maybe it was because of Dee's condition."

"Condition?" Mandy was grateful they'd made their way back around to Dee. "You mean her depression?"

"Yeah, that and her behavior after we left Petersburg. We departed around seven p.m., and it was later that night Deidre hallucinated having seen someone go overboard. She ran up to the bridge and insisted on a water search, which the captain immediately performed. Also, the crew combed the ship and counted passengers. All of them were accounted for. But Deidre wasn't satisfied and as time went on, she became more adamant that someone had gone into the ocean that night."

"Hallucinated? Did she take into consideration that maybe it was a dream or a nightmare?"

"Deidre claimed she'd just fallen asleep but was awakened by a scream. By then she'd gotten a little strange. Well, not strange so much as she isolated herself and didn't socialize with the crew like she used to. When she was working, she wasn't her old self and didn't seem very happy. Then, shortly before we were to arrive in Juneau where you were getting aboard, she was visibly worse. It didn't make sense, because I know she was looking forward to seeing you."

"Do you have any idea why she was getting worse?"

"No, I was puzzled by it then figured it was another step down into her depression."

"That must have been hard on you, given you'd become friends. Well, more than friends like you told me."

"More like devastating. I thought our relationship was going to turn into something really good, and I haven't felt that way about anyone else in a very long time." Britt's eyes watered.

Mandy shook her head. "I'm so sorry." The Dee that she knew had been a pretty upbeat person and had never, as far as she knew, been treated for depression or any mental illness that would account for hallucinations, nor had Kera ever mentioned that. On the other hand, Dee had decided to take a leave absence from her job in Michigan because she felt confused and down about her life. She wanted to have space to think and deal with things of her past and to get her life on a positive track. Mandy thought Dee enjoyed her job on the ship at first and was feeling better, but as time went on, she and Kera noticed Dee was sounding down again. That was the reason Mandy had decided to come to Alaska—to cheer Dee up.

But hallucinating?

"Do you know if Dee was on anything that might have caused that reaction?" Britt asked.

Mandy shook her head again. She was certain that when Dee left for Alaska, she wasn't on any kind of medication. Maybe when she started feeling more depressed, she sought medical help for it, and the medication wasn't working. Maybe it even had a negative effect on her. That certainly was known to happen to some people.

"Or any other condition we're not aware of?" Britt looked as confused as Mandy felt. "I'm aware that drugs are easily obtained in Alaska. I don't know if she—"

"Dee didn't do illicit drugs. That's not in her character." Mandy was about to mention that Dee was always chewing Kera out because of her pot-smoking, but Mandy stopped herself. From her table close to the lounge, she'd spotted Kera coming out from behind the bar. She was signaling her relief guy that she was leaving for a break. Mandy realized that Kera was going out on the deck to smoke weed and would no doubt have a lingering odor from it. She modified her statement. "Well, she's smokes pot now and then, but that wouldn't cause anything like hallucinations."

"She's not the only one on the crew." Britt snickered. "But I didn't know that about her. She never mentioned it to me."

"She's always tried to cover it up as best she could with fabric spray and breath mints." Mandy smiled. She'd made sure Kera had some of each with them when they came aboard. "She says it helps when she's nervous."

"I'd image she'll be using it more, then. It's got to be so hard on her, trying to pick up her life again. I worry she'll never get her lost time back." Britt sighed. "Is she even getting a glimmer of what happened to her?"

"No, nothing. Not yet, anyway." Mandy knew Kera wanted people to think Dee had a chance of retrieving memory, all in hopes of whoever pushed Dee off the cliff—if that's what happened— would get worried and show his or her hand. Mandy took a deep breath. This whole escapade was not only crazy but damned dangerous. She couldn't imagine it ending well.

CHAPTER TEN

Dee's Journal

I can't believe it's the Fourth already. Yikes! The season is almost half over.

We docked in Juneau today. They're having quite the celebration here according to the captain and the crew. They said the passengers and I are in store for a great fireworks display tonight. Yeah!

I'm glad I brought my journal with me. I've been able to detail in words much of the landscape, smells, textures, and sounds. With my camera, I get the visual. Breathtaking! I will always be able to remember the beauty of this place, whether or not I come back for another year's cruise season.

Going back and forth between Ketchikan and Juneau has really been fun. I wondered if I would be bored by it when I first signed up, but I love it. Always something new. It's never the same experience, either in the scenery or the animals we spot along the way. Two bears yesterday! The passengers are always different, except for one guy who has taken every cruise so far. I need to take a pic of him. Mandy and Kera won't believe me if I try to describe him.

I go to bed every night dead tired, but it's worth it. I've learned so much about this area, plus everything Mick has taught me about the boats and other stuff. Today I helped him repair the motor on one of the skiffs. It's more like I learned about the inner workings of the motor, not able to offer much help. It was so fun. Mick and I took it for a spin around a small island, and it purred nicely, as he put it. The skiff we worked on is an old metal boat that had been his dad's fishing boat back in the day. He and his father spent a lot of time in it. Good memories for him. Mick's able to have it here, even though it looks out of place—all the others are much larger and inflatable skiffs—because it was part of his employment package that he'd insisted on. I'll have to remember the next time I go for a job to think what I can put in an employment package. Hmm. Maybe an annual vacation to Alaska. Ha-ha.

Mick is easy for me to work with, not a big talker, more a matter-of-fact kind of guy. I like that since I chat all night with people at the bar. I appreciate not having to do that when I'm off bar duty. Mick told me a couple of days ago that the captain trusts me and wants to talk to me about doing something else but didn't say what. Interesting. It sounded like another responsibility. Of course, it would be. If so, I don't know where I would fit anything more into my day. I do welcome something new, though, since things have become so routine now that I don't have to concentrate on what I'm doing as much. Not like I used to.

Having my duties down, I function pretty much on automatic. I don't like that because it gives me too much time in my head. My thoughts keep going back to my personal life—my default setting it seems. I keep reminding myself that my original goal was to come here to try to get perspective and think about things. When I do, I end up diverting myself so I can turn away from the pain. Otherwise it feels overwhelming. Big time. Makes me feel heavy, tired, want to go to bed. Good grief. I thought I'd gotten over the losses: My mother and father, way too soon. Wrong. My disastrous marriage. Wrong. My miscarriage—thanks to my bastard ex-husband. Wrong.

Thinking about it now, I can sack it all up in one emotional garbage package and stamp it—loss of the big beautiful picture I had for my life.

If I accept my loss, that means I need to make a new picture and I have no idea what that looks like. It scares me.

I have a dark hole in me that I avoid, avoid, avoid. It depresses me. At times I feel so out of it, I don't even want to hang out with other crew members. I just want to be alone. Work is my drug of choice, and sleep is my break.

I guess this all leads me to look forward to another job challenge, if presented. That's why I'll, no doubt, accept whatever it is the captain wants and trusts me to do. Bring it on, as my sister would say.

Another thing, which I already knew about myself—I hate conflict. Hate to be a part of it. Hate to be in it. So, when Roni and Britt had a run-in today—not their first—I just wanted to leave and find a remote cabin. The latest flare-up happened when Agnes spilled red spaghetti sauce on Roni. Britt had told Agnes the sauce bowl was getting low, so she filled another large bowl from the pot on the stove and was on her way to take it out to the buffet table. Unfortunately, Roni was sitting near the buffet. When Agnes walked behind her, Roni pushed her chair back and into Agnes—accidentally of course—but it spilled the hot sauce on Roni, no doubt burning her. Agnes was horrified and tried to apologize, while Roni grabbed cloth napkins and tried to wipe it off, screaming at the poor woman that she'd purposely dumped it on her. It was clear that it was no one's fault, just a freaky bad-timing thing.

All this happened in the last half hour of the lunch period, but there were still about ten passengers present. They all sat in disbelief. I'm not sure which was more shocking, the burning hot sauce all over Roni's shirt and pants or Roni's raging reaction toward Agnes. Her bellowing brought Britt running out of the kitchen just as Roni grabbed Agnes by her blouse, and it looked like she would punch the poor woman. Britt pushed Roni out of the way and escorted a crying Agnes back to the galley with Roni close behind. When Britt realized Roni was following her and Agnes, she yelled at her to get away from them. Roni didn't. So, Britt put an elbow into her gut, sending Roni down on her knees, doubled over, gasping for air from the sucker punch—I guess that's what they call it.

At the time, I stood there as dazed by the incident as the passengers. I know that had it been Kera, she'd been in the fray the second it started up. When I got over being completely stunned, I asked the passengers to take their plates into the bar area to finish. I helped Roni get back to her cabin, even though I felt no sympathy for her. Good grief, how she'd treated Agnes. Unbelievable!

Later, I talked to Agnes who was still crying and feeling guilty about what had happened. I tried to calm her down and reassure her that I saw the whole incident, that it was truly an accident, and would vouch for her. Britt didn't blame Agnes either.

I don't know what the heck is wrong with Roni. Why does she treat the native workers badly? The social worker in me tries to understand that woman. She's a veteran and probably saw combat and has PTSD, like Kera. That may be why she's quick to anger and has difficulty with control. But it seems there's more to it with her. It's like she has a mean streak running under all of it. Kera has the same issues but has worked hard to keep herself in control. Even at her worst, she was never mean. And another thing. Roni flirts with me. Makes me really uncomfortable. Why on earth would she think anyone would respond to her is beyond me.

I wonder what will happen when the captain hears about this, although he doesn't tend to get involved in disputes between workers. This might be different. This time it was in front of passengers. Big difference. I can't believe he won't do something.

CHAPTER ELEVEN

Kera

I think I could get used to being a bartender. I'd thrive. No one can sneak up on me here with shelves of various bottles of booze and beer taps behind me. The bar wraps around a corner with a good view of the lounge area and into the dining area, too. Gunslinger's syndrome, wanting my back to the wall so I can keep track of the whereabouts of folks. Helps keep my anxiety at bay, which I need, especially not having Lakota with me.

Damn, I miss my pooch. I don't have her set of eyes and ears watching and listening for me, but at least I'm able to duck out on my breaks for a few tokes. There are places I can be alone around here, unnoticed. My medical card to smoke weed from Michigan probably won't do me much good here. Hmm. I wonder what the laws are in Alaska, or if it's frowned upon here on-ship. No matter. I need it. If I'm careful to only use enough weed to take the edge off, it should keep me functional. I make my way to the top floor of the ship and stand behind a stack of equipment where no one can see me. It's really windy. The smoke gets blown away and hopefully the smell. Earlier, I saw a guy coming back from here. He had the smell of relaxation on him. I don't know what would happen if anyone saw us but so far no one seems to pay any attention.

I don't have as many nightmares like I used to, but last night I had one of my whoppers. I woke up in a sweat, soaked the bed sheets, yelling. I had a hell of a time getting out of it. Actually, I didn't come out of it by myself. Mandy helped me calm down. I hate those nightmares about Iraq—bombs exploding, body parts rushing past me. The worst part is seeing my old girlfriend flying into a million pieces. I wonder if that nightmare will ever go away. That moment in my life along with the other experiences in Iraq are the subjects for my flashbacks. At least I have fewer of them, but they sneak up on me in times of stress. Sometimes I can stop them in midstream but not always, especially if I don't see them coming.

I draw my last toke and make my way back to my post. The bar stays open, officially, until eleven at night, though I'm not supposed to push anyone away if they still want to drink. That is, within reason. Wonder who decides what is *within reason?* According to several crew members I've talked to, this kind of adventure cruise doesn't attract the hearty party crowd. It seems to be true.

Not everyone is adventurous. There are several couples here where one of them is clearly just accompanying the outdoorsy partner. The tagalongs read books, play board games, or disappear into their rooms until happy hour. I think I see one of the tagalongs coming into the bar now just as I'm trying to clean up for the night. *Damn.*

"Is it too late for me to get a drink, my dear?" It's Bev, the older woman who'd shepherded her cheating partner, Charlie, away from the bar last night. I was surprised when I saw the two of them take off in a kayak today. I'm sure Bev didn't do any of the paddling. She's the "I'd-rather-read-a-book" type.

"Nope," I answer. "What can I get you?" I wanted to tell her that it was too late and to go to bed.

"Pappy Van Winkle's Family Reserve, on the rocks," she says and bellies up to the bar.

I open my mouth to tell her once again, since I told her twice now, that we don't have that expensive-as-shit brand of bourbon. She should know that this isn't a fancy cruise. It's for outdoor type people. I'm about to remind her when she waves me off.

"Okay, okay. I know you don't carry the good stuff, so give me what you got. What was that nasty stuff? Old Crow." She grimaces. "How perfectly, bloody dreadful."

I'm thinking that's going to be her usual, that is after I remind her that we don't have her hoity-toity bourbon. I noticed we also had Wild Turkey bourbon, not displayed, as well, but there was a note on it that it was to be used only for mint juleps. I didn't let Bev know we had that. I don't know how good it is, but if it was good stuff, she'd have thrown a fit and insisted on it. I don't need the grief.

Bev made a pit stop here before dinner. At that time, she also bitched that we didn't have an onsite hairstylist since her gray roots were showing through her stark-black dyed hair. After she was done with her complaints, she told me that she and Charlie had a fight on a kayak trip this morning, though she didn't get into it. I've gotta believe it had something to do with Terri, "The Tart." That's what Bev calls "the other woman," in her somewhat Americanized English accent. She also updated me on all the things I supposedly already knew before my accident. I learned that Bev came over here years ago to go to college, then to law school, and never returned to England. From her jewelry and dress, I would guess she's doing well for herself, though not so much in the romance department.

"Coming right up." I reach for a glass for her "perfectly, bloody dreadful" bourbon. I got a feeling I'm not going to be leaving at closing time tonight. This woman wants to talk. Too bad we don't have a hairstylist aboard. I could use the relief. Who knows, though. She might say something I need to know. So far, I haven't been able to glean anything from anyone that seems helpful or useful. I know I'm going to hear nothing but complaints about Charlie and The Tart.

"My downfall," Bev starts off, "is I'm not attracted to women of my age. They're too, too…" I can tell she's trying to come up with words to describe her peers. Then her face lights up. I'm about to get the rest of it. "Too boring, too opinionated. Set in their ways." I nod, like I agree.

"And," Bev picks up the drink I placed in front of her, "I have to admit that I have a thing for young bodies." She chortles. "That's my confession for the day."

Her moment of mirth is one of a proud cougar, but she quickly returns to a distressed aging woman, motioning with her glass that it's time for another round. In her smoker's gravelly voice, she complains about not being able to smoke at bars anymore.

Like, what's become of the world? I suddenly realize that I don't know what the smoking rules are on this ship, so I guess I should ask someone. Whatever. It won't stop me from my weed. That's medicinal.

Bev sits directly in front of the bar's sink, so I decide to wash glasses. I was so busy earlier that I didn't have a chance to keep up. Besides, it gives me a good reason to hang out and listen to her in a skimming-the-surface sort of way and tune back in if I sense she's coming up with something important.

"I've told Charlie," Bev points her finger and shakes it, "that I was not—big emphasis on the *not*—putting up with her straying anymore. I'm all over that, way over."

Her familiarity with me must be because she buys that I'm Dee. She seems to have forgotten about Dee's amnesia. At any rate, I'm benefiting from the comfortable relationship she had with Dee. Bev no doubt spent many hours on the bar stool spilling her guts to my sister. Because Dee's a social worker, Bev probably got some good advice from her. Something I won't be that good at. Then I remember Dee told me that she doesn't give advice. She mostly just listens and lets people vent, occasionally pointing out alternatives.

Shit, I can do that.

"Oh my. I forgot. With your loss of memory, you don't recall all our conversations. I'm sorry, I'm so wrapped up in my own problems, I—"

"That okay. You can fill me in on any details if I need them. I'm still here to listen."

"That's kind of you." Bev doesn't miss a beat and moves on. "Charlie has a problem with straying. Oh, she always comes home. But when she gets a whiff of women in heat, she takes off, for hours, sometimes days." Bev shakes her head. "Like I said, she always comes back, pulls out an excuse from her back pocket, and expects things to be all right with me. In the end, she knows where her bread is and who's buttering it. The bloody little jailbird."

"Jailbird?" That gets my interest, big time.

"She won't tell me how long she was incarcerated or what for, but she says it's in her past. I suppose I could have found out. Frankly, by the time I knew she'd been in jail, I was hooked on her and I didn't want to know. But I guess her criminal record is why she can't find work."

It occurs to me that having Bev for a sugar mama must be a last resort for Charlie, or at least she sees it that way.

"She's almost thirty years old and has never held a real job or any job at all." Bev looks up from her drink she's been glaring into. "She was a princess growing up in an upper middle-class family and never had to do anything or fend for herself, as far as I can tell. Can you imagine?"

"No. I can't picture myself living off from someone else." I say.

"You pointed out to me that I had choices," Bev continues, "and that I was free to let her go. I've been thinking a lot about what you said and am ready to act on it if I see any more hanky-panky from her and that tart! I mean it, this time, and I bloody well told her so."

I wonder if Bev told Charlie that Dee suggested she had choices. If so, Charlie couldn't have appreciated that comment from Dee. Still pushing my sister off a cliff because of it would seem a bit heavy-handed.

"Of course, she denies everything. I know she's been involved with Terri The Tart for some time now."

"How did The Tart," I stay with Bev's name for Terri, figure that bonds us, "get on the same cruise with you and Charlie?"

"Oh, Charlie doesn't realize I know that she's the woman Charlie's been running around with behind my back, so she managed to get her on the same cruise as ours. Can you imagine the vaginal balls that woman possesses?"

Vaginal balls?

"Charlie claims she's never seen the woman before. Huh!" Bev rolls her eyes. "I didn't give it away that I know who The Tart is. Anyway, even if I did accuse Charlie, she'd just deny everything. Always does."

I nod as I swizzle clean the beer mugs in the dishwater.

"But," she continues, "I feel like I have to catch them doing something red-handed, like, you-know-what." Bev smirks. "At least that's my bottom line."

"That line's pretty low, Bev." My comment surprises me. That bit of insight came flying out of my mouth before I gave it thought. What the hell. It's true and Bev needs to hear it, whether or not Dee would've said it.

"I know, I know, but that's what I'm able to live with. I've promised myself to stick to it. This time I've made the consequences clear to her, and I think she finally believes me." Bev slams down her fist on the bar to convince me or maybe herself. "I giveth and I taketh." She purses her lips. She downs her drink and sets her glass firmly on the bar. "The flow of money will cease. Her name will never see the light of day on my will. The bloody little bitch will have to go to work, with or without a criminal record."

Watching Charlie and Terri last night at the bar, I would bet Charlie will be looking for a job real soon.

* * *

It's late, past two. Mandy is probably asleep by now, so I open the door as quietly as I can. The light is on, and she is sitting up on the bed in her clothes. She looks as though she's seen a ghost.

"What's wrong?" I ask.

"Look at this." Mandy hands me a sheet of paper with cut-out words pasted on it—probably from a magazine—that reads:

I know what you are up to.

My heart starts thumping in my chest. "Where did you get this?"

"It was on our bed." Mandy seems frozen in place, barely breathing. Finally, she says, "Someone came into our cabin. So much for the honor system. I hate that we can't lock our door when we're out of our room."

"You've been sitting on this all night, waiting for me to finish at the bar? Why didn't you come and tell me?"

"No, no, I couldn't sleep. About eleven thirty, I went up to the deck and sat in a chair for a while, watching stars and trying to relax. When I came back, it was here."

"How long did you stay out there?"

"I just got back here about five minutes ago."

"Fuck!" I thought I was doing so well, at least performing to a passable version of my sister. But someone has caught on.

"What do we do now?" Mandy flips her feet onto the floor and stands up.

"I guess we wait and see what happens. Whoever sent this didn't threaten to expose me, I mean us. It's that she or he—maybe even they—know what we are up to."

"Someone wants to blackmail us?"

"Honey, I don't know. We need to stay calm and hang tight until we're contacted again."

"What if they don't? What if they just turn us in to the captain? Good god, what will he do? What will happen to us?"

"Wait, wait." I hold up my hands to try to calm her down. Her panic is taking over my ability to think this through. "Whoever sent this isn't going to expose us, at least not at this point." I sit down next to her and put my arm around her. "Or they wouldn't have gone to the trouble of writing this." I hold up the note. "They're after something else. So, they'll be letting us know."

"This is freaking me out."

"At least we've stirred the pot."

CHAPTER TWELVE

Mandy

Mandy stared at the note, cobbled together with words cut out from a magazine—probably from the pile in the lounge. If it weren't so scary, she'd find it humorous. Seemed like something she'd see on a rerun of some old movie or from an Agatha Christie TV mystery series. On the other hand, she had to admit that it was clever in its simplicity and lack of technology that otherwise might be traceable, not that they had any means to trace anything here on a ship. She imagined a pair of hands, rubber-gloved, carefully cutting out each word and pasting it onto the generic white paper.

But whose hands?

Before Kera left to help Roni with the morning kayakers, they tried to consider who might have left the note and why. What did they want? They obviously know that Kera is pretending to be Dee. But how did they figure it out? Maybe Dee confided in someone that she had an identical twin.

If only she could go back to bed and escape under the covers. She sighed. That wouldn't stop another note from coming from whomever was doing this. Good god.

She told Kera she would see if she could learn anything today, but there'd be no chance of doing that if she stayed locked up in her cabin under her covers. She took a deep breath, let it out slowly, and told herself to put on her big-girl panties and get out there.

Mandy grabbed a plate and headed to the buffet table. She didn't have much of an appetite, and acid roiled in her stomach. Still, she scooped up some scrambled eggs with cheese sprinkled on the top, a piece of bacon, a slice of toast, and poured herself a cup of coffee.

When she glanced around for a place to sit, she noticed Britt eating by herself. Britt had told her that she often took her meals in the dining room with the passengers, because one of her assignments was to make sure people were happy with everything on-ship. Well, she was a passenger, and she definitely had an issue, not that she'd mention this one. Mandy made her way over to Britt's table.

Britt looked up as she approached.

"Mind if I join you?"

"Please do." Britt moved a clipboard to make room for Mandy's tray. "Hope you slept well."

"I'm still not used to the rocking of the ship and the sound of the diesel engines. I wake up a lot, but I think I'll make it through the day." Mandy forced a smile. She was determined not to give her nervousness away to anyone.

"I know what you mean." Britt said. "That was hard for me when I first started working on the ship, but you'll get used to it. After a while, the rocking will feel comforting and the engine sounds will become background noise. At least it is for me."

"As long as the rocking stays gentle, I'll be okay." Mandy dreaded the mere thought that they could be at sea in bad weather.

"Don't worry about that. If there were going to be a big storm, the captain will get us to a safe place to ride it out." Britt took a sip of her coffee.

"That's comforting."

"How's Deidre doing? I saw her heading out to help Roni with the boats earlier. I'll be heading out that way myself as soon as I make sure the galley staff is doing okay." Brit jotted down something on her clipboard.

"Dee said she slept well last night, and her ankle is feeling better. She's planning to use her cane to get around instead of her crutches, so she can be more mobile. I don't know how much help she'll be to Roni, but Dee is determined."

Mandy thought it a good idea to mention the cane. This morning Kera had decided that she needed to move more freely so she could "snoop around" better. She hoped Kera didn't get so involved that she'd forget to at least limp. Sprained ankles didn't heal that fast.

"It won't take Roni long to clue her into what needs to be done. There are things out there that she'll be able to do. Speaking of how Dee's doing, has she regained any memory?" Britt looked hopeful. "I know it's selfish, but I want her to remember what we had together." She sighed.

"No, I'm sorry. Nothing yet."

"I guess I'll have to be patient. It might take a while."

"Or she may never remember. The doctor said it could go either way." Mandy shrugged and bit off a small piece of her bacon.

Britt stood up. "But at some point, I want to tell her about *us*. I can only imagine how not remembering a piece of her life is difficult for her. It's hard on me too. I miss her so much. I know that sounds funny, right? Being around Deidre and knowing that she doesn't see me as I see her is really making it crazy for me." Britt picked up her tray. "I better get out there on the platform to make sure we get those folks in the kayaks and on their paddle boards. There are a lot of sign-ups for water equipment this morning."

"Ker-, uh, Dee won't be able to help that much to—"

Luckily for Mandy, a female passenger passed by the table and caught Britt's attention. She asked Britt what the topic was for the nature talk tonight. Mandy hoped to God she hadn't screwed things up, because for a second, Britt looked confused when Mandy muffed the names.

"See you later." Britt smiled at her as she left.

Whew! Seems she escaped that gaffe.

Her head felt like it might explode—too many unknowns, too many potholes to trip her up. She went back to her eggs but still had no appetite. Her food was cold and even less desirable now. She peered out the window at the ocean and tried to decide what to do next. She drew a blank.

She sipped on her third cup of coffee, hoping for an idea. Finally, she decided to check out the stacked magazines in the lounge as well as a few scattered about in the dining room. It wasn't as though she expected to find someone fast at work gluing words to paper. Searching for a magazine with cutouts was at least a start. Maybe she could ask around to see if anyone saw someone clipping. But why would she be asking that?

Then, an inspiration came to her, though a scary one to be sure. Since all the cabins were unlocked, unless someone was inside and had locked it, she could sneak into passenger cabins when people were out. She could check to see if anything looked suspicious, like cut-up magazines or a glue stick and scissors, or even paper fragments. Probably the best place to start would be with the people who had left the ship to participate in the recreational activities. By checking the sign-up board, she would be able to determine who had activities planned and what cabin they occupied. The tricky part would be to know whether the person shared a room with someone else who might still be in it. Then she remembered seeing a diagram of the cabins that indicated whether it was a single or double occupancy.

Her enthusiasm for coming up with something that might produce results was quickly quashed. This was something Kera should do, not her. But Kera was busy carrying out Dee's chores.

It was up to her.

Prickles of fear crept up her back to her neck.

* * *

So far, all the passenger cabins that Mandy checked had netted her nothing other than nerves-induced sweat. As she was about to sneak into the next cabin on her list, she noticed Wally with his own personal mat heading up for the yoga class. Since he seldom did anything else, she decided to use the opportunity to check out his digs. When she opened the door to his cabin, she immediately noticed photos adhered to the walls by old-fashioned corner stickers. A lot of pictures. As she studied them, she realized that they were either pictures of Dee by herself or snapshots of her with other crew members.

Good God, Dee is in every one of them. That's sooo weird. More than weird. He's a sicko. The pictures were hung neatly, and the rest of the room was also neat to a fault. Being in his place felt creepy.

My god, he's obsessed with Dee.

Mandy took a deep breath and started searching the room. She pulled out a suitcase from under the bed and opened it. She found clothes folded with tissue paper to keep his garments from wrinkling, even his boxers. She quickly glanced in a second suitcase and found a travel printer, a box labeled as printer cartridges, and several packs of photo paper. Okay, this is sick. She quickly shoved the two cases back under the bed and left. She couldn't get out of that place fast enough.

She went through nine passenger units that morning, snooping, invading—the law would call it, breaking and entering. Since the doors weren't locked, maybe no breaking. Maybe they'd consider it not honoring the honor system. She was beginning to sound like one of her clients, playing stupid to justify her actions.

Before each cabin search, she'd assessed the likelihood of being able to get in and back out without being seen. Terri's, or The Tart's, room was next and would be her last cabin intrusion for the afternoon. Her nerves couldn't handle any more pressure. The Tart hadn't left the ship, but Mandy had spotted her in the bar area working on a puzzle with two other passengers. She appeared engrossed in that activity. Hopefully, Mandy had enough time for a quick look-see.

All the clutter in Terri's room was in stark contrast to Wally's cabin. It was so bad Mandy could barely open the door to get into the place. Getting in was just half the battle. Her ability to move around was hindered due to the wall-to-wall clutter. The Tart hadn't taken the time to organize her space and hadn't put anything away previously worn or used, including a wet towel that smelled. A suitcase sat on top of the bed with its contents strewn throughout the small quarters.

"What a slob. How am I supposed to see anything in this chaotic place?" Mandy muttered, a little louder than she intended. As she was picking up the various items to check what lay under them, she heard someone walking down the hallway. She froze.

No one would be coming this far down the hall unless they were heading for either cabin 113 or 114, and she was in 114. She listened and to her horror determined that the footsteps had passed room 113. Only seconds…

Before she'd started her break-ins, Mandy decided that if she were to get caught in someone's room, she'd plead confusion. Being new to and not knowing her way around the boat might work as an excuse. At least it would be worth a shot. But the problem with being in this particular room was that it was located at the end of the hall. The room she shared with Kera was in the middle of a row of cabins. On another floor.

She quickly glanced underneath the bed. Since nothing had been stowed there, it looked like there'd be enough space for her, but the bed was not very high off the floor. It would be a squeeze for her. There wasn't another choice. She kicked a pile of clothes aside in order to jam herself underneath. Her feet barely made it all the way before the door opened and someone entered.

She presumed it was Terri the Tart, who then began to ruffle through her suitcase, tossing articles of clothing onto the floor.

"Where the fuck is it?" the voice said. Then there was the sound of a slammed suitcase. The lime green sneakers moved out of sight. Mandy remembered Terri wearing them at breakfast.

"It has to be somewhere, damn it."

Whatever you're looking for, it's not under here, slob.

Mandy's heart galloped like a runaway horse. It would be just her luck that even though the woman hadn't bothered to stow away any of her things, she'd still check under the bed.

Terri plopped down on the floor in a place where Mandy had a side view of her sorting through a pile of clothes. She pulled out a black-laced teddy. "Ah, there you are."

Mandy was only too aware of the fact that if the woman were to peek down a couple of more inches, she'd be able to see her wedged under the bed. My God, what could she possibly say? Her pre-planned excuse of, "Oh, sorry. I wandered into the wrong cabin and found myself under your bed," was beyond unbelievable. Sleep walking maybe? That was the only explanation she could think of that put a nice spin on an otherwise criminal behavior, more commonly thought of as attempted robbery. Her breathing had become so heavy she wondered why the woman couldn't hear her. She tried to quiet herself by imagining herself in yoga class.

There was a soft knock on the door.

"It's me, Charlie."

"Come on in, sweetie."

"Wow!" Mandy heard Charlie's low-pitched voice. She'd obviously seen The Tart's teddy.

"Just for you, baby. I'm wearing my silky best."

Mandy heard some movement. The mattress squeaked from two people falling onto it with their legs dangling over the side.

"Time for our little nap, wouldn't you say, honey?" Charlie's voice.

The suitcase was swiftly pushed off into a pile of clothes.

Giggles.

Mandy couldn't help smiling. Then it occurred to her that she'd be under the "little nap" they were about to take. *Good god!*

The kissing and cooing began and went on and on. No attempts to ignore it worked. Embarrassment meshed with her preexisting fear of exposure and jail time. This was going to be one of the most unpleasant experiences she had ever had.

After what felt like an eternity, she heard Charlie say, "I'm nervous about Deidre."

"Why?"

"When I sat at the table with Mark and William at lunch today, Mark—I learned that he's a doctor—said that there was a good chance Deidre could regain her memory. Maybe not all of it, but pieces of it."

"Really?" Terri asked.

"Yeah, and that wouldn't be good, as you well know. Be sure to keep your eyes and ears out for anything anyone says that suggests she's beginning to remember things, anything at all."

"I will, sweetie, but we got better things to think about and do right now. We want to have our special time before you-know-who gets back to the ship."

"Uh-huh. Okay. But—"

"Shhh."

Making love and listening to it under a bed were two very different experiences. Not only that, but the mattress wasn't that thick, and it lay on a wire mesh structure. It made movement something close to a trampoline experience for the participants. Being under it all made her feel an unwillingly part of Charlie and The Tart's sexual frolicking affair. Moans, groans, and squeals continued above, along with a squeaky bed. Below, Mandy incurred bumps to her head and other body parts, as well as a self-inflicted— since she chose her location—wound to her dignity.

My god, how long have I been under here?

It finally ended with sounds of contentment, followed by an announcement over the speaker that the bar would be open for happy hour in thirty minutes.

"Whew. I think I just had my happy hour," Charlie said with a big sigh of a job well done.

"I could go down for more of that, Charlie."

"Oh, me too, babe, but Bev told me that she'd be returning around five. Frankly, I don't trust her. She's got me on a short leash. I can't afford to lose the purse string to my financial well-being." Charlie snickered. "Unless, of course, you come into some money and can afford me."

"You keep promising me that you have a plan to leave her and still get enough of her money to live on," Terri said in an irritated tone. Quickly, her tenor smoothed out and flowed like warm cream. "My sweet baby love, how can you possibly keep having sex with that old bag? Especially when you have me? It must be terrible for you." Mandy almost gagged at the fake compassion.

"Believe me, it is." Charlie apparently bought the empathy act. "I have a plan. Bev promised to put me in her will when we get back to California. I'll be the only benefactor. Besides, Bev wants to get married as soon as we can. Things are looking good, but I need to behave myself until I can get a solid and permanent place in her will, like my name on a marriage certificate."

Silence. Mandy could feel the awkwardness of it from under the bed.

"Then when I divorce her, or maybe something horrible happens to her," Charlie snickered, "I'll be a very rich woman. Hang in there, babe, and keep the faith."

"Yeah, yeah, I know. It's just that I get tired of all the hiding, only having you when you can find a time to get away, and then it's limited. I'm certain she's suspicious that something's going on between us. Otherwise, she wouldn't have pulled you from the bar the other night."

"I've got everything under control. Don't worry." Charlie was beginning to sound annoyed by the subject. "I just need to keep things under control for a little longer."

A stage sigh from Terri.

"And remember," Charlie said. "Even though she saw us, she doesn't really want to know—really know, that is—what's going on. We have that in our favor. Bev doesn't want me out of her life. She thinks if she threatens me, I'll do whatever she wants. I've been with her a long time. The most important thing to her is that I don't flaunt it and humiliate her. When she worries that a friend or colleague might be onto me having someone else on the side, she becomes threatening, says she will cut me off, blah, blah, blah. She hasn't in the past. I'm certain she won't now." Charlie's last words lost the bluster.

Terri didn't say anything to Charlie's rant, and Mandy wasn't able to see her facial expression. She had to believe that Terri was a bit incredulous. At least if it were Mandy, Charlie's words would have brought on a disgusted eye roll.

"I got to get going." Charlie stood by the bed. "Hey, don't get into too much of that, okay?"

"If you would stay a little longer, you could get high, too. I scored lots of different goodies before I got on the ship."

"I wish I could, babe."

There was patting sound on the bed as Terri said, "Aww, come on honey. Sit back down. You can stay for a little longer."

"No, I really can't, but you enjoy." Charlie walked out.

"Shit!"

The Tart obviously didn't get what she wanted, for which Mandy was grateful. "Oh well. I guess it's going to have to be a party of one."

Mandy could only hope that her party wouldn't last very long.

* * *

Her back was killing her. Mandy had no idea how much time had passed since Charlie left, but it was sheer torture for her cramped body. Terri was indeed having a party by herself. Her mood swung from happy singing to sad crying to pissed tirades and back again, like an out-of-control carousel.

That is, until it became just plain bizarre.

Terri started talking to someone she perceived was in the room. At first, Mandy had thought she was talking to her, like the woman now knew that Mandy was under the bed. When the conversation between The Tart and the Whoever didn't seem to need her input, and no one else had entered the room, Mandy realized that Terri had an imaginary friend. She was hallucinating under the influence of whatever pharmaceuticals she'd downed.

Shortly after Charlie left, Terri plunked down on the floor. She landed near where she had previously donned her teddy. She lay there, mumbling and gesturing to her imaginary friend or friends, for a while. Then her arm flopped out and down with her hand landing on a plastic baggy containing some pills. That delighted her. She tried without success to open the bag with her fingers that didn't seem to be working very well. She resorted to her teeth and ripped it open. She washed the pills down with a bottle of what appeared to be whiskey.

A call to dinner came over the speaker. Mandy hoped that would inspire her to get dressed and go eat. But The Tart either didn't hear the call to dinner or food didn't appeal to her. Surely, the woman would pass out before too long. Mandy couldn't imagine how anyone could drink and take that many drugs and stay awake...or alive.

An announcement rang out over the ship's speaker. "Will Mandy Bakker please come to the lounge. Mandy Bakker to the lounge, please."

Why were they summoning her? The only answer she could think of was that it had to do with Kera. My God, did something happen to her? Was she hurt? Mandy had no choice. She had to get out from under the bed and leave that room, regardless of what would happen between her and Terri the Tart.

She inch-wormed her way back out, peeked over the foot of the bed, and caught the attention of the wild-haired Terri.

"Welcome, my better-late-than-never new friend," she slurred as she lay melted like a puddle on her back, her body out of touch with her muscles. Her head slopped over to one side. She peered through glazed-over eyes, and her lips twisted in a crooked smile. "Hi there, honey." Drool drained out of the corner of her mouth. "I'm so glad you could make it to my party." Then, she slushed out, "That will teach my girlfriend not to leave me, won't it?" Her eyelids slid shut.

Mandy took the cue and tiptoed to the door, put her hand on the knob ready to escape. She didn't take her gaze off the woman. The Tart's eyes lifted before she could get out. Mandy dropped her hand, not sure what to do next.

"Here, have some of this." The Tart pointed with a limp finger at an empty bottle of whiskey that had been tossed to the floor. "It'll make you feel better. All my friends love it, and it's made me feel so much better."

"Thanks, but I have to go now." Mandy opened the door and left, but she could hear the woman's final beckoning.

"Hey, come back. The party's just getting started."

CHAPTER THIRTEEN

Dee's Journal

Heading to Juneau to meet up with Mandy. I'm so excited!

Got all new passengers, except for good ol' Wally who, as promised, is back on board. He hasn't missed a cruise and has taken to giving me a slap on the back when he sees me out from behind the bar. Says either, "Hey, Deidre, how's it going?" Or, "See you tonight at the ol' drinking hole." Cracks me up. It's like serious business between us. I suppose it is for him. He tells me all his woes. It's sad. His life has certainly been one of an outcast. Feel bad for him. I wonder what he'll do when the season is over. Wouldn't be surprised if he wants to stay in touch. I'm a sucker for people who don't fit in. I might have made a lifelong pen pal. Yikes!

I saw something today I wished I hadn't. When I helped with taking a group on a hike this afternoon, two of the women suddenly came up missing on a head count we do several times on each hike. It fell to me to go back and find them while the group waited. When I spotted them off the trail—a real no-no—they were going hot and heavy at each other. I called out to them and they untangled and appeared startled. Why I don't know. What on earth would make them think we wouldn't go back looking for them? What really amazed me was that they didn't seem embarrassed. Instead, they acted pissed that I found them and expected them to stay with the group. I waited for them to get themselves together and follow me back. When they came up to me, one of them, Charlie, said that I'd better not mention to anyone what I had just seen, "if I knew what was good for me."

Her attitude didn't make a lot of sense until I realized she happened to be the partner of Bev, the woman who gets really drunk and blabs onto me about "her Charlie" who strays. Bev has been Charlie's sugar mama for some time now but told me she's considering cutting Charlie off. Charlie knows about her threat. Instead of falling in line with Bev's demand, she apparently chose to threaten anyone who might tell Bev what's going on. That accounted for the clenched fist she presented to me along with her warning wrapped in a snarl.

That woman scares me, so I'm recording this on paper. If anything happens, I'll have her threat documented.

I need to think of something else so I can get to sleep tonight. I'll sign off and read my book.

CHAPTER FOURTEEN

Kera

I'm looking forward to doing something besides serving drinks. Roni asked me to help on the boat launch platform since Britt was busy and might not be able to get out there. I need to remember that I'm supposed to have a sprained ankle. I can't shed my cane for any reason. It's easier at the bar to fake it because customers see me hop from one place to another while I work. They don't notice if I accidentally put my foot on the floor and allow all my weight on it. Out on the platform, I'll be more exposed.

Roni pulls her head up from one of the life jacket lockers she's ploughing around in and smiles at me. "Hey, thanks for coming out, Deidre. I know you're limited in what you can do, but I think fitting folks with these"—she holds up a life jacket she's just pulled out—"should be doable for you."

"Should be an easy enough job."

"But before you hand out any of life jackets, make sure the customers are first signed out on the board over there." She points. "It's important that we keep track of our passengers' comings and goings. Need to make sure everyone gets back."

"Will do." I limp over to Roni who then leaves to work the boats and paddle boards.

"If it's too much, let me know," she calls back. "Don't forget to put on a life jacket yourself."

"Okay." I grab a preserver. I hate these damned bulky things. They make me feel confined, but I'm not out in Lake Michigan by myself where I can do as I please. Dee wouldn't hesitate to don one of these orange beauties. Like a good girl, I slip the bulky jacket on and buckle the damned thing up.

The passengers are excited, though I hear nervousness in some of their voices. To my left, a male couple argues in loud whispers. One wants to go out in individual kayaks, and the other insists on a tandem. I wish they'd come to a damned decision or at least move out of the way. A woman is upset because she wanted one of the paddle boards, but they're all taken. Roni promises to make sure she gets one on the next ocean outing. The woman joins one of the two groups who will head to shore for a hiking trip. The naturalists who will be leading the hikes lecture the groups about the dangers of the Alaskan wilderness. They impress upon them to hang together and not wander off. One of the group leaders glances my way, like I'm an example of what happens when you don't stick with the group. Glad I can be of service. Jesus.

As I pass out and fit the jackets, I check out the faces and manner of everyone. I try to figure out if anyone seems overly interested or acting weird—even slightly so—toward me. I'm expecting a blackmail message anytime, a follow-up to the note we received last night. I don't think it'll come by someone whispering something in my ear or handing me another letter with pasted cutout letters. But I'm looking to see if someone tips their hand in some way.

At any rate, things need to come to a head ASAP while I'm still on the ship and people are contained. It would be a complete disaster if I had to figure out who is out to kill my sister after everyone has scattered all over the goddamned place. What I need is to have someone make the next move, soon.

Before long, Wally has his hand out for a life preserver. As he takes it, he flashes a quirky smile, so quick it's like he's embarrassed that he'd allowed it to cross his face. Then he says, "See you tonight at the ol' drinking hole."

"Uh-huh." What else could I say.

I wonder about him and his obsession with my sister. He's moved up on my list, although it's hard for me to think he's out to kill her. More like he's begging for attention when he's at the bar. He fucking feeds off it.

The next person in line taps her foot and holds a hand out for a life jacket. I reach in for another one even though I have one ready to go. I put the brakes on my handing-out process. I don't respond well to people being impatient with me. It brings out a passive-aggressive vein that runs through me, like when someone beeps their horn when the light turns green and I haven't gotten my foot on the accelerator fast enough.

Wally looks back at me as he heads for Roni's line.

"Have fun," I call out to him, hoping to make amends for not giving him more attention.

The guy gives me another weird smile. Or maybe it's indigestion. It can't be easy being Wally. I watch him climb into a kayak and paddle off by himself. Too bad. I feel sorry for the guy, but I've got so much going on in my mind.

I look back to the foot-tapping woman. Her name is Alice. Foster's lager is her drink of choice. She reminds me of someone who walked out of the woods at the Michigan Womyn's Festival. She's decked out in her green leafy outfit, nose ring, stomach popping out at the middle with gold navel ring, and elfin shoes, obviously not concerned that this is the land of hiking boots. This area is a rain forest. Maybe she thought it was a tropical rain forest instead of temperate rain forest. Her black curly hair swirls like a nest that's been attacked by a bear. I finally toss her a life jacket.

The last in line is Bev. I don't usually see her until the bar opens. She gives me a wink like I'm in on something with her. Well, in her case, I guess in way I am, given I'm her barmaid and in her mind, her confidant, her therapist, her enabler.

Bev takes the jacket. "Thank you, honey. I'm being brave this morning, and I'll be going out again this afternoon. I'd appreciate you having my drink ready. I'll need it after today. Make that two drinks." Bev raises two fingers for me to see.

"I'll do that." I help her adjust the straps on the life jacket.

I've taken care of everyone, and they're on their way. It's time for me to get lunch. Roni thanks me for the help and asks if I can work with her a little longer. Then she asks in a semi-flirty sort of way if I'd like to have lunch with her when we finish up here.

Whoa. That seems out of left field. Did Britt have competition for Dee's attention?

* * *

I'm starving. Roni and I are late for lunch. We head for the galley. One of the kitchen workers clears off the buffet table while another busses the dining room tables. There's an opening from the dining room into the kitchen where I'm able to see the stack of dishes and pots and pans. Lots of work for a few workers.

"Hey, don't put away the food yet. We haven't eaten," Roni growls at them as she grabs a tray. "Jesus Christ. I've told you before to make sure I'm back from the launch platform before you clean up. And stop banging those chairs around. You're getting them all nicked up. Jesus, they cost money, you know." Roni looks at me as though I must agree with her. Frankly, I don't see any nicks.

I glance away, not wanting to side with her, while both women stop what they're doing and give Roni a "I'm-looking-through-you stare." They go into the kitchen. One scrapes dirty dishes, while the other stacks them. They're stone-faced and attack their jobs with angry energy.

Roni and I fill our plates from the buffet table. I choose the chicken salad sandwich, vegetable soup, and canned fruit before I join Roni at the galley table.

"Got enough food there?" Roni says to me in a mock sarcastic tone. "Damn. I must have worked you too hard."

"No, not really."

Her expression turns thoughtful. "I have to say I've never seen you eat that much."

"Just enough work to give me a big appetite, I guess." I realize that I've always eaten more than Dee but eating more than my sister shouldn't give me away. I decide not to make a big deal of it and overexplain like people who lie are prone to do.

Roni laughs. "Well, I've never seen you pile your plate like that before."

"Maybe there's a hole in my ankle where food's escaping." Apparently, she and Dee have eaten together quite a lot.

Britt walks through the area and into the kitchen. I can hear her giving the kitchen staff instructions about the evening meal. She strolls over to our table and narrows her eyes at Roni. "The captain says he needs you on the bridge as soon as you can. I'll take care of anything that's left to do out on the launch. You better hustle."

Roni returns the hateful look and checks her watch before she snaps, "Don't you worry about me and my responsibilities."

"Isn't that why you got kicked out of the military? Falling down on the job and not listening to orders? Or was it your bouts of bad temper?" Britt offers, like dangling raw meat in front of a lion.

Hmm. This is interesting.

Roni face reddens, and her glare is hot enough to burn a hole through steel. "I'll go up there when I'm fucking ready to go." Then she turns to me, totally calm like she'd just opened her eyes from meditation. "I see your ankle is doing a lot better. How about your memory? Anything coming back yet?"

Wow, that's talent...or scary.

I have a mouth full and therefore have time to think through what to say. I want to be ambiguous, give them the ideas that my memory's trickling back but not all there. I shake my head as I chew and swallow. "A few minor things, here and there, but nothing much to speak of."

They both raise their eyebrows.

By getting it out there that I'm beginning, though ever so little, to remember things, I'm hoping to up the pressure on my sister's would-be murderer. I figure Britt and Roni will get the word around, at least to the crew, then it will leak on down to the passengers. As much as everyone on this ship pretends otherwise, I know that I'm a popular topic for gossip.

* * *

I open a few new bottles that will be needed, fill some nuts dishes, place them around the lounge, and return to the bar. A folded paper under the tips jar catches my attention. I open it up and see that it's another note from whoever it is who knows what I'm up to. It's in the same style as the last: *I'm watching you and your memory problem!*

I look around the bar, but no one is in the vicinity. I check the time. It's still a little early for customers. Whoever left that message for me isn't likely to stand around and watch me read it, like a pyromaniac watching the blaze he's set. I know the note wasn't here when I checked on the supplies this morning, but there has been plenty of opportunity since then for just about anyone to slip it under the jar.

Hmm, I wonder, does this note mean that they don't believe Deidre has a memory problem, or they don't believe I am Deidre.

I try to think it through. Either way, I figure whoever tried to kill my sister realizes that I'm a threat. They probably think that Mandy is too. People know she's a lawyer and Deidre's friend and is someone who would question the odds of Deidre's having another nasty accident. Their next attempt on my life has to be foolproof. But they'll have to wait for the right opportunity to come along to finish the job—some kind of a deadly event that couldn't be called into question by anyone, especially Mandy. It feels like the oxygen has gone out of the room. I suck in several deep breaths, let them out slowly concentrating on staying in the moment.

I stuff the note in my pocket and wonder what kind of shitty situation this might have put Mandy in. I need to keep a closer eye on her and insist she be extra careful. Otherwise, Mandy might be included in the next attempt on Dee's life, whether planned or by mistake. Shit, they might try to get us both in one fell swoop.

As I worry about how I've put Mandy in harm's way, I realize she should have shown up here by now. Jesus, where is she?

Mandy wasn't in the cabin when I changed into dry clothes. I know she didn't have plans to leave the ship today, she probably changed her mind and decided to do an afternoon trip. All tours should be back any minute now. She probably did do a trip, maybe felt she needed to check something out or hang with someone who was going off-ship. That doesn't give me a lot of relief now that I worry her life might be in danger.

My anxiety is blowing through the roof. It's one thing for me to stick my ass out there, quite another to have Mandy's ass out there, too. Jesus, I couldn't take it if something happened to her.

Shit, shit, shit. I can't live through another disaster, another death of someone else I love. The pictures of Iraq are coming faster, getting clearer. I'm disoriented and suspended between the bar on the ship and the checkpoint in Iraq...at the point of no return...

My girlfriend, Kelly, is about to blow up. She's looking toward me. I know what's going to happen, I've seen it before, a million times. I rush to her but too late. Her body explodes. I fall from the released force, look up and watch her fly into pieces. Blood, skin, and bones splatter everywhere, fly in my face. The stench of death. Sand stings my eyes, blinding me and filling my lungs, stealing my breath.

Someone rolls me over onto my back. A blurred face stares down at me. I can't make it out. Who is it? The lips on the face are moving like horizontal dancing worms. I hear random sounds, words strung together, senseless, out of order. Maybe a different language.

I'm wringing wet. I don't know where I am, but I'm in tight quarters. I hear heavy breathing. It's me.

Another blurry face appears behind the first face. More garbled words come from the dancing worms. Yet, I still can't make any sense of what's being said. A hand comes toward me and something cold pats my forehead, hurts, burns. I close my eyes, turn off the sensory stimulation.

I'm overwhelmed.

I hear Moran's voice. She's chanting to the beat of her drum, and the drum is pulling me. Then Lakota's tongue slurps my cheek. I open my eyes, still blurry in ambient shade of twilight. Moran and Lakota watch over me then slowly fade away replaced by an image of another woman, fuzzy, but coming in now. Gradual, like adjusting the focus on a camera shot.

I'm almost there…

"Are you okay?" It's Britt's face not Moran's. Britt is kneeling and bending over me. She asks again, "Are you okay?" She holds something icy to my forehead then pulls the cold away. I see that it's a rag, soaked red.

"I think so. Yeah, I'm okay. Really. I'm okay." I figure that I must have smacked my head on something when I fell. Of course, I'm not going to admit I had a flashback.

"I've called for the staff nurse," Britt assures me.

I nod and feel woozy. I don't know whether it's from hitting my head or just my usual grogginess coming out of one of my episodes.

"She must have banged her head on the bar going down, but it looks like the bleeding has stopped." I see Bev's lips moving as she peers over Britt's shoulder, wide-eyed. "My guess is her fall was because of her sprained ankle. Probably put weight on it and down she went." Bev is giving her version as to what she imagines happened to me. "I just came in from kayaking, and I heard this loud noise coming from the lounge area. At first, I couldn't figure out where the noise came from. Then I heard her moaning and looked over the bar. There she was, flat on her back on the floor. It scared me to death!"

Thank you, Bev. She has just handed me my story of what happened.

* * *

The nurse insisted I lie down for a while and that Mandy keep an eye on me. She said she'd be back to check in to see how I was doing in a few hours. Until then, the guy who covers for me would take over at the bar. When the nurse returned, I insisted I was fine. She was hesitant and eyed me suspiciously. She finally cleared me to return to work as long as Mandy was there and watched me carefully.

Mandy has taken the nurse's instruction to heart. She sits with her drink at the bar with her eyes glued on me. It terrified her when she heard herself paged on the loudspeaker. She told me that her heart jumped up into her throat and was having a hard time finding its way back into her chest. She thought I'd been killed. When we got back in our cabin, I told her it was only a flashback and that I'd smacked my head going down. That explanation didn't give her much relief.

When Mandy told me about her day searching through the passenger's cabins, I was both alarmed and proud of her. Alarmed at what could have gone so wrong had she gotten caught, but proud she had the courage to do that sort of thing. Had my employee and friend, Vinny, told me over a game of pool and a beer about being stuck under a bed while a couple screwed, I would still be laughing my fucking head off. In Mandy's case, not so funny.

After telling me about all the places she'd searched and found nothing, Mandy finally tells me about Wally's obsession with Dee and what she'd overheard Charlie say about being worried that Dee might regain her memory.

Holy shit!

I add up what I know about Charlie. She has a prison record. She's living off Bev while fucking women on the side, and she's into drugs. From serving her at the bar, I know that she drinks Bud Light—classless choice of brew, in my book, but that doesn't mean anything. I try to come up with a motive. Why would Charlie want to hurt my sister?

And Wally? His obsession with Dee? Somehow, I don't see the guy pushing my sister over the cliff. He doesn't have the body bulk. Then again, if it were unexpected and from behind... He's certainly fixated on her, no doubt about that. All those pictures of her? He could be a sicko serial killer or one of those obsessed weirdos who doesn't ride the rails of reality and ends up killing what he can't have. Jesus! Still, I don't believe Wally's my bad guy, but I'll keep an eye on him.

CHAPTER FIFTEEN

Dee's Journal

Getting close to Juneau. Yeah! Can't wait to have Mandy here and be able to talk to her. I have sooo missed her this summer.

I miss Nona already. I think I could have had a close friendship with her. We'd spend a lot of time working together and had gotten to know and like each other. She's a straight woman and it was frankly easier to have a friendship with her because there were never any misunderstandings between us regarding romance.

I keep struggling with my depression and have to push myself to do anything that isn't related to my job. Feel so depleted most of the time. I was wrong to think that running away and occupying my mind with other things would heal me. I did plan to do some self-healing, working on my issues. Not! After this cruise season, wherever I go or whatever I do, I need to find a therapist to help me with the pile of grief I carry around and can't seem to dump. I promise myself, here in writing, that I will get a therapist! I promise. I promise. I promise!

But I really wonder... Does anyone ever get completely over grief?

On a positive note—and I'm glad I have something good going on—I love helping native people get jobs. I do think the native women who are on our ship have to work way too hard and definitely need more help. I heard one of the women, Coleen, complain about their workload. I talked to Captain James about how long they work and how little rest or relaxation they get. He listened and agreed and said he'd look into it and see what he could do. He's a good man, but he told me he'd have to take it to corporate, a hard sell. Still, he thought he could come up with something that wouldn't have to be cleared by the higher-ups.

Nona has a good soul and has been concerned about how Roni treats the native workers, too. She wasn't there when Agnes accidentally spilled spaghetti sauce on Roni, but I told her about it later. I must confess to you, dear journal, I never did let the captain know about that incident as I had planned. That very night, just before the nature lecture, he got up in front of the crew and passengers and complimented Roni on some cruise line award she'd received. He went on to let everyone know how devoted she was to the passengers and all her other job duties. I was afraid that if I had told him about what happened between Roni and Agnes, it wouldn't have gone over well. I'm not sure when or if I should say anything at this point. Maybe the next time—and I'm certain there will be another Roni outburst—I'll let the captain know about it. I promise myself this—in writing!

Wally has been getting on my nerves lately. I try hard not to show it, but I don't have the patience with him, not like I had earlier in the season. Just haven't been able to give him the attention he demands and seems to require from me. Don't know if I have the energy to do any better. He ticked me off when he grunted after I told him about Mandy joining the cruise in Juneau. Jealous little snot.

I'm tired, so signing off for now.

CHAPTER SIXTEEN

Kera

The nurse came to my cabin to check on me this morning. She said I have a concussion—which she'd already told me last night—even though I've consistently denied any of the symptoms. I didn't want her to put any limits on me. She tactfully avoided my bandages that covered my supposed head wounds from my supposed cliff plunge. I guess that was because when the word came down from the captain that no one was allowed to talk to me about what had happened, it apparently applied to absolutely everyone, even the nurse. Or at least she thought it did and adhered to his command. That's a lot of power and I was grateful for it and reinforced the notion that she didn't need to worry about it. She kept shaking her head as I refused to admit symptoms, other than the lump above my eye which was hurting. I sat across from her as she jotted down copious notes on her pad—covering her ass, no doubt, so she won't lose her medical license. I tried to see what she was writing but I'm not skilled at reading upside down—though I did make out the words, "not allowed," and "she claims," and "refuses" and "uncooperative." That's all true. I made it clear, like I did last night, that the bandaged area of head hadn't hit anything and my ankle was okay and wasn't further injured it. Besides my head, I didn't want her checking my bogus bad ankle still wrapped in Ace bandages.

Last night, the nurse hadn't asked for much in the way of details about why I fell. I certainly didn't volunteer any info at that time. This morning, she questioned me. I stuck with Bev's explanation that I had tried to put a little too much weight on my foot, and it threw me off balance. Then I added another culprit as to why I took a nosedive behind the bar. I said there was spilled beer on the floor from pouring beer into mugs from the spigot. That part is true. To make my point, I handed her my pants and shirt that had mopped the boozy floor when I landed there. I wanted to convince her I hadn't had a seizure or something even more severe. My soaked clothes seemed to satisfy her, and she was pleased when I said I'd be asking for a floor mat to keep it from happening again. Of course, the mat won't stop a flashback. Wish it would. Before I returned to my post last night, the word had apparently gotten out about my fall. All the beer behind the bar had been cleaned up. Hell, there had to have been a lot more suds there than usual, given I had had a mug of it in my hand when I hit the deck.

The nurse finally left just as Mandy was bringing us both some coffee from the dining room.

* * *

Mandy hands me the coffee and sits beside me on the bed. I insist that she give up the room invasions. I could tell she was still shaken from yesterday. We decided she would hang out around the ship to check to see what's happening and maybe take part in the snorkeling, since I noticed earlier there were two slots left open for that activity. I know she'd love it. She instantly agrees to that plan. When I ask Mandy why she's rubbing her stomach, she tells me it's upset from all the coffee she's been drinking and perhaps she should have some breakfast to settle it. I figure that her upset stomach is most likely due to her snooping escapade. I suggest she go to the yoga class this morning to help calm her nerves.

Besides not being honest with the nurse, I haven't exactly been truthful with Mandy either about not feeling well. Otherwise, I know she'd be freaking out right now. She doesn't need more stress.

I'm not trying to be superwoman, but I don't have time for a concussion. I've had several concussions in my life and recognize the symptoms and know I can function with them. Although a short nap is in order.

* * *

I'm jarred awake by a nightmare, a recurrent one that has its roots in Iraq. I wonder if I'll have that nightmare for the rest of my life. Maybe someday, the film will get old and break like on the old movie reels. I wait for my breathing to settle down and wipe my sweaty forehead with the pillowcase.

Ouch! I forgot about my goose egg.

There are ten minutes left before the kitchen closes for breakfast, so I grab my cane and limp off as fast as I can while still maintaining ankle-injury credibility to anyone who could be watching me. The cane slows me down, which isn't a bad thing. I'm still dizzy, and on top of that, I have a hell of a headache. I forgot to take the pain meds that the nurse gave me last night. I go back to my cabin to grab them before heading back to the dining area.

All the passengers have eaten and are gone except for Roni and Mick who are eating in the cafeteria area. I scoop up some scrambled eggs with sausage, a bagel and cream cheese, and a couple of slices of watermelon. I decide to sit with them.

"Mind if I join you?" I know they didn't see me approach. I've obviously startled them. Whatever they were talking about comes to an abrupt stop.

"Sure, sure," Mick says with a mouthful. He kicks out a chair for me without missing a beat with his fork.

"I hope I didn't interrupt your conversation." From the expression on their faces, I know I have.

"No, not at all. I'm about done." Mick checks his watch.

"How are you doing this morning?" Roni asks me.

"Fine." I'm not going to let anyone know how I feel, or I'll be relieved of duty. I give her my cobbled version of what happened behind the bar, though I'm sure she's already heard it from others.

"I'm so sorry," Roni says. "If there's anything we can do to make your work environment better, I—"

"Well, my slide to the floor was mostly due to the beer suds on the floor. It happens when I fill the mugs at the tap. It slops over some, especially when I'm busy. Then there's water from the sink. It spills due to the ship rocking. Sometimes, it gets slippery back there."

"We can't have that." Roni appears genuinely concerned. "No one's complained about that before. What do they do in other bars?"

"They have rubber drainage mats, ones with holes in them for the liquid to seep through. It keeps the floor from getting so slippery."

"Why haven't you mentioned that to us before?"

I shrug my shoulders. No doubt my reflex shrug was as good an answer as anything that might burst out of my mouth. Nothing I have to back-peddle from. Hell, how would I have any idea if Dee ever complained about not having a mat? Is Roni feeling guilty for not providing one and a possible lawsuit? Or is Roni testing me?

Roni seems content with my reaction.

"As a matter of fact, if you're feeling okay," Mick says, "I sure could use your help this morning. I have another leak in the air-conditioning system in a passenger's cabin. Water's leaking onto the passenger's bed. I have a ton of other things to get done today. Since you have some experience with fixing that sort of thing…"

I can't very well say "no" to him, can I? Dee must have learned some shit about the air-conditioning, not that I know anything about it. Or is he quizzing me, too? Is that what they were discussing before I came to the table? How they'd both test me?

Sweat oozes out of me. How can I gracefully deal with fixing an air-conditioning problem that I know nothing about? All I can do is hope they will buy the idea that my loss of memory of people and places also goes along with learning about air-conditioning systems, even though my ability to bartend wasn't a factor. *Ah-ha*. The light bulb comes on in my brain, finally. Like me, Dee acquired bartending skills in college. But she only recently learned about their air-conditioning system. I know for sure she wouldn't have picked it up anywhere else but here on this ship. If they think that they've snagged me in a lie, I'll explain the difference—bartending is an old skill.

"I'll no doubt have to be retrained on how to do that," I say. I watch Mick's facial expression.

"I'm sorry. I forgot. No problem," Mick says. "We'll get the tools, and I'll show you the room and give you a quick refresher."

"Yeah, that would be a recent skill I've learned from you, not an old one from another time." There…just in case there's any doubt. Neither his or Roni's expression gave me a clue as to whether I was being tested.

Roni wipes her mouth with a napkin. "Deidre, I could use your assistance this afternoon. Britt said that you seemed good enough, now, and suggested that you could help on the launch today. We really need a third hand. But only if you feel up to it. I know you got your bar shift later and I don't want to—"

"Should be no problem." I hope my headache feels better by then.

"I gotta run." Mick gets up. "Take your time with your breakfast. Make sure you wear your long pants and a jacket. You'll be crawling around all the pipes. It's damned cold." He leaves.

"Yeah, this time of year it can get downright frigid there," Roni says. "It was cold on the platform when I went out there early this morning. The weather's supposed to be chilly all day, so be sure to dress warm."

Roni decides she'll hang with me while I eat. She's attentive and nice to me but says little that gives me a clue about anybody. It's not like I can ask her, the second-in-command, anything about me/Dee and what happened. Periodically, I catch her staring at me, like she's trying to evaluate me. She asks questions like, do I remember this or that? It makes me have to think fast if it's something I should know now, or did I only know it before my fall from the cliff—like do I really have amnesia? Then she goes on to other things, such as, am I "feeling okay, these days?" and "is my vision clear?" and if I'm sleeping well, and any "dreams" that are hard for me to sort out? I guess that's her euphemism for hallucinations. The last set of questions were likely her effort to try to determine if I'm sane and fit for duty.

I gobble down a slice of watermelon, totally forgetting that Dee doesn't like the stuff. She can't even stand the smell of it. I realize by the look on Roni's face that she's aware of Dee's distaste for the fruit. I decide not to address the matter as it might make her more suspicious if I stumbled around trying to justify my melon slurping. I say something to the effect that I'm so thirsty these days that I need to get juice wherever I can. Then I change the subject. I need to be more aware and remember what Dee likes to eat and what she doesn't. I better not eat any pork. Dee has a thing for pigs.

I excuse myself, telling Roni that I'll be sure to be there in the afternoon to help her and Britt on the launch platform. She gives me a wink.

Maybe she admires my fortitude.

* * *

I probably should get to the bar. Everyone's back on-ship, most of them ready for drinks. Roni, Britt, and I finished getting the inflatable skiffs back up on top where they're stowed for the night. There won't be any more trips until tomorrow morning. Roni and Britt stay to finish buttoning up all that needs to be done on the platform, while I head for my station in the lounge so I can prepare for the onslaught.

I'm almost finished setting things up at the bar. It's still early to open up, but what the hell. I signal for the few folks who are already in the lounge to come over to the bar and I'll take their order.

I'm handing out drinks when I see Roni rushing into the lounge. "Deidre, the captain wants me on the bridge," she says. "I need to get up there, pronto. There's some problem." She realizes that a few passengers have overheard her and look concerned, so she turns to them and downplays her message. "Hey, it's nothing serious, I'm sure, most likely he needs to pee, that's all." She chuckles then turns back to me and lowers her voice. "Britt's still out there on the platform finishing up, but she can use help so she'll be able to get to her other duties. I need you to head out there now. I'll see if I can get someone to tend the bar until you can get back. It shouldn't take long at all." She scans the lounge. "It's early, anyway, and not that many customers here."

"Not a problem." I don't mind having more time out on the platform. I'd rather be outside any day, especially around water. I toss my rag in the sink and leave the bar. I'm glad that one of Dee's duties has been to be the on-call person when Britt or Roni can't finish buttoning up for the evening. Mick told me that it was a position of trust to make sure all was checked out at the day's end. Of course, Mick could do it too, but he is called only as a last resort due his needing to be on hand for any technical duties and emergencies. I'm glad I know what has to be done to finish up for the night. And since Britt will be out there, too, all should go fine.

"Thanks," Roni gives me another friendly wink. I wonder how sure she is that I'm okay to perform my duties. Did I pass my test today? She calls out after me as I leave the lounge. "I quickly checked the passenger in/out board before we started putting things away, but we always give it a second look to make sure we don't miss anyone. It's protocol."

"Sure thing."

* * *

I suck in the ocean air, wishing I could hang there for a couple of hours and not have to return to the bar. Britt sees me and asks if I'd be comfortable taking care of the rest of it as she needs to get back to wrap things up, "stuff that needed to be done, hours ago." She wipes her brow with her arm, looking harried. I give her a thumbs-up, and she smiles and mouths a "thank you." Before heading back into the ship, she reminds me to check the passenger board. It's good to know they take that seriously.

The gear is pretty much picked up and put back when I notice another life jacket that's not been stored, probably tossed by a passenger who was in a hurry for a drink. As I walk over to it, I notice the in/out passenger board and am reminded that I'm supposed to double-check it. I fetch the life jacket, put it away, and go over to the board. As I scroll down the list of names, I see that there's one name at the very end that hasn't been checked off as having returned from the last outing. It's a woman named Ruth Zappa.

Shit. If this woman didn't just forget to sign in, then she must be still out there, and it's getting dark. Jesus!

I rush in and catch the first crew member I see and ask him to hurry and find Britt to tell her that I need her out on the platform. I emphasize that it's important. ASAP. As I wait for her, I scan the water to see if Ruth might be on her way in.

"What's your problem?" Britt asks when she comes out.

"Over there." I motion in the direction of the passenger board as I walk back toward it. "Look, there's a name here, and it's not checked off. I thought I'd better show you before—"

"Are you sure?" Britt scowls and checks the board.

"Right here." I point to the name at the bottom of the list.

"Oh my god, that's not good. Damn." Britt runs her finger up and down the list of names several times.

"She's the only one who seems to still be out there," I say.

"Let's hope so. I'll go in and page her. It wouldn't be the first time someone forgot to check in." Britt rushes back into the ship.

I hear Ruth Zappa's name on the loudspeaker, several times. I try to place who the woman is, what she looks like, but I can't. Really, I reason, I haven't had time to get to know everyone onboard. She must not be one of the regulars at the bar.

After a few minutes, Britt comes back out to the platform. Her expression tells me that she hasn't gotten any response from her page.

"I have some folks searching for her but so far, no luck. Let me check this board again." Britt runs her finger down the list and stops and glares at the board. "Damn it, the woman forgot to put her room number on here. No matter how many times I give that instruction, someone inevitably forgets."

"Do we know what group she went with?" I ask.

"It shows here," Britt points to the board, "that she didn't go out with any group—which is probably why no one has reported her missing. And, if she came on the cruise as a single that might also account for why no one has noticed that she's not back."

"How many kayaks do we have?" I'm looking up at the top of the deck where they're stowed.

"Twelve singles and eight tandems. Would you please go up there and do a count for me?"

"Sure enough." I head up to the top deck of the ship and come back with the bad news that we do, indeed, have one missing single passenger kayak.

"Oh shit. She's probably still out there. We need to get someone out to look for her, fast." Britt looks thoughtful. "We're so damned shorthanded on this trip. I don't know who we could get to do it?" She scratches her head.

"Shouldn't we let Roni know about this? She's in command right now. And she might know who could help with—"

"No!" Britt pales, looks like she might vomit. "Roni hates me and will have my head if she finds out that I didn't check the board, and a passenger's been missing this long. She been trying to get me fired for a long."

"Actually, she asked me to make sure it was double-checked." I confess.

"Doesn't matter. Believe me, it's considered my responsibility, not yours. I can't believe it. I checked it the first time but didn't see any names not check off. I should have checked it before I went in because I outrank you, not to speak of the fact that you are—"

Nice of Britt to stop before she says that I'm impaired or nuts or whatever.

"Well, it's my problem, not yours, Deidre, and I need to take a skiff out to search for her. I'll be lucky to make it off this boat alive letting this happen, along with not getting my work done." She sighs. "God knows I'm not going to leave this job with any recommendations for future employment."

I don't feel like fighting her for the responsibility of this situation, but I'm feeling bad for Britt. She's clearly panicky and desperate. I'm a sucker when it comes to jumping in and helping people; actually, it's pretty much my job description as a detective.

She looks at me, her eyes seem to be pleading for me to say that I'll do it. She probably doesn't want to out and out ask because of my injuries and what the captain might say about sending me out. I figure that since Dee has piloted these boats and that she knew how to do it before she came to this job, it's an old skill that a "brain injured" Dee should be able to do without being retrained. And, since I've driven these crafts myself pretty much all my life on Lake Michigan, it's not a problem for me.

We hear footsteps behind us and turn to see Mick. He's fumbling around in the stationary toolbox located near the life jacket storage unit.

"Hey Mick," Britt calls out. "Are you real busy?"

"Hell, yeah, real busy. Probably be up all night," he says, "Need to try and fix a diesel engine. Goddamned captain doesn't call me right away and ends up making things worse. I got a damaged part now. The man thinks he knows shit, but he doesn't." Mick huffs. "Wish he'd just go back to driving the frigging boat."

There goes Britt's hope that Mick might come to rescue her. What the hell. Ruth has probably lost track of time out there. I would love a nice buzz around the small islands in this bay, and someone needs to get out there as quickly as possible to find this woman.

It's obvious that Britt's waiting for me to jump in.

"I'll do it," I tell her.

"Thank you. Thank you so much. You are a lifesaver!" Britt looks like a ton of bricks have been lifted from her. She reaches out and puts her hand on my shoulder. "It's not just that I probably couldn't find anyone else to help me, especially someone who's not invested in making a big deal out of this," she adds with a thin smile. But then she quickly points out, "This is a big deal, for sure. But I got a ton of stuff to do before tomorrow morning or my ass will be in a sling, if it's not already." She shakes her head.

"Got you." I say. I figure she's counting on me, her girlfriend—even if I'm supposedly not aware of that—to be on her side.

"Oh shit." She wrinkles her brow. "All the skiffs are bedded down. How am I ever going to round up a crew to help me get one down here?"

I understand the problem. It takes a lot of help to bring down the skiffs. They need two people on the top deck who attach ropes to the skiffs, then lower each boat down individually to two waiting members of the crew.

"Do you suppose you could take out Mick's old fishing boat?" She's pointing to the old metal outboard sitting on the platform.

I see that Mick is still messing around in his toolbox, I call out to him, "Hey Mick, would you mind if we use your boat?"

"No problem," he says without raising his head from his task, too preoccupied to ask why we want it.

"How come he doesn't stow it up with the other skiffs?" I ask Britt, not wanting to bother Mick or risk getting him involved in what we are doing.

"He says he wants to be able to jump in it anytime and not have to go through bringing it down from the top, so the captain lets him keep it there."

"Okay, why not? I'll take it," I say. This wouldn't be the first time I've been in one of those old tubs.

Britt gives me her toothy smile. "Thanks, Deidre. You're truly saving my ass by doing this." She takes a step toward me, like she's about to hug me, then must think better of it and pulls back.

Britt gives me a push off into the water and away I go. The old metal skiff has, no doubt, a lot of years on it, but it seems sturdy.

Reminds me of the many old fishing boats people use back home. I'm more partial to it than the inflatable skiffs. It's got character. I check the motor to make sure it has enough gas in the tank. It's almost full, so I start it up and take off in search of Ruth.

There's a bit of a wind out here, which makes the water a little choppy, but I love it this way. The problem is these waves aren't good for a kayaker, especially if she's not very experienced.

I know I really can't afford the time out here. What I need to be focused on is who might have attacked my sister, not searching for someone who doesn't understand returning to the ship before dark. But as I scan the inlet, I can understand how someone could lose time out here as they take in the beauty of the inlet's high-treed cliffs and waterfalls.

There are a lot of small islands in this bay, so I circle around them to look for her. I see otters everywhere, several holding paws. I pass by one with a baby on her tummy, knocking the cute factor off the charts. I wish I could stay out here for hours and hang with these furry guys.

Suddenly, my boat stops, even though the motor hasn't quit. The first thing I worry about is the propeller. Has it gotten wound up in all the kelp that I'm trying to avoid but not always succeeding? I turn off the motor and pull it up.

There is no prop.

Jesus!

The damned thing had to have been loose, just waiting to drop off, when I left. *Fuck.* I should have checked it before I went out. I look all around the craft. No paddles. At least I was always smart enough to carry paddles in my boat on Lake Michigan.

Now what in hell am I going to do?

I suppose if I sit here long enough someone will eventually come look for me, as well as Ruth. But how long will that be? God damn it. The wind is getting stronger and the waves are kicking up higher. I unhook my life jacket so I can zip up my sweatshirt that's underneath. Then I pull up my hoodie and tie the strings together tight. That helps some.

Looking around inside of the boat, I try to find something that will help me out of this mess, like anything I could paddle with or form into a paddle. Not a damned thing. In my search, I notice some water trickling up into the bottom of the skiff.

What the fuck!

I watch in disbelief as the ocean water seeps in. As it oozes its way in, I can see that it's increasing in volume. With my hand, I check along the seams of the hull and find where the water is getting access. It's leaking in from around two of the rivets.

Shit!

I look closer and discover that there are marks and dents that suggest that the rivets have been damaged, like pounded and pried on, which would explain the loosing of the seals. Jesus. Someone has messed with this boat, and it must have been fairly recently. Mick told me that he took it out not that long ago.

I can't come up with a reason that anyone would damage his boat. Does someone hate Mick? Then a thought creeps into my brain.

Did someone plan all along to get me out here and put me in this situation?

Have I succeeded in getting the person who tried to kill my sister to finally come after me?

But how could anyone possibly know in advance that there would be a missing passenger tonight and that I'd end up searching for her—and in this particular craft? Really, it doesn't seem possible that it could be a planned attempt on my life. Too many coincidences, too many variables.

The most important thing for me to focus on right now is how I'm going to get the hell out of this mess. I'm in deep shit. The water begins to pour even faster into the boat. The volume will most likely only increase as the area around the leak weakens further. How long can I sit here until someone comes?

Or will anyone even come?

Doubt seeps into my psyche like the water seeping into the craft. Not good, but I can't seem to stop it. Will Britt remember, in time, that she's sent me out in the ocean? I know she's frantically busy elsewhere and upset and anxious about not having things done. Her job is at stake. I take a deep breath, then another. I remind myself not to give in to panic. Stay calm, I tell myself, or I'll never get out of this predicament alive. Keep thinking. Keep looking for a way.

Damn it, there's got to be a way.

The only thing in this old clunker boat that could be used for bailing is a flimsy drink container from a fast food restaurant. That's another thing I could kick Mick's ass for. There's no bilge pump or even a bailing can that I could use to pump or scoop the water out.

What the fuck is wrong with Mick? Where are his emergency supplies? Knowing what I know about him, I would have guessed that he's a guy who'd insist upon stringent safety precautions. Guess not.

The prop had to have been loose from the get-go to have fallen off so soon after heading out here. I have the life jacket, but it won't help me get to the ship. It's not like I can jump in the water and swim back. The ocean is so fucking cold that my muscles would cramp up, and hypothermia would set in before I could reach the ship.

Another factor, not in my favor, is that I'm behind an island completely out of sight of the ship. As I look around, I can't see any other boats, let alone Ruth in her kayak. Not one single soul except for some otters who don't seem to be interested in my plight. I'm envious of their fur coats, coats that would keep me warm enough to swim back to the ship.

I take the paper cup and begin to bail. I know it's useless, but it makes me think I'm doing something for myself. Already, the paper cup is breaking down. I'm hoping sooner or later, Mandy will notice my absence.

She's my last hope.

CHAPTER SEVENTEEN

Mandy

The yoga class started too early in the morning to Mandy's liking, especially on a vacation. Well, what was supposed to be a vacation. Still, Mandy valued the morning class that was offered. The woman who led the class was into the spiritual well-being part of it, as well as the physical conditioning. Mandy counted on it being a brief hiatus from the stress she's felt every second of the day since she boarded the ship and began living a charade. Being there felt to her like walking on thin ice and being totally certain that at some point she'd break through.

At any one moment, it was difficult to know just how well she was pulling the whole ruse off. There were times when she saw people giving her or Kera strange glances, but she couldn't discern if it was because people doubted them, or simply because the whole situation was weird for everyone. And apparently the person sending them notes had indeed figured out their scam, making it feel like the boogieman was around every corner, ready to pounce.

Shivers crept up her spine when she thought of what had happened yesterday as she crawled out from under Terri the Tart's bed. She wondered how far gone Terri was. What would her reaction be when the drugs wore off and she saw Mandy for the first time since that encounter? Would the drugs erase the whole bizarre scene?

Then, when she entered the lounge and saw Kera on the floor behind the bar being tended to, her heart flew up to her throat. My god, she thought that Kera had been shot or stabbed, maybe even dead. Remembering that moment made her stomach turn over. Every day the stress weighed on her and gathered momentum. Conceivably, there'd be the morning that she wouldn't be able to get out of bed.

She also feared that someone might have seen her leave Terri's cabin. She'd told Kera that she didn't believe anyone noticed, but she couldn't be certain. When she slipped out of the room, she thought she saw a shadow of a person move across the intersection of the two hallways located ahead of her. But it was such a quick glimpse. Good god, this trip started out to be a vacation cruise with Dee, but it has turned out to be a nightmare.

Mandy lumbered up the steel stairs to the deck where the yoga class was being held. The crew was busy lowering the last of the skiffs and kayaks from where they'd been stowed for the night.

She kicked off her slippers. The sun-heated surface of the deck's floor warmed her feet, mitigating the chilliness of the morning ocean breeze. If it weren't for the circumstances of this cruise, she would have been enthusiastic and invigorated by the freshness of this start of her day. But as it was, she could only hope for a moment or two of respite.

"Hi Mandy, get your mat and come over by me." It was Alice. Mandy remembered Kera's name for the woman, "wood nymph."

Alice was friendly and more verbal than Mandy's liking, especially when she wanted to concentrate on her yoga. But what was most disturbing and invasive was the woman's personal hygiene. Cleanliness wasn't one of Alice's virtues. Working out next to her was more than Mandy believed she could endure again. She experienced that at the last yoga class and once was more than plenty. But she didn't know a tactful way to explain to Alice that she didn't wish to be next to her. One of Mandy's problems, according to Kera, was that she was too nice and never wanted to offend people. For a fleeting moment, Mandy envisioned diving over the rail to escape Alice. Looking down at the water, she figured she probably could pull off a one-and-a-half summersault. She'd done plenty of them in college but not into freezing cold ocean water. She took a deep breath of fresh air that she feared would be her last for a while.

"Hurry, we're about to start," Alice called out from her spot.

"Okay." Mandy smiled half-heartedly and ambled over to the pile of mats. She pretended to search for just the right one, hoping if she lingered long enough, some unsuspecting person might plop down next to Alice.

"Saved a place for you." Alice patted the space next to her as Mandy snailed her way over toward the group.

"Thanks." Mandy reluctantly settled down next to Alice and crisscrossed her legs. The woman was dressed in camouflage green yoga pants, a sunflower yellow top, and a yellow band snugged around her snarled black hair. Dirty feet with chipped red polished toenails topped off her presentation. It was the very same costume Alice wore to the last class.

Alice stretched her arms and legs. "I'm sore from yesterday."

"Me, too." Mandy shook and rotated her shoulders to loosen muscles that felt as though they'd petrified into knots. It was clear to her that her discomfort had much more to do with the stress from her present life circumstances—including being stuck and cramped under Terri the Tart's bed—than the previous yoga class.

"I like your friend, Deidre. She's always nice to me. Not everyone is." Alice glanced around as though maybe she'd spoken too loudly. "How's she doing anyway?"

"Better."

"The word's out that she's regained some of her memory. Is that true?"

Hmm. The word had even reached Alice, the person who most people avoided. Mandy wasn't certain how to respond to Alice's inquiry. Thankfully, the yoga instructor began the class, distracting Alice as she went into a yoga posture.

At the end of the class, Mandy lay on her mat to hang on for as long as she could to the looseness her muscles had gained from the workout. She knew only too well that soon enough they'd be back knotted up tight.

"Say," Alice whispered, "I haven't seen that woman who has the prosthetic leg in a while. Have you? I admire how flexible she is and how much she's able to do. It's quite amazing, don't you think?"

"I've never seen a woman with a prosthesis," Mandy said. "Unless of course she's always had long pants on, so I didn't notice." "Oh no. She wears short pants every time. I respect her for that. She obviously doesn't let it bother her. I don't know how she lost her leg. Well, it's not all her leg, just from the knee down. She seems to be able to do anything any other person on the crew can do, and she's got great upper body strength, too."

"She's a member of the crew?"

"Yup."

"Huh. I've never seen her."

"Maybe she's been too busy to come anymore," Alice said. "I haven't seen her around for a while. They probably got her shoveling coal for the engine."

Shoveling coal? That was a weird comment. Maybe Alice thought that since the woman had great upper body strength, they'd consigned her to a coal bin. Mandy laughed to herself, not mentioning that the ship was propelled by diesel engines. The picture in her mind of a woman shoveling coal in the bowels of the ship reminded her of her grandparent's coal bin. Remembering that time from her youth helped keep her anchored in the calm state she'd achieved from her yoga exercise. But all too soon, she felt the peacefulness slip away with the rustling of people getting up and stacking their mats.

Back to the shoulder knots.

* * *

After yoga, Mandy went back to her room, read her book, and fell asleep. She woke up starved. She checked the time. It was noon. She grabbed her novel and padded down to the cafeteria.

One of the good things about Alaska was that you could get your fill of fresh salmon, Mandy's favorite fish. That was what was on the menu for lunch in the form of grilled salmon sandwiches. She fixed her plate with all the offerings and found an empty table by the window. Several passengers had offered to have her sit with them as she passed by their tables, but she politely declined. She insisted she was reading a good mystery and couldn't put it down. The real reason was that she wanted to be by herself, at least for a while. She craved a break.

She glanced up as Mark and William strolled by with their trays. They caught her eye, so she couldn't very well ignore them when they stopped by her.

"Must be a compelling book you have there," Mark said. "I take it you're not looking for company?" He smiled in a way she knew he wouldn't take offense.

"Yes, it's a page-turner. I can't seem to stop reading." She closed the book, using a finger to hold her place.

"I won't keep you from it then other than to ask how Deidre is doing. I heard she took a tumble last night. If she has any concerns, I'd be willing to check her out."

"Thanks, Mark. That's so kind of you. Nothing like having a doc aboard when accidents happen."

"I'm sure the nurse did a fine job. Just thought I'd offer."

"Thanks, I'll tell her."

"If you don't mind me asking, how is she doing with her memory issues?"

"She's getting a little recollection back, mostly about job stuff. I try not to ask her about it too much. It makes her nervous when I do." Mandy hoped that that last statement would find its way to the passengers so they'd stop asking Kera about her memory. Even though Kera very much wanted people to know she was beginning to recall a few things, Mandy didn't like it at all, because it made Kera a walking target. Since Mark was a doctor and used to keeping patient confidences, he most likely wouldn't pass anything on. But William was right there, and he had heard what she'd said. He'd probably send out the word to any curious person. God knows, gossip would make its way around this small ship faster than a runaway virus.

Mark and William moved on, and Mandy quickly resumed reading, determined not to look up again and find it necessary to be friendly. She'd almost finished her lunch when she felt a presence, like someone was hovering nearby. She snuck a glance up and saw Wally with his tray standing several feet away. My god, he was staring at her. He didn't say anything, but he didn't drop his gaze, either. The guy was definitely weird.

"Hi, Wally." She expected that by acknowledging him, he'd move on.

He nodded but didn't budge.

"Is there something I can do for you?" She smiled like she might to a child.

He indicated with another nod and a questioning expression if he could sit down.

"Uh, well, sure." Mandy gestured toward the chair across from her. She couldn't believe he wanted to have his lunch with her. After all, he was obsessed with Deidre, but this might be interesting. Since Kera wanted to know if Wally knew anything, this could be her opportunity to find out if he did. She closed her book. She watched as he carefully took every dish off his tray and arranged it, just so. Then he shook out his napkin and gingerly tucked it in the neck of his shirt, still not talking.

Hovering over his bowl, he seemed to be waiting for a cue of some sort to dig into the clam chowder.

"I had some of that, too." Mandy pointed to her empty soup bowl. "It was delicious, I'm sure you'll love it?"

Wally didn't raise his head from over his chowder but nodded. He scooped soup onto his spoon using a broken off piece of his roll to keep the chunky liquid from spilling over. Then he pitched the soup into his mouth along with the soup-soaked piece of roll.

"I appreciate the food they feed us. It's always fresh and hot or cold as it should be, even though it's buffet style." Mandy waited. Surely, he'd say something soon.

He moved to his coleslaw, regarded it like it was something foreign, but then licked his soup spoon clean and dug into the slaw.

"The salmon we get here is great, isn't it?" Mandy took a bite of her sandwich. She noticed he also chose salmon for his sandwich. "I had halibut yesterday and it was good, too." She took another bite.

He dove into another spoonful of slaw without acknowledging her comment.

Good god, why did he decide to join her, anyway? He just sat there like a mechanical dummy, not saying or responding to anything she said. She could be reading her book, but now she felt obliged to talk to him. She watched him, trying to understand why in the world he'd chosen to join her.

He bit off a chunk from his sandwich, chewed and chewed and chewed, until it had to be minced into tiny pieces. He smacked his lips and patted them with his napkin.

She had to admit that watching him was in a strange way captivating. She decided to take another crack at starting up a conversation.

"Has the food been to your liking, Wally?" She mentioned his name, hoping it might shake him out of his stupor.

He still didn't look at her but extended his tongue out to the side of his mouth trying to snag a crumb of the roll that stuck to his face.

That did it. She decided not to make any further attempts to carry on a conversation that he clearly wasn't interested in. She opened her book and went back to her lunch. She pretended to be involved with the story when, in fact, she was unable to stop glancing up at him on the sly.

He kept using his tongue to clean around his lips. After a few excruciatingly awkward and unsuccessful attempts, Wally finally captured a second bit of gooey dough that hung from the other side of his mouth. Then he went back to his soup. Unfailingly, he patted his mouth with his napkin after every third bite or slurp, even if it was unnecessary. She noticed that he only moved to a different serving of his food after eating three of whatever he was currently engaged in. Three spoons of soup buoyed by bits of soup-soaked roll—dab the lips. Three spoons of slaw—dab the lips. Then back around to his soup again.

Now he was on to his salmon sandwich, three bites and three pats of his lips. Wally reached for his glass of water and sipped three times. Of course he would, she giggled to herself, this guy is definitely into threes. Next, he cut into his dessert—a piece of yellow pound cake with lemon frosting, then back around again to the rest of the food. Apparently, he made no differentiation, no break, between the main course and his dessert.

As he made his way through what was his last round, she noticed something else. He ate the servings in alphabetical order— clam chowder, coleslaw, salmon sandwich, water, and… *Oops. The cake is in the wrong order.* She was strangely disappointed until she remembered the cake was a yellow cake. That must be how he views it. So, everything was in its correct alphabetical order. And it was interesting how the last drop or crumb of everything ended at the same time. Did he intend to do it that way? If so, it had to take some real planning to be able to figure it out. The guy was fascinating. Absorbing. Bizarre… Kera would call it fucked up.

Still, he hadn't said a word to her in all that time. It made her almost want to study his behavior at another of his meals so she could test her hypothesis. The key word was *almost.*

Then, quite unexpectedly, he looked up at her and said, "I saw you coming out of Terri's room yesterday."

"You what?" Mandy felt her jaw drop.

"I said," he dabbed his chin three times again, "you were in Terri's room."

She scowled. For a moment, she forgot that The Tart's name was really Terri. Then she remembered that she had seen a figure of a person in the hallway. It had to have been Wally. She didn't know what to say to him or what he expected from her about it. Before she could come up with anything, he spoke again.

"Charlie would be very upset that you were in there with her little floozy girlfriend."

Good god, he thinks I'm interested in Terri the Tart. What could she say to him? Certainly, she couldn't tell him the real reason why she was in Terri's cabin. And it was clear that he expected an answer about this, and if she didn't give him some plausible explanation, it probably wouldn't go well for her or Kera. Wally the Tattletale would likely let someone know, like the captain or Roni or whoever.

Finally, her response came to her. "Yes, I'm sure Charlie would be upset. Then again, she's cheating on Bev, now isn't she?"

"Touché," he whispered, his eyes wide with delight. "Charlie deserves it, doesn't she?"

"I would say so." Frankly, Mandy didn't know where to go from there. She waited to hear what Wally would say next.

"It'll be our little secret. I wouldn't want to see you get hurt. Charlie is not a nice person." He put his fingers over his lips and giggled.

"I appreciate that."

"I so like secrets," he said with an Alice-in-Wonderland Cheshire cat smile that promptly faded into his normal flat affect, with a faint twist of pouty annoyance. "Well, most secrets, anyway." He stood, put his dishes on his tray, nodded at her, and left.

What a peculiar man. She felt confident that he wouldn't say anything to Charlie, because it seemed that he would enjoy sharing a secret with her. For him, it would be a connection with someone, something he probably yearned for but obviously had difficulty procuring. But for insurance, she'd have to make sure Kera knew about Wally having seen her in Terri's room and how important it was for her to keep Wally happy.

* * *

Mandy knew she'd regret later that she didn't take advantage of the scuba diving opportunity she'd planned on, but exhaustion overcame her. She decided to hole up in her cabin and finish her book. Physically, she felt fine, but the mental and emotional stress had returned in full force. It seemed like she was walking through waist-high sludge with nerves that were on fire. She'd read almost all the novel but realized she had no idea what had taken place in the story other than it was a mystery—she'd read that much on the jacket of the book. She thought it took place somewhere in Europe, and the protagonist had red hair and a fiery temper. Oh yeah, and large breasts that housed a pistol, or maybe it was a knife? She flinched. No, it had to be a gun.

As she thought about the cleavage being a storage place for a gun—a hiding place a guy didn't have—she considered where Kera hid hers. The pistol she'd brought with her wasn't her regular one that she carried at home, but a smaller one she'd described to Mandy as her vacation piece, not seen, not suspected, and waterproof. Kera hadn't expected to need one, but "you never know," as she'd put it. Given the situation they'd gotten into, Mandy appreciated Kera's having it. She holstered it low, just above her ankle, which is why she decided to wear the long pants of her uniform instead of shorts, no matter the temperature. Luckily, the weather generally called for long pants.

Tomorrow, they would dock in Petersburg, which was primarily a fishing village. One of the crew described the town to her as a mere speck of a place, but nevertheless a taste of civilization and a spot where you could get a pretty good pizza. It also had cell phone reception that most often worked. Mandy hoped she'd be able to contact Moran to see how Dee was doing. Maybe Dee was conscious by now and could let them know how she'd fallen from the cliff. If it had been an accident or, god forbid, a suicide attempt, Kera could give up on the bad guy premise and not have to worry that someone was out to hurt them.

Mandy closed her eyes and drifted off only to suddenly jerk awake from a nightmare. In the nightmare, she was climbing the stairs to the deck to attend her yoga class. As she reached the top, she saw a large man grab Kera. He and Kera struggled, but he prevailed and tossed Kera overboard. He saw Mandy and ran off down another set of stairs. She screamed for someone to stop the ship and go back and save Kera, but it seemed nobody could hear her. The more she replayed the nightmare, she realized they heard her but didn't respond. It was as though nobody cared. Her scream was so loud in her dream, it woke her up.

Her heart pounded like a bass drum. Her blouse was soaking wet, like Kera experienced when she awoke from one of her wartime nightmares. Mandy checked the time. Kera had to have long finished her work on the platform and started her shift at the bar. That nightmare had been so real. It was crazy, but she needed to confirm that Kera was still on the ship and alive. She changed her blouse, dragged a brush through her hair a couple of times, then headed to the lounge.

She spotted Bev who was perched on her usual stool at the bar, but Kera wasn't behind it. Mandy's heart began to beat fast again. She told herself that Kera had to be stuck somewhere, called to do something elsewhere on the ship, and would show up soon. Maybe if she sat and chatted with Bev, she'd distract herself until Kera arrived.

"I'm waiting for your friend." Bev said, tapping her fingernails on the bar. "Dan, there," she pointed to a guy, "got his drink. He said Deidre was here but left and said she'd be back. That was quite a while ago, from what I understand."

Mandy sat down on the stool next to her. "She'll be back any minute now, I'm sure." Mandy's words were meant more for her own sense of well-being than for assuring Bev.

"My drink tonight can't come too soon." Bev's laugh contained more irritation than mirth. "As it was, I was late getting here."

Mandy looked around and expected to see Kera hurrying into the lounge. But no Kera. "I could use a drink myself." Mandy looked over at the opened bottle of pinot noir behind the bar. She thought it'd be easy to step behind the bar and make them both feel a lot better.

"Damn. Deidre should be here any second. She doesn't usually leave me just hanging here, like this." Bev checked her watch. "There's sure lots of stirring going around here, just not at the right place." Bev gestured at the row of bottles sitting behind the bar. Her irritation was increasing exponentially. "Things need to happen here. Soon." She emphasized the point by wrapping her knuckles on the bar.

Maybe waiting with Bev wasn't such a good idea. Now that Bev had mentioned it, Mandy noticed that Roni and Mick and a few other crew members were whizzing back and forth through the ship, seemingly preoccupied with something. It wasn't their normal behavior this time of the evening.

More passengers filed into the lounge, wondering, no doubt, what the holdup was about. Mandy found herself clicking her nails on the bar.

Charlie waltzed in, spotted her sugar mama at the bar, and strolled over. She sat down on the other side of Bev and threw her arm over her shoulders. She glared at Mandy.

Had Wally said something to her? He promised to keep it a secret but as Britt said, he enjoyed telling on people. Then again, it could be that Charlie worried that Bev and she had something going, sitting at the bar together.

Just then, Roni rushed into the lounge. Before she could get by them, Mandy reached out, grabbed her by the arm, and asked, "What's going on? Is there something wrong?"

"No reason for anyone to get concerned," Roni said in a low voice. "We're having some engine difficulties, but Mick is on it. Not to worry." She patted Mandy on the shoulder as she broke loose from Mandy's grasp. Before Mandy could regain her attention and ask what was keeping Deidre, Roni was off.

Mandy reassured herself that all had to be well or Roni would have said something to her. If Roni was needed to help Mick, then it would make sense that Kera must have been suddenly called to help finish up on the launch platform or was needed to help in some other capacity. After all, the crew was shorthanded.

A nightmare is just a nightmare, not reality.

CHAPTER EIGHTEEN

Kera

"How'd you get stranded out here?" A guy tosses me a rope to pull my clunker in and snug our boats together so I can board.

"It seems no one from my ship realizes I'm not on it. Man, I owe you a big one. You were literally my only chance."

"Really? You're telling me they don't have any form of accountability in place when peeps come and go?" The guy looks like he can't believe it. "I'm Jason, by the way."

"It's a long story," I tell him to keep from going into it all. I am so damned cold it feels like I'll never be warm again. "You'd think they'd be looking for me." I snicker for effect. "I'm a bartender, amongst other things, and people get restless when happy hour comes around when there's no booze being served up." I do finger quotes for "happy hour" then stash my hands under my armpits for warmth.

"Does the bartender have a name?"

"Sorry, I'm, uh, Deidre." I might not have been smart enough to check the skiff before I left, but I am with it enough, surprisingly, to finally get my sister's name out. Score one for me.

"Well, Deidre, for the sake of the rush hour bar traffic, let's get you back." Jason ties the rope to his boat and secures the connection so that Mick's tin can will ride alongside his, much like a calf whale and its mother.

Jason tells me that no one on his ship had seen me at first. I'd frantically waved my life jacket when I first spotted his ship coming in. It then occurred to me that even though my smartphone didn't have any reception out here, it did have a flashlight app which I used to SOS the incoming ship. Luckily, I caught the short window of time when my light would be visible to the incoming liner before it moved passed me and out of sight.

"What's wrong with your motor?" Jason asks.

"The prop fell off." I hate telling him that fact, because it is such a preventable thing and makes me look like an idiot.

Jason shakes his head. "Deidre, you should check those things out before you take off." He secures our coupled crafts and sits down.

"I know, I know. I don't have an excuse. I was worried about a passenger's whereabouts and took off like a bat out of hell. I failed to do a safety check. Just wasn't thinking."

But I'm sure thinking now. Thinking a leaking boat and a loose propeller isn't about my neglect. I'm pretty damned sure that I stirred up Dee's attacker like I intended, but I let my guard down. Lapses like that could cost me big time. It almost cost me my life.

The only thing that saved my ass was the epoxy putty I found in my pocket from when I helped Mick with the air-conditioning system. He uses that stuff because it works around water. I was fucking lucky to have forgotten to return it. I didn't have much of the putty and didn't know how effective it would be because it's supposed to dry first. What I had was enough to slow down the ocean's attempt at sinking the old skiff—and claiming me as well. Still, Jason's showing up was none too soon.

I tell Jason that I'd just gotten started with my search for a passenger when I broke down out here. My plan was to cover the water as well as to circle all the small islands to make sure she wasn't near or on any of them.

"So, where have you searched for the woman?" he asks.

Even though, more than anything, I'd like to get back on-ship and warm up, I need to find the missing woman. If I'm cold, she has to be freezing her ass off and scared as hell, thinking no one will show up.

We take off with Mick's boat in tow and head toward the closest of the small islands to see if we can find the woman and her kayak. I'm going to be late for my job at the bar, but at least I'm alive. Maybe my early birds to the bar will clue someone in that I'm not on board.

My teeth are rattling.

* * *

By the time Jason and I pull up to the launch platform, I'm seething. Frozen. Bordering on hypothermia, no doubt. Jason and I searched all over for the Zappa woman. All the while, not one skiff from the ship came out to look for me to see what had happened. Maybe I overestimated the importance of the bar job.

I thank Jason, though I don't know how to show enough appreciation to the guy who's just saved my life. He hands me the rope that's connected to Mick's skiff so that I can pull it up onto the platform. I wave him off. Probably will never see the guy again, but if I do, I told him he's got a steak dinner and all the beer he can drink coming.

After a quick hot shower to stop my teeth from chattering, I go through the dining room and head for the lounge, most of the passengers look up like it's no big deal I've been away from my post. All of them are beer drinkers. Then William stops me as I pass by his and Mark's table and asks if he can get some of the good stuff now. He drinks rum and coke. At least he missed me. Well, he missed his booze.

In the lounge, I see Mandy behind the bar. She's slinging mugs of beer like a pro. I wonder where my stand-in guy is. He can at least do the beer and wine. I guess they could be having him do something else, like looking for a lost passenger.

Mandy spots me approaching. Her face lights up. "Hi Dee. Do they have the engine problems taken care of?" She smiles as I make my way behind the bar. "It's certainly taking a while. Hope everything is okay," she says. She searches my eyes for the answer. I nod halfheartedly.

Engine problems? I'm bewildered as hell. Everyone, including Mandy, is under the impression that I've been helping with some engine issues the ship is apparently having. That's why people in here think that I've not been at my post, tending bar.

I'm not going to mention anything to Mandy, not while Bev is sitting right there and can overhear me. I can't very well let a customer know that I've been floating out in the ocean in a goddamned sieve. Besides, I'm not sure I should tell Mandy, not at this time, anyway. She continues to keep hanging in there with me, even though she's a nervous wreck. I'm afraid to stress her more. It might paralyze her, keep her from being able to function at all.

"Let me get your hard stuff," I say to Bev and fix her a double bourbon over ice. I go on automatic bartender mode while I make a stab at gluing together the events of the last hours.

Bev pushes her half empty wine glass away, disgust on her face. "Thanks, Deidre. Finally the good stuff…well, Old Crow is barely tolerable, but it's better than that nasty wine."

I notice Gerald, my backup guy, making his way into the lounge. I ask him to tend the bar for a bit. Before I can inquire as to why he didn't come in to take over when I didn't show, he says that he'd just gotten up from a nap and came to the bar to grab some orange juice. And that no one let him know he was supposed to relieve me. That would account for his no-show and his bedhead. He probably has no idea about what's going on. He tells me Mick woke him and asked him to check on something, so he can't help me right now.

"What do you have to do?" Mandy asks me.

"I need to talk to Britt."

"Last time I saw her," Bev pipes up, "she was going into the kitchen. I tell you what, folks are running around this place like chickens with their heads cut off."

Mandy nods her head in agreement with Bev.

"Yes sir-ee," Bev goes on. "Even our esteemed captain and the second captain—if that's what she's called—have been speeding back and forth between the engine room, the bridge, and who knows where?" She shakes her head. "How are things going with the engine repair, anyway? Looks like we're stuck here and not able to get into Petersburg. When do—"

I interrupt her. "I don't know but I need to leave. Be right back." I don't mean to sound rude, but I'm beyond niceties.

Mandy eyes me, undoubtedly wondering what's going on. She doesn't say anything, though I can see she's confused and probably worried. But I can't talk about it, not now.

Now, I'm determined to go and find Britt and ask her why she hadn't even checked out how my ocean search was going? I was out there way too long or at least too long for what was happening with my boat. Wasn't she even curious, if not worried? Jesus. What in hell is so fucking more important than a lost passenger? Then it suddenly occurs to me. Ruth must have shown up on the ship and no one bothered to send someone out to let me know? Is this a case of incompetence or uncaring? I guess they didn't want to go to the trouble of getting a skiff down. Figured I'd show up when I showed up—even if it's next week! Surely Britt must care. Aren't I, her girlfriend, doing her a big favor? Her lifesaver? Shit, I know she's stressed and busy, but...

Bev looks annoyed. I'm leaving, and she doesn't know when she'll get her next drink. What the hell. I grab the bottle of bourbon and place it on the bar next to her. She won't even have to stretch her arm to get it. It's against ship's policy, but I don't give a shit. No doubt it's against some bartender union rule, and I don't give a shit about that either. Hell, it's probably even illegal. I don't give a fuck about any of it. I'm just sorry I can't stay and have a drink, myself.

* * *

I find Britt in the kitchen, chewing out a woman in the back of the galley about something. I've never seen her be like that with a worker. She's overwhelmed, I know. It has to be why she's acting that way. A flash of guilt crosses my conscience. Because of my injury—well, Dee's—it adds to everyone else's load, along with the sudden engine problems. A lot of stress going around. The momentary guilt fads fast, and I'm back to being mostly pissed at what happened to me.

"I need to talk to you Britt." I call out so she can hear me.

Britt turns, looks surprised to see me. "Just a minute." She turns back and says something to the woman, then hurries over to me.

"Was the missing woman found here on the ship?" I ask before she has a chance to open her mouth. "Because I—"

"Uh, no. You didn't find her?" She looks puzzled.

"What's going on here?" I ask her. "Doesn't anyone care that I was out there, almost drowned, no one came looking for me."

Just then, I notice that Mandy has followed me into the room and is standing beside me.

"What!" Mandy's eyes pop to the size of saucers. "You almost what? Drowned?"

I give the *Reader's Digest* version of what happened. Even with leaving out the worst parts, Mandy's all but hyperventilating. Britt's jaw drops.

"I'm so sorry," Britt says, looking horrified. "I got scared when you didn't return with the woman yet, so I decided I finally had to let Roni know what was going on. Luckily, she didn't kill me on the spot, just said she'd handle it, so I thought everything was being attended to. Obviously, I had no idea you were in distress."

"I can't believe," Mandy says, her voice shaking, "that this whole situation is being taken so lightly. How could you treat Dee like that?" Mandy glares into Britt's eyes.

I'm certain what Mandy is trying to communicate to Britt with her glare is that Britt, as Dee's girlfriend, should never have sent me out there in the first place, especially not in my condition and to at least have continued to stay involved. Since I'm not supposed to know about Britt's relationship to me, I couldn't address that aspect of the debacle. Glad Mandy did.

"All I can say is, I'm so so sorry." Britt says, glancing between both Mandy and me. "I'm under so much pressure, and now Roni is beyond pissed at me. I'll no doubt lose my job over this. I know that it's no excuse, but it's all I got."

"Okay, okay," I say. There's nothing else I can gain talking to Britt, other than get more "I'm sorry." I want to talk to Roni. Mandy follows me out, hurling one last glare at Britt as she headed back to the lounge. I'm going to search out Roni. But before I do, I have a stop to make. I've got a bone to pick with Mick.

* * *

When I open the door to the engine room, I find Mick in serious conversation with the captain. I want to tell him that his goddamned skiff leaks. He no longer has a prop on his fucking motor, and I was almost a goner. Furthermore, what I most want to know is, did he have any idea about the condition of his fucking skiff when he said I could take it out? But from the expressions on both their faces, I can see that my fiasco trip into the ocean would be small potatoes to them, given what they're dealing with. After all, I'm alive, aren't I? So, I close the door. "Shit."

I head up to the bridge, taking two steps at a time, forgetting my supposed bad ankle. I check around, relieved that no one has witnessed my ascent. I put my hobble back on for the rest of the way.

Roni's on the bridge. She watches me as I limp on over to her. "Did you find Ruth Zappa?" she asks.

"I assume by the fact that you're asking me that, Ruth must not have shown up on the ship?"

"I paged her several times since Britt told me she didn't check in." Roni shakes her head. "Nothing. Damn, I sure wish Britt had told me about this earlier. I've had it with that woman and her incompetence. The blame for this squarely rests with Britt, not checking the board before she went in to do other things and leaving the rest of the platform clean-up to you. A head is going to be on the chopping block over this." Her voice lowers, and she seems to be talking to herself rather than to me, "And it's not going to be mine." She takes a deep breath. "Anyway, after Britt told me, I've been trying to find enough people to get a skiff down so I could get someone out there to help look for her."

Trying! What the fuck? Doesn't this situation rise to the importance of a four-alarm fire? I try to stay calm. Breathe, breathe, I tell myself. I level down, for the time being, enough to make the decision not go into what happened on my ill-fated search. What the hell, what good would it do for Ruth or me. But I'm frustrated and pissed. A woman is missing and I'm watching two people not having paid attention to what's important, and one who seems more concerned about shifting the blame to the other one rather than focusing on a missing passenger.

"Did you search the area thoroughly and check the coastline along all the little islands to see if she got out of her kayak?" Roni's finally back on task.

"I did."

"Did you circle around several times?" She has the nerve to ask me, like maybe I hadn't done a thorough job when she's the one who dropped the ball.

My built-up rage releases like a popped balloon in my head. I stop myself from responding, say nothing. Again, I breathe in and out several times, searching to regain my composure, instead of blasting out about my breakdown in the ocean that could have cost me my life. I could let her know about the water coming in through newly created leaks from two rivets and my prop falling off due to a loose nut. I could mention how I froze my fucking ass off and am still fucking shaking from the cold. I could tell her how fucking scary it was thinking that I would die.

But I don't. I swallow hard and continue to stuff my anger.

Roni tilts her head, waiting for my answer.

"She was nowhere to be seen," I say, almost calmly. "I didn't find any kayaks or signs of life other than gulls and otters." I keep forcing my rage into the pit of my stomach and slow my breaths so I can focus on what's important right now—the missing passenger. "Didn't you see Zappa's name on the list when you checked it before you left Britt and came in to take over the helm?"

"I was in a big hurry. You know that! I sprint when the captain calls for me." She glares at me and my perceived impertinence.

I guess I stepped on Roni's authority. Too fucking bad.

"Besides, I know I told Britt when I left that I didn't get a good look at the board and asked her to follow up," Roni says. "I meant right then, not just the last check before she left. She knew that." She scowls.

The way Roni said that, I'm not sure she told Britt that, nor did Britt mention that to me. Back to ass-covering, maybe.

"Let me try paging her again. It could be that she's on the ship and never heard me calling her name."

I think that's already been done enough times, bitch, but whatever. Shit, maybe I'm being too hard on her, maybe she's doing all she can and still run the ship while the captain works on the engine. I don't know.

I say, "How about I check the sign in-and-out board again? Maybe if she's back on the ship, she heard her name paged and realized she'd forgot to sign in and went back out and took care of it."

Roni nods. "Good idea. I'll keep working on things from up here."

I hustle my ass down the stairs and through the ship to the launch platform to check the board. I run my finger down to the last name on the list where Zappa's name was located, but I don't see it anymore. Gone! I'm willing to consider that maybe her name was out of place, alphabetically, and I didn't realize it at the time. But all the names are clearly in alphabetical order. I start at the top of the list again and carefully go down, one name after another, to make sure. I still can't find the woman's name on that board.

It's as though she never was a passenger on the ship.

What the fuck?

Surely, I'm just not seeing it, like a negative hallucination, not seeing what's there. I'll look again. I could use more than the lights from the ship to get a better view. I take out my phone flashlight and methodically run the beam down the list. This time I'm better able to make out the vacant line at the bottom where Ruth's name was when I saw it earlier. Now, I can make out smudge marks on that line. The X in the adjacent column next to her name was smudged out too. That's the column that indicated she'd taken out a kayak. So now, there's no sign of a Ruth Zappa taking out a kayak and therefore not bringing it back.

Jesus! Someone has obviously erased it.

I look closely again where her name is rubbed out. It was obviously done in haste, because it wasn't wiped clean. Looks like maybe smeared with a tissue or a finger. I can faintly see that a name was there but not whose.

I know damned well, though, that the name was Ruth Zappa.

And there's also a missing kayak.

* * *

When I got back to Roni, she tried to pull up her roster list on her computer to check for the missing woman's name but, for whatever reason, she couldn't access it. As she was doing that, she came up with a possible explanation for the erasure—Zappa's name was there, but someone on the crew had realized that it was a name from a past cruise and wiped it off. I figured that if that happened to be true, the erasure had to have been done sometime after Britt and I saw the name on the board, making it necessary for me to go to search for her. But I'm not convinced a crew member would do that and not tell Britt or Roni. I don't say that. Roni doesn't want to hear that from me.

Her second hypothesis was that it might have been a prank. Some goddamned prank, if you ask me.

She lets me know she'll inform the captain and he will certainly suss out if either of those things happened, an innocent but irresponsible erasure or a prank. Whichever, she assures me that there'll be consequences. Meanwhile, she promises me she'll keep trying to bring up the passenger roster.

In the end, probably because the name wasn't there anymore, it was made crystal clear to me that I didn't need to be concerned. Her whole demeanor toward me was one of treating me like I might be having difficulty with reality.

And I thought I had passed her test earlier.

I suppose having had emotional issue and hallucinations, head injury from falling off a cliff, then recently slamming my skull into the bar, that someone might come to that conclusion. But I bet she doesn't want to believe Ruth was a passenger and therefore a missing person. An incident like that wouldn't make her look like an award-winning assistant to Captain James or the company.

But I know what I saw…and what I didn't see.

* * *

When I enter the lounge, I notice that Bev's bottle of Old Crow is drained dry. Mandy, on the stool next to her, is leafing through a magazine as though all is well with the world. But her hands are shaking.

Mandy looks up. "What did you learn?"

"I'll tell you later when I'm finished here." I signal with my head that Bev may be listening. "But as for the problem with the engine, not much. They're still working on it." I push open the Dutch doors that lets me in behind the bar.

Mandy lifts her glass and signals for more wine. "I need another drink after this day."

I nod in agreement.

"I wonder what happens if they don't get the engine going?" she asks.

"I'm certain they'll get it moving," I assure her, not that I have a clue. "If not, I suppose they'll send another ship to get us." I uncork another bottle of wine and fill her glass.

Bev peeks through her glazed eyes. "That could seriously mess with people's plans. I have things to do when I get off this godforsaken boat," she slurs.

I shrug my shoulders. "That's true but what you gonna do? It is what it is. Your life will go on, regardless." I have no patience for people who get all disturbed that life doesn't follow their plans. "You'll undoubtedly make adjustments," I tell her.

Bev looks at me like her therapist just bitch-slapped her. She picks up her empty bottle and stares into it, obviously hoping there's a drop left. I know I should cut her off, but I'm not in the mood to give a shit or argue, so instead I open a new bottle and pour her another, though only a half glass.

"Thanks, dear." She doesn't seem to notice it's half full with plenty of ice. "You're a peach."

I've been forgiven.

In comes Charlie. She bellies up to the bar, puts her arm around Bev, and gives her a peck on the cheek.

Bev glares at her through bloodshot eyes. "Where have you been all evening?"

"Hey, my love. We had a great dinner together, didn't we?" Charlie tries to pull Bev closer but Bev's not having any of it.

Bev checks her watch. "That was several hours ago, then you up and disappeared. Where'd you go?"

"Remember, I told you I wanted to take a shower and change my clothes. I decided to take a nap." Charlie's eyes are pleading for Bev to swallow her latest story. She gives Bev a sideways squeeze with the arm that's wrapped around her.

Bev turns away from Charlie and glances up at the ceiling. "Charlie thinks I buy all her shit, but I don't." Her aside statement takes on the quality of a garbled Shakespearian soliloquy. Her eyes remain locked upward like more's to come.

Charlie doesn't respond. She's probably been part of this drama before.

"She'll fuck anything that crosses her path," Bev says to me and slaps her drink down on the bar.

Apparently, that's Charlie's cue to jump in. "Bev, honey, that's just not true."

"For starters, there's that little tart you've been fucking." She gestures widely, almost falling off the stool, obviously trying to indicate that the woman is somewhere on the ship

"God damn it, Bev. I'm not doing anything with that woman. I've told you that, over and over." Charlie narrows her eyes as she turns away from Bev and mumbles—to no one in particular— "fuckin' dumbass bitch." Then she shifts her attention back to Bev who's still glaring at her. In a petulant teenage tone, Charlie says, "We talk now and then, but that's it. Stop making something out of nothing."

I glance at Mandy. She rolls her eyes.

"There's also that woman who works on the ship." Bev adds.

"What woman?" Charlie's either truly perplexed or she's a great liar.

"Well," Bev says. "I've haven't seen her lately, but I saw you eyeballing her the minute we boarded."

"What the fuck are you talking about?" Charlie acts simultaneously confused and indignant.

"I don't know her name. She had one of those fake legs."

"I...I never hit on her. Besides, that woman's straight."

"So, how on earth did you find out she was het? Huh?" Bev snickers. Before Charlie can answer, Bev continues, "Must have been a little embarrassing when she let you know she wasn't your type. Serves you right." She turns back to her glass.

"I didn't hit on her. Someone must have told me." Charlie's voice is getting louder.

I glance around at the people left in the lounge. The combatants have drawn the customers' attention. For the most part, though, people are being discreet, taking quick and sneaky glances at Bev and Charlie.

"I haven't seen her around lately or I'd ask her," Bev says. She tips her glass up to her lips, empties it, and smacks it down. She signals me to pour her another drink.

I say, "Bev, I think you've had enough." I take her glass and put it in the sink. She protests but doesn't put up a big fight.

Charlie grabs her arm and in a low but firm voice tells her it's time to go to bed. Bev is beyond tipsy. Charlie offers her arm, but Bev pushes it off.

With the main attraction leaving, it instigates an exodus. Soon, no one remains in the lounge other than Mandy. She gives me her second eye roll of the evening as Bev and Charlie turn the corner and out of view.

"So," Mandy asks, "what did Roni have to say?

I tell her what went on with my conversation with her. Then I explain what I saw at the sign in/out board and Roni's speculations as to what might have happened. Mandy didn't buy them any more than I did, but we're of the opinion that Roni believes I'm crazy and doesn't think I should be involved any longer.

"I'm exhausted," I tell her. "Let me clean up here. Why don't you go back to the room?"

"You look a bit rough around the edges. How about I give you some help?" Mandy slips off the stool.

"No, honey, it won't take me that long. Not that much to do, really." I've goofed by calling her "honey," damn it. We check around to see if anyone entered the lounge and overheard my gaffe, but no one's in the area. Mandy sets her almost full drink on the bar and heads off to our cabin.

As I work cleaning up the area, my mind buzzes around like a fly, landing on everything that has to do with Ruth Zappa. I can't help but believe that it's connected, somehow, to my sister.

Maybe a good night's sleep will help. I can only hope.

CHAPTER NINETEEN

Kera

I wake to pounding on my cabin door. I disentangle my legs and arms from around Mandy and roll out of bed. I cover up her unclothed body with a blanket and toss on my pajama bottoms and a T-shirt on my way to the door.

It's Roni. "Two things. We won't be getting into Petersburg today. It's possible we could make it in tonight but probably more like tomorrow."

I grunt, nod, and listen for my assignment. I'm not one to wake up and immediately be on top of things.

"We obviously didn't plan for any outdoor events today, since we're supposed to be in Petersburg," she says. "That means that our social director, Cheryl, will have to come up with some on-ship activities to entertain the passengers this morning. We'll also have to see about what to plan for this afternoon, if we're still stuck here, at least until happy hour." Roni grins, knowing pretty much everything stops for happy hour.

"Do you have any idea what the holdup is?"

"We're waiting on a part for the engine to get here. They'll fly it in on a float plane."

"What do you need from me?" I ask.

"First, I wanted to let you know that I talked to the captain about the Ruth Zappa thing. He agreed with me that it was either a name from another run or that someone was messing with the board. And as I assured you, he'll look into it when he can. Right now, he has a million things on his mind."

"Were you able to get to your passenger roster?"

"Yes, I did. There's no Ruth Zappa on the passenger list." Roni gives me a look that tells me she's now certain I was wrong and am to be treated with kid gloves.

No matter how hard I try to make sense of it all, it doesn't compute for me. And where does my being left out in the ocean figure into all of this? I obsess over a possible connection between Ruth Zappa's disappearance and what happened to my sister. Something doesn't smell right.

* * *

I see Roni eating her breakfast. I grab a cup of coffee and sit down with her. Who knows, I think optimistically, I might learn something.

She gobbles her food like she's in a hurry. "As soon as I finish here, the captain wants me to take over on bridge so he can work with Mick in the engine room. The captain thinks he knows quite a lot about these diesel engines—or at least he says he does." Roni lets out a snicker that tells me she doesn't believe he knows that much. "I've been mulling over the Ruth Zappa thing," she says.

"Oh?" I'm surprised she brings that up, maybe she anticipates my bringing it up and wants to get the first lick in.

She lifts her fork and taps at the air. "I keep thinking about it and am convinced, like we talked about, that either it was a name of someone from a previous cruise and her name didn't get erased, cleanly, or it's a not-so-funny prank."

She glances up at me, like she's hoping for a nod from me. But I'm frowning.

She stabs another chunk of her scrambled eggs and says, "Look, Deidre, I can tell you still aren't convinced, but think about it, no one has reported her missing. If a woman was missing, don't you believe someone on the ship would be wondering about her? Asking about her?"

"Not if she didn't come here with anyone else."

Roni swallows and waves off my last consideration, then says, "She certainly would have made some friends, and for the amount of times she was paged, no doubt someone would have wondered about where she was and why she wasn't responding and let us know."

I figure that if Roni's convinced that there's never been a Ruth Zappa on this trip, she must think it a waste of her time to keep on this. And it's apparent to me that she doesn't want to worry the preoccupied captain who, though he's been informed, is overwhelmed by problems with the ship. And on his part, he most likely wants to believe that Roni has a handle on the situation and buys into her list of various hypotheses.

I change the subject. "I suppose that since you'll be on the bridge this morning, you'll need me out on the platform?"

"Not right away because Cheryl's working with the crew to plan some inside activities for our guests this morning. She's great at setting up entertaining activities inside. If it appears that we'll still be held-up here in the afternoon and the weather looks good, we might do some outdoor things and will need your help out there. Why don't you kick back for now?"

"Thanks, I'll do that." If I didn't think so before, I'm convinced I'm on my own in my concern for the Zappa woman. I've got to know more, and now I'll have some free time to work on it.

I get more coffee, set it on the table across from Roni, then grab a bowl and fill it with oatmeal and fruit. That's comfort food in my book. My mom used to make it for Dee and me, and it was the real stuff, not those little packets you mix with hot water. I noticed Quaker Oats cylindrical boxes in the galley, so I know this is the real deal.

The oatmeal's good, just not the right consistency like Mom's. Roni doesn't say much more to me, but patronizingly pats my shoulder when she gets up to leave. For sure, she thinks I've lost it. I finish up and head back to my cabin.

Mandy's sleeping. I quietly get dressed and go out to the lounge to check on bar supplies I'll need for today. I finish at the bar and go up to the bridge where I know I'll find Roni. I realized after Roni left our table at breakfast that I hadn't brought up that the reason I went out in the first place was because of a missing kayak, so who took that kayak if not a passenger.

Roni glances my way as I approach. Her expression says it all, *don't bother me with the Ruth Zappa thing.* I'm not easily dismissed, not now, not ever. My parents found that an irritating characteristic of mine. I tell her that there was a missing kayak when I counted them for Britt, only eleven, so that's why I ended up taking Mick's boat our for the search.

"I'm sure you miscounted."

"I'm sure there was a missing kayak," I snap. I shouldn't have spoken to her that way but, damn it, doesn't she think I'm smart enough to have counted more than once? She goes back to tending the boat, thinking I'll leave, no doubt.

I'm not ready to be dismissed.

Given the kayaks have been stowed up here since my count last night, it would be an easy thing to prove that a kayak is missing. Hell, they're within spitting distance of the bridge. Roni wouldn't have to be gone from her station more than a few minutes, so I can prove to her I didn't miscount.

She glares at me, expecting her words and frown should send me on my way.

"Would you be willing," I ask, "to take a quick walk over with me and see if there's a missing kayak? If there's not, I promise I won't bother you again about this."

"That's a deal I can't refuse," she says, her lips forming a smirk.

I'm relieved. Finally, I'll get her to see that there's only eleven kayaks, there. We head over, both of us count.

None missing. Twelve kayaks.

God damn it, I know there were only eleven last night. I know it! But I also know that my credibility has been blown.

* * *

I'm back to wondering about the passenger's list. When Roni was able to get her computer's passenger list up, did she miss Ruth's name? I know she's stressed by the engine problems, delay and plan changes. Plus, she looks exhausted. She could have overlooked it. Because she appears convinced that my head injuries have gotten the best of me, she might not have even checked the roster. Wouldn't surprise me. Like she has more important things to do than entertain a nutcase. Not only that, I'm sure she doesn't want to have a missing passenger situation and not wanting to see the

name can result in a blind eye. I've experienced that myself. I need
to be certain there's no Ruth Zappa on that list.

Surely Captain James has a list of passengers on his laptop
as well. I'd really like to get a look at his roster. Getting on his
computer is a long shot. But long shots are all I got. Hmm, since
he's such a busy guy, he might not want to deal with a password to
open his computer. I don't. Passwords just take time, and I forget
them. Even if I can't get on, he might have a hard copy laying
around.

When I last saw the captain this morning, he was headed for
the engine room. I can't remember if he had his laptop with him,
although I've noticed he's always carrying it when he's going from
his room to the bridge and back. But why would he take it to the
engine room. First, I need to check if he's still tending to the ship's
engine problems, and if so, does he have his computer with him? If
not, I can try to get into his quarters. Since he's been busy running
back and forth dealing with the engine, I'm hoping he isn't locking
his door. Unlike the rest of us, he's able to secure his quarters.

I stand in the hallway that leads to the captain's stateroom and
attempt to look like I'm doing something when someone walks by.
At first, I think that it's lucky there's a daily activities board located
on the wall not far from Captain James's door. Problem is, there are
no outside activities today. The activities listed yesterday are wiped
clean, and the social director hasn't posted anything yet, due to
having to come up with a last-minute activities schedule. As I start
down the hall, the captain whips by me and goes into his quarters.
That gives me a jolt, as well as a reminder that I will need to get in
and out of his place, quickly. His movement around the ship is now
completely unpredictable. Besides, there's absolutely no reason for
me to be in his stateroom.

After about five minutes, I realize I can't stay here like I'm
stalking someone. I scoot into the lounge where I'd seen a clipboard
earlier that some crew member had apparently forgotten and left
on the bar. I snag it and hustle back to a spot where I can view the
captain's door and see when he leaves his room. Over the years,
I've learned that people with clipboards and company ID's hanging
around their necks—or in my case, a uniform with name tag—look
like they have some authority for doing whatever it is they're doing.

After about forty-five minutes, the captain finally comes out
of his room and whizzes back by me. I watch as he heads in the

direction of the engine room. I wait for a few minutes to make sure he doesn't turn around and come back. Feeling like it's now or never, I hustle down to his room and hope he didn't lock his door.

I turn the knob and push the door open.

Standing there is Agnes, about to leave. We're both obviously stunned at seeing each other.

"Agnes, what are you doing?" That's as far as I go because I realize that she could easily ask me the same question. But Agnes won't be asking me. She has guilt splashed all over her face and doesn't respond. "Oh," I finally say, giving her words to use, "You had to deliver food to the captain, eh?"

Of course, I don't believe the alibi I gave her. I know that she's been in that room with him all the time I've been watching— enough time for a quickie, maybe more. But I want to give the woman an out if she wants it. Hopefully she'll afford me one, too. By the expression on her face and her furtive movements in straightening her clothes and smoothing back her black hair, I'm certain she'll take the deal.

"Uh-huh." Her face is flushed. She glances around me like she's ready to bust out of there and is mapping out her path. "Uh-huh," she repeats. This time it's clear she's catching on to the gift I've just handed her—my generous explanation for her being in the captain's room.

I'm guessing she's afraid I might gossip to others. So, I add, "Don't worry. I won't say anything to anyone. It's none of my business, okay?"

She nods, though it's clear she's apprehensive. I step to the side to make room for her to move past me. In her own embarrassment, she didn't ask me why I was entering the captain's quarters. Then I figure that she might have thought that since I'm staff, the captain sent me to get something he'd forgotten. Or it could be she's too upset about being caught there that she wasn't thinking about what I was doing at all.

I watch her scurry down the hallway. In one way, I can't blame the captain for falling for her. She's a beautiful woman. But she's an employee and a woman who, in my opinion, can't stand up for herself, let alone to her boss. If the captain came on to her, she probably wouldn't have the wherewithal to say no to him. And she needs a job.

I quickly pop into his stateroom. I glance around the space, which isn't exactly the lush accommodations that big ship captains enjoy, but way better than anyone else's on this ship. He has a small desk and on it is his computer. That's a relief. It shouldn't take me too long.

No luck. I guess at a few passwords that a captain might use, like naval-related words, such as the name of his ship, maybe his drink of choice. But nothing works. Realizing I could spend a very long time and still not come up with the right one, I plough through some paperwork on his desk, dig into his drawers, but come up with nothing even close to a list of passengers. I try to put things back in the same condition I found them, get my clipboard, and open the door a crack to check the hallway. I don't see anyone. I get the hell out of there, fairly confident that I've gone undetected.

Since I can't figure out what my next move will be, I decide to hang out at the bar. I can pretend that I have something to do there, while I ponder how I can come up with an official passenger roster.

As I enter the lounge, I meet Roni. She says that she's been looking everywhere for me because Cheryl needs someone to help her organize people and activities this morning. I agree to do that, even though that kind of job requires an aptitude that doesn't square with my personality or skill set.

Then it fucking hits me. Cheryl, being the social director, must have an official passenger list, not only on her computer but probably a hard copy as well. I glance over and she's talking to a woman. Hot damn, as my dad would say, she has clipboard. She's scrolling down with her pencil, maybe to find that woman's name on the list. Now she's flipping through several pages. There are about sixty passengers on this craft and, given the number of pages she's thumbing through, I bet that list contains every name. I have renewed hope.

I give Roni a big smile and let her know that I'd be glad to do whatever I can to help. What I mean is, I'll do everything I can to get my hands on the paperwork Cheryl's holding. Roni flashes me a smile and says she appreciates my flexibility.

With the word out that we won't make Petersburg today given engine problems, and probably no outdoor play, the passengers hang in the lounge to see what's in store for the morning. Cheryl gives me the choice of heading the bingo group. Really? Bingo?

Somehow, I don't see adventure cruisers big on bingo. Or, my other choices are dominos, one of the versions of Trivial Pursuit, or a scavenger hunt that I would have to put together. Cheryl tells me that the scavenger hunt should be something "befitting this particular ship." She's come up with a "great prize" she will reward winners—two free drinks, every day, for the rest of the cruise. Now there's something to shoot for. With Bev aboard, it's good they limited the prize to two drinks.

I'm all over her plan for the scavenger hunt. Once I get it going, I'll be able to send peeps out looking for things and have a cup of coffee and figure out how I'm going to snag Cheryl's clipboard. Mandy agrees to come with me when I flatter her with the fact that I'll need her people skills. But it's the truth. She's got great skills in that area.

I gather my ducklings and find a place in the dining room for us to huddle. I make sure they know what the winners will receive. The booze does seem to be a great motivator. They're excited. Alice, the "wood nymph" or "the odiferous"—Mandy's handle for her—is at the rear of my group.

Sitting down at a table, I quickly put together a list of items to be fetched, while Mandy divides up people into groups of two. She comes up with an uneven number of participants, and it's no surprise who doesn't get a partner. Mandy agrees to team up with the nymph, because my sweetie is kind like that. Not only that, but she probably worried there could be a rebellion by the unfortunate person who got stuck with her.

It occurs to me to keep Mandy close by in case I might need her. I make her group's list of scavenger items that are within hollering distance. That leads my mind directly to the clipboard, I want, snugged in the crook of Cheryl's arm.

Hmm…I have an idea.

With the scheme I have in mind, I need Mandy to help me and maybe even the nymph. I call Mandy over to ask for her list of items she's to get and jot down, "clipboard." Then I whisper the rest of my plan in her ear. She nods and takes off with Alice.

After I've given each group their list and answered their questions, I make my way through the crowd to Cheryl. I whisper in her ear my idea as to how she can calm the group and make them happy. She smiles and nods.

I go to the bar and set out as many appropriate glasses as I can find on several trays. I take out orange juice and champagne and begin to make mimosas. I look around in search of Mandy and finally see her. She nods at me to indicate she and the nymph have all their easy-to-find items, except for the most important one. As I'm finishing up the first tray, Mandy and the nymph walk by. Mandy acts as though she has just noticed me busy at work making drinks. They stop in front of me.

"Do you suppose we could have one of those?" she asks with Alice standing next to her, looking on.

"Sure," I say. "I'm making all these for the folks this morning who are participating in the games. Help yourselves."

Mandy scans the room. "Oh my, you have quite a few yet to make in order to get to everyone."

"True that. I'm going as fast as I can," I add, in a planned exasperated tone so that it's natural that Mandy comes up with an offer of help.

"Do you have anyone who can help you distribute those?" Mandy asks innocently for anyone in the vicinity to hear.

I shake my head. "It'd be great if I had a bar waitress about now, but I'll get the job done, sooner or later. This was a last-minute idea, otherwise I would have a head start on making these drinks."

Mandy turns to Alice. "How about we help her with this?" Mandy gives her a wink. "After all, we have all but one of the items left to get." She whispers in Alice's ear. Alice gives her a knowing look and a conspiring smile. Mandy hands her a tray, and Alice takes off in the direction of Cheryl. She passes out plastic glasses filled with mimosas as she goes. I continue to stay busy with my drink-making as I watch out of the corner of my eye. Mandy follows Alice as she walks over with her tray.

To my delight, it happens as smooth as if it'd been rehearsed. Alice lifts her tray to Cheryl so she can take a glass. On cue, Mandy "accidentally" bumps into Alice, which causes her to spill the remaining drinks onto Cheryl. Cheryl is soaked with mimosas as plastic glasses hit across the floor.

The shock of the cold wet drink elicits a scream from Cheryl, drawing the attention of everyone within hearing range. A mini chaos ensues as the social director sets her clipboard aside and grabs a wad of napkins. She pats at her clothes to soak up the spilled mimosas.

I watch as Mandy slips through the crowd, clipboard in hand. Mission accomplished.

I can't help but smile. That's my girl!

* * *

"With everyone aboard all day and mingling about, my nerves have been on edge," I tell Mandy.

Soon, the people will fill the bar for happy hour. The only thing that keeps me going is that I have my back to the wall and had two shots of whiskey that burned down my throat. I'm usually strictly an IPA woman and am not used to the hard stuff. Bell's Two Hearted is my liquid drug of choice, which they don't have on board, and is most likely not even available anywhere in Alaska. But I needed something to relax, fast, so I had a couple of swigs from Bev's bourbon bottle.

"Take it easy on that stuff." Mandy says in a motherly tone. "You're not used to drinking that hard stuff. You're likely to start wobbling."

She has no idea how much I can handle without showing it. I don't think that's a good thing, just a fact. I nod and let her know I have no intention of getting wasted. Especially now that I'm totally convinced that Dee was pushed over the cliff, and that whoever did it was out to finish the job by setting me up to be out searching for a nonexistent passenger in a damaged boat and a loose prop.

"I keep feeling like I'm in the twilight zone," I say to Mandy. "I can't believe that I didn't see Ruth Zappa's name on Cheryl's list. I must have checked it ten times."

"I know. When you handed it to me after Alice left, I went over the list again and again." Mandy shakes her head. "It's like we're trapped in an Alfred Hitchcock episode. It's spooky and scary."

"Yeah." It does feel crazy, no Ruth Zappa and no kayak missing? I either am crazy or something weird is going on here.

"You're not crazy, Kera. And it scares me."

I wish I could say something to quell Mandy's fear.

When we were back in our cabin earlier, she said she was ready to jump ship and take her chances with the sharks and freezing water. Even though she's a great swimmer, I knew she wouldn't really jump. She just wanted to be transported out of this mess. However, I didn't want to take a chance, given her frazzled nerves.

I told her to forget about sharks, that from this far out in the water, she'd die from the freezing water before she made shore. That wasn't the right thing for me to say. She glared at me. I ended up having to rub her back and talk her down. Live and learn.

Waiting for the happy hour crowd, Mandy and I talk about the bizarreness of the Ruth Zappa situation and what part it might have in what happened to Dee. Mandy can't get it off her mind, not that I can either, but it's wearing on her. She's terrified. I can't afford to go into my fear. I have to stay in the what-do-I-need-to-next mode.

Mandy raises her empty wine glass to signal a refill.

I pour her a half glass, but after this drink, I'll cut her off. She's a lightweight and though I don't mention it to her, she needs to maintain a fine balance between calming herself with wine and keeping her wits about her. In other words, stay sober.

"Do you think Britt has a hand in all this?" Mandy asks.

"No, in fact she was going to do it, herself. I only offered because she was upset about not being able to get her work done. I didn't have to say I'd do it. She even asked Mick when he was out there if he was busy. How would she know the condition of Mick's boat and motor? Besides, she's Dee's girlfriend."

"Do you think Mick had any idea his boat was damaged?"

"I don't think so. I doubt he'd ever damage or allow his rivets to be damaged. It's his dad's boat, and it has sentimental value to him."

"Unless there was a very good reason for him to do so. Don't you think he could fix the damage?" she says.

"I suppose. After all, the old clunker has more than one dent in her. What's one or two more, I guess. Still, I don't think so."

"So, we're back to Roni and why she might want Dee dead." Mandy shakes her head. "What could have possibly happened to make anyone want to do that to Dee?"

"Yeah, we need a motive."

We quiet down when Bev saddles up to the bar.

"How's it going?" I ask her and pluck the bourbon off the shelf to make her a drink.

Bev sports the smile of a cat who's eaten the canary. "I'll tell you one thing. I've been able to keep track of Charlie since we couldn't leave the boat today. And I got some time with her in the sack." She holds up her glass in celebration.

I grab an empty glass and clink it with hers. I'm glad I don't have Charlie's task of servicing two women. Mandy's more than enough for me to handle, although the stress of this trip has put a big damper on our libidos.

When Bev showed up at the bar, Mandy left, knowing Bev would be more likely to talk to me if she weren't around. I've decided that I can't pussyfoot around anymore by playing it safe, waiting for someone to hand me some useful information. That strategy isn't getting me what I need. The clock is ticking. I need to get more aggressive.

Bev's glass is close to empty, so I pour her another one and say, "I'm beginning to get some flashes of memory back, but it's been hard for me, not remembering things. Yesterday, Roni was telling me about something she and I did several cruises ago and that helped bring back a little."

"I thought people weren't supposed to talk to you about anything so as not upset you." Bev slurps the drink I gave her.

"It seems the restriction has loosened up a little," I lie, "and I'm feeling more upset that I don't know stuff than I'm sure I would if I did. It seems to me that I should be the judge, don't you?"

"Yes." Bev raps her fist on the bar, as though it were a judge's gavel. "It definitely should be up to you."

"I was wondering, do you have any idea who my friends were on-ship? You know, crew members that I hung out with? I know you were on the ship only a short time before my…uh, accident."

"Hmm." She puts her hand to her chin. "I really couldn't say since you worked with many members of the crew. And I saw you working other places on the ship when you weren't on duty here at the bar. But I couldn't say if any of your coworkers were your friends."

"Did you ever see me with anyone when I was completely off duty?" I say, pushing her a little more.

She taps her newly painted fingernails on the bar as she thumbs through her memory. "Come to think of it, there was this woman that I saw you joking around with several times. And I saw you both eating together at the pizza parlor when we stopped at Petersburg on our way up to Juneau."

"Do you know her name?"

"No, but in fact she was a member of the crew because she wore the uniform you all wear."

"Could you point her out to me when you see her next or tell me what other things she does on-ship?"

"I think she helped with getting people equipped with the skiffs and other equipment. She also instructed them in how to use the stuff. Not sure what else she might have done."

"Why did you say 'might have done'?"

Bev cocks her head, like she hadn't realized that she'd used the past tense when speaking of the woman. "I guess because I haven't seen her since I saw you two in that restaurant in Petersburg."

"Can you describe her to me?" I push another drink on Bev. I want to keep her lips flapping and tongue loose.

"She's blond, no maybe light brown hair. Shit, I don't really remember. I'd just be guessing. You both were sitting in a booth. I only saw her a few times. Oh, wait. I remember. She has a leg missing. Well, she wears a prosthetic. When she wears long pants, you'd never know. She walks so well with it."

I haven't noticed anyone with prosthesis. But like Bev said, if this person has been wearing long pants, I wouldn't know.

"Was anyone else with us?" I ask.

Bev shakes her head.

Wally walks up to the bar and takes a stool next to Bev. He doesn't acknowledge me or give me eye contact. Guess he's traded me in for Bev and wants me to know it. Interesting that he's hit it off with Bev. The other night I saw him talking to her, or more like she was bending his ear. They're perfect for each other that way—she talks, and he listens. He seems to have connected to Bev, and she's respectful toward him, unlike many other passengers.

Bev turns to Wally and asks him, "Hey, do you know the name of that woman who has a fake leg?" That description was less than respectful to the woman with the prosthesis, but I'm not about to call her out on it.

Wally thinks for a minute and says, "Nona."

* * *

I rest my cane at the foot of the bed, sit down, and kick off my shoes. I am gaining a new respect for career bartenders who spend the better part of their lives on their feet. Mandy props a pillow against the wall for her back and sits down on the floor across from me.

I tell her what I'd learned tonight about the woman with a prosthetic leg, Mandy's eyes widen.

"Oh my god! I've heard about the woman with a prosthetic leg. I never mentioned it to you since it didn't seem relevant to anything."

"Really? When?"

"It was Alice who told me about her when I was at yoga class. She talked about a woman who had a prosthetic leg and was really good at yoga."

"Did she mention her name?"

"No, and I had no reason to ask. It was just in passing that Alice told me. Come to think of it, Alice said she hadn't seen her around in a while and wondered why she'd stopped coming to class."

"Wally said her name was Nona."

"Clearly this woman was a crew member," Mandy continues, "because Alice thought that maybe she'd been given another job. Oh, I remember. She thought the woman might be assigned to shoveling coal to feed the engines on the ship." Mandy laughs.

"I take it you didn't tell her this ship doesn't run on coal." I laugh too.

"I didn't have the heart. She seemed entertained by the thought of the woman down in the bowels of the ship, shoveling coal into a big furnace."

"So, Alice hasn't seen her lately, either. She didn't happen to mention the last time she saw her, did she?"

"Uh, no. But since we've never seen her, it had to have been before we boarded in Juneau."

"Bev said she saw her when I—well, Dee and Nona—were eating a pizza at a place in Petersburg on the way up to Juneau."

"Dee and Nona must have been friends, then."

"At least they liked each other enough to eat together. Don't you think she would have come around to ask how Dee was doing?"

Mandy nods. "I would think so."

"That says to me that she's definitely not down in the belly of the ship shoveling coal into the diesel engines...or she doesn't get breaks."

Mandy smiles.

"I wonder if it was Nona that Dee thought had gone overboard," I say. "I learned that people got back aboard the ship around eight p.m. that night, due to the ship leaving. That would be the night that Dee thought she heard someone go overboard. Nona hasn't been seen since then. We need to find out who Nona was with that night and what happened to her."

"Since Nona was a crew member, don't you think there would have been a big uproar about Nona gone missing?"

"You'd think!" That pops me off the bed, and I start pacing back and forth in the tiny space of our cabin.

"That's so weird, Kera, and spooky, don't you think?"

"Yes. We have a vital missing piece here. We need to find out why or what caused a crew member to disappear, and yet no one seems disturbed about it. I just know that my sister's fall from the mountain is connected to it all."

Suddenly, a look comes across Mandy's face, one that says she remembers something. "Kera, oh my god, I think I've seen that woman, Nona."

"Really?"

"Yes, but not in real life." Mandy looks as though she's seen a ghost.

"What do you mean, 'not in real life'?"

"I saw her picture in Wally's cabin."

"What?"

"I forgot about that woman until now, that is, because she didn't seem notable at the time. We weren't looking for a woman with an artificial leg. She was merely another of the many people in all the pictures of Dee on Wally's wall. What grabbed my total attention at the time was that Dee was in all of them, every last one, and that was what bothered me and made it feel all creepy."

CHAPTER TWENTY

Dee's Journal

Wally loves mint juleps. On the first cruise with him, he was disappointed and pouty that I didn't have all the ingredients for that drink. When he said he was going to come on the next trip, I made sure I had everything I needed for a mint julep, including having purchased Wild Turkey bourbon. Our other bourbon, Old Crow, wouldn't do. Lucky for Wally, the captain okayed that expenditure, but said to stash is away and only use it for that particular drink, and only if someone asked. So, I was prepared for the Kentucky Derby's drink of choice, at least according to Wally. He told me that every May, on the Saturday of the Kentucky Derby, he went to a bar and had his drink while he watched the horse race. He's proud of his Derby tradition and has taken the mint julep on as the only drink he'll "allow to flow over my lips, derby or no derby, Saturday or not."

For me, Wally will be one of those people who I'll never forget. I think he'd make a good a character in a book. But I go back and forth from feeling sorry for and being wary of him.

His facial expressions are strange, no matter what he's feeling. He has several different looks. One is like a happy face, the kind that teachers scribble on your paper when you've done a good job. Then there's his tight-lipped smile that never makes its way up to his eyes. He uses that smile when he's standing back from the crowd or group and watching people, or when he's watching me when I come and go. Makes me feel like I've left the bathroom with toilet paper stuck in my pants and trailing behind me. Then there's his "I-didn't-get-my-way" look. It's a protruded bottom lip pout. I get this one when I don't give him attention, or he has to wait too long for a drink. Another emotional expression he uses is a pinched-lips look with darting eyes, like he's angry and is looking to make someone miserable. That last one sort of scares me, like tonight, when I was so darn busy.

Everyone was drinking and happily discussing their adventures. With each drink, the stories were getting better and more harrowing. Wally stood off to the side listening, but as usual, not joining in. He wore his happy-face smile. At one point, he asked me for another drink. I had five orders ahead of me and ran out of glasses, so I needed to wash some. All the while, I forgot about his mint julep. With anyone else, they would have just reminded me. Not Wally. He didn't even go to his pouty look. He stood in the back of the lounge with his pinched lips and glared at me. It was as though I had betrayed him in some horrible way, like handed him over to a Nazi firing squad. When I saw that expression on his face, it startled me. Then I felt a shiver go down my spine. I signaled him to come to the bar and told him I was sorry I forgot him and went about making his drink. He waited until I set it on the bar in front of him then he walked away, not taking the drink with him. It was rude, to say the least, but mostly bizarre. I wonder what he'll be like tomorrow. I hope he doesn't go on the hike like he said he would earlier. I plan on going. Don't need his creepiness.

If that's not enough, there's Charlie who said she's also going on the hike tomorrow. Good grief, I need a break. At least I won't be on duty for that hike, so no responsibility for what she and her friend are up to hiding in the brush. In fact, I think I'll find a good spot, let the others go on while I sit and watch the waves and meditate. I need it.

CHAPTER TWENTY-ONE

Mandy

Tying her bathrobe's sash snugly around her, Mandy padded down to the huge silver coffee urn in the dining room, not feeling a bit conspicuous in her nightclothes. She was following a morning ritual practiced by most passengers on the ship. The smell of freshly baked cinnamon rolls floated through the air and set off hunger rumbles in her stomach. She filled two Styrofoam cups and started back to Kera who was still in bed. Because of the short time she'd been on the ship, Mandy hadn't developed sea legs. With the ocean kicking up waves this morning and rocking the ship, she could barely keep her balance, let alone carry two overfilled containers of coffee.

The hot liquid splashed over the top of both cups, burning her fingers. "Ouch, ouch, ouch."

"Here, let me help you." Britt rushed over and relieved her of the cups. "Oh my, look. Your fingers are beet red."

"Thank you. It's really my fault. I should have put lids on them or at least not have filled them so high." Mandy wiped her hands on her robe and blew on her fingers.

Britt went to the urn stand and returned with lids. "Capping them is a good idea, even when the waters seem calm. You never know when a gust will come up and rock the boat. Sea legs help, but not always."

"I should have known better."

"I've been so busy lately since we're a bit shorthanded. I haven't had a chance to ask you how Deidre is doing?"

"Her ankle is much better and she's not as sore as she has been." Mandy wanted to ask Britt if being "shorthanded" also had to do with a missing crew member, as well as Dee's injuries, but thought better of it.

"That's great. I've been concerned about working her so much. She doesn't complain at all, but—"

"No, quite the opposite. It's been good for her."

"Has it helped with her memory? I've heard some of it is coming back, at least in bits and pieces."

"I think being able to do her jobs has made her feel useful and lifts her spirits." Mandy sidestepped Britt's question. She wanted to avoid talking about the memory stuff.

"I don't want to be a pest about it, but has she remembered anything about our relationship?"

"I'm sorry. I know that's important to you, but I don't think so. At least she hasn't mentioned it." There was no way she could avoid the question this time. But she needed to be careful how she answered it.

"Well, it's returning somewhat anyway, right?"

"She says that things come back, like you mentioned, in bits and pieces. But the dots don't connect for her."

"I guess I need to hang in there and cross my fingers that she'll remember me at some point." Britt's said, "Staying busy has helped me deal with it, but I miss her. A lot."

"If anything comes up, I'll be glad to let you know," Mandy assured.

Mandy did feel bad for Britt. If Kera had lost memory of her, it would feel devastating, a lot more upsetting for her than for Britt who had just started a relationship with Dee.

"Thanks. I'd better get back to the kitchen and make sure things are progressing. By the way, I had them bake cinnamon rolls, Deidre's favorite." Britt winked. "Don't tell her. Let her nose lead the way."

"I promise she won't hear it from me." Mandy flashed Britt a conspiratorial smile. Britt took off for the kitchen. Mandy made a mental note to make sure Kera remembered about her sister's love for cinnamon rolls, in case Kera didn't know it. That way she'd be sure to make a fuss over them.

Mandy continued on her way with the coffee. As she turned to go down the hallway leading to her cabin, Roni came toward her.

"Hey, Mandy, would you remind Deidre that she has the day off. Not that she probably forgot, but just a reminder. I don't know the full nature of her memory problem, whether it's just an incident memory difficulty or day-to-day stuff as well."

"No problem." Mandy started to explain but decided not to give out more information than she needed to—something all witnesses should follow in court trials.

"Okay, thanks Mandy."

Before Roni walked away, Mandy said, "I'm so glad we've finally made it into Petersburg. When will we be due back on-ship today?"

"Deidre will be free all day. However, if she goes into Petersburg, she'll need to return in the evening an hour before the passengers' boarding time. You'll find all the passenger information on the schedule."

"Where are people supposed to eat if they remain onboard?" Mandy wasn't sure if Kera wanted to leave the ship for the entire day. As for her, she'd like to get off and hire one of those float planes, hop aboard and never return.

"The kitchen crew remains on-ship for those who want to stay here. The food is something simple, both for lunch and dinner. For drinks, we'll have complimentary bottles of wine set out as well as beer and sodas. Oh yeah, let Deidre know she needs to get those out before she leaves for shore. Most passengers want to take in Petersburg and end up eating in town. I would assume that people will be especially ready to get off, since they were stuck all day on the ship yesterday."

"It's a historic fishing village, quite quaint." Roni held up two fingers as she turned to leave. "There are only two places to eat in town. I like the pizza place, myself."

"Thanks. I'll let her know."

As Mandy approached their cabin, she noticed a folded piece of paper taped to the door. Roni might have put it there since she'd come from that direction—probably last-minute directions from her. Mandy balanced the coffees against her chest, pulled the paper off, then stepped into the cabin. Kera was still sleeping. As Mandy set down the Styrofoam cups, Kera opened her eyes.

"What do you have there?" Kera asked as she rubbed her eyes.

Mandy opened the note and let out a big sigh. "Good god. It's another message from the creep."

Kera sat up. "What's it say?"

Mandy read it then handed it to Kera.

You will pay! And it won't be long now. Have a good day. A hand-drawn smiley face followed the message. Otherwise, it's the same cutout letters like from the other notes.

"Jesus!"

* * *

Mandy made her way to Wally's cabin. Kera had asked her to find the picture of Nona that Mandy had seen there. Her body felt as though it were wound up in knots and might unravel or maybe explode at any moment. Good god, when will this all come to an end? And to what end?

She realized her breathing had become increasingly shallow to the point that she was barely taking in any air at all. Probably why she felt faint. She leaned up against the wall and took in a few deep breaths to try and calm down.

There was nothing, really, Kera and she could do at this point about the third note, other than, as Kera put it, "watch their backs and carry on" and wait until something presented itself. Like what? A gun jabbed into their backs? A strong heave up and over the ship's rails, sending them into the ocean? Mandy tried to stop picturing bad endings, things she couldn't do anything about at this moment. Fretting didn't help her nerves and it didn't help their situation. She needed to stay focused and on task.

She was on her way to Wally's cabin to locate the picture of Nona. Having to sneak into Wally's creepy room, once again, scared her to death. Suddenly it occurred to her—none too soon she figured—to first check around the ship to see if she could find Wally and make sure he wasn't in his cabin. As she approached the dining room, the luscious aroma of cinnamon made her mouth water. It reminded her that she'd forgotten to tell Kera to fuss over the cinnamon rolls. As Mandy entered the dining room, she caught a glimpse of Kera in the kitchen, talking to Mick. It occurred to her to go up to Kera and whisper in her ear about the rolls, but that would have been weird. Surely Kera would remember her sister loved cinnamon rolls.

She glanced around the dining room and spotted Wally at his usual table for two, alone, meticulously attending to his breakfast. *Sad, on so many levels...* Aware of how long it would take him to eat due to the rules around his food ritual, she calculated that she'd have plenty of time to get the picture as long as he didn't go back to his cabin for some reason.

She remembered, the picture with Nona in it was a snapshot of a group of women with their arms around each other's waists, like in a chorus line—without the leg kicks. Mandy hadn't noticed who else was in the picture other than Dee. At the time, all she wanted to do was to get out of that cabin as fast as possible. As she recalled all the women were dressed in the cruise line's uniform. The person who had to be Nona caught Mandy's eye because, ironically, she was the only one in shorts. That's why Mandy noticed her prosthesis.

When Mandy arrived at Wally's cabin, she checked around to see if anyone else was in the area. Thinking it was clear, she put her hand on the door latch and was ready to enter when Britt buzzed around the corner and into view.

"Hey, how's it going?" Britt flashed a smile.

"Okay." Mandy quickly pulled in the door that had slightly opened.

"Did you lose your way?"

"I think so. Should have turned the other way, right?" Mandy gestured in the opposite direction. "I still get confused as to where I am, can't get my bearings, but I think I see my mistake now."

"That would be the right direction all right, but unfortunately, the wrong floor." Britt's smile was kind.

"Good God. I really got disoriented." Mandy watched Britt's reaction to make sure that she still bought her story.

Britt nodded. Her eyes fell on Mandy's hand still on the door handle. "You almost went in. That could have been an embarrassing moment for you."

"For me and whoever." Mandy removed her hand. Her heart throbbed. She was hot, so hot that the sweat trickled down onto her forehead and into her eyes. She was certain she would faint, so she leaned her back against Wally's door.

Britt retrieved a tissue from her pocket and handed to her.

"Thank you." Mandy dabbed at her stinging eyes. "I think the boat's pitching doesn't help my directional abilities, either. I'm a bit dizzy." Her legs started to wobble. She needed to calm down fast before her guilt showed through, along with her fear of being exposed.

"Good thing I came along." Britt took hold of Mandy's arm. "You're not the only one who's made this mistake." Britt chuckled "So, don't feel bad."

Mandy figured that Britt must think her a wimp for getting all discombobulated over something as minor as mistaking someone else's cabin for hers. Though being a wimp was a far better misunderstanding than for Britt to believe that Mandy was breaking into Wally's room.

"One time, there were two guys in their cabin, and they forgot to lock it," Britt said. "A passenger, who'd probably had too much to drink, was in a neighboring cabin, inadvertently opened their door, and found that couple engaged in a nooner." Britt shook her head. "Boy, did I get an earful on that one."

"Nooner?"

"Yeah. You know, love in the afternoon."

"Oh, that certainly would have been awkward. At least he was a neighbor."

"Yeah," Britt said, "and you're not even drunk." Britt's laugh faded into a thoughtful expression.

Mandy knew the second those words came out of her mouth, it was the wrong thing to have said. Good god, Britt must be mulling over the fact that a drunk only missed his cabin by one door, and there was sober Mandy who found herself in the wrong end of the ship and on the wrong floor. She decided to play up her disorientation. She blotted her brow with an already soaked tissue. "Oh dear, I don't feel very well."

"And you don't look very good, either." Britt said. "Maybe you should sit down for a moment. I don't want you fainting on me." Britt's concern seemed real, so if she'd had second thoughts about Mandy, it didn't seem like she had them now.

"Thanks, but I think I'll be fine, really. This isn't the first time the boat's rocking has gotten to me. I find if I stand here a moment and get my bearings, I'll feel better." Mandy figured she must look terrible because Britt eyed her, probably ready to catch her, thinking she'd fall at any moment.

No doubt she was pale from fear. At least she could take solace in the fact that Britt bought her rocking boat explanation. Plus, it was a split second of grace that kept her from getting caught breaking into Wally's cabin.

Oh god, that last thought didn't help calm me down. I have to pull myself together. I obviously don't have Kera's cool.

"You'd better move over to the wall," Britt said. "If someone opens that door to come out, you don't want to fall in." She helped Mandy find a place close by. "There, that's better."

"Thanks."

"I got to get back to work. Are you sure you'll be okay? I can walk you to your cabin or to the nurse, if you'd like. It'd be no problem."

"No, that's sweet of you, but I'll be okay."

As she watched Britt head down the hall, Mandy thought that going to her cabin and lying down sounded like a really good idea. She'd probably curl up in the fetal position. She didn't know if she could handle another attempt at breaking into Wally's cabin. How much of this could she take without having heart failure?

She propped herself up against the wall for a few minutes and sucked in more deep breaths. She didn't want to let Kera down.

All right, I need to put on my big-girl panties and get with it.

She looked around again and saw no one. Before she could chicken out, she darted over to Wally's room and slipped in.

It was creepy again seeing all the pictures of Dee. She quickly spotted the picture she had come for. It was the one with Nona standing between Dee and Britt.

Mandy grabbed it and got out of there, as she closed the door she spotted Charlie coming her way.

Good god!

Stunned again by the unwanted appearance of a person who would question her coming and going from Wally's cabin, Mandy's legs turned to wet noodles.

Charlie had a way of carrying herself with a swagger that said to the world, "get out my way and don't mess with me." When Charlie's gaze landed on Mandy, she squinted her eyes, and the swagger intensified.

"What the fuck are you doing in this hallway?" Charlie said loudly. "You got no business being here."

"I was coming to find Wally and—"

Though Mandy's heart thumped, she grew angry that she was answering Charlie. She didn't need to tell Charlie why she was there. Now that Mandy thought of it, Charlie didn't have any business being in this hallway, either—except Terri the Tart's cabin was two doors farther down from Wally's. But that was a fact Charlie wouldn't want to admit to any more than Mandy wanted to talk about being in Wally's cabin.

"You were with Terri, weren't you, you bitch!"

"I certainly was not!" Mandy slipped the purloined picture into her pants pocket while Charlie locked gazes with her.

"Then what the fuck are you doing here?" Charlie was now in her face.

Mandy took a deep breath. She'd be damned if she'd let this woman intimidate her, which of course Charlie was doing a good job of right then. But Mandy was determined not to show her fear. "It's really none of your business, Charlie, and frankly, I could ask you the same thing," she said as calmly as she could.

It was obvious Charlie wasn't about to play defense. "You're worse than your friend, who's going to get her—" Charlie stopped in mid-sentence then said, "I know you've been with Terri before. Believe me, she's paid the price for it. If I see or even hear of you being within ten feet of her, you'll pay for it," she growled. "Got that, bitch?"

Mandy quickly lost her fake bravado. Besides, she didn't want to get into a brawl with Charlie. Mandy wasn't a physical person and would lose…badly. As a lawyer, she fought with words. She could tell that Charlie would rather throw a fist than work through it with civil conversation.

Charlie pushed past her and huffed her way down to Terri's room.

Mandy didn't want to hear what would happen next. As she hustled away, she still wondered if Charlie had seen her leave Terri's room after she's crawled out from under the bed. Or maybe Wally broke his oath and told her…

And what did Charlie almost say about Dee and then pulled up short, switching to accusing Mandy of having been with Terri?

CHAPTER TWENTY-TWO

Kera

The pressure is on. Whoever's responsible for those notes is about to blow my cover…or worse. Not to speak of the fact that Mandy is in harm's way as well, thanks to me. God damn. That little smiley face on the note is the touch of a real psycho.

Jesus, I gotta figure this out fuckin' fast!

I hated asking Mandy to get that pic. I'd feel better about doing it myself. But I need to hunt down Agnes. Damn, I hope she feels like she owes me a favor. At least I'm counting on it. I kept her secret and didn't put her in a world of shame about her and the captain. I need at least one employee on this ship to ignore the captain's orders and talk to me about Nona. My hurdle will be getting her alone.

"Morning." Mick slaps me on the back, coming up from behind. "Wonder what we got going for breakfast?" We headed to the buffet table. "Yum, I could smell the cinnamon rolls as soon as I woke up." He spots the scrambled eggs with the cut-up sausage links in them, scoops up a hungry-man sized portion on his plate, then slaps the cinnamon roll on top of the eggs.

Across the serving table, Wally seems stuck on which meat to choose, then he takes some bacon. But he thinks better of it and puts it back. With his fingers. Yuck. I'm glad I got to the meat before he did.

Britt comes out of the kitchen with a fresh supply of the cinnamon rolls on a large tray and a bowl of mixed canned fruit. She spots me and holds the rolls up to me before setting them on the table.

"No thanks," I say. "But I'll have some of that fruit."

"How can you pass these up?" Britt looks puzzled, like she can't believe I've declined her offer, or maybe I insulted her in some way.

"They smell great but I—"

Roni shows up. Before I can tell Britt that I'm not a fan of cinnamon, she says to Britt, "I won't refuse these yummy things." She takes two. "I'll take Deidre's share," Roni says and heads off toward the bridge and yells back to us, "I'll let the captain know that the buns are hot out of the oven."

I grab the rest of my breakfast, throw a piece of toast on top and plop down at the crew table. Agnes is in there with another worker. While I'm thinking about how I'm going to get Agnes alone, Mick shows up with his tray, kicks out a chair, and sits down. For the time being, I decide to change direction, since there's no way I can get to Agnes right now.

"Did you hear what happened to me the other night?" I ask him. I'm not going to put the emphasis on the missing person with him. Since I haven't been able to talk to him yet about the condition of his beloved skiff to check out his reaction, this will be a good time.

"Britt told me you got stranded out at sea because the prop came off, and some guy from another ship picked you up."

"Right," I say. "It was my bad. I didn't check it before I left."

"Yeah, I was in a big hurry and failed to check it once. Luckily, I had a radio on me and it happened in daylight." Mick scooped his eggs.

"It was my fault, for sure. But did Britt tell you the part about the damage to your boat?"

"No." He seems surprised about that.

"Several of the rivets had—" I stop in mid-sentence. I was going to say, "been tampered with," but I don't want to imply that it was foul play. Instead, I say, "Ah, several rivets were loose and let water into the boat."

He arches his eyebrows. "Really? Without a prop and water leaking in…That's not a good situation to be in."

"You're right. And—"

"I have another prop for it, so that part is an easy fix." He seems to be mulling over his boat's problems in his head. "Hmm, Britt didn't tell me about the boat leaking, just the lost prop. I'll check it out after I get the ship's engine problems taken care of. I better stash the old girl away till I have time to repair her. Been so damned busy with other shit, it'll take me a while to get to it." He gulps down the rest of his food and leaves.

I wonder, since he didn't ask me any of the details of my misadventures on the ocean in a leaking boat without a prop, does he even give a shit about what happened to me? What did Britt tell him about it? Did she give him the whole story? How I could have drowned? Shit, I could be dead. I was lucky as hell to have been rescued—and not by anyone on this damned ship. Jesus, I'd think he'd want to ask me about that.

I push the rest of my food from one side of my plate to the other and wait for a chance to talk to Agnes. Then an opportunity presents itself: Agnes tells her coworker she needs to go to the bathroom, or at least that's what I think she must have said—she spoke in her native language. She heads toward the bathroom door just off the kitchen. The coworker is busy and doesn't notice me following Agnes, who opens the door, and I slide in with her. Needless to say, this is inappropriate behavior on my part. But I'm desperate.

She looks dumbfounded—as she should be.

I'm afraid she might scream so I put my hand over her mouth and whisper, "I'm not going to hurt you Agnes. I just need to talk to you a minute. Are we cool?"

She nods her head. So, I let my hand fall away.

"I want to ask you a few questions, questions no one else will answer for me. Whatever you decide to say to me, I won't ever let anyone know it was you who told me. I promise." I'm hoping she considers the fact that I haven't told anyone about finding her in the captain's quarters. She has very little status on this ship, and her affair with the captain would most likely rile a few crew members if they found out. If someone told upper management, it'd be more likely she'd get the boot, not the captain. Agnes doesn't say anything for a minute but finally nods. I'm relieved. I figure it could have gone either way with her.

"What you want to know?" she whispers back.

"I heard I was hallucinating, you know, before my accident. Do you know anything about that?"

She clenches her teeth in a grimace, like when someone doesn't want to give you bad news. "I never saw you do it, but people say you did."

"Did they say what my hallucinations were about?"

"You have one hallucination I know. You say someone go overboard."

"When did I have that hallucination?"

Agnes wrinkles her brow. "It was in night. You told the captain, so he stops the ship and searches all the waters."

"Just that one hallucination?"

"Only one I heard."

"So, did I keep having that hallucination, over and over, or just once?"

"I think only one time. You very upset. No one believes you."

"Agnes, are you in the bathroom?" I recognize Britt's voice from outside the door.

"Uh-huh," Agnes responds, her eyes wide.

"Get on out here, for god's sake."

I whisper in her ear, "Tell her you're not feeling well."

Agnes nods then says, "My stomach hurts, and I puke."

"Oh. I'm sorry, Agnes." Britt's loud sigh makes its way through the door. Then she mutters, "We're already so shorthanded." Another sigh. "Hope you get to feeling better soon."

Agnes makes a sound like she's heaving her guts out.

I'm impressed with her. She's getting on board with my lie. A few second later, we hear Britt's footsteps leaving the kitchen, but I know she'll be returning. I don't have much time left to get information from Agnes.

"So," I continue, "no one believed me, right? But I thought it was real. Not a hallucination. Is that what you're saying?"

"Right. They don't believe you cause captain did big search in ocean and counts. Everyone aboard."

"Did I say who I thought went overboard?"

"You say you didn't know. You see it out of your cabin window, but it's night and couldn't tell who it is. People first think you had nightmare, but then they say you had a hallucination—some say delusion—that someone fell overboard."

"Do you remember what night that was?

"I remember, okay. It was the night we left Petersburg for Juneau. Everyone on whole crew had to get up and help look and count all passengers. But no missing person."

"Did they check to see if all crew members were onboard?"

Agnes closes her eyes tight as if trying to recall. She opens them and says, "I don't know. Don't think so, cause all crew is out counting passengers."

"Were you counting passengers?

"No, I'm not crew. I just cook."

"Did anyone come around and check whether or not you were on board?"

"Hmm." Agnes put her finger to her lips. "Don't remember someone doing that. But maybe." She shrugs. "Don't know for sure."

"How are you doing in there, Agnes?" Britt's voice again.

Agnes looks up at me, like she's forgotten her lines in the script. I whisper to her to tell Britt that she's still feels sick. Agnes doesn't say anything but instead sticks her finger down her throat. This time she really throws up. Under other circumstances I might consider that overacting, not to speak of nauseating for me, but given the severity of our situation, it was spot on.

"I guess that answers it," Britt says. "As soon as you can, you need to go off duty. You shouldn't be in the kitchen and handling food when you're sick."

"Yes, ma'am," Agnes says in a sickly tone and flushes the toilet.

Britt walks away.

"Do you know what happened with Nona? You know her, right?"

Agnes nods.

"She was on cruise when it started out," I say to Agnes, "but she's not on it now."

"The captain is real mad at her."

"What did she do?" I ask.

"She didn't come back to her job on-ship."

"When did she leave her job?"

"In Petersburg. Captain thinks she found a guy and stayed with him, because she did same thing last year. So, he says she do it again."

"Why do you think he took her back, if that's what she did last year?"

"Nona knows lots about all jobs. She promises him she wouldn't do it again." Agnes's eyes widen, almost childlike, and says, "He won't put up with it anymore. He won't ever take her back again. That's what he says."

"Just one more question, then you better go to your quarters like Britt says."

She nods.

"I don't understand," I say, "why Captain James doesn't want me to know anything about my hallucination. Do you have any idea about that?" I figure that Agnes sleeps with the guy, and he might tell her, or she might overhear conversations.

"He says it upset you. He tells all the workers not to bother you, you need time to rest and get better. He thinks you might get upset and start to hallucinate again. I think he protects you."

"Thanks, Agnes. You've been a big help to me." I promise her again that I'll not say a word to anyone about what she told me. Then I give her a quick hug. "You go out now, and I'll figure out a way to slip out of here."

"I got to pick up my stuff before I leave," she says. "I cough, you come out." She follows that with, "I'm not bad person."

"I don't think you are."

Her face tells me she wants to say more, but she's decided not to. She opens the door and leaves.

She's helped me out a lot, but there must be something more, something I didn't ask about. Maybe she wanted to explain about her relationship with the captain. I don't know if the guy is married. Anyway, I make a mental note to let her know that I don't judge her. It's none of my business, and frankly I don't care who anyone sleeps with as long as it's not kids and it's consensual...

If it's hets, I tell them I don't like them *flaunting* it. I love throwing that shit word back their way, even if only under my breath.

* * *

Earlier, from the deck I spotted a statue that looked like a fisherman and a red-and-white striped sail attached to an old Viking vessel. That's where I told Mandy we would meet—after she swiped the picture of Nona and I finished getting stuff ready for those who planned to stay onboard today.

As I leave the ship, I see her sitting on a bench close by our meetup spot. I have my fingers crossed that she was able to get that snapshot of Nona. Since she's sitting there, I'm assured that she's not stuck under Wally's bed. Thanks be to the Goddess, as Mandy would say.

I buzz on over and plop down beside her. "Got the pic?"

She hands it to me. While I study it, she tells me about how Britt almost blew it for her and about her confrontation with Charlie after snagging the pic. I have to say, my sweetie is quick-witted and strong-minded, qualities I love about her. It makes her a good lawyer, too. But having to venture back to Wally's cabin and deal with shit has obviously had an unnerving effect on her. Her hands shake.

"I'm sorry, honey, that you had to do go there again." I pat her leg. I wish I could hold her, but this wouldn't be the place to do that. I turn my attention back to the picture. "I see Dee's also in it. And Britt. All with smiles."

"Like I told you, Dee's in all of Wally's pictures."

"We got to figure this out, fast, since that last message makes it clear that time is running out for us." My eyes meet Mandy's which are full of terror. Jesus, I realized how stupid it was of me to have said that.

I offer her a piece of gum and take one for myself. That's all I can do for her at this moment. Chewing might help her nerves. It does mine, although a couple tokes would be more effective.

We sit there while I tell her about my adventure in the bathroom with Agnes and what she had to say. I'm forced to do this in bits and spurts, because crew members coming off the ship and heading for town stop by our bench to offer us suggestions for places to visit while in Petersburg.

"Agnes is sure Nona didn't get back on the ship, and she had gone off with some guy?" Mandy asks me.

"At least it's the version of that night everyone believes. It might be true since she left the ship before with a guy, here in Petersburg last year. Maybe she met up with the same guy. Who knows? But I won't be happy with the boyfriend hypothesis until we're able to make sure that that's what really happened."

"Okay, we know now what Nona looks like." Mandy holds up the picture. "Now we try to find her, right?"

"Yeah, good thing we have the picture since we don't know her last name. We'll have to show it around. Let's be very careful not to let members of the crew see us doing this, I don't want to have to explain what we're up to."

Mandy nods.

"Study her face." I hold the picture so Mandy can see it. "If she's in Petersburg, we might spot her on the street."

Mandy looks skeptical. "What are the chances we'd be that lucky?"

"Looking around, I can't believe there are more than five or six thousand people who live in this town. It's conceivable that she could be out and about today. Anyway, we can't ignore that possibility."

"This picture isn't all that clear." Mandy frowns at the snapshot. "I'm not sure I could identify her from this."

"Yeah, but it's all we got to go on."

"What if we do find out that Nona is here. What then?" Mandy pulls her hoodie sweatshirt over her head.

I pocket the photo when I notice Wally coming in our direction. If he does see me, he's not acknowledging it. He saunters along in front of us, affecting a bit of a swagger and not looking in my direction, pretending to study the old Viking vessel.

When he finally leaves the area, I get back to Mandy's question. "If Nona is here, then I have to believe my sister is psycho."

Mandy scowls at me.

"I don't mean to disparage Dee," I say, "but like me, those of us with mental health issues have our own lingo for our whacky conditions. Many of us value our dark and politically incorrect sense of humor. It's a coping mechanism. Although, we don't appreciate those outside the sisterhood making fun of us."

Mandy's scowl hasn't left or been replaced with a smile—which I was going for—but instead, it is joined by considerable irritation as she amends my terminology by correcting me. "Don't say 'psycho.' Say she has emotional problems."

"Whatever." I adore Mandy, even when she's reprimanding me about my lack of PC-ness.

"You shouldn't say those things about yourself," she repeats.

It's all "blah, blah, blah," to me.

I soldier on with what I want to say. "If not psycho—I mean emotionally distressed—she probably had a nightmare, and she mistook it for being a real event." I know from personal experience how vividly genuine those horror dreams can seem, even in the light of day.

"If that's the case," Mandy says, "then Dee's fall is not connected to Nona's disappearance, and Nona flew off with her beau."

"That would follow all right, but we're not at that place, right now." I stand up. "Come on. Let's find out what we can." I almost said the time-is-running-out thing again, but this time I caught myself.

Since we only have one picture of Nona, Mandy and I will have to stay together as we search the town. That's probably just as well since people would most likely expect us to be wandering around with each other. The good thing is, the borough of Petersburg's small enough that we can get around on foot, and we should have plenty of time to search the public areas.

I was about to suggest we go to the police station first, then I notice a cop in front of a store talking to another officer. I ask Mandy to keep an eye out to check if any crew members are watching me as I approach the uniforms.

"Hi there." I shake hands with them. I show the picture and point. "This is Nona, a friend of mine, who used to work with me on the cruise line." This is one of those times when it's great that Dee and I are identical twins, since Dee's in this picture with her arm around Nona. They'll think it me.

They examine the photo. The older cop takes it, holds it further from his eyes, and studies it. "What's her last name?"

"That's my problem," I say. "I don't know. She's not from Petersburg, originally. She told me she was getting married to a guy from here and would be changing her last name to her husband's, but I forgot what it was, and I don't know where she lives." I hadn't anticipated his question, but I was able to ad lib it.

The older cop shakes his head. "I don't think I've seen her around." He hands the picture to the other guy.

"No, I don't recognize her, either. It's kind of hard to see her face clearly. I'm new on this job and to this town, so I'm not a good one to ask. I haven't seen anyone who looks like her, though." He hands the photo back to me. "What do you call it when someone has a leg thing like that?"

"A prosthesis," I tell him.

"Well, I'm sure I would have noticed someone wearing one of those."

"Jim," the older cop says, "unless she's wearing shorts, like in the picture, you wouldn't necessarily know. It's been chilly around here, so she'd probably be wearing long pants and you wouldn't see her prosthesis. She might have a bit of a limp, though." He turns to me. "Does she?"

"Just a little," I tell him. I really have no idea if she does. I think that these days, most artificial limbs are really good, and she probably doesn't have one. I decide if I see a woman whose gait's a bit off, I'm going to make it a point to get good look at her face.

"Sorry we can't be of help, miss," the older cop says.

"Thanks anyway."

I meet up with Mandy, and she assures me that she didn't see anyone in a cruise uniform while I was questioning the police officers.

"Hey, lady," the older cop calls out. "You might check with the guys at the firehouse. They're not full-time because they're all volunteers, but I heard they're having a meeting this morning sometime. If I'm not mistaken, one of them was getting married, or got married, or maybe got unmarried." The cop laughs. "Could be any of those."

"Will do, thanks."

I figure the fire station is a good idea, so Mandy and I check it out but none of them knows or has seen Nona.

Our next stop is the post office. It turns out to be just a room where they have personal and business boxes, along with a stamp dispenser and a place to weigh packages. There's a woman in there who's about our age getting postage for several packages. I give her my spiel about looking for my friend, but she doesn't recognize Nona's name or picture.

"We're not getting anywhere." Mandy says as we leave the post office.

It's clear Mandy doesn't have a realistic sense of what investigative work is all about. I've told her before that it's time consuming and tedious work. It's not like on the TV shows where everything is solved in an hour's time, minus all the commercials. I try to encourage her by telling her that we've eliminated a lot of possible sources of folks who might have seen Nona. She shrugs, apparently not impressed.

"Come on honey, let's move on."

Even though this is a small town, there are many more places to check out than I originally thought. We come up with the most likely spots Nona might frequent like the retail establishments. We'll do restaurants after the lunch crowd leaves to minimize the likelihood of bumping into someone from the ship. That's a better time anyway, because the employees will be less busy and more likely to talk to us.

Since it's lunch time, most shoppers and tourists aren't in the business area. We start at the end of the main strip and walk by several empty shops where someone's dream of a successful business died. We come to the last store with windows that display T-shirts, sweatpants and sweatshirts, mostly the kind that appeal to tourists. Nona might not be interested with such a store, but we decide it's worth our effort.

"Look, honey." Mandy points across the street. "There's a bench where you could make a call to Moran about Dee. Why don't you take advantage of the fact no one's around to overhear you? I'll check with the clerks in the shop while you make your call."

"As long as you feel comfortable doing it on your own." I'm anxious to find out how my sister is doing. Not knowing has been eating away at my guts.

She waves me off and goes in the store. Just as I pull out my phone and start to cross the street, out of nowhere I hear a screeching of tires. I look up and see a black pickup flying right at me. I try to jump back up onto the curb, but I'm not fast enough. The truck hits me on my left side and knocks me to the pavement.

Mandy runs out of the store as I am picking myself back up. She helps me over to the stoop in front of the store.

"Oh, my god. Are you all right, honey?" Mandy sits down next to me and starts checking me over. I try not to flinch as she pats my left side.

"I think so. Jesus, I almost got killed." I look down the street. The black truck is nowhere to be seen.

"I didn't see what happened, but I heard the noise from inside," Mandy says, her eyes wide. "You didn't look to see if a car was coming?"

"Yes, I looked before I crossed the street, Mandy," I snap. I feel like my mother is scolding me.

"You had your cell phone out, and I just wondered if you saw the vehicle coming."

I try not to let her parental tone annoy me. It's the tone that both she and my sister use on me, from time to time. I realize it happens when they're scared for me, but still, I find it irritating. I decide this is no time to get into an argument about it. I'm sure we're both getting tired and edgy. Instead, I say to her, "Besides, it wasn't a car. It was a two-passenger black pickup truck."

"Where does it hurt?" Mandy's still checking me over.

"Pretty much everywhere."

"We need to get you medical attention."

"We don't have time for that." I get up. I grab my left side as the pain gets up with me, especially in my left shoulder and down my arm. When I noticed the truck barreling toward me, I turned and jumped back. By doing that, I avoided a full body hit, but my left side wasn't so lucky.

Mandy picks up the cane that I've pretended to need and hands it to me. She links her left arm in my right. "You know what. There's a medical center in this town, and we're going there."

That tone again… But I hurt too much to grumble at her.

* * *

When we leave the medical facility, it's after five o'clock. I'm already starting to bruise. I have a sprained shoulder, so I'm sporting a sling to keep it steady, along with the cane. I didn't need the cane before, but it's now actually helpful thanks to the sprain occurring on the same side as my fake sprained ankle. I have pain meds, which I don't intend to take. I can't afford a muddled mind.

Of course, the medical people called the cops and I ended up talking to the older cop that I saw earlier. I gave him the description of the truck. He took my info and said he'd get back to me if he found anything out.

Mandy was in the waiting room while I waited my turn in the examining room and finally got the doc to check me out and send me for X-rays. I tell Mandy the medical results of my being the bull's-eye of a hit-and-run. As I'm telling her, I'm also planning where we should go next.

Mandy breaks into my thoughts. "I called Moran while you were in there to see how Dee is—"

"How's she doing?" I feel my heart fly to my throat. Mandy lightly rubs my back.

"Good news, honey. The doctors brought Dee out of the coma, and she's doing well."

"Did you get to talk to Dee?" I ask.

"No, she was having tests when I called. If everything turns out okay, Moran expected Dee will be released and home in Ketchikan before we arrive there."

"That's great!" My heart slips back down to its place in my chest. "Did Moran say if Dee had any idea what happened to her?"

"Apparently Dee doesn't remember anything about the incident, or being depressed, or thinking someone went overboard."

"Well, she's okay. That's the most important thing. God, I'm so relieved." I say. "But damn, we're left in the same place as we were when she was in a coma. We still don't have any pertinent information about how she got injured. The most important question still is whether she was pushed over the cliff."

Mandy nods. "Ironic, isn't it? Dee really does have amnesia."

"Shows it wasn't a stretch for me to claim loss of memory. But back to what happened to Dee. Between me being sent and left out at sea in a leaky boat without a working motor and almost getting killed by that goddamned truck, I'm ninety-nine percent sure she was forced off the cliff."

"Are you sure that the driver of that pickup targeted you?"

"I am. Jesus, that truck was hell bent for me."

"The driver could have been on drugs or drunk or a jerk—or all three. He could've been somebody who doesn't like people from the ship hanging out in his town, so was taking it out on you. It might not have anything to do with what happened to Dee. Besides, who in this town wants to deliberately hurt you? I realize that someone on the ship may have done something to Dee, but we are off-ship now. I think it's unlikely that anyone from the ship has a truck stored here."

"Yeah, I haven't been here long enough to have offended a townie." I'm mulling things over in my head. "If someone on that ship's scared, how hard would it be to find an asshole willing to pick up an extra chunk of money for a job that takes a vehicle and a few minutes of work?"

"Did you get a look at the driver?"

"No, it all happened so fast. I'm convinced the driver of the truck isn't the one I need to focus on. I think it's whoever hired him."

* * *

Mandy and I visit most of the stores, but no one recognized Nona, not even the clerks in the grocery store. That, I believe, is significant. Doesn't everyone have to buy groceries? Unless, of course, Nona and her boyfriend have gone completely off the grid.

Since Bev saw both Nona and Dee together in the pizza restaurant, Mandy and I decide to have dinner there. Who knows, maybe someone from the waitstaff remembers Nona or has seen her lately.

The bell on the door jingles as we walk into the smell of Italian spices and Tony Bennett singing, "O Sole Mio."

I hear, "Hey, over here."

Britt is waving us over. I don't want to sit with anyone from the ship, because it will put a serious damper on me trying to find out anything about Nona, but I can't come up with a reason why we wouldn't join her. So, we head to her table.

"My god, what happened to you?" Britt shakes her head.

"I tripped at the curb when trying to cross the street." I'd prepared that line ahead of time. I decided not to mention the truck's role in my accident. Since I'm supposedly unsteady due to my bad ankle and am already using a cane, I have to believe people will readily buy that I had clumsily tripped.

"I'm so sorry, Deidre. You sure didn't need that. Come on. You and Mandy sit down if you'd like and have dinner with me. I wasn't sure if I'd get things done on-ship in time to be able to come here to eat. Seems everyone from the ship has already chowed down and left. Anyway, I hate eating alone and would love your company."

Out of the corner of my eye, I notice Britt gives Mandy a wink. Mandy plays along and smiles back at her. It's their little secret, but I wonder how much longer Britt will be able to hold out telling me that she and Deidre had been involved.

"We'd love to," Mandy says. Apparently, she couldn't come up with a reason not to sit with Britt, either.

I grab the menus cradled between two adjoining moose figurines and pass them to Mandy and Britt. The waitress is looking me over, wondering no doubt what happened to Deidre.

"I can be clumsy," I say to her and laugh. I don't want to go into it.

"I'll say." She shakes her head then starts taking drink orders. When she gets to me, I ask her what's on tap, she says, "Your usual. We haven't changed anything since the last time you were in, honey. Still have the wine you like, too." She gives me a wry smile.

Shit, I didn't expect that response. Seems Dee's been in here a few times and has left an impression or at least the knowledge of her drink order to this waitress. I smile and tell the woman I'll take my usual beer. I had no idea Dee was into drinking beer these days.

As we wait for our drinks to arrive, Britt asks me about my arm and what the tests showed and if I think I can carry on with my bartending responsibilities. I joke that if I can work with only one functional foot then I should surely be able to carry on with only one functional arm.

When our server returns with our drinks, she asks for our food order. We each decide on the eight-inch personal pizza. Mandy and Britt give their toping choices, but when it comes to me, unfortunately, the waitress doesn't offer up Dee's usual toppings. Dee and I have shared the same pizza in the past, but I can't remember what it might have been since she tends to order it, as I'm not fussy and like just about everything. I'm starving, so I decide to order what I want—the all-meat pizza. I need the protein.

Britt looks at me, disbelieving. "What?"

I realize I made a huge mistake, something I could've avoided. I should've remembered Dee wouldn't order an all-meat pizza—even if she has amnesia. She's not a vegetarian, but in the past few years she's been on a health kick and went veggie.

"Okay. What do I usually order on my pizza?" What else can I say?

The waitress glances around the table with an expression of total bewilderment. I'm tempted to tell her that if she'd been so kind to clue me in to what my usual pizza choice is—as she did my beer—she wouldn't be perplexed right now.

"You never eat meat on your pizza," Britt says, looking perplexed. "You ask for all the vegetables they have except for green olives or onions.

"Usually, you order a veggie pizza, but often you have some meat on it," Mandy quickly adds, helping me to mitigate my blunder. "I don't know what you order here. Maybe you need something more hearty today."

I can see the wheels turning in Britt's head…and not in a good way. "It's interesting that this morning you didn't want a cinnamon roll either, which I asked the chef to make especially for you since you love them so much. You've never turned one down before. And now you want an all-meat pizza, something—"

"Is there anything else you ladies would like?" the waitress asks. "If not, I'll put this order in."

I can tell the poor woman doesn't know what to think. We all shake our heads, and she leaves. The brief interruption seems to have given Mandy a moment to come up with an excuse for me.

"It's strange," Mandy says, "but I read about something similar in one of my professional magazines. The woman in the article also had a head injury. Her tastes changed rather dramatically after the injury, not just in food area but in other things as well—like music, her favorite book genre, movies. Can't remember just what else. There were some medical hypotheses offered by the experts as to why it happened. Hmm, but I don't recall what they were."

"Huh." Britt tapped her fingers on the table. "That's weird. It doesn't make sense to me, but whatever."

I wish I could get into Britt's head to find out what she's thinking, she's probably trying to decide what she believes.

"That seems really bizarre to me too," I say, "that my tastes could change like that. But this whole experience seems so strange and unreal." I shrug my shoulders. "I guess anything's possible."

Britt nods. "As they say, stranger things have happened."

"I know," Mandy chimes in, "if I hadn't read about it myself, I'd have a hard time believing it."

I feel like I might have dodged a bullet thanks to Mandy, but if Britt has had any doubts about me, my all-meat pizza order and turning down the cinnamon roll didn't help my case. I can only hope she doesn't spend a lot of time thinking about it.

Britt looks at me. "I hope our food gets here quick. We need to get back to the ship soon, at least you and I do. We only have about forty-five minutes before the crew is due to board." She turns to Mandy. "Since you're a guest, you get an extra hour to play around here if you would like."

We make small talk about the cruise until our pizza arrives twenty-five minutes later. Then we chow down as fast as we can. The pizza's good. I wish I didn't have to gulp it down so fast. We pay the bill, and Britt runs to the bathroom.

Since we've walked into this place, I've noticed the same waiter glancing our way—specifically at me. When we stand and are about ready to leave, the guy comes over and says to me, "Looks like you took quite a beating."

"Yup," I say then throw him the old line, "but you should see the other guy."

He politely laughs. "Hey, I was wondering about the woman you were with the last time you were in here. I was hoping—"

Before I respond, Britt rushes up behind me. "Come on, Deidre. We need to hurry to get to the ship on time. Captain James doesn't look favorably on the crew being late."

In general, I'm usually the one flying in at the last minute. Britt, I've noticed, has the mentality of a sergeant. She's always early.

"Sorry. I got to get back to the ship," I tell the guy and follow Britt out the door. Mandy's behind me.

I stop and turn around to Mandy and whisper, "Go back and see if you can find out what that guy wanted to say to me."

Mandy nods.

I trail behind Britt a few steps. She doesn't seem to be aware that Mandy isn't with us. When I catch up with her, she finally notices. "Where did Mandy go?"

"She told me she wanted to see if she can pick up a T-shirt and pair of sweats she was eyeing earlier."

"Oh, no problem," Britt says. "She has time before she needs to board."

"Yeah, I hope she finds what she wants."

Britt smiles and helps me hobble along.

CHAPTER TWENTY-THREE

Mandy

As Mandy walked back to the pizza place, she mulled over the dinner with Britt and Kera. She couldn't believe her lapse, not remembering to tell Kera to be sure to eat one of the cinnamon rolls. Under the stress of having another note delivered to them, it had slipped her mind. Now, to add on to that, Kera ordered the all-meat pizza. She wondered if Britt had any uncertainty about "Dee," especially with these blaring food choices that Dee would never make. Had Britt bought the on-the-spot story of taste changes due to a head injury? It did seem that Britt had come around to accepting it as a possibility. Another possible problem, since Britt was so close to Dee, it wouldn't be surprising if she might notice subtleties of differences between Kera and Deidre. It wasn't likely she would try to Google all the possible effects of a brain trauma, since there was little or no Internet reception while on the ship. Mandy took a deep breath and let it out slowly. She had never felt so much stress and for such a long time in all her life. It wasn't merely from what was happening at any given moment, but what might happen, or what people might be thinking.

Good god!

Mandy slipped back into the restaurant and to the table she, Kera, and Britt had occupied. She waited and tried to spot the waiter Kera had mentioned. Finally, he emerged from the kitchen carrying a tray of food for another table. When she signaled to him, he nodded, finished his food delivery, and came over.

"My friend had to get back to the ship," Mandy said when the ponytailed waiter got to her table. "She wanted to apologize to you for taking off like that. She'd be in real trouble with her boss if she were late getting aboard. She asked me to find out what you were going to ask her. Something about a woman?"

"Yeah, I was wondering about the woman she was with the last time she was in here," he said as he brushed his mustache with his fingers.

"When was that?" Mandy wanted to make sure if he was talking about Nona.

"That would be when the boat docked here for a day on its way up to Juneau last week sometime. I can't remember the exact day. She promised she'd meet up with me here when the ship docked today on its way back to Ketchikan."

"What was her name?"

"I was afraid you might ask that. I...uh...can't exactly remember." A wave of embarrassment crossed over his face and settled in. "I mean, I did know it...well maybe. But that night we got to drinking way too much. I don't recall her name, if in fact she told me." He grimaced, looking embarrassed.

"Not to worry. I've been out drinking before where experiences and names evaporated from my memory forever." That wasn't true, but her goal was to win this guy's trust, like when she cross-examined someone on the stand. She didn't want him to feel judged.

"Yeah. You know how it is when you first meet someone, you don't always remember their name after they've told you. Then as the evening rolls on, you feel embarrassed to ask again, especially after you've gotten really close with that person." He chuckled, sheepishly. "I think there's some rule that says you have to at least know the person's first name if you're going to lay your lips on theirs."

"Sounds like you made quite a connection with her."

"Yeah. I liked her a lot. Would want to see her again. I really would. I thought we had something going, you know?" The guy seemed sincere.

"Back to her name that you don't remember. Does Nona ring a bell?"

"Could have been, but I'm not sure." He shrugged his shoulders. "Like I said, we were both drinking and having fun and it was late when she left to board the boat. If I knew her name, it got lost in the booze."

"Are you saying the woman you were with got back on the ship?"

"Well, yeah, of course. It's her job."

"Did you see her actually get on?"

"I walked her to the ship and waved goodbye to her. That I remember."

"Did you stay there long enough to see the ship leave the dock?" Mandy wanted to make sure that there was no doubt that the ship left with the woman on it.

"Yeah, she sailed off into the sunset, as they say, except it was more like moonlight in my case."

Mandy nodded, encouraging him to say more.

"Maybe she stayed on board this time to avoid me. If that's the case, I'd like to at least know that." The waiter sat down across from her. "I took the day off so we could be together. But when she didn't show or even try to contact me…" He let his voice trail off. "Maybe she couldn't remember my name, either. Anyway, when she didn't show, I took over this shift tonight for a friend who wanted to go to a party."

"Hey, Barry!" a husky voice belted out from the kitchen. "Hustle on over here and get this order. It's getting cold!" The guy looked at Barry as though this wasn't his first offense, and he had had it with him.

"Sorry." He jumped up. "Got to get back to work." As he headed for the kitchen, his voice trailed back, "I guess I got stood up."

"Hey, just one more thing," Mandy called after him. "Did the woman you were with have a…?" But before she could ask about the prothesis, he disappeared into the kitchen behind the swinging Dutch doors.

Mandy heard the same guy chewing Barry out for not attending to his job. She figured that even if she waited for Barry to come back out of the kitchen, he wouldn't want to give her any more time for fear of getting into more trouble. Besides, he apparently accepted the fact that the woman had ditched him, so why talk about it further? But she wished he'd remembered the woman's name, because it'd just occurred to her that Dee could have been sitting in the restaurant that day with more than one woman. And, good grief, she hadn't found out if the woman he was with had a prosthesis, which was the question she was trying to ask when the boss barked at the waiter, sending him off. That should have been her first question right out of the gate, even though it would have sounded a little weird and non-PC.

Even though she didn't have much hope of gleaning anything more from Barry, she waited around for a while anyway. But after his food delivery to a table, he tore back to the kitchen, obviously avoiding her gesturing to have him come back over.

She knew a shut door when she saw one.

* * *

Mandy walked toward the dock. She had time left before boarding, but there wasn't any place she wanted to go. She ambled toward the ship. As she got closer to the dock, she noticed two women sitting on the bench by the old Viking ship where she'd sat with Kera. One of them was on her phone, and the other woman played fetch with a large, white curly furred dog. As Mandy walked up, a tennis ball flew her way with the dog in chase.

"Watch out!" the women who'd tossed the ball shouted. "I'm sorry. I didn't see you heading this way."

Mandy caught the ball mid-air, but the dog was so hell bent on getting the flying object, it plowed her over.

The woman ran over to Mandy and helped her up. "Oh my lord. I'm so so sorry. Are you okay?"

Mandy didn't feel pain anywhere. In fact, she couldn't help but laugh. "Don't worry I'm fine, no damage done."

"I'm so grateful you're not hurt. Had I seen you coming, I wouldn't have tossed the ball in that direction."

Mandy twisted her torso, arms, and legs around to ensure she didn't have pain anywhere. The dog sat in front of her, ball in mouth, clearly waiting for Mandy to take it and throw it.

"Your poodle reminds me of another dog who's very close to my heart," Mandy said as she patted the dog's head. "Her name is Lakota, and she's crazy for balls, too. She also has tunnel vision when the ball is tossed for her."

"I'm glad you're understanding. When that ball's in the air, Sakari sees nothing else. But it's really my fault," the woman said. "I should have paid better attention to where I was tossing that ball. By the way, my name is Jan, and if you're hurt, I'll pay—"

"It's okay, Jan, really." Mandy brushed off her clothes. "I'm fine. All my body parts are still intact and moving okay."

"What kind of dog do you have?" Jan asked.

"She's not mine. She's my girlfriend's dog, and she's a mix of German Shepherd and Rottweiler."

"Sakari is actually not a poodle but a Labradoodle, a mix of two very rambunctious breeds, I'm afraid. We have a very hard time wearing that girl out. Which is why we bring her down here and let her play hard, most every day, both morning and night."

"How fun for her. We do the same thing with Lakota, only we run her on the beach of Lake Michigan."

"I bet that's a great place for a romp."

"It sure is. She can run for miles, up and back, up and back. My girlfriend and I walk, maybe a mile, to and from, and Lakota will cover probably fifteen miles of sand, at least."

"How wonderful for Lakota," Jan said. "We especially like our time here when the boats are due to come in or leave in the evenings. But I suppose you get great views, too, on Lake Michigan."

"Very similar, I'd say." Mandy ran her fingers through her hair, hoping to put it in pre-tumble condition.

"It's such a beautiful image to watch the silhouette of ships as they come into view or disappear into the sunset. It's like all is well with the world, whether it is or not. At least it's a moment when it feels like it is."

Mandy wished she could have that experience right now. She'd love a few moments of feeling all is well in her world. "Sounds wonderful. Are you familiar with the various ships that come and go here?" She thought it was a stab in the dark, but just maybe these women had been here the night Nona boarded.

"Oh yes, we have our favorites." Jan laughed. "For instance, see that green one docked over there?" She pointed to Dee's ship.

Mandy nodded.

"That one is definitely a favorite. From what I've heard, it is the best of the adventure cruise ships that regularly come in here."

"That's nice to know," Mandy said with a smile. "That's the cruise I'm on."

"My cousin works on the docks, and he says the captain is a good guy, always respectful and even tips him. Not many captains do that."

"Yes, he seems like a good guy." Mandy had very little contact with Captain James, but it was good to hear he treated people, other than just the passengers, well.

"We grew up here," Jan continued, gesturing to the other woman who was on the phone. "Carol and I are from fishing families. It's a tradition to send off those who head out to sea to get food for their families. That's dangerous work. The ocean can be cruel and unforgiving, we're all too aware of the fact that they might not come back. When they arrive here safely, we hurry down to the docks to meet them and show our appreciation for their work. We want them to see our joy that they've returned. At least in our case, I guess the tradition has extended to all the ships. Even though we're retired, we obviously can't make every return. But we get down here as often as we can. It feels good." She smiled like a proud mother as she looked at Sakari. "It makes my pooch feel good, too." Jan took the ball from Sakari and gave it a toss.

"By any chance, were you down here last week when that ship was leaving for Juneau?" Mandy gestured toward Dee's ship.

"Uh, yes, we were. Why?"

"I was just wondering if you happened to see a woman board late just before the boat left. She might have been a little tipsy." Mandy wished she had the snapshot of Nona, but it was with Kera.

"No, can't say as—"

"We might have, Jan." The woman, Carol, had ended her call. She got up from the bench and joined them. "Remember? She was in crew uniform shorts. We noticed she had an artificial leg. We wondered how she'd lost her leg, like if she'd been in the war. She was with a guy. They kissed, and she ran up the gangplank, wobbling quite bad. We didn't think of her as tipsy at the time, but that maybe her leg was making her unsteady. We watched her all the way up, worried that she might not make it."

"Oh yeah, now I remember," Jan said. "They waved to each other for a long time as the boat departed. We thought it was sweet and romantic. You know, like something out of a movie. Is she a friend of yours?"

"No, I was asking for a friend." Mandy had nowhere to go with the conversation unless she had the time and inclination to tell them the whole story. She hastily said. "Hey, thanks, but I have to get going. I promised to meet my friend on-ship for a drink."

CHAPTER TWENTY-FOUR

Kera

I spent almost an hour trying to calm Mandy. I finally got her relaxed enough to fall asleep by telling her funny stories about Dee and me when we were kids. I would have rubbed her back, but any attempts to do so hurt my shoulder. She was keyed up from having to wait for me after my shift. She wanted to tell me about Nona's boyfriend and the women at the dock who verified that Nona had gotten back on the ship that night. I guess that truck almost mowing me down didn't help Mandy's nerves, either.

I'm sleepless, wondering what my next move should be. It's not like I can go to the captain, Roni, Mick, or anyone since I have no idea who in hell I can trust. I told Mandy, to help her sleep, that I would contact the Coast Guard about Nona's mysterious disappearance. In reality, I have no way of doing that. Luckily, she didn't ask me how I thought I could contact them since there's no cell phone reception out here in the open waters. There's ship-to-shore communication, but that's located on the bridge. Because there's someone at the helm at all times, it's not an option. That leaves me with no chance of getting any form of private communication with the outside world. Makes me feel like a caged animal.

Maybe the only hope we have is to wait until we get to Ketchikan and contact the authorities. They'll be able to ask questions and demand answers regarding Nona's sudden disappearance, like was she the person Dee saw going overboard? A good chance, I'd say. But did Nona jump, accidentally fall because she was drunk, or did she have help plunging into the ocean? I'd put my money on her being helped over, especially because of all the shit that's happened to Dee and, subsequently, to me. There must be a connection.

I can't figure out how the threatening notes tie into all this, though. I suppose it will become clear when I'm confronted as an imposter. That's too late for my liking. One thing is certain, I need to be ready to dodge another attempt on my life, as well as keep Mandy from harm's way. We have tonight, tomorrow, and until almost noon the next day to find out what's going on around here. That's when we're scheduled to dock in Ketchikan. It's a lot of time for things to go bad for us, but it's very little time to figure out who fed Nona to the sharks. Who tried to destroy my sister's body by sending her down the mountain? And who tried to run me down in Petersburg?

When we arrive in Ketchikan, passengers will scatter far and wide. A lot of the crew members will head for other assignments. Not having the entire original cast of characters confined in one place will seriously jeopardize my ability to get to the bottom of all this. Feeling the time crunch ignites my anxiety. The mobility in my neck has about twenty degrees of flexibility. Damn. I need some relaxation. I best venture outside, hang by a rail, and let the THC in my weed do its work. It shouldn't be difficult for me to find a good place do my healing smoke, given most people are asleep at this time. I'm glad I don't have to worry about weed smell on my clothes as I smell it on a lot of workers and passengers alike. Doesn't seem to be a big deal.

September's night air sends a chill through me. I zip up my sweatshirt and pull the hood up over my head, light up my pipe, suck in my medicine, hold it in my lungs, then let it drift out into the breeze. Once…twice…three…four drags. Already my anxiety barometer has dropped from about-to-jump-out-of-my-skin to high-normal—that's about as relaxed as I ever get anyway.

I take in the night sky. It glitters with flickering dancing stars, their lights replicate in the water's surface and make the water and sky merge, the horizon indistinguishable, irrelevant. It's as though I'm floating in a night-sky bubble and have been released from this planet and am stepping out into a soft universe...

Until a scream yanks me back. It sounds like it came from a woman. A second scream, but it's quickly muffled, like a hand's been slapped over the mouth. It's followed by the sounds of sobbing.

I snuff out my pipe and go inside. I hear someone crying from a cabin close by, the cabin where the two housekeepers sleep. Frankly, it puzzles me as to why these two housekeepers rate their own cabin. But Dee got one. Maybe it's from a drawing or a crew member of the month reward.

No one's around. I don't know if anyone else heard the shrieks. The cabin is away from the bridge, probably out of earshot, and there's just a skeleton crew in the evenings. Or it could be that people are ignoring the scream, like in the case of a domestic disturbance—maybe that's what it is. Many people view it as "it's none of my business." I've never looked at it that way.

I knock on the door. The sobbing stops, replaced by sniffles, then silence.

I knock again.

Whispers.

"It's Deidre," I say, in a soft voice. I don't know if these native women trust Dee at all, but I give it a try. Still no response. "Uh, hey, is there something I can do to be of help?" I say into the silence.

Still nothing. I conclude I'm either not wanted there, or they figure I can't do anything for them. I decide to go back to my cabin.

"Deidre?" A voice from inside comes through the door.

"Yes."

The door cracks open enough for me to see an eye peek through, but the opening remains narrow as the lone eye looks at me, then searches around me.

"I'm alone," I say.

The door opens barely enough to scrape my body through.

The eye belongs to Agnes. Behind her are two native women. I've had little communication with either of them, but I know their names.

Lillian has dark hair that forms a long braid down the middle of her back. She sits on the bed with a wad of drenched toilet paper pressed to her nose, sniffling. Her eyes are puffy red, and her face is filled with anguish. Her dark watery eyes dart around the room, fearful, untrusting. Why, I don't know.

The other woman, Coleen, stands to the side of Lillian and strokes her back in a comforting motion. The first time I laid eyes on Coleen, I was awed by how perfectly symmetrical and sculptured her facial features were, like her carver had spent an extra amount of time on her face. She too has a long braid, but hers comes together and drops down over to the right side of her head. Her eyes are raven black. I have difficulty deciphering her pupils from the irises. I gauge both these quite beautiful women to be around the same age, somewhere in their mid-to-late teens, but it's hard to tell.

"What's wrong, Agnes?" I haven't moved away from the closed door. I don't want to upset these women any more than they already are. Besides, the room is no larger than mine and four people stuffed in the small space is a bit of a crunch.

"These girls," as Agnes refers to them, "are having a bad day. No big problem." That's all Agnes says.

Really? In my book, screams and sobbing mean a whole lot more than just a bad day, but I feel like I need to tread lightly and not challenge what Agnes has said or do something that might scare the women.

"Okay," I say gently, "but is there something I can do to help?"

"No, they'll be all right. Their work didn't go so good. I stay with them for a while." Agnes looks over at the women who both have their eyes glued on her. I know there's silent communication going on amongst the three of them, something my Euro-American white ass isn't supposed to have an ability to decipher.

"Okay," I finally say. "I'll be in my room if you need me, Agnes, no matter the time."

She nods and her lips curl slightly into a hint of a smile, but her eyes are saying something different.

* * *

On my way back to my cabin, I think I hear footsteps behind me. But when I turn around, no one is there.

That's creepy.

I keep walking but feel like a mouse is running up and down my spine, giving me goose bumps.

I hear the footsteps again.

I whip around. This time someone is there.

It's Mick. He's doing a slow drumbeat with a huge wrench that he's tapping into his hand. That mega tool could leave a sizable dent in my head. I turn to face him, ready. Dee isn't a black belt like I am. In this case, I can't be concerned about stepping out of my role. Besides, with my one arm stuck in a sling, I'm going to have to rely on a whack of my cane or a well-placed kick, if necessary.

"You're out and about pretty late," Mick says. He stops about four feet from me. Still brandishing the tool.

"Went out to stargaze. It's a beautiful night." I try to keep my voice level, but my gaze is glued on his hands, especially that piece of iron he's using as a drumstick. A much better weapon that my cane.

"Yup, a good night for it all right. No clouds."

"Uh-huh." I'm so focused on him, I'm sure I haven't blinked.

It occurs to me why, when I thought I heard him the first time, I didn't see him. At that time, I had just gone by the opened door of the engine room. If he's up to doing me harm, he could have momentarily stepped in there, out of sight, when I turned around to see who was behind me. This last time, when I whipped around, there was no place for him to hide. But I go on as though everything's fine, like I don't suspect that he was about to use that piece of iron to split the back of my head open.

"I came in because I heard a scream. Didn't you hear it?" I ask.

Frankly, I don't see how Mick couldn't have been aware of that piercing sound. He wasn't that far from the housekeepers' room. It seems to me that anyone on this floor who was in one of the hallways would have heard it. Maybe anyone who might have been aware of the disturbance wanted to ignore it.

"Scream? No." He has a puzzled look on his face—or he's putting on a look of bewilderment for my sake. "Who screamed?"

"I don't know," I lie. "I guess it could have been my imagination." Since I'm supposed to have been mentally unstable and likely still am, he can write it off as one of my hallucinations. I let it drop, because if he's guilty of anything regarding the scream, he's not going to admit it. If he had nothing to do with it, I don't want to talk to him about Agnes and the other two women.

The captain rounds a corner and comes up behind Mick. "Hey, what's up, you two?"

"Had to stop by the engine room and get my wrench," Mick says. "I saw Deidre out here wandering around, so I was going to ask her for help. I just needed her for a minute or two." Mick glances at me and then back at the captain.

Jesus, that's sure not what I thought you were up to, Mick.

"It can't wait till morning?" The captain raises his eyebrows. "Mick, my man, you put in long hours of hard work every day. Surely you don't need to be laboring at this hour." The captain puts his hand on Mick's shoulder.

"I suppose, but I was busy earlier putting a new prop on the motor of my skiff. I was trying to see what I could do to repair the old girl's leaks, though not much accomplished on that front. I'll have to deal with them when I got more time. Anyway, I didn't get some things done around here that I wanted to do. So, I decided—"

"Still, you need to sleep, Mick," the captain interrupts. "At least once a week." He laughs and shakes his head.

"True, but I was lying in bed and couldn't stop thinking about what I didn't get done in the engine room."

"It's not an emergency, right?" the captain asks.

"No, but I thought that if I just got up and fixed the damned thing, maybe I could get some sleep."

"I tell you what," the captain says as he winks at me. "We've got to let Deidre get her rest, too. I can give you a few minutes of my time before I have to take over on the bridge from Roni. Besides, with only one functioning arm now, I don't think Deidre could help you that much."

"I only needed her one arm for a few minutes to hold something for me." Mick chuckles. "I wasn't planning on keeping her up all night."

No, it looked to me like you were planning on putting me to sleep forever!

Mick and the captain walk back toward the engine room. I hear Mick telling the captain that the job can wait till morning and he was going to head for bed… Hmm.

I go on to my cabin. My body feels like I've been revved back up and am ready to burst out of my skin. I slip into bed with Mandy and curl around her. I only hope she can't feel my agitation.

CHAPTER TWENTY-FIVE

Dee's Journal

It's Charlie again. She is the most difficult passenger we've had on any of the cruises this season, and according to most of the crew members, the worst one that anyone has had to deal with, ever. The crew can't wait to be rid of her. One guy suggested we lock her up in the engine room and let her deal with the diesel fumes and loud noise. It's hard for me to be civil to the woman, let alone nice. She functions on threats. I guess she's mostly bluster... I hope! She's probably gotten her way in life being that way, but it's obnoxious and I'm sure she's scary to people in her way, and when I've been in her path, she does frighten me. But I try not to let her see it.

Today she didn't like her lunch, so she went into the kitchen to harangue Agnes. She was carrying her plate of perfectly good food. I thought the dish she'd prepared was different but very tasty and quite creative. In fact, I had earlier complimented Agnes on it. Charlie's gripe was that the sauce was not the correct kind for that particular dish—like she's some great chef? I'm not sure what she thought Agnes could do for her, other than stop what she was doing at that moment and redo the sauce. I was having my lunch at the time and witnessed what was going on between the two of them.

Agnes didn't stand up for herself, as she certainly had the right to do. I don't know if it's her personality or her culture or fear for her job—or perhaps, all of those—that causes her to be incredibly submissive. She kept her head down and continued to apologize to Charlie as though she'd actually done something wrong. But her cowering didn't stop Charlie's tirade. In fact, I believe it served to egg the bully on. It was clear that Charlie liked a willing victim and kept hammering the poor woman.

I felt like I needed to step in, tactfully, and help Agnes but I initially hesitated. The captain keeps emphasizing that we all need to make the passengers happy—the customer is always right sort of thing. I hate that! The captain doesn't directly say it, but it's certainly his underlying message to the crew. I had to intervene, job or no job. Earlier in the season when an employee didn't completely abide by one of the captain's rules, though he had every right to do and say what he did, he was fired on the spot. (A lesson to us all!). I can't always go by every rule—or a stupid belief system—all the time, not if I want to have any self-respect.

Before I knew it, Charlie, with her plate of food in hand, demanded that Agnes leave the galley and go with her. She didn't tell Agnes why or where she wanted Agnes to go. Agnes was terrified. I could see her trembling.

When I caught up with them out on the deck, Charlie had handed her plate to Agnes and was insisting that she feed the food to the fish. Before Agnes could obey the big bully, I grabbed the plate out of Agnes's hands. By that time, I was angry and unable to control myself. I'm sure my face was blood red when I told Charlie she was out of line and was never to treat another person on the cruise like that again, or she'd have me to contend with. (There went my plan for a tactful approach.) In most verbal battles, I'd win, but if it came to a physical showdown, I'd be out of luck, not merely out of a job. Anyway, I took Agnes's arm and pulled her close to me, which brought Charlie's fists up, ready to let me have it. When I realized what I had done, I was trembling, too.

Luckily for Agnes and me, Britt came out, saw some of the action, and stepped in. She placated Charlie while I took Agnes back to the galley. All the while, I assured her she'd done nothing wrong. Later that night, when Britt talked to me about the incident, she wasn't upset with me. She said Charlie was an asshole and was glad the captain hadn't been around to see it. (Thank you, Britt!) I don't know what Britt said to Charlie, but she didn't go to the captain to complain. Whew! Still have my job. But we've got to get to Juneau and back to Ketchikan with that bitch aboard. That's the second time Charlie and I have had a run-in with each other.

My mission: avoid her, avoid her, avoid her.

When I took Agnes back to the galley, she had tears in her eyes. She thanked me for helping her but worried about the consequences for me standing up for her. I let her know that I didn't care. There was no way I'd stand by and let that happen to her or anyone else. More tears ran down her cheeks. Then she said something really strange that I'm still wondering about and trying to make sense of: "You do have good in you. I guess everyone does." Then she went back to her work in the galley.

At the time, I was perplexed by her comment and wanted to ask her what she meant by it, but Britt showed up and requested my help on the platform. When I saw her later, it didn't seem appropriate somehow.

I'm still shaky from the whole thing.

CHAPTER TWENTY-SIX

Kera

Trying to sleep when I'm on hyperalert mode is downright impossible. There's nothing like having a guy slink behind me with a wrench in his hand to keep me feeling jumpy—for hours. But being in this nerved-up condition, ready to pounce, is no doubt why I hear soft footsteps outside my cabin. I wouldn't be surprised if it's Mick with his wrench standing there.

I jump out of bed and fling open the door. *Wally.* "What the hell are you doing out here?"

"Uh…I was just walking by. That's all." Wally's eyes are popped open wide. He quickly slips his right hand behind his back. He stands at an angle that doesn't allow me to observe what's in that hand. I crane my neck around to try to get a glimpse of whatever it is. As I do, he makes an adjustment with his stance, so I can't see.

"Really," I say sarcastically. "At this time of night, you're walking past my door for exercise or for fun?" I know where his cabin is, and it's not on this floor. There's no good reason for him to be down this hallway unless he's up to something, such as stalking me. I certainly wouldn't put it past him to be lurking around my sister, i.e., me. He's the kind of freak to do it, probably out to get a few new snapshots for the picture gallery on his cabin walls—maybe hoping to catch Dee in her pajamas. The bastard is obsessed. *Creepy… Maybe, worse than creepy.*

"Yes," he says. "I'm getting my exercise. There are no rules that say I can't walk around the ship. That's all I'm doing."

He looks guilty as hell.

"Is that why you're walking on your tip-toes." I don't bother to disguise that I don't believe him.

"I was not on my tip-toes." He's obviously insulted by my characterization of his walk-by of my cabin. "I was only walking softly to be considerate. I didn't want to disturb others, so I've been trying not make a lot of noise." He gives me a look like I accused him of slapping his mother.

"Well, now. Isn't that considerate of you." I don't believe this jerk at all. Not for one minute. And he knows it. God damn it. He's up to something. He starts to slink away. Apparently, he thinks or hopes that it's all over. It's not. I grab his arm and pull him around. That's when I get sight of what's in his hand. It appears to be a piece of paper. I snatch it from him. Holy shit, I think I might have discovered my secret note sender.

"That's mine! It's no business of yours." He grabs at it but only gets the air as I pull the paper away from his reach.

"Oh no. I need to see what you got here, buddy." I put my hand—from my good arm—on his forehead because he charges at me like a wounded bull. I push him back, hard, against the wall.

"Give it back to me or I'll tell the captain," he says in his whiny voice. "I'll tell him that you hurt me."

"You just do that, Wally. I'm sure he'll be very interested in what you've been up to these days." I unfold the paper. It is, as I suspected, pasted letters forming his next threat to me:

Your unveiling will be tomorrow!

"Well, now, I guess you and I have something to talk about, don't we?" I grab the jerk and yank him into the cabin.

"What's going on?" Mandy says, jarred awake by the ruckus.

Luckily, she's wearing pajamas. Lately, due to our unpredictable circumstances, she felt it necessary to make sure she'd be ready to jump up and run at a moment's notice.

I slam Wally down on the floor since we don't have the luxury or space for a chair. I'm not about to let him sit down on the bed by Mandy.

"Guess who came to deliver us another lovely message?" I hand over the paper to Mandy.

Mandy reads it, looks at Wally, then back at the note. "Really, Wally. You're the one doing this…" Mandy hesitates then says, "to Deidre?" She shakes her head and glares at Wally.

I imagine that her hesitation was due to almost calling me Kera, but I figure that it really doesn't matter anymore because Wally obviously knows I'm not Dee and is out to expose me. I wonder if he's the only one who knows…and how it's tied to the death attempts on my sister and me.

"I caught him red-handed." I rub my arm, it hurts. I used my good arm to battle him, but somehow, my injured shoulder and arm must have joined the fray.

Mandy shakes her head. "I guess I didn't search his room well enough," she says, then covers her mouth like someone who'd just let the cat out of the bag.

Wally didn't seem to hear her or was probably too preoccupied by his circumstances to absorb it. At least he didn't say anything.

"Okay, Wally," I snarl. "It's time to spill your guts." I'm sitting on the edge of the bed holding Wally by the collar of his shirt. "Why in hell have you been dropping these little shitty notes in my path?" His eyes look like they could pop out of his head. I bet that he's never heard Dee talk like this, let alone swear at him.

His bulging eyes dart around the room. I suppose he's looking for an escape, but my leg is in his flight path to the door. I'm so angry right now that if he did try to run, I'd place a swift kick to his groin. I have no idea how he fits into what's been going on around here, how he's come to know that I'm not Dee, but I'll do whatever it takes to get it out of him. Before I decide what to say or do, I'll see what I can squeeze out of him. I want him to tell me what he knows and how he knows it.

His body is rigid, tight, like a sitting tin soldier. He stares straight ahead, not blinking. His mouth is half open, but he doesn't say anything. It's like rigor mortis has set in on him.

I prod him with my foot. "We're waiting."

Mandy looks at me at me like I'd kicked a dog.

Really, Mandy?

I give her my it-was-just-a-nudge expression as a response to her accusing scowl. She has to admit it was effective, because it obviously shook him from his stupor. He starts babbling, but unfortunately, his words make no sense.

"You're going to have to do better than that Wally," I snap at him. "I'm not an indulgent person, never have been, and since the war it's worse. Far worse. I'm losing my patience with you." Oops! That war comment is not something Dee would say, but again, he doesn't act like he heard it or that it registered with him. I glance at Mandy. It doesn't appear she noticed my slip, either.

I'm quite sure that what's clogging him up is that he felt like he had the upper hand and now finds himself at a disadvantage. He's trying to figure out how to right the situation in his favor. If there is a way for him to do that, I'm not going to give him time to figure it out. We're doing this my way, not how Dee would approach it.

"Speak up, buddy!" I pull my foot back and prepare to nudge him again.

He notices. "I did it because you're mean to me."

"Mean?" What the fuck is he talking about. "How am I mean to you, Wally? Other than make your drinks and be nice to you."

"You're pretending to have amnesia so you won't have to be my girlfriend anymore," he whines. His bottom lip protrudes like a pouty kid whose had his little blanket taken away from him.

I try to sort through what he just said. I glance over at Mandy and can see that she confused, too.

"Girlfriend? What in hell are you talking about?" Jesus, this guy is delusional. He fucking thinks Dee is his girlfriend?

Mandy sits up, swings her feet to the floor, and leans in toward him. Given the size of the room, they're only inches apart. She asks in a tone usually reserved for a six-year-old, "Since when has Deidre been your girlfriend, Wally?"

Wally squirms. Still no eye contact with either me or Mandy.

I don't have patience. If I were alone with him, I'd kick his sorry ass. He's been tormenting us with these threatening notes all because he thinks I'm being mean? Jesus. Okay, I know I need to back off. Mandy's method, I have to admit, will get better results. She's used to dealing with people on the stand. I hold myself back and give her a chance at it. If that doesn't work, we do it my way.

Mandy reaches over and touches Wally's shoulder. "Please, Wally. I just want to help you. Really, I do."

I'm about to puke.

Wally's head rises slowly then stops. Mandy reaches out and puts her hand under his chin so their gazes meet. "You like to think that Deidre is your girlfriend, don't you, Wally? After all, she's always been very kind to you."

"She was kind," Wally blurts out. "Then she went and pretended she doesn't know me. That's not kind, not at all. And she kicked me!" Wally snaps a glance at me then back to Mandy, the person who understands him.

Finally, it dawns on me. Jesus! Wally said it, straight and clear. I was so caught up with the idea that he thinks Dee is his girlfriend that I didn't hear what else he actually said.

He thinks I'm his girlfriend, Deidre, who's come back from the hospital, and that I'm pretending to have amnesia—just so I can ditch him.

Wow. Deranged.

It's pretty sad when I allow an ounce of compassion into this picture. These notes aren't connected to Dee's attack on the cliff. The guy's acting on his own, and he doesn't have anything to do with all the other shit that's going on around here. This is Wally's own pile of delusional shit, no one else's. But to be sure I'm not missing something, I let Mandy continue her connection she has with him.

"You were sending those notes to punish Deidre, weren't you?" Mandy says. "You wanted her to feel pain like you were feeling. Isn't that right?" Her words are kind, understanding, and flow out like an elixir.

Wally nods and almost smiles at Mandy, grateful that someone knows and understands his agony. I know I need to jump in here, from Mandy's brief glance in my direction. I'm still trying to organize my thoughts to make sure that Wally isn't putting on an act for me.

"Does anyone else know about what you've been doing, making these notes?" I ask him.

He shakes his head then drops his gaze, like a shamed kid.

"Didn't you think that doing this could get you in trouble?"

He shrugs his shoulders. "I guess I do now." He glances up at Mandy, his protector, just in case I start kicking (nudging) him again.

I think I've heard enough. I sit down on the bed next to Mandy and finally don my sister's persona. "Wally, you've made me very upset. I thought we were friends," I say with emphasis on the word "friends," purposefully ignoring his crazy-ass belief that Deidre's his girlfriend. I try to set him straight about the actual relationship he has with her. If, indeed, she ever thought of him as a "friend" instead of the needy pain in the ass that I've experienced.

Tears roll down his face. I don't think his crying has to do with being caught in the act. More likely, the tears have to do with my cracking into his world of pretend and delivering a kick-ass dose of reality, something he didn't want to hear.

"I'm sorry, Deidre," he whimpers. "I didn't mean to upset you."

I'm about to ask him how in hell he expected me to react to his threatening notes, but I stop. It's not a place I need to go with him.

He sniffs. "I didn't know you could be so mean."

"It just shows how far you pushed me, doesn't it?"

"Uh-huh." He peeks up at me and then quickly back down.

He somehow breaks through my anger. I'm beginning to see him as pitiful and actually feel sorry for him. He's taking all these cruises just to be near Dee, someone who talks to him, someone who notices and is nice to him.

Mandy hands him a box of tissues.

He blows his nose, honking like a goose. "I'm sorry," he whimpers. "I didn't mean to upset you, I just wanted to…" He can't find the words to finish his sentence. He grabs another handful of tissues and honks again, which brings a boatload of nasal debris. I turn my head. When I glance back at him, I notice that his gob of tissues is soaked through. He sees it, too, and remedies the problem by wiping the gooey hand on his pants.

"Don't worry, Wally. I won't tell anyone what you did to me," I assure him. I most likely wouldn't under normal conditions, either, but given the other shit that I'm trying to deal with on the ship, it would serve no good purpose.

* * *

By the time Mandy and I finished with him, Wally had collapsed—like a stabbed inflatable air dancer you see at a used car sale. His remorse dribbled on and on, until I put an end to it. I swear, had I asked, he would've walked the plank by the time we picked him up off the floor and prodded him out the door.

Even though we're still no closer to finding out who tried to kill my sister or why, at least we don't have to be concerned about another nerve-rattling note showing up. But the bad thing is, I still have a bull's-eye on my back. Sometimes you just can't win.

"Wow," Mandy says as she crawls back into bed, "what a night. I sure wouldn't have guessed it was Wally."

"He's one sick puppy—a very annoying sick puppy."

"Yup." Mandy tries to fluff a foam pillow. "He exhausted me and after all that, I'm not sure I'll be able to sleep."

"Hopefully, we both can get some rest because tomorrow's our last full day to try and figure things out." Just thinking that thought pushes my panic button.

"Kera, don't you think it would be wise to be grateful that Dee is alive and well and for us to just ride this cruise out? After all that's happened to her, I'm sure she'll be more than willing to go back to Michigan with us."

"I truly wish that was possible, but we can't, honey. Somebody wanted to kill Dee, and still does, or they wouldn't have tried to run me down in Petersburg. Until we find out what this is about and who's behind it, we'll never know what threat Dee poses to this person or persons. Even if I were ready to give up on searching out who did this to my sister, what would keep whoever from tracking down Dee when she's back in Michigan?"

"Yeah, I guess you're right," Mandy says.

"Let me get ready for bed. I can't massage your back, but I think my shoulder will allow me to rub some oil on your body. That should help to relax you a little." I change into my pajama bottoms and T-shirt.

"I'm not sure if I'll ever be able to relax again, but I might, someday... Like when we're finally out of here and back home in Michigan." Mandy's faint smile doesn't reach her eyes. I know she's trying to be positive and I appreciate it.

"I'll be right with you," I say. "Just looking for the rubbing oil you brought."

"I think it's in the bathroom in my toiletry case. It's a small bottle, greenish, if I remember right."

"Oh, yeah, I got it." I have to brush my teeth, so I load my toothbrush and toss the massage oil to Mandy's outstretched hands.

It doesn't make it that far and hits the wall and drops in the crack between the bed and the wall. "Sorry. Bad shot."

"Where did it go?" I hear Mandy rummaging around trying to find the bottle. "It's got to be here somewhere."

"It couldn't have gone too far," I say through a mouth full of toothpaste.

She shakes the blanket and sheets, even looks into our pillowcases. There's no way the bottle could've bounced off the wall into either of the pillow coverings at the head of the bed, but she's in desperate need of an oiling.

"Good grief. I saw the bottle flying in this direction." She scowls. "It's here somewhere on this bed. It has to be."

I swish out my mouth and join the search. "Maybe it fell down the crack between the bed and the wall."

"I ran my hand along the edge, but it wasn't there." Mandy shakes her head. "The crack is pretty tight. I can barely get my hand all the way down, so I don't think the bottle could've slipped down there."

"Let me check anyway. That bottle's not that thick." It's a tight squeeze, but I'm able to fit my fingers down the crack and push them toward the floor. I move my hand sideways toward the foot of the bed. Just before I get to the end of the mattress, my longest fingertip brushes what feels like it could be a bottle. At least it's solid. "There's something here."

"The bottle?"

"I don't know yet. Probably." I force my hand down farther in order to grab or at least try to pry loose whatever it is that lurks there. But the palm of my hand is a little too big to shove all the way down through the crack. "I can't get to it."

"Hang on a minute," Mandy's says. "I saw a shoe box yesterday under the bed. It had pens, stationery, envelopes, and stuff like that in it." Mandy gets out of bed and retrieves the shoebox.

"Stationery? I didn't know anyone wrote letters anymore." Then I think about the lack of Internet around here and remember that Dee had sent me a postcard.

Mandy hands me a ruler to use and says, "Dee sent me a card at the beginning of the cruise season. Since then, it's been phone connections with her when she's ashore."

I dig down and realize whatever it is that I'm trying to pry up is larger than the massage oil and doesn't feel like it either. I get it up enough that I can use my fingers. I pull out a small leather-bound book. Or at least that's what it looks like.

Until I realize it's a diary...

Dee's!

CHAPTER TWENTY-SEVEN

Kera

"Good God!" Mandy exclaims. "I never knew Dee kept a journal, but I suppose she got one so she could record her experiences here. Makes sense."

I'd already opened the journal to be sure it's Dee's. I can tell by the handwriting that it is. I start glancing through the first pages.

"Kera, do you think you should read it?" Mandy acts like I should put the diary down as though these are normal times, and I should honor my sister's privacy. I would do that...normally.

"Honey, we have to look through here. It might give us a clue about what was going on with her."

"I know, I know. You're right. It just seems so wrong, even now."

I haven't taken my eyes off Dee's words as I scan through pages of what appears to be periodic entries, maybe seventy-five or more pages. She starts out by describing her flight out to Alaska, finding her place to live in Ketchikan, and the beginnings of her new job. I skim through these.

Mandy scrunches in close to me. "Can I look on with you?"

"I'm sorry, of course." I move the diary so she can better see and read along with me. "I got excited. Didn't mean to be rude.

Hopefully, there's something here that might turn out to be helpful to us."

We leaf through her first entries.

"Most of it, so far, is upbeat and shows that she's enjoying her job, even though she says here," Mandy points to the page, "that she misses us."

"We know she was unhappy with her life when she left and had been for a while," I say. "From her entries it sounds like she was doing the right thing for herself by getting away from her life in Michigan."

"I agree, but somewhere along the way things turned for her."

We move on through her pages, not seeing much that would be helpful, other than to realize that my sister's emotional pain was returning, little by little.

Mandy shakes her head. "It's sad. I know Dee told us that she felt she hadn't dealt with all the grief she's piled up with all her losses and believed this would be a good move for her. I was never sure how Alaska would help that, other than be a nice experience. Dealing with her grief seems like a therapy issue, not a vacations issue."

"Uh-huh." I'm listening, somewhat. I'm getting the thread of her analysis of my sister's mindset, but I keep plowing through the pages. I need to find out who went after my sister, almost killing her, not try to understand her reasons for coming here in the first place. Mandy doesn't seem to notice my lack of attentiveness and keeps talking.

"…I so wish she can someday make it through her pain and end up on the other side, feeling good and—"

"Look." I point at a passage. "She talks about Roni's temper around the crew. But she says here that Roni's been really sweet and nice to her."

"Hmm, I wonder," Mandy says, "if Roni has feelings for Dee?"

"Maybe, but being sweet and nice to someone doesn't mean romantic feelings."

Mandy raises an eyebrow. "But Roni doesn't seem to be sweet and nice to many members of the crew. I wonder if Britt might have had some competition."

"I hope not. Roni's a jerk. I'd think my sister would see that pretty fast. I can't see her falling for that woman. In fact, she shouldn't be falling for anyone. Remember? She said she was going to lay off romance. Period." I look up at Mandy.

Mandy nods. "But even if Dee wasn't interested, maybe Roni didn't get it. Or Dee was concerned about Roni's temper and worried she could lose her job so didn't completely close the door to her. Roni's her boss. It would be a difficult situation for her."

"And inappropriate on Roni's part," I add.

"Doesn't matter, Kera, happens all the time."

"I hope my sister didn't have to deal with that," I say.

"If Roni was interested, it must be encouraging to her that you, well, Dee, can't remember that Britt and you were involved. It would give her a second chance, if she wants one."

"Yuck."

"At any rate, with Roni's temper and position," Mandy continues, "if I were Dee, I'd hate to have to let Roni know that I wasn't interested in her. We know what a bitch she can be to people who anger her."

My imagination is now running a film clip of Roni behind my sister pushing her over the cliff. With Roni's body build, it wouldn't take much of a bump. Then, when I think about it more, probably not the case. The woman's got a bad temper, but she's ambitious and wants everything to go perfectly. I don't think she'd be willing to risk her career and end up sitting in jail. I can't see her premeditating a bad end for my sister… But I also know that people don't always act logically or in their best interests when it comes to their emotions, especially unrequited love. Then I remember Roni being in the Iraq war, maybe having PTSD. That doesn't help her case. PTSD or not, we got damaged there.

"Look here, Mandy. She writes about Mick's boat. Doesn't say anything about it being damaged. He even took her out in it. He wouldn't have done that if it were leaking, which confirms that someone tampered with it. But when and who?"

Mandy points to a passage in the diary. "Dee's writing about being depressed."

"Yeah, looks like she's figured out like you did that Alaska and a new job is a diversion, not a necessarily a place to heal." I smile to myself, I guess I was paying attention to Mandy's ramblings more than I thought.

"Uh-huh. But look here. It's another bitch moment on the part of Roni. This time, it's directed at Agnes."

I find the place that Mandy points out and read that Britt comes to Agnes's rescue. It brings on another moment of conflict between Roni and her. Jesus, this time it's physical as well, and in front of the passengers.

"Seeing the staff fighting like that had to freak out the passengers," I say. "I wonder if the captain knows anything about Roni and Britt's nasty relationship."

"Look at this. She's writing about Roni and you. Dee's referring to PTSD issues Roni has, but she also points out that, although you too have problems with anger and control, you don't have Roni's mean streak." Mandy glances at me. "I would've added here that you've done a lot of work to learn how to your control your issues, honey."

"Just a lot? And anger?"

"You're better, much better on both fronts."

"But not cured, right? Is that what you're saying?"

"I'd say your anger is more appropriate...most of the time."

I decide to cut off the conversation about my anger and control. It can't lead to any place good, and Mandy and I sure don't need to get into a fight right now. Ha. I believe I've just demonstrated my improved *control skills* by not engaging further. I wonder if Mandy's noticed that. And I do believe I deserve to be angry at whoever it was that tried to kill my sister. I'd say that it's spot-on appropriate.

"Dee writes here," Mandy says, pointing, obviously wanting to move away from igniting our issues. "Dee didn't like Roni's advances and wasn't at all interested in any romance." Mandy looks relieved.

"Apparently, Britt hadn't entered the scene yet." I look at the date of my sister's entry. Makes sense, timewise. Britt said it was a recent budding relationship. Knowing Dee as well as I do, she means well, but her track record is one of getting involved, even though she loudly protests to the contrary.

We move on through the diary and take note of Wally's being a pain in Dee's ass as well as being smitten with her. Obsessed is a better word, I'd say. He took all the cruises she was working on. Even though she's aware that he's taking her picture, I bet she had no idea he was pointing his camera at her secretly, as well. If she'd seen his room, which I assume she hadn't, it would've freaked her out.

I'm not feeling sorry for him right now. I'm back to wanting to wring his fucking little skinny neck.

"Read here." Mandy shows me the paragraph her eyes are glued to. "Charlie threatened Dee sometime when Dee and she were on a hike. Look. Dee says that Charlie was cheating on Bev, messing around with someone, and Dee saw them. It's when they were on the way up to Juneau. Yeah, the date is right."

I take a closer look. "Well, well, well. Charlie threatened my sister." I wonder why Charlie went to jail or prison—whichever it was. I wish Bev knew and could have told me why. Was it a crime of bilking money out of older women, like a sugar mama? Or was it because of something of the violent nature? Or both?

"Do you think Dee might have threatened to tell Bev about what she saw?"

"Or it could be that Charlie assumed my sister would?"

"Or worried she would."

"Bev is Charlie's meal ticket, and Bev tells me she's determined to dump Charlie if she messes around anymore. Or I should say if she gets caught with Terri the Tart. But I don't know. Murder? That's a—"

"But you told me that Charlie doesn't seem to want to go to work," Mandy says, "that she enjoys her life by living off her sugar mama." Mandy shakes her head. "She's never worked, so no skills and a prison record. I've seen people in court kill for less. And she has an attitude of entitlement."

"Okay, let's move Charlie up to the top of our suspect list for now."

"I didn't know we had one."

"It's up here." I tap my head.

Mandy rolls her eyes.

"Hey, look at this." I show the place where Dee mentions Nona, how they work together and became friends.

"Another confirmation for us about the existence of Nona as a crew member on this ship—who strangely isn't here anymore."

"Yeah," I say. "The question is, why?"

"We absolutely know now that she got back on board that night in Petersburg and somehow disappeared from the ship the same night."

"Do you think Nona knew that Charlie threatened Dee on the hike?" Mandy yawns then adds, "After all, Dee and Nona were friends. Maybe Nona confronted Charlie, they got into a fight, and Nona got pushed overboard."

"That's one possible hypothesis." I try to decide how likely it is. "I know that it's getting really late, honey." She's finally given in to her repeated attempts to quash her yawns for the last fifteen minutes. "But we need to finish reading this." I pat Mandy's thigh as though that might keep her awake.

"I know, hon." Mandy works to keep herself awake by lightly smacking her cheeks.

"Nona's knowing about the threat to Dee could certainly be possible since they were working together and were friends. But I'm not sure Nona would confront Charlie about that. However, we don't have any idea what might have happened between Charlie and Nona. God knows, Charlie is on the lookout for a fight. We can't exclude the possibly that Nona had her own run-in with Charlie."

"But how would Charlie have known that you'd be the one sent out looking for a missing person and then have time to damage Mick's boat and loosen the propeller." Mandy put her hand over her next yawn.

"I agree. That doesn't seem likely. But at times, events seem unrelated, but when you fill in the empty spaces, it can turn out differently. That's a concept I like to keep in mind when I'm on a case. At this point, we don't have all the other pieces of the puzzle that fit around Nona's disappearance and the attempt on my life."

"Attempts." Mandy corrects me.

"Yeah, right."

Makes me sort of thankful that Dee's in the hospital, and I'm here in her place. I know it's said that a cat has nine lives, but I don't know how many lives I've been allotted. I'm quite certain I'm close to running out, given my present profession and time in Iraq.

"Here's something about Charlie again," Mandy says as she turns the page. "This time she's after Agnes over the food she'd cooked."

"Jesus, what a bitch. If I were Dee, I'd… Oh look, good for my sister, she stood up to Charlie and for Agnes. You rock, Dee."

"Yes, but maybe another reason for Charlie to seek revenge."

"Check out this last line." I run my finger along the sentence where Agnes says to Dee, *You do have some good in you. I guess everyone does.*

Mandy and I look at each other, in disbelief. We're taken aback by Agnes's words to Dee, and Dee was surprised, too, according to what she wrote in her diary. If there's anyone on this earth who's a good person, it's my sister. That's why a person like her goes into social work. She likes to help people, always has, and has worn herself out doing it. I consider why anyone would say that, and especially Agnes.

"We're almost to the end of her entries," Mandy says. "Shows she's still depressed, which squares with what people have told us."

"Uh-huh." I'm reading further down. "But down here, she's talking about something else, something that she's anxious about."

"Anxious, for what?" Mandy asks. "I know she was anxious for me to come so we could have—"

"No, no. Anxious as in nervous, upset."

"Hmm." Mandy turns the page back to check the date. "Isn't this the night that Nona went missing?"

"It sure is."

* * *

There are only a few more pages of entries left in Dee's journal, so we're moving close to the end of her writings. Mandy and I take a deep breath and hope for something more solid to go on. Mandy volunteers to read the rest of what Dee wrote out loud to me so we will be at the same spot:

Since last night, I feel like I've been given a sort of social banishment or shunning by the crew. They hardly speak to me and when they do, it's only because they need something or want me to do one thing or another. Apparently, it's only the crew members who've heard, I'm sure. I've noticed them whispering to each other while glancing at me, thinking I'm not noticing.

Very unnerving.

Eye contact from any of them is rare and accidental if it happens. I guess looking directly into the eyes of someone who's mentally unbalanced is a scary thing, so they pass by without even a nod and pretend not to see me.

For the most part, I think passengers know little, if anything, about me seeing someone fall into the ocean, so they're still okay with me. I'm sure the captain doesn't want the passengers to know about it, if he even thinks it's true. Can't really blame him for that.

I'm guessing everyone on staff thinks that I didn't see anyone go overboard. Really, who'd want to believe that? The captain talked to me tonight—he actually did look me in the eyes. He assured me that his search of the waters last night was very thorough and nothing or no one was found. He must have repeated that five times.

He gave me a few ideas as to why I might have thought a person hit the water, such as dolphins or orcas playing around the ship, but I wasn't convinced. And he knew it. I told him that none of his explanations accounted for what I'd witnessed, which was something falling into the water from above my cabin. Then he suggested I might have had a nightmare, and I would certainly not be the first person to worry about accidentally falling overboard then have a bad dream of that sort. It felt like he was assuring my six-year-old self. He guaranteed me that tumbling overboard only has happened in very rare occurrences, and it had never happened on one of his ships. (Doesn't that make him due?) Then he told me again that the crew had thoroughly checked on everyone and he'd been assured that all had been accounted for. What could I say?

Shortly after he left, the nurse came to my cabin in order to evaluate me, though she claimed it was to learn if I was sleeping well, which I haven't been, ever since I found out. And because of what happened last night.

Mandy turns to me and asks, "Found out about what? Did Dee mention anything about that in any other place in her journal? Did we miss something?"

"No, I don't think so. Keep reading." I'm lying on my back on the bed, my hands under my head, staring up at the ceiling, hoping Dee has left us a good clue of some kind. We sure as hell need one.

I'm certain her visit was at the captain's directive, since he could see I wasn't convinced it was a nightmare. At first, I thought she bought it—or pretended to—when I told her it wasn't a nightmare. Then she implied it was probably a hallucination. I asked her if it was her experience that people often hallucinated on cruises. I was being sarcastic, but she took me seriously and said, "Only if they forget their meds." I assured her that I've never had a need for any anti-psychotic medication before and sincerely doubted that I needed it now. At which point, she went on to tell me about how years ago, sailors had hallucinated mermaids. I told her that I didn't think I was that desperate for love—that's what Kera would have said. It's funny how, periodically, I catch myself channeling my sister.

Mandy turns to me and snickers. "Dee's got that right. It is funny how you two throw out each other's lines, every so often. But mostly Dee does it. You should channel Dee a little more often. It'd sweeten you up." She winks.

"She quotes me more than I do her because my lines are better than hers."

Mandy rolls her eyes and reads on:

The nurse shook her head with my wry comment about not being desperate enough to imagine a mermaid, but it stopped her cold from going on with another hypothesis. I'm glad I borrowed Kera's sarcasm as it is often effective, where my own attempts to shut people down from what they're saying doesn't cut it. So, thank you my dear sister. (I probably won't tell Kera about this. She's got a big enough head as it is.)

"See. What did I tell you?" I give Mandy my self-satisfying glance.

Another eye-roll. Mandy begins reading again:

After the nurse left, I looked for Nona but couldn't find her anywhere. I asked Mick if he'd seen her. He told me she'd "abandoned ship again," in Petersburg for some dude who lived there. I know she was hanging out with a guy but had no idea she'd intended to do something like that or that she'd done it before. I would've thought she'd tell me that. I guess I've misjudged her. It's weird, though. I swear I saw her come back onboard just minutes before we left port. I know I didn't dream that...

Good god. Maybe I'm fooling myself. I'm beginning to wonder if I did hallucinate seeing someone go overboard or seeing Nona return to the ship... Maybe I do need anti-psychotic medication. Makes me feel crazy.

It's hard to hang on to what I think I know when I'm the only one who believes it.

What I do know, for sure, is that Nona was scared about what we've been involved in and she wants out. So do I. Bad. How horrible. I'm sick to death. But I don't know how we can get out of it—though maybe Nona did find her way out.

I pop up. Mandy and I lock gazes. "Jesus! "What in hell did my sister get herself into?"

CHAPTER TWENTY-EIGHT

Kera

To say my night's sleep was fitful would be to exaggerate how much rest I got—or Mandy, too, for that matter. We both bounced around in bed like two fresh-caught fish flopping in the bottom of a boat.

We stayed up late trying to figure out what Dee and Nona might have been involved in that was upsetting my sister. I have a friend who says that the less you know about something, the longer you talk about it. I agree. But I do believe that whatever it was they were caught up in, it had to be the reason for Nona's disappearance and the attempt on Dee's life—and of course, the subsequent attempts on my life.

Last night, Mandy and I agreed that I would go to the galley early in the morning to talk to Agnes. I figured she might know something. After all, she sleeps with the captain—boy, did Mandy's eyes pop when I told her that one. Maybe Agnes overheard something from him or, hopefully, she's picked up on conversations around the galley that might be helpful, at least to some degree. Of course, everything depends on her willingness to talk to me. But I know she was about to tell me something the other day when I spoke to her in the bathroom, and she suddenly stopped. I would sure like to know what she decided not to say.

I check the time. It's 5:02 a.m. I know Agnes starts preparing food in the kitchen around this time, if not earlier. I would guess Coleen and Lillian will be there, too, but none of the non-native members of the crew whose jobs are in the galley will be up at that time. Agnes has made that quite clear to me. It's fucking obvious that the cruise line takes advantage of the native workers. They slog hard and long hours since they're responsible for all the housekeeping chores as well as food prep and clean up. Though every one of the crew works hard, the natives put in more hours. And I don't see the native workers have any time off to enjoy the various fun stuff that other crew members get to do. I did ask Roni why that was. She told me they didn't seem to want to join in, that they like to stay to themselves. I have a real hard time with that explanation because I don't see how, with all the work they have on their plates, they'd have time—even if they wanted to participate in anything. It's more like the native workers are taken advantage of because they need jobs and don't have lots of other choices up here.

I head to the galley. I hope I can get Agnes to leave for a few minutes to talk to me. Since she runs the kitchen operation— though under Britt's supervision—she should be able to. If she's willing, that is.

I'm in luck. Agnes is over at the coffee urn in the dining room. I hustle over to get to her before she leaves.

"You're up early." She smiles.

"If you don't mind, I'd really like to ask you a few questions."

Agnes's expression changes to one that lets me know she'd really rather not. She quickly glances around. She presses her lips together, tight. Not a great sign, but at least she didn't run from me.

"I promise I won't keep you long," I say. "I know you have a lot to do."

"What?" she asks in a quiet voice.

"I found a journal I was keeping. You know, before my accident." At any second, someone could interrupt us, so I get right to the point. "There was something in it that I don't remember or even understand. I hope you can help me."

She scowls.

"I wrote that I was upset about something but didn't say what it was. Do you have any idea what it might have been?"

"Upset because people didn't believe you, like I say."

"No, it was something else, something before that."

She shrugs her shoulders.

"I wrote that Nona was upset about it too," I add, hoping to jar her memory, if that's even her problem.

Agnes's eyes bore into mine, like she's trying to figure me out but still doesn't say anything.

I push on. "It seems that I'd gotten into something that made me upset and scared, apparently neither Nona nor I understood it, or maybe we didn't at first but then later did. I don't know. That's why I want to ask you. I really need to know what it was."

"I can't help you." Agnes rubs the back of her hand across her sweaty forehead, wipes it on her apron, and looks toward the galley like she's ready to bolt in that direction.

"Does that mean you don't have any idea what it might be, or you don't want to talk about it?"

Watching Agnes's expression soften, I get the feeling she might be getting ready to tell me something. She starts to speak, then her eyes suddenly indicate that there's someone coming up behind me. I hear the footsteps closing in on us.

"You're up early, Deidre," Britt says as I turn around. "What on earth gets you going this time of day?"

"Honestly, I don't know what woke me up, but I couldn't go back to sleep. I thought I'd come out and see if there's any coffee brewing yet."

Agnes plugs in the urn she just filled and says, "About half hour coffee is ready." Then she leaves toward the galley.

Damn, damn, damn. I've just lost my opportunity, and this is my last full day before we dock in Ketchikan. Who knows if I'll get another chance to talk to Agnes?

"Hey," Britt puts her hand on my shoulder. "We have an early group going out this morning. Since you're up, would you mind helping me get the kayaks ready? Brian and Jared are lowering them down from the deck right now. All you need to do is guide the kayaks, nothing heavy. You should be able to easily do it with one arm."

"Sure." What else could I have said?

"Then you can come back here for your morning joe. Maybe I'll even join you." Britt winks, more flirtatious than merely friendly.

Well, well. She's getting bolder. Maybe she wants to come out as my girlfriend before the end of this cruise...

Jesus, that's all I would need right now.

* * *

By the time I finish on the platform and get back to the galley, Agnes is knee-deep into food prep. Coleen and Lillian, side-by-side, peel, chop onions, and toss them into a large bowl. This time, I don't have time to be super worried about Coleen and Lillian being around. I need to find out what Agnes was about to tell me before Britt showed up.

"All done," I say to Agnes as I enter the galley. "What's for breakfast?"

Agnes's gaze remains on what she's doing. She signals with her head for me to check the menu board outside the galley.

I walk over to it. "What's this?" I crane my head around and stick it through the open service area so I can talk to her.

"What's what?" she says, still avoiding me.

"I can't read it, or it's something I don't know." I'm hoping to give her an excuse to come over and help me out. It looks like it's some name for scrambled eggs, probably an Alaskan dish, maybe Inuit.

Agnes wipes her hands on her apron and walks over.

"That." I point to the word. I don't give a shit what kind of scrambled eggs they are but continue with my fake curiosity in case anyone is paying attention to us.

"Fluffy," she says, looking at me like... *What the hell? You think that's some kind of Inuit word?*

I ignore her sarcastic expression and jump right in. "What were you going to tell me, Agnes?"

Her lips are pinched, again, no words.

"Come on, Agnes. You were going to tell me something more before Britt showed up. I really need to know. Please. I won't tell anybody." I'd get down on my knees and beg. I feel that desperate.

"That's not the problem, you—" Agnes stops, looks over at Coleen and Lillian who, though they can't hear, are watching us.

"Look, you know you can trust me. When you tell me something, I keep it to myself." I can feel Agnes' penetrating gaze, like she's trying to find a reason to believe me. Damn it. She knows I didn't say anything about her coming out of the captain's quarters while she was adjusting her clothes. Agnes has reason to trust me, at least as far as I know.

"Hey, Deidre." Roni's heading toward me.

Not again. Shit, shit, shit.

"Did Britt give you the disembarking procedures?" Roni pats me on the back. "It gets pretty busy around here with passengers leaving. I jotted down some things that have to be done during that time and gave them to Britt to give to you."

"Thanks, I appreciate that, but no, she hasn't given them to me yet." What I want to say is *get lost.*

"Next time you see her, remind her. I saw her tuck them into her pocket." Roni turns to Agnes. "I've been meaning to show you where—" Roni steers Agnes toward the storeroom.

Agnes turns back to me. "I give you my recipe as soon as get break. I bring it to your room? Or—"

"Yeah, my room would be great. Thanks, Agnes."

Whew!

* * *

It's been fifteen minutes. I'm waiting for Agnes, worrying that she might not show up like she said she would. Mandy's getting things together and packing them in her bag, so she'll be ready for tomorrow morning's docking. I suppose I should be doing the same thing, but all I can do is pace.

"Sit down, Kera. You're making me nervous." Mandy zips her duffel bag.

"If Agnes doesn't show up, I'll have to go and look for her. If that's the case, it means she's probably changed her mind and decided not to talk to me. She'll be making herself scarce."

"The woman went to the bother of making up an excuse to meet you here," Mandy says in a calm voice. "That says to me she'll come."

"Yeah, well…" I check the time. "She should be here by now. Roni was just going to show her something in the storeroom. How long can that take?"

"Agnes was working on breakfast, right?"

I nod.

"Well, that may seem a bit more critical to her now, and it would be strange if she left the galley to talk to you when she has to do her preparations for breakfast. You know she can get in trouble easily with Roni."

"I know, I know. But we don't have much time."

"Have some patience. From what you've told me, I think she'll be here. At least allow her ten more minutes before you go looking."

"Humph." The best I think I can do is five minutes. After that, I'm out of here to hunt Agnes down. Mandy gives me her *look*. She knows the clock's ticking fast for me, and it won't be long before I take off out of this room. That's why she said ten minutes, because she was going for five. We know each other only too well.

Our heads turn toward the door in response to a soft rapping. Mandy nods as if to say, I told you she'd show up.

Indeed, it is Agnes standing at there, hands wringing. I take her arm and guide her in, more like pull her.

"I'm sorry it took me so long," Agnes says as she glances over at Mandy. She seems unsure if it's all right to talk with Mandy in the room.

"It's okay," I assure her. "You can say anything in front of Mandy."

She starts glancing around our small quarters like perhaps someone else could be hiding somewhere. She hasn't stopped with her hand-wringing. Her lips are pinched. A bad sign. I search for something to say to help loosen them when Mandy jumps in to help.

"Agnes, I'm Deidre's best friend. You don't have to worry. Whatever you say, I won't repeat to anyone." Mandy pats the bed for Agnes to sit down. "No matter what you say, you're safe with us," Mandy says in a soft sweet tone.

It's the same sensitive voice she used with Wally, but this time it's with an adult tone. I'm sure she uses it to her advantage in the courtroom, too, when she needs it. Besides that, Mandy's big innocent green eyes and girl-next-door looks could get just about anyone to spill their guts.

Agnes addresses Mandy, "I don't think Deidre will like what I have to say about her."

That's takes me aback.

"Whatever it is," Mandy says, "she wants to hear it, Agnes."

"But she might get mad at me and punish me."

Punish?

"No, she won't. Deidre wants to know what you have to say." Mandy glances my way, signaling for me to show that I agree with what she'd just said. Agnes's gaze moves to me as she waits for my response.

"I need to know, Agnes. I know whatever it is that you have to tell me is really hard for you. I respect that. I'll be grateful to you no matter what it is you have to say about me. I promise. I just really need to know."

Agnes looks back to Mandy like she's waiting for conformation that I'm telling the truth. I hold my breath as Mandy gives her a nod to go ahead.

What the fuck did Dee get herself into?

Agnes takes a deep breath and turns back to me. Her expression looks like she's about to be force fed slimy worms. "Deidre, you are part of the ship's jobs program."

"What jobs program?" I ask. That doesn't sound bad. I haven't heard of any such program, but I haven't been on the ship that long either. What the hell? What can be so unspeakable about a jobs program?

"The one that takes girls to get jobs." Agnes stops right there and looks as though she's sorry she came here and might flee at any second.

"Takes girls? What girls?" I ask as gently and softly as I can, trying to prevent her from bolting.

"Girls who want jobs." Terror fills Agnes's eyes and her face has turned white as a sheet. She glances at the door. "Don't think I say any more. I'm sorry." Her lips twist tight.

How do I keep this woman from bolting?

"Look, Agnes..." I say in the kindest voice I can come up with, trying hard to keep or, in this case, gain her trust.

Mandy puts her hand on her shoulder and gently says, "Take a deep breath, Agnes. You're looking really pale. You need to breathe deeply."

"From reading my diary," I say to Agnes, "I know that Nona and I were involved in something we wanted to get out of, something we thought was not good, like perhaps it was something we didn't know we were getting into at first. But we wanted out. I'm prepared for whatever it is that you tell me."

No, I'm not.

Furthermore, I'm feeling really confused about a jobs program that's not good, because a program that helps people get jobs sounds like a positive thing to me.

Agnes's gaze is fixed on her feet, but she mumbles to us. "You and Nona told native girls who need jobs that you could get them work."

"Work where?" I ask.

"On cruise lines, maybe other places too."

"You mean like you, Coleen and Lillian?"

This continues to sound like a positive thing, like something I'd like doing. It certainly sounds like something Dee would get involved in, given her social worker mindset, heart of gold, and always wanting to help people. True, they're worked too hard and—

"What are you not telling us, Agnes?" Mandy asks. "You know, the part that would upset Deidre. The bad part."

Agnes turns toward me but keeps her gaze on the floor as she hesitantly says, "These girls you find don't get real jobs." She takes a deep breath and blows it out. "They get treated bad, don't get money for their work, and don't get cruise line jobs." She finally looks up to Mandy, seeming to look for Mandy's reaction to what she's just said. Mandy kept her cool.

"What!" I blurt out. That was not cool and not helpful.

Agnes's head snaps back, startled, but with Mandy's gentle touch on her shoulder and kind smile, Agnes takes another deep breath and moves on. "They get taken to other place and can't ever leave and go back home." A tear rolls down Agnes's cheek.

"Holy shit!" Once again, that came out way too loud. Now it's my turn to take a deep breath or two, calm myself to make sure my voice comes out in a whisper. "D…uh, I've been involved in human trafficking? That's what you're saying?" I glance over to Mandy, her mouth hangs open, but her lips don't move. She's speechless—a condition I've never seen her suffer from before. She looks like someone told her the Pope has a wife and five kids.

"Did I know," I ask Agnes, "that I was sending these women— really girls—into this situation?"

Agnes shrugs. "I guess."

"How do you know I knew?" I can't believe, no I know, my sister wouldn't intentionally do such a thing. I'd bet my life on it.

"Dee wouldn't do that," Mandy says in my sister's defense.

Agnes shrugs again.

"Do you think I knew when I initially got into the so-called jobs program that these girls were actually treated that way?"

All Agnes can seem to do is shrug, shake her head, and look terrified. Her skin still hasn't turned back to its natural pecan shade.

"So, Coleen and Lillian are part of the so-called job's program?" I ask. "They've been taken into the slave trade, too? And they're forced to work on this ship and won't get paid?" I keep posing questions I now know the answers to, because I can't seem to take in what I'm being told. Jesus. There it was right smack in front of me and I didn't have a fucking clue. Well, I saw how hard they worked. Still, it didn't scream slave trade.

"They don't get paid. But they won't stay here. They leave the ship when we dock. Men wait in boats and take them right off the ship, way before passengers get off. They take them to other places and sell them. I don't know where they go. We get more girls when we go back to Juneau."

"Are all the women working in the kitchen being sold?"

"No, just Coleen and Lillian. Other kitchen helpers work on-ship all the time."

"You're telling me this ship picks up young women in Juneau, ones who want jobs, then takes them to Ketchikan and sells them off as slaves?"

"Uh-huh. They work on-ship till get to Ketchikan then are gone. They think they pay their way there by working on-ship." Agnes stops, takes a breath, looks each of us in the eyes and decides to continue. "When ship gets to Ketchikan, girls think they get to go to a place where are good jobs and can make good money and send some home to family."

"Jesus." It then occurs to me. "Agnes, you've been made a slave too, haven't you?"

"Yes, but I always stay on this boat."

"You're here to work and, well, do whatever the captain asks of you, right?" I didn't want to say, "be his sex slave," since that would embarrass Agnes. But we all knew what I meant.

She nods and drops her head.

"Jesus!"

"Why haven't you told the authorities?" Mandy asks in a gentle and non-accusing manner.

"I'm afraid."

Mandy scrunches up her face. "Of what?"

"They say my family will pay consequences." Agnes raises her head, tears and terror in her eyes. "They say they will kill them."

"Who is the 'they'?" I hold my breath. "Did my sis— Uh…Did I ever tell that to you?"

"No, you never say that to me. I'm with captain two years, way before you come to work here."

"When did Coleen and Lillian start here?"

"They got on when you come back from hospital."

"In Juneau, you mean?"

"Uh-huh. The captain says I need to teach the cleaning and kitchen work. That's what I do for all girls who are in program. They work on this ship until they get dropped off in Ketchikan. They think they learn so they can work other places, maybe on big ships, maybe in fancy hotels, until…well, until they find out the truth. I don't know where they go after they leave here. They think they get good jobs on big ships or other good places."

"When are the young women told about what's really going to happen to them?" I ask.

"I don't know when. Probably, like me, not until they're bought by someone and they have no say."

"So, Lillian and Coleen don't know, yet," Mandy says. "Right?"

"They know now. I had to tell them. Lillian got homesick and says she wants to go back to her family when she gets to Ketchikan. She has brother there, thinks he will take her back home. I got scared for her and her brother cause people in the program are mean bad people and will hurt her and her family, if she doesn't go with them. So, I have to tell her she can't go home and what will happen if she tries. This upsets her, really bad." Agnes starts sobbing now.

Mandy gives her some tissues and puts her arm around her. That calms her and she seems ready to talk.

"What about Coleen?" I ask.

"She didn't say she wants to go back home, but she was there when Lillian tells me that. Coleen gets all upset too."

"Oh, that had to be the night I stopped by and wanted to know about the screams I'd heard. And I saw Coleen and Lillian were upset, right?"

Agnes nods.

We all grow silent. Mandy looks like she's been hit by a stun gun. I can barely breathe. It's like all the oxygen has been sucked out of the room.

Jesus, what did Dee get herself into?

And where do we go from here?

* * *

After repeatedly reassuring Agnes that Mandy and I will not be letting anyone know what she told us, she returned to the galley. Mandy walked her back for support. We told her we'd try to help her and the other two young women. From the look on her face, I thought that telling her we'd help them frightened her more than assured her. I asked her why it scared her. She told me that trying to do something made her more nervous. Something bad would happen to all of them and their families, if word got out about what was going on, or if they ever got caught trying to escape.

She has obviously been living with only fear and little hope.

I swore to her that I'd see to it that nothing bad would happen to them. It was a promise I had no right offering, but she wanted, needed, to believe in it. So, she did...or at least she appeared to. I'm sure, though, that she'll have big-time second thoughts on that one. I sure as hell would.

The only thing I know for certain is that the captain is part of this operation. But I don't know whether this slavery ring is only his undertaking, and he's the big boss of it all, or if he's just a cog in the wheel of a much bigger operation. Either way, he's in it. Big time.

Now I need to figure out what to do.

Before Agnes left, I asked her who else knew what was going on? She said Nona was the one who recruited her to this ship, two years ago. It was just recently Dee joined in to help get the girls into the program. Other than the captain, she didn't know if anyone else was involved. As far as she knew, the rest of the crew bought the story that the jobs program was a good thing for the girls. In fact, she said, when the girls leave, the crew gives them a send-off and wishes them good luck on their new job location. It's a happy event.

* * *

The door opens and it's Mandy with coffee and food. Boy, do I need the caffeine and nurishment. Mandy and I have some work to do and not a lot of time. We dock tomorrow morning. Some ideas of what we might do next are floating around in my brain, but need a lot of details worked out.

How good they are, or how effective they'll be, is another thing.

CHAPTER TWENTY-NINE

Kera

Mandy and I drink our much-needed coffee. I tell her about the plan I've cobbled together while she was getting us coffee and breakfast rolls.

"In the early morning while it's still dark," I begin, "we'll leave the ship in Mick's boat with Agnes, Lillian, and Coleen."

Mandy wrinkles her brow. "You were about to sink in that leaky tub when you were out in it the other night searching for that woman. Why would you think all of us could get to shore in that sieve before it sank?"

"I checked with Roni about the ship's scheduled docking. I have it figured out, time and distance wise. We're due to dock in the morning around nine. If we grab the boat and take off around four or four-fifteen in the morning, the ship will have made it within range for us to make it to Ketchikan safely, and arrive there before the ship makes it in and gets a docking space. Even if we're spotted leaving, the skiff will be faster than the ship. Mick's motor has the power."

"They could send out one of their skiffs and chase us down."

"Not possible, Mandy," I assure her. "It would take them far too much time to get a skiff down from the top where they're stored for the night. Even if they tried, by that time we'll be long gone."

"Did you forget about Mick's prop being lost?"

"Mick had an extra one, and he's already replaced it," I say.

Mandy still looks skeptical. "Would we have enough fuel to get that far?"

"He has a large gas can, filled, already in the boat. I checked that out."

Mandy frowns. "Still, like I said, that boat leaks."

"That's true, but I think we can get in to dock before we take on too much water, and, I'll bring extra bailing cans."

"Think!"

"Well, I—"

Mandy's large green eyes widen even further. "You're counting on us to bail in order to make it?"

"I'm sure we can make it. The bailing cans are just an insurance policy," I say with as much authority as I can muster.

"But Kera, there'll be five of us in the boat, won't that one, slow us down, and two, with the extra weight allow in more water? You said the water was coming in faster as you sat there hoping to get rescued."

"I know where there's more epoxy putty I can use." I picture Mick's supply closets. There isn't that much of the putty left, but enough, I hope. What I say to Mandy is, "I'll plug it up where it leaks. When I was out in the ocean that night, I didn't have much to work with and it didn't have any time to dry by being out of the water. But now, I can patch it up, at least well enough for the trip to shore. I'll do it tonight on my break. It won't have time to be as solidly dry as I'd like, but for sure, better than in the ocean the other night."

Mandy holds her head in her hands. She's told me, and I've witnessed, that she does that when she thinks her head might explode. Mandy's one of those people who thinks of every possible eventuality. I appreciate that about her, and in many cases and in most situations, it's a good thing. But I can't possibly cover every angle or make every step a solid certainty. I'm trying to find a way out of this mess on a wing and a prayer. If I were to consider everything that could go wrong, I'd come to a dead stop. I need to figure out the most likely possible path that will get us all out of this shitty situation, if we're going to have a chance at a happy ever after.

"I wish," Mandy says, "we could get our hands on one of those reliable inflatable skiffs they have."

"Me too, but Mick's boat is the only one that's stationed on the platform, and it's the only one I can get to. There's no way I can lower another skiff in advance without help and being noticed. Mick's rig is our only hope."

"Why don't we wait until we dock and get the authorities to help us?"

"Remember Agnes said that a boat with the kidnappers is always at the dock waiting to whisk the girls off immediately. Essentially, these young women never even set foot on land. They'll be escorted to a waiting boat that takes them to wherever."

"I don't like not getting the law involved. It—"

"We don't have the time or cell reception to try and get ahold of them this far out, let alone convince the authorities what's going on here. All we can do is contact them after we get the women to a safe place. Otherwise, we risk getting them snatched out from under us and taken off to who-knows-where."

Mandy looks sick. "There must be another way."

"If there is, I don't know it, and I don't have the luxury of time to figure it out."

"You're right, honey," Mandy put her hand on my shoulder. "I just want to get them safely on land before the bad guys get to them. Can't you leave when we're closer to shore and have a better chance of making it?"

"Mandy, we have no idea who or what lies on the other end of the handoff. But I have no doubt these people are mean-assed dudes who will go to any lengths necessary to keep the *job's program* from public view and intact. They'll be waiting there. Any attempt to get the women off will be noticed if we do it in broad daylight before the boat even docks. We'd be spotted immediately and tracked down. Obviously, we won't be appreciated by invading their *program* and exposing their operation. Believe me, they'll do anything to eliminate our existence. They got a lot to lose."

"Yes, I know." Mandy nods with a sober expression. "People in this line of work play rough. I know."

"We don't know what Nona or Dee did, but they had to have crossed these people in some way, made some bad mistake, or they might have threatened to expose them, I don't know. Whichever it was, Nona ended up losing her life."

"And Dee came close to suffering the same fate," Mandy adds. "My god, where does this all end up?"

My stomach swirls and chops what's left of my last meal when Mandy reminds me of what could have happened to my sister. I swallow hard to keep from barfing. I can't imagine being on this earth without my sister. Thoughts swirl in my head and land on the picture of someone pushing her off the cliff. I'm not only sick to my stomach but downright pissed, angrier than I can ever remember ever being. And that's saying something. But I guess that's a good thing. Anger gives me energy and fuels my resolve—not that it needed much powering up. In fact, I need to calm my engines down a bit.

Stay cool. Stay cool. Breathe.

* * *

As my mind races, I pour drinks, open bottles, and try to carry on a conversation with my bar folks, like it was just any other night.

After Mandy and I talked about our plan to get the women off this ship before it docks tomorrow morning, I found Agnes and explained my strategy to her, step-by-step. To say the least, it terrified her—at first, anyway. She was less wary after I reassured her as best I could that I was certain it'd work.

Shit. Certainty is a lie, under any circumstance.

Finally, she agreed to talk to Coleen and Lillian and see if they would be willing to go along with the plan. Just before I came on my bar shift, Agnes let me know that they were apprehensive but were on board with it, mostly. They worried what would happen to them if caught trying to escape. Not only were they worried for themselves but also because their families would be in jeopardy as well. That's a heavy burden for the young women to carry. God damn, that's weighing on me, too. If I fail to pull this off, it's not only about Mandy and my safety—and ultimately Dee's too. A lot of people are going down with me.

"Oops," I say to Bev. I've overloaded her glass.

"You're way too good to me tonight, Deidre." Bev laughs and grabs the glass before she thinks that I might try to rectify the overfill. "I'll need to have someone carry me out of here if you keep this up."

Charlie, sitting beside her, rolls her eyes and snickers. "So, what would be new about that?"

Bev grabs my cane that I'd left hanging on the edge of the bar and holds it over Charlie's head. I'm sure Bev would really like to bash that stick on Charlie's skull, but she's acting playful about it—at least for now.

Charlie holds up her arms in defense and mocks fear. "Don't. Don't. I'll be good. I promise. I promise."

Bev starts in on Charlie. "That'll be the day."

My attention leaves the couple's relationship antics. In my mind, I'm plotting my next move, like how I need to sneak out on my break and do my best to fix the leak situation on Mick's boat. And hope no one is around to question me why I'm fiddling with his boat on my break. Earlier, I grabbed some epoxy putty from Mick's storage unit and have it in my pocket. When I was out in the ocean, the epoxy didn't have time to dry, so it didn't hold well. It slowed the water seeping in a tad but that didn't last very long. The sooner I can get out to the platform and put the putty on, the longer it'll have to cure. At this point, I suppose a few minutes here or there won't mean much. The problem is, I need at least seventy-two hours for it to get hard enough for any real durability. I've got about eight hours, max.

I know nothing about Ketchikan. Never have been there, haven't even sent a card or letter to my sister's address. I've always called or texted her. I realize now how stupid—more like negligent—it is that I don't even know where she lives. I am aware that it's a boarding house or something like that. When we get to Ketchikan, where am I going to stash Agnes, Coleen, and Lillian if I don't know Dee's address? Then I remember that Mandy will no doubt have it, probably in her phone. Damn. What am I thinking? I can't take the women to Dee's pad. Her address is no doubt available to the captain and maybe some of the crew. I need another place.

As though lady luck heard my concern, a customer walks up to order a drink. I notice she has a brochure of Ketchikan in her hand.

"Hey, does that have a street map in it?" I ask.

"Yes, it does." The woman flips open the map and lets me look at it.

I want one for myself. I step out from behind the bar and get that same brochure. Sure enough, it seems quite detailed, not only does it have the streets of the town but icons of places such as restaurants, stores, and places of interest. That's a start. Unfortunately, it doesn't include an icon for a place to stash people or help me know where Dee lives.

Roni strolls up to the bar as I return. "Hey, how's it going?"

"Doing okay. Want a drink?"

"No can drink. I'm heading for duty."

"All night?" I ask.

"Until seven a.m."

Hmm. It will be Roni I'll have to hide from when I take off in the skiff with the women. I wonder how I could distract her from—

"It would definitely be frowned upon by the company," Roni says. "Not just that, it's hard enough for me to stay awake as it is but to have alcohol would seriously jeopardize my ability to keep my peepers open."

"I know what you mean." I pour her a Coke. "Here, this will help keep you awake. I've never been a night person myself." That's not really true for me. It's the mornings that gets to me, but it's important to keep her on this subject of having to stay awake on the night shift.

"Thanks. You remembered my soda preference." She takes the Coke. "Yeah, about four thirty, I'm fighting sleepiness, big time."

"What do you do to combat that?" I ask.

"I'll drink another Coke along with caffeine pills," she says and sits down and puts her soda on the bar. "Helps, for sure, but makes me a bit jumpy. It's still better than falling asleep at the wheel." She laughs.

"That's for sure. I'm glad I started you off on your road to a caffeine high."

She picks up her drink, chugs it, then slams the glass on the bar and says in John Wayne style, "Pour me another one."

I play along. "Sure enough, partner."

"I notice you're checking out Ketchikan."

"Uh-huh." I set the glass of Coke down in front of her.

"Hey, I don't want to pry...uh...or embarrass you in any way, but do you know where you live there? I mean—"

"Actually, no." That makes me wonder how Dee and Moran will find the place when they get to Ketchikan, if Dee doesn't recall. Then it occurs to me that the captain undoubtedly gave the hospital that information when he tried to visit Dee. They'll be able to get the address, if necessary.

"I can access that info for you if you want. Your address will be in the computer somewhere."

"I don't think that will be necessary. My friend Mandy told me she has it. I wanted this map so I'd have an idea when we dock where things are." I smile. "You know, where and when to turn left or right."

"Got ya." Roni takes a sip from her glass. "I'd tell you which direction to turn to get to your place, but I've never been there. When the crew gets together after we return, which we often do, it's always at a bar, not at anyone's place."

Captain James ambles up behind Roni and taps her on the shoulder. "You're on." He signals to me with a hand gesture by tipping a phantom glass to his lips. I pour him a whiskey and water. "Craig's up there keeping us on course. I hope," he says to Roni. He snickers as he looks around to see if anyone heard him.

"Yeah, he's good for a short break," Roni says. "He's learning. I think he's coming along, actually, for as long as he's been at it."

"When he can do more than one thing at a time, he'll be a big help." The captain slugs down the rest of his drink and indicates he'll have another one. "Hell, at this point, all he has to do is follow the coastline around and in."

"I remember when I was first learning," Roni says, "that's how I was, too—glued to one thing and not able to attend to much else."

Captain James chuckles. "I remember that too. But that period in my career was a long time ago for me." He pulled on his beard. "Too many years ago."

"Well, it's time for me to get up there," Roni says. "Will Craig be able to spell me tonight?"

"Yup," he says. "Craig will get a couple of hours rest after you take over, but he'll be on call for you tonight for your break. Or cat nap, I should say." He smiles. "I don't know how she does it. She can take a fifteen-minute snooze, a few swigs of Coke, and gets refreshed." He turns to Roni. "I'll relieve you around seven. I need to get going myself, see if I can catch my forty winks."

As Roni sets off for the helm, the captain turns to me and says in a low voice, "Which frankly, I've not been getting much of lately. I suppose it wouldn't be cool for the passengers to know that their captain suffers from sleeping issues and may not be as alert as he should be." He gulps the last of his second whiskey, places his glass on the bar, and shuffles off to bed.

I wonder how he can sleep at all being involved in the slave trade.

Fucker!

* * *

The lounge thins out to a few stragglers, but they're on the verge of leaving. I'm left with just Bev and Charlie at the bar. Everyone seems to have turned in earlier than usual, probably to pack their suitcases to get ready to disembark tomorrow morning. I'm anxious to get out of here and return to my cabin to finalize my plans for tomorrow. No doubt Mandy is a nervous wreck about it all. But I can't shut the bar down as long as a passenger wants to drink—a point they stressed, unless it gets to be an unreasonable hour. Since this is the last night I'll have to work here, I really don't give a shit about rules and would be more than willing to send them away. But I also don't need to be drawing any attention to myself by not following the rules. Unfortunately, I can't claim that ten o'clock is unreasonable. But maybe I can nudge them along.

I move over to where Bev and Charlie are perched on their bar stools, not talking, both staring into their drinks. "Do you two have much to do to get ready?"

They glance up at me, not seeming to understand what I'm getting at.

"You know," I explain, "to get ready for going ashore tomorrow."

Charlie looks to Bev like she had no idea the trip will be ending when we docked in the morning then seems to remember. "Hmm. I guess I have lots to do, especially since I haven't been too neat, and my stuff is scattered all over."

"That's for damned sure," Bev says as disgust flashes across her face, intense enough that I know it's not just a problem between them during this trip.

Charlie ignores her.

Bev isn't done. "Your stuff has a way of spreading everywhere and migrating out of your living space to other living spaces, doesn't it, my dear?" The sarcasm drools out of both sides of Bev's mouth. Oh shit! This isn't the direction I meant for this to go. All I need now is for them to have a full-out bar fight tonight.

"Hey," I spread my hands out to separate the combatants, like a referee in a boxing match. "How about I send you off to your cabin with a fresh drink on the house. You know, so you can get ready for your morning departure."

I realize I'm sending a brewing fight to their cabin—especially giving them another drink in hand—but if it happens, it happens, and it would be someone else's problem. I'll be out of here.

* * *

"Agnes just left," Mandy says as I enter our cabin.

Mandy sits on our bed as she folds and rearranges clothes in her bag. Like everything is normal. Even though she's not going to be able to take her things with us in the skiff—who knows if she'll ever see them again. I don't think I've mentioned that to her yet.

The calm scene feels like a mind-fuck to me.

"What'd Agnes want?" I sit down next to her and kick off my shoes.

"Agnes said she didn't think it was a good thing if she left in the early morning with the girls. She's afraid that her moving around might make the captain suspicious, since it would be earlier than she usually gets up. Apparently, he's a light sleeper."

"He did mention something about not being able to sleep well, but I thought that was about the time she got going in the morning. Frankly, it wouldn't surprise me if she's scared, or maybe she thinks if she stays, it gives the other girls a better shot."

"Uh huh." Mandy says. "She's a little older than they are and takes on a motherly role with them. Also, her being around here would raise less suspicion."

"I think it can still work out okay for her." Mandy picks up her water bottle, takes a swig, and sets it back on the floor.

"How so?" I haven't had time to mull this new development over.

"If all goes according to plan, when we get on land we'll be able to move the young women to safety and contact the authorities. Agnes, even if she remains on the boat, will eventually be set free. If for some reason we aren't successful—"

"This will be successful." I stop Mandy in her tracks before any more negativity fills her head. In my mind, it's never good to start something and think it's not going to work out. I'm not a fool, I try always to have a contingent strategy—at least when there is one.

"All right." Mandy gives in to my need for a positive outlook. "But in order to be successful, it seems to me we need to be able to sneak off the ship and out of sight, undetected. How do you think—"

"First off," I interrupt, "it will be at a time that most people will be sleeping, crew and passengers alike."

"But whoever's at the helm will most likely spot our boat with the ship's lights or, if not hear the noise from the outboard motor."

"Uh, I've altered my originally plan a bit."

"Oh?"

"Well, it would all work out better if you didn't come with us in the boat, either."

"What!" Mandy's eyes grew large and her voice rose. "You're leaving me here? I know I said five in that tub was dangerous, but now it would be four and I don't want to be left on this ship without—"

"Hear me out," I say, gesturing for her to lower her voice. "I've thought this through, and it will be better." I understand why she's shocked by my new idea, and I don't like leaving Mandy here. But I think she'll be out of harm's way staying aboard. Also, it will make us all safer by her playing a key role in our takeoff. Our skiff will more likely escape, unnoticed.

"Okay," she says reluctantly, and picks back up the thread of our conversation. "Why do you think I should stay onboard?"

"Like I said, Roni will be captaining the ship tonight. In order to pull this off, I need to know when exactly Craig relieves her. Roni told me the other day at lunch that she gets relief only once a night, around four o'clock. She mentioned that time again this evening. That will work out perfectly, since that'll put this ship close enough to shore for me to take off and make it in Mick's skiff to Ketchikan."

"You mean before the leaky boat fills with water and sinks into the ocean." Mandy takes a deep breath and rolls her eyes...for the umpteenth time.

"I'll have bailers with me. We won't sink so I'll have extra time to get to the dock."

"Still, Craig will be on duty."

"Yes, but from what I've heard about him, he's not a great multi-tasker." I grab Mandy's water and drain the bottle.

"What's that got to do with anything?"

"That's where I hope you'll be able to help me."

Mandy raises her eyebrows. "Doing exactly what?"

"If you stayed behind on the ship, you could clue me in, so I'll know for certain that he's at the wheel at his designated time. Then you'd create a distraction. My plan is that you would go up to the bridge around—"

"You mean, run on deck bare naked in the middle of the night?" Mandy says with a sarcastic grimace.

"It might work. It'd sure work for me, but we can't count on Craig being heterosexual." I snicker but notice that she looks a bit put out that I might think her body wouldn't disrupt the concentration of even a gay guy.

"Well, sweetie," Mandy says in mock annoyance, "what do you have in mind for an effective distraction?"

"We'll have to work out all the details, but what I had in mind was for you to keep watch so you'll know when Craig relieves Roni. That's when you show up and distract him. I'll have Coleen and Lillian in the skiff. We'll paddle it up close and tuck it in near the ship, just short of and in line with the ship's bridge on the port side. Without using the motor and the three of us paddling, we should easily be able to reach that side of the ship without being seen or heard. When you execute the distraction, you'll flash the light from your cell phone down from the deck, three times, like in code. That will be my cue to start the motor and take off."

Mandy looks like she's contemplating what I'd described, then says, "So, the idea is that I'll need to distract both his eyes and ears."

"Right. It's to our advantage that he's a newbie and is currently doing an on-the-job training kind of thing. Hopefully, you'll sidetrack him long enough for us to get out of sight and earshot."

"But won't that put the ship in jeopardy?"

"What do you mean?"

"If whoever is piloting the ship takes their attention off where the ship is headed, it might make for—"

"Don't worry, honey. This ship is not traveling that fast, and there's not much in its path to run into. It's not like driving I-94 into Detroit. Besides, it can be set on autopilot."

Mandy takes a deep breath and rubs her hand across her forehead. She exhales and utters, "Good god."

"Now we need to think of a distraction. Something that pulls his attention away long enough for us to get out of there."

"Let me think." Mandy seems to have set her fear aside and is on board with my plan or is at least resigned.

"Like you said," I tell her, "it's going to have to be an event that distracts visually as well as cover the sound of the motor—or a big enough diversion that the motor's sound is ignored.

"Hmm. What if I claim I couldn't sleep?" Mandy says. "That way, I decide to check out the helm, since passengers have been invited to do that. Then, as I have Craig explain things to me, I suddenly act as though I have severe pain, like maybe a heart attack. Having a passenger in the midst of a heart attack would definitely pull his attention away from gazing out at sea or thinking about the sound of a skiff's motor."

"Good idea, that would probably sidetrack him from seeing me leave, as well as hearing my outboard motor—especially if you moaned or carried on a bit." Then as I watch that scenario play out in my head, I see the flaw. "But the problem in that set-up, honey, is that all the attention would be on you. How would you be able to signal me?"

"Oops." Mandy put her hand over her mouth. "That was dumb."

"No, no, don't think that way. We're brainstorming. We need to let ideas bubble up so we can check them out—without worrying that we're coming up with something stupid. I've already tossed aside a few ideas of mine before they made it out of my mouth."

We sit on the bed side by side, thinking. Each of us shoot down ideas that pop up in our heads as well as the ones we verbalize. So far, nothing. The fact that Mandy can't be the center of the distraction has put a damper on a workable plan.

Mandy finally breaks our silence. "Okay, let's go back to my plan, I go up to the bridge under the pretense that I'm not able to sleep and want to check out the helm. But I add a noisemaker this time, and it's not me."

She's piqued my interest.

Mandy continues. "I'll stop by the maintenance closet and get a metal bucket. I've seen them in there when the door's been open. I'll take one up with me when I'm sure no one's around. When I reach the top of the stairs, I'll peek around to make sure Craig isn't looking my way, then I'll kick it down the steel steps. Metal pail on steel steps should be noisy enough. Craig will undoubtedly be alarmed and will check out the noise. That's when I'll slip over to the side of the deck and signal you. Of course, that doesn't guarantee you a lot of time to get away unnoticed."

"It has the sound blocking factor and would get Craig out of the wheelhouse for a few minutes, depending how long it takes him to realize it's only a falling bucket. But I don't know the timing on that would be tight, as you indicated. Hmm…"

"If only we had someone to help us," Mandy says. "Obviously we can't use Lillian and Coleen. They need to be in the boat. And Agnes can't leave her cabin before—"

"Wait, wait, we do have someone. Before I ask this person to help, I need some materials to put my project together."

"You're going to ask who? And what project?"

My mind is racing. "I'll need Ping-Pong balls. Cheryl? Isn't that her name? The social director?"

"Yes."

"She has them in a bag in her closet." I decide to skip over the *who* and hope Mandy gets so involved in what I'm asking her to get that she forgets to ask…at least for now.

"Ping-Pong balls? Really?" Mandy scrunches up her nose and looks at me like I've lost my mind.

"Yeah, and I'll also need a glue gun and a pair of scissors." I hand Mandy a piece of paper and a pen. "Would you start a list so we don't forget anything? I know Cheryl has all this stuff. I saw it when she had her arts and crafts projects out. Do you remember the weird salt and peppers shakers she showed me that she made from Ping-Pong balls? Can you imagine coming on a trip like this and doing arts and crafts? But whatever."

"Well," Mandy interjects, "it went over pretty well for some folks when there was an engine problem. Still, I don't get what you're doing."

"Oh, I'll also need some sparklers. I saw some under the bar by the beer mugs. I'm not sure why they're there, but probably left over from Fourth of July doings. That should do it." Mandy is shaking her head and looks skeptical. She probably really thinks I've lost it.

"Okay," she says, "but can't you just give me a hint as what you're going to do with all that stuff?"

"Don't worry. You'll see soon enough. The clock's ticking. I really need you to go out and find these things and bring them back here, ASAP."

While I go recruit a partner in crime.

Mandy puts the list in her pocket as she walks to the door. She turns and says, "You could at least tell me what you're going to do with all this stuff I'm getting"

"Build a bomb."

Mandy gives me a look as if to say, "Sure, Kera. Do you really think I'm buying that one?" But she leaves anyway.

CHAPTER THIRTY

Mandy

Mandy slipped out into the hall and pulled the door shut quietly, careful to not make a sound. She didn't want to wake anyone and bring attention to her wandering the hall at that hour. Worse yet, what would she say if someone asked about what she held tightly to her chest?

She was about ten minutes ahead of the time frame in which Roni took her usual night shift break from the helm and when Craig was supposed to take over. She wanted to get to her hiding place as soon as possible.

The thunderous storm that had started about an hour ago caused the ship to sway and groan. Luckily, it covered any sounds from her footsteps, although she was still careful to be quiet. As she slipped into the cabin's corridor, the ship's lights flickered. It was eerily absent of human noises. Only sounds of the grinding and creaking of the ship's joints could be heard with an occasional clap of thunder. The piercing snaps of lightning startled her. She felt like she was on a ghost ship from scary movies she'd seen as a kid.

Her back prickled, making her shiver.

Rolling thunder sounded overhead. The ship rocked, tossing her against the corridor wall. Besides having difficultly navigating the hallway in these conditions, she wondered how anyone could sleep with the ship pitching side to side. Yet, no one emerged from their quarters.

A door creaked open…then shut.

She almost dropped the device that would cause the planned distraction.

The dim light in the corridor flickered and died.

Total darkness except for an occasional flash of lightning. The rocking ship tossed her to the side and smacked her up against the wall again. She reached out with her free hand to stabilize and help her move along. She needed to get to the stairs, conceal the homemade smoke bomb under the stairwell, then get back to the supply closet where she'd hide until Roni's replacement took over on the bridge. That's when she'd go up to the helm and distract Craig with lots of questions.

Smoke billowing up to the helm was to be the distraction. Smoke screams emergency, as Kera put it, something he'd have to attend to immediately. While Craig tried to find out what was wrong, Mandy would go to the side of the ship and signal Kera that it was safe to take off for Ketchikan.

Mandy was flabbergasted at Kera's ingenuity and further impressed that Kera possessed the knowledge to build a smoke bomb. And out of Ping-Pong balls, of all things, along with the grocery list of stuff Kera had sent her to search for. She was always surprised and often troubled by the tricks Kera had up her sleeve. She sighed then focused back on the plan. Kera would ignite the Ping-Pong bomb Mandy was about to hide under the stairwell, then she would need to make a mad dash to her waiting skiff with Coleen and Lillian already situated. The device would take a while for the smoke to float up to the bridge and alarm Craig, which Kera was counting on in order for her to have time, barely, to get to the skiff.

Now that she thought about it, what if the smoke drifted somewhere else instead of up the stairwell? The openness of the area and any possible cross breezes might cause problems. What if someone lingered in the area and Kera couldn't set it off in the allotted time? Or after she set it off, she got caught and that'd be the end of them all? These possible plan-busting scenarios kept rearing their ugly heads and seriously undermining her confidence—not that she had much to begin with.

Good god.

Last night, she and Kera were both so exhausted and desperate to get a few hours of sleep that they didn't deal with these details or possible unplanned outcomes. Since Kera didn't bring them up, she probably hadn't thought of them either.

And now the storm. How would the skiff survive that? More importantly, how would Kera and the women survive?

Another worrisome and possible snag in the plan came to her, besides potential problems setting the smoke bomb off. How would Kera have enough time if there were any issues in getting the women ready and into the skiff? Didn't Kera have too much to do before taking off? That pricked her memory. Kera said something about someone helping? Mandy never got back to her about that.

Who?

Most likely Kera didn't even say that, Mandy decided. Surely, she'd imagined it. Fatigue and fear do funny things to the brain. Like wishful thinking. God knows there was no one on board that would help them. Mandy took a deep breath. She'd have to let it all go. There was nothing she could do about anything now. Worrying about stuff would end up immobilizing her. The only thing she could do was hope all would go well. Plant the bomb under the stairwell, get into the closet, and wait for Roni to take her break, then head up to the helm and engage Craig until Kera lit the bomb and the smoke did its part.

Her positive self-talk wasn't helping her mounting anxiety, more like fear and panic were setting in. Her legs shook.

What else didn't they think of?

A hand touched her shoulder from behind. Large…a man's hand.

Her heart jumped up into her throat.

The hand moved over her mouth, and an arm pulled her in. "Don't scream," a voice whispered in her ear. "It's okay."

She was able to pull the hand away from her mouth enough to ask, "Who are you?"

"It's just me, Wally," he said softly. "I'm here to help you." He lifted his hand completely away. "I didn't mean to scare you, but

I couldn't call out to you and risk that someone would hear me."

"What do you mean you're here to help?" Mandy couldn't comprehend why Wally would be here and that he'd be someone to help her.

Surely this isn't who Kera had in mind...

"Deidre came to me last night and asked me to set off the smoke bomb after you go up to the bridge."

"What?" Mandy didn't know what to think. Kera never mentioned anything about involving Wally in their plan. And why would she do that after what he'd pulled on them? What was Wally up to? Yet, it was clear that he knew what they were up to.

"I know she said that she wouldn't get a chance to tell you, and I'm sorry I scared you like that, but—"

"Why would Deidre ever trust you with anything, Wally? Especially after the stunt you pulled." Mandy's anger and anxiety caused her voice to raise.

"Shhh." Wally smacked his hand back over her mouth. "Deidre told me what's been happening on this ship. I think it's horrible. Besides, I owe her a favor after what I did. So, anyway, here I am."

Mandy pulled Wally's hand away from her mouth. "Really, she asked you to set off the smoke bomb?"

A flash of lightning lit up Wally's face. He was beaming. "Yup, I get to light the smoke bomb and make sure it floats up the stairwell." Wally showed her a towel. "See this? I can fan the smoke to the bridge if I need to."

My God! Now we're counting on Wally! No wonder Kera didn't tell me.

"Deidre said you were going to hide out in the maintenance closet until it's time to go up there. I thought I would wait there with you."

I'll get you for this Kera.

"Well, okay, I guess." What else could she say? She cringed as she thought of all the ways this could go wrong.

CHAPTER THIRTY-ONE

Mandy

Craig was busy giving her explanations for just about everything on the bridge, but Mandy wasn't absorbing much. Any other time, she would have been interested and grateful for the care he was taking to show her the workings of the ship. But she was too stressed with worrying that things wouldn't go as planned to pay attention. What would she do if any part of their scheme didn't work? How could she plan for that? Mandy didn't like surprises. In court, she prepared as best she could so that nothing would come up that she wasn't ready for, at least nothing big. But here and now...

"And this is the..." Craig continued, not seeming to notice Mandy's inability to focus on what he was showing her.

When she'd approached Craig, he was rather excited that she wanted him to show her around and to explain the workings. Apparently, the ship's guests mostly requested the tour of the bridge from the captain or Roni.

Craig droned on as he pointed to something she couldn't see very well from where she stood. Didn't much matter, she couldn't concentrate on what he was showing her anyway. Whenever she thought he wouldn't notice, she glanced over at the stairwell. She waited for the smoke to make its way up and become visible. Then she would signal Kera in the skiff below. Once Wally ignited the smoke bomb, it shouldn't take long to see the smoke—the stairs weren't far from the helm, and Wally was there with his towel to fan it up.

Craig began explaining the controls, still oblivious to her lack of attention.

She'd been up at the helm with Craig for a while, but it was difficult for her to determine how long. It could have been only minutes, but it felt like hours. When she was a child, her Aunt Margaret used to tell her how long something would be by using a "felt-like" yardstick of time. Aunt Margaret described what an hour at the water amusement park "felt like" versus how long an hour "felt like" while Mandy rode in the car to get to that amusement park. This definitely "felt like" the hour it took to get to the water park, maybe longer.

Come on, Wally. Fan that smoke up here.

Craig tapped her on the shoulder and pointed. She glanced where he pointed but was too distracted.

Did Kera tell Wally that the smoke bomb needed to be set off well before Roni finished her break? Was Wally even still down there? Did he get scared and run off?

Good God, what's Wally waiting for?

"This is where I control the…"

"Interesting." She hoped she sounded engrossed when Craig turned to her.

"Do you want to steer the ship?" Craig asked.

"Yeah, sure." Anything to keep Craig engaged in his efforts to entertain her. She put her hands on the wheel. The feel of the wood reminded her of when she was a kid. She had a sandbox that had a ship's wheel, much smaller of course, but the wood felt smooth like this one. She and the neighbor boy liked pretending they were sailing in the ocean and fighting off pirates. She was in the ocean, alright, but fighting off panic.

"You really don't need to do much but keep her steady." Craig instructed. "She doesn't tend to make any fast moves." He chuckled.

He stood behind her, explaining something. Out of the corner of her eye, she watched for smoke. Still nothing.

"Wally!" the captain's voice boomed out. "What's going on, here? What in the hell are you doing with that towel? Jesus Christ, there's smoke!"

That's when she noticed it. The smoke had started trickling up the staircase.

Wally shrieked. "I'm, I'm, I'm…well, I'm trying to put out the fire, captain. See here, captain, we got a fire on the ship. It's coming from under the stairs. I'm just trying to—"

"What the hell?" The captain's voice rung out.

"I'm trying to put out the fire," Wally repeated. "I'm using my towel to smother the flames."

Pretty good improvising, Wally. That is, until you mentioned the nonexistent flames. Mandy rolled her eyes.

"What flames? Where?" The captain coughed. "I just see smoke. That's strange. Where's the…What the hell?" The captain's voice was muffled, like he was holding something over his mouth and nose.

Craig's jaw dropped at the sight of the billowing smoke. He set some controls and ran over to the stairs, looked down, but recoiled when the smoke reached his face. He rubbed his eyes and began coughing. Then he ripped off his shirt, covered his face, and ran through the smoke to the stairs. Mandy followed him until he headed down the staircase. That's when she diverted and ran, coughing, to the side of the ship.

She peered over the rail and saw the women and Kera in the skiff and gave them the signal to take off. Away from the smoke, she was able to clear her lungs. As she watched Kera motor her craft out of there, it gave her a sinking feeling. Now she was left on this ship, basically alone. But even worse, Kera was out in the ocean in an old metal boat that was less than fit for the task of getting them to Ketchikan.

CHAPTER THIRTY-TWO

Kera

In these damned choppy conditions, thanks to the storm, the ocean is sloshing water into the boat with one surge after another. Mick's old skiff is clearly on its last legs and does all it can not to give up and sink. All along, I haven't been overly confident that my patches would stick in calm seas, let alone in this storm. Who knows if the putty on the rivets is holding at all? It's hard to tell with all the water in the hull, which is a big clue that I'm trying not to think about. But it's nothing I can fix at this point.

With every swoop of wind, we're lifted high on the wave, followed by a hard slap down when we hit the ocean's surface. I feel like we're on a dilapidated daredevil ride at an aging amusement park—but there's definitely no fun being had by anyone.

I'm not sure if Coleen and Lillian have forgotten their bailing task or whether they're too scared and worried they'll be tossed over. They aren't following my instructions.

"Bail, bail, bail!" I yell, but I'm mostly drowned out by the tumultuous storm. "Or we won't be riding the waves for long."

I'm smacked in the face by a sheet of water. I try to wipe it away, but my jacket sleeve is already soaked.

Jesus. What a fucking night to have to make our escape.

I told Coleen and Lillian—even demonstrated—how to hold on with one hand and bail with the other. Still, Lillian clutches to her seat, water up to her ankles. Only occasionally does she dip the can to scoop. It leaves me with no choice but to scream, over and over, to keep bailing. Coleen makes more of an effort, but inevitably, her attention leaves our threatening water situation and turns to Lillian to comfort her. All the while, Lillian holds onto her seat with one hand and wraps the other around her stomach, like her guts might spill out. And now... Jesus, she's crying. So, in effect, I don't really have a bailer. There goes my backup plan for us to stay afloat—not that it was much of a plan given these weather conditions and my obviously failing rivets.

"Lillian wants to go back!" Coleen yells out to me.

"What?" I yell back at her. God damn it, I heard what she said. I just can't believe she said it. I realize Lillian is scared. We're all scared, but—

Coleen cups her hand around her mouth and yells back at me. "She's afraid that her family will be murdered because she ran away from the ship!"

I understand Lillian's concern. I do. I sympathize. But we talked about this before they boarded the skiff. We went over it several times and they agreed to this plan. Granted, Lillian had been more difficult to convince, but I assured them that I would immediately go to the authorities once we got on land. The slave traders would be arrested, and she and her family would be okay.

"We can't go back, Lillian," I shout back. I shake my head. I can't believe Lillian thinks that, at this point, we can turn around and go back to the ship without being seen.

There's only going forward, whatever that brings.

Lillian screams so loud it pierces through the storm.

"Lillian, damn it," I yell. "You need to realize that we can't return. There's no going back at this point. If we're going to have a chance at making it, you need to stop your damn screaming and help Coleen bail."

The lights of the ship are behind us, but so far there aren't any search lights casting out from it, like when they're concerned something might be in their path or they're specifically searching for something. Hopefully, they're busy dealing with the smoke bomb. I won't use my flashlight, although I wish I could occasionally check to see where I'm going. My plan is to keep the land on my left, stick as close to the shore as I can, and follow it around until we get to Ketchikan.

The ship has dropped out of view. We must have curved around the shoreline enough to be out of sight of it. I quickly flash my light and see that we're still snug to the shoreline, though I've been able to vaguely make it out all along. I also want to check out any rocks in our path, for sure they've got some big ones around here. I only spot them when I'm almost on top of them and have to make a fast maneuver to get out of their way. I determine that we're not in danger, at least at this moment, so I snap off my light to avoid being seen.

Due to the cloud cover of the storm, I get better glimpses of the shoreline when there's a flash from the lightning—so far, so good. Hugging the land keeps me on track and not going too fast allows me to watch out for and avoid any boulders and other obstacles that might be in our path.

Coleen has returned to bailing. Lillian is bent over, face in her lap, holding onto her seat with both hands. I guess that's all I can hope for, to have Lillian keeping quiet and Coleen bailing. It's barely enough to keep us on the water, not under it. Though the skiff bounces around, Coleen only occasionally grabs the side to hold on. She seems pretty sure of herself now and not terribly affected by the conditions. I can't help but believe that she must come from a family of fisherman by the way she's handling herself under these circumstances.

Oh shit. Lillian is barfing now. Her upchuck is slopping around in the water. Some of it heads toward Coleen. She scoops most of it out with her bailer and goes on with her task. Damn it, part of it is comes my way. I lift my feet until the boat spills it back toward the women. Coleen takes care of the rest of it.

As hard as she tries, Coleen can't keep up with the incoming water, so I ask her to toss me Lillian's can. The amount of ocean we have in the skiff is not just from the ocean's spray, it's from the rain as well. Although I can't see the spots that were leaking before, I know that my makeshift patching must be blown through, big time.

I have second thoughts about the decision for Mandy to stay on the ship. So many things could go wrong there. Of course, so many things can and are going wrong out here in this storm, too. But how many options did I have in this situation? If I had a lot of choices, I wouldn't have asked or counted on Wally to help me. I intentionally didn't tell Mandy about Wally. I figured she'd think it was crazy to trust him to help us. Telling her would have made her even more leery of what we were trying to pull off. As I tried to work it out in my mind, I didn't know how I could possibly do it all, timewise, and not be seen. I figured Wally was a guy who might want to redeem himself in the eyes of his "girlfriend" Deidre.

Jesus, I hope I called that right.

I don't know how long we've been bouncing around out in this storm. It seems days, but it must be about twenty or thirty minutes. I'm too busy bailing and steering this old thing to get out my phone to check the time. I keep getting glimpses of the shoreline with the lightning strikes, so I know we're successfully sticking to the shoreline. We should still be on course. According to my calculation, we will be seeing Ketchikan soon. Damned soon. But we keep taking on more of the rain and ocean.

Damn. I don't know how much longer we can survive out here in this old sieve.

CHAPTER THIRTY-THREE

Kera

Damn. This is taking too long.

I was sure we'd be to Ketchikan by now. Roni let me see the ship's location on the map tonight and our ETA for docking. What could be wrong? I don't think I got turned around, since the shoreline has always been and is still to our left. But something seems off. Or I've totally miscalculated how long it would take to reach Ketchikan. Damn, I'm not a neophyte when it comes to navigating in large and rough water in a small boat like this. Lake Michigan can be as wild as the ocean, and I've been out in it, at night and gotten myself back home. The lake taught me well. I take a deep breath and try to focus on avoiding protruding boulders.

We've been way ahead of the ship for some time and out of sight of it, thanks to our gradual curving around the coastline. I've been about as patient as I can be. Damn, where in hell are the lights of Ketchikan?

I'm confident I've made decent time, even with the rough water. Maybe the city is just ahead but lost power in the storm and went dark. No, even if it did, I'd still see lights on the big ships coming in or already docked there. Unless they too lost power... No, they wouldn't all lose power at the same time.

I stop bailing, pull out my flashlight, and scan the area.

Lillian starts crying again and quits bailing. She'd only just begun to help out a few minutes ago. I raise my hand to my forehead to keep my brain from exploding from irritation. My fingers hit a dangling strip of gauze that's come undone. No wonder, in this weather with all the rain and me sweating. I'm lucky that it hasn't become totally released from my head. I stuff it back up under my cap and pull my hat back down tighter. I can't fix the bandaging now. I probably don't need it anymore. At this point, it doesn't really matter if the women think I'm Dee. But I won't take it off. It would confuse them more than they already are, especially Lillian who's emotionally unstable.

I'm sure—well mostly—that we left the bay where Petersburg is located and haven't mistakenly got turned around and reentered it. Otherwise, the land would be on my right and I'd be seeing Petersburg's lights ahead of me, which I don't. I keep scanning the area with my light, not that it projects very far. Damn it. The land has been on my left all the way. I've made sure of that, so I must be headed in the direction of Ketchikan.

So, where the fuck am I?

The last thing I want to do is to ask for help from Coleen or Lillian. Although if Lillian weren't here, I'd discuss our situation with Coleen, who keeps bailing like a machine. I'd have her on my team any day. But if I bring up my concern around Lillian, she'll become even more histrionic.

I fuckin' don't need that.

Then it hits me. The problem is, I've religiously followed the coastline, and at some point, it had to have taken me around and into another bay. It has to be a bay that I didn't notice when I looked at the navigational map. That means if I were to keep going around in this bay, I'd eventually make my way back out into the ocean and on a path to Ketchikan.

If I'm right, which I'm sure now that I am, instead of following around the bay, I could make a shortcut by crossing over to the other side. Then continue to keep following the land on my left. From there, I should be on my way back out into the ocean water and on course to my destination. I hope I can make good time and get back out into the ocean fast enough, well before the ship crosses the mouth of this bay—if it already hasn't. First, I need to add some gas to my motor. This little side trip cost me some fuel, besides time.

* * *

Shit! Ahead of me I see the ship. It's starting to cross the mouth of the bay ahead of me just as I'm about to get there.

Fuck, fuck, fuck!

If I leave the bay and go out into the ocean right now, I'll be spotted, especially since the storm clouds have let up. Even though there are still clouds, they're thinner and have breaks in them allowing for some starlight.

My heart flips over in my chest as the ship turns on its searchlight and scans. Before the light gets to me, I'm able to make an abrupt ninety-degree turn and scoot toward a small island in the bay that's halfway to the other side of this inlet. I hope I can get over there and out of sight before the searchlight picks up my skiff. My clunker barely makes cover before I see the light trail behind me. Whew!

I'm sure the captain isn't the only one looking for us now. He's undoubtedly alerted the bad guys out there who are waiting for the delivery of Coleen and Lillian—and now, me.

God, I hope Mandy is okay.

My heart's thumping so hard, I can feel it in my ears. In the back of my mind, I knew there was a good chance that our absence would be noticed before we docked, though I really hoped it wouldn't.

Our plan was for Mandy to depart immediately upon docking and to not worry about any of her possessions or luggage—to immediately get the hell off and out of sight. Thanks to the city map I found, we figured out a meet-up place. We both made sure to charge our phones, so they'd be ready when we got close to land. But if they were to suspect her of having a part in our disappearance, I don't think I should try to contact her. She could be in a situation where the sound of her phone might give her away, plus I don't think we're close enough to shore yet for either of us to have reception.

I work on my breathing...in and out, in and out. I can't allow myself to think about what might be going wrong on the ship. I need to stay calm to prepare for what might come next, and when it's time, keep moving.

My phone rings.

What a weird sound to hear when I'm out in the ocean in this situation. Surreal. Maybe it's my alarm clock. I shake my head. No, I'm not waking up. I'm not in a bad dream. I'm still in the ocean.

But since my phone's working, it has to mean we're pretty close to Ketchikan, at least within cell phone reach. Maybe it's Mandy. I fumble around in my jacket pockets. It's not there. I feel around and find it in my pants.

I see Vinny's name on the screen. What a time for him to call me. I can't believe it. Weird. I wonder if something has gone wrong with a case he's on. Well, I'm not really doing much but hiding behind an island from bad guys. I'm struck by irony of it all. I decide to answer it. Hell, might just as well find out what's going on in Michigan while I wait for the ship to pass by.

CHAPTER THIRTY-FOUR

Mandy

Mandy put her hand over her nose and mouth keep the smoke at bay as she made her way down the stairwell. She got to the bottom just as the captain fully realized that it was truly a case of all smoke and no fire. He was livid and blamed Wally for the whole incident. He didn't listen or believe Wally's protests to the contrary. So far, Wally hadn't betrayed her or Kera. He kept saying that he thought there was a fire, and he was trying to put it out and that maybe he exaggerated the part about the flames.

The captain had Wally by the collar of his shirt and lifted him so that only the toes of his shoes touched the floor. "I don't believe you, you little creep."

"I didn't do anything. I promise I didn't."

"Who else would do such a stupid thing?"

Wally's eyes bulged. "I didn't, I—"

"Who made this stupid smoke bomb then? Huh?" The captain's voice was getting louder.

People opened their doors all the way down the hall and peeked out. Others were leaving their cabins and gathering nearby to see what was going on, coughing and covering their faces from the smoke.

"I don't know, I don't know. I was just—"

"You will never board my ship again. Not one foot! Never!"

Hearing the captain tell Wally that he couldn't be on Dee's ship concerned Mandy, given Wally's obsession with her. How would he react to not being able to see Dee again? She watched him intently.

"You've been on every damned cruise of mine this summer," Captain James said. "I should've guessed you were up to something, but why this?"

"But, but..." Wally looked over at Mandy.

She stared back at him with her Aunt Margaret's stern eyes and raised eyebrow. She didn't dare leave until she knew what Wally would do or say. Would he take the blame for setting off the smoke bomb or continue to plead ignorance and innocence? Or would he give her and Kera up to the captain? If he did the latter, she'd need to go into hiding somewhere on the ship...fast. Just in case, she backed away until she was on the fringe of those gathered. She was ready to bolt on a moment's notice.

"If you don't tell me the truth this time, I'll have you arrested when we get to shore." The captain almost pulled Wally up off the floor completely. Those watching gasped.

"Okay, okay."

Mandy quickly slipped away while all eyes were focused on the captain and Wally.

* * *

"Agnes!"

"Yes sir?"

"Have you seen Deidre's friend, Mandy, this morning?" The captain barked out his words as he stomped into the galley.

"No," Agnes said curtly, maybe too curtly.

Mandy's heartbeat doubled, maybe tripled, as she listened from inside the galley's tiny bathroom. She tried to determine if Agnes's answer sounded guilty. Agnes had hidden her in the bathroom when she'd flown into the galley after leaving Wally to his about-to-give confession to the captain.

"And Coleen and Lillian, they haven't come in here this morning? Is that right?" The captain undoubtedly knew the answer, but he was obviously fishing to see how Agnes would handle that question.

"Uh, no. I was about to go and find out why the girls didn't show up. I needed to first finish getting food out of the freezer to thaw.

Good answer, Agnes. He's trying to trick you into confessing that you know what's going on with them.

"They won't be helping you this morning, Agnes. They've left the ship with Deidre in Mick's goddamned skiff. You're sure you didn't know anything about—"

"No, captain, no. I would tell you if I know."

"You better not have known," he grumbled.

Footsteps moved across the galley and drew closer to the bathroom.

Mandy reached up and locked the door.

"Who's in the bathroom?" The captain asked. Mandy watched the knob turn back and forth.

Mandy was sweating from fear and the close quarters, mostly fear.

"No one. Uh…well, I locked it. The toilet isn't working good. Mick said he was busy but would fix it before the trip back to Juneau. I don't want anyone to pee and not flush. I don't like to smell—"

"So, how are you going to open it for Mick to fix? Huh?" the captain asked in a sarcastic voice.

"I got the key, of course," Agnes snapped back and then her tone became more deferential. "I keep it locked, so the crew—ones who don't work in kitchen—don't come in here and use it. It smells up the place, and they get in my way."

"You should put a sign on it then."

"Good idea."

"Humph." Footsteps stomped off.

Mandy took a deep breath and let it out. Her heartbeat slowed down to double time.

*　*　*

Agnes brought her a cup of coffee and a bagel with cream cheese on it, but Mandy had little appetite, though she appreciated the coffee. Probably shouldn't have drunk it though. She certainly didn't need to kick up her anxiety any more than it already was.

Mandy heard, then saw a flurry of downloads coming in on her cell. The ship must be within a cell tower's reach. That meant they had to be close to Ketchikan. She quickly shut down her phone. All she would need is for it to ring or chirp when someone, besides Agnes, was in the galley.

Agnes peeked in to ask how Mandy was doing. Mandy noticed that she had taped an out-of-order sign onto the door. She offered Mandy more coffee, but Mandy refused. Just as Agnes was shutting the door, Mandy heard the captain's voice again.

"We've searched everywhere on this damned ship," he growled as he entered the galley.

Mandy had no idea if Captain James had noticed Agnes closing the bathroom door. If he did notice…

"Give me some of that coffee," he told her.

She heard coffee pouring into a cup right outside the bathroom.

"God damn it. I have five people scouring the place and still not a sign of her and nobody seems to have seen her. Are you sure that you haven't, Agnes?"

"I have not seen her." Agnes's voice was stern. Light footsteps walked away.

The captain slurped his coffee. It sounded like Agnes was now scouring something.

"You better not know a fucking thing about this, Agnes."

Scouring stopped. Silence.

"In fact, it's hard for me to believe you don't. You talk to Coleen and, what's-her-name, uh, Lillian every damned day. You must have known something was going on."

More silence until the scouring started up again.

"Well?"

"I told you, I don't know nothing about nothing." Agnes's voice didn't hold the same resolve as before.

Mandy held her breath and wondered when it would occur to the captain that the only place that probably hadn't been checked was this bathroom. What would it take for Agnes to breakdown and confess like Wally did? The captain had shown how intimidating he could be. Agnes had to be terrified of him.

This time heavy footsteps left.

Mandy took in a breath.

* * *

By the slowing and maneuvering of the ship, Mandy thought that they must be close to docking. When would it be safe to leave, she wondered. Hopefully Agnes would check for her as best she could, so Mandy would know when it'd be clear for her to get out of that bathroom. She and Kera had settled on a meeting place in Ketchikan, but she needed out of here first.

"Hey, Agnes. How are things going in here? We'll be docking soon." The voice was that of a woman, but who?

"I'm almost finished."

"I hope so. You'll need to direct the incoming food delivery shortly." It was Britt's voice.

"I know."

"The captain's still looking for Mandy. Did she come in here?" Britt's tone didn't sound angry, more of a sweet honey quality to it.

"No, I told the captain already I didn't see her today."

"Well, I just thought she might have come in after you talked to him."

"Nope."

"You do realize, don't you," Britt's voice stayed sweet but with a tinge of threat to it now, "that if those girls get away, it won't just be bad news for the captain and me. It will be bad news for you, too."

It took a minute for Mandy to absorb what Britt had said before she realized that Britt had to be involved in the human trafficking ring, too.

My God!

"Why me?" Agnes sounded confused. "They make me be here. I didn't do nothing bad. Nothing."

"That's not what the captain and I will tell them, Agnes." The previous kind and understanding, good-cop voice had morphed into the bad cop.

Silence.

Mandy was back to holding her breath, sweating, waiting, praying…

Hold on, Agnes, hold on! We just need to get to dock and you'll be a free woman again… I hope.

Footsteps approached the bathroom door. The doorknob jiggled back and forth.

Mandy held her breath.

"I'm not convinced this bathroom is out of order, Agnes," Britt said. "Open it!"

CHAPTER THIRTY-FIVE

Kera

Wow, I can't believe Vinny is in Ketchikan and all because he happened to call the hospital the day Dee and Moran left for Ketchikan. He probably got an earful from Moran about what I was up to. I'm glad she convinced him—or he convinced himself—that I could use some help.

I don't know why Rob flew his plane back to Michigan early. I thought we'd agreed that he would stay in Alaska until I was ready to go back. Something must have come up. It worked out for the better, since he was in Michigan and able to give Vinny a speedy lift out this way. I guess I'll have to thank Rob for not hanging around. I hope I live through this and can pay him back.

I'm close to Ketchikan's port as I follow about a kilometer behind the ship. I hold tight to the shoreline. Vinny said he'd scout out a spot for me to put in, someplace shallow before I reach the docks. He'll signal me with a flashlight when he sees me. It's almost daylight now, so his signal shouldn't be as noticeable as if it were really dark. Hopefully, it'll be good enough for us to pick up but not so bright as to draw attention from other boats in the area—like the one coming for Coleen and Lillian.

"You said you had a gun?" Coleen whispers to me, her eyes wide. She'd overheard me talking to Vinny. She'd followed my gaze when I spotted a yacht not that far from us.

"Yes." I pull up my pant leg and show it to her.

I also have two extra magazines in my pocket, not enough to hold off a gang of bad guys, but Vinny will be armed, too.

"I'm scared of guns." Lillian's eyes are saucer-sized. She stares at my piece like it might discharge at any moment.

"You should be more scared if Deidre didn't have one," Coleen tells her in a tone that sounds like she's lost her patience with Lillian, too.

There's no doubt in my mind that the captain has notified the guys at the other end of this human trafficking ring, and they're already looking for us. There's another problem. Our little tin craft is riding lower in the water, not only risking a total drop to the ocean's floor, but also our sinking outboard motor is struggling as it tries to push this bathtub to shore. It could—should say, will—shut down at any moment.

Lillian, whimpers, "I'm so scared." She's up to her calves in water, but at least she's stopped sobbing.

Coleen grabs my bailing can, hands it to Lillian, and hisses at her, "You need to start bailing if we're going to make it. Deidre has to watch for boulders and look for the signal from her friend."

To my surprise, Lillian takes the can and begins to heave water out of the boat. Maybe she finally decided we might make it. I don't want to discourage her, but we still have some major hurdles in order to get her to freedom.

"Look." Lillian points. "Flashing light."

Coleen and I follow the direction of her outstretched arm.

I see it. Has to be Vinny. I turn our skiff toward the light.

Then I spot a boat out a ways but headed in our direction. It's yacht-sized, a suitable vessel to pick up Coleen and Lillian and transport them to wherever they're supposed to go. But that craft is way too large to get close to the shallow waters at the shore where we're headed. It will need the deep water of the docks to put in, but it's definitely headed our way. Hmm. I bet they'll drop anchor in deep water and use a dingy to come ashore. We need get to land. Fast. I ask the engine to give it all she's got.

She gives it a last shot and dies.

We coast in a little until the waves have their way with us. Without being able to steer, we get tossed about and end up wedged between two boulders. I don't have time or ability to dislodge the boat. The water isn't as frigid as out farther in the ocean but it's damned cold. Luckily, we don't have that far to go.

I hope the women can swim.

I forgot life jackets.

* * *

Though struggling, Coleen makes her way through the water. In places, it's shallow enough for our feet to touch bottom but actually easier to swim. Lillian is having problems. The waves beat her around, and she's barely able to maneuver through the water. I grab her by the front of her sweatshirt and flip her on her back. It's almost all I can do to get myself to shore in these conditions but I also have to try to help her. The waves try their best to take me under, and it doesn't help that Lillian is back in panic mode.

I hear a dog's bark coming from shore. I look up to see what appears to be the shadowy image of a dog next to Vinny.

Damn, it's Lakota.

My dog jumps in the water and swims out our way. She must have heard my voice, or Vinny sent her out to help.

Lakota finally gets to Lillian and me. I swear I see a smile on my pooch's face.

"Good girl, Lakota!" I pat her on the head.

Lakota yips back at me.

"Here, take." I hold Lillian's sweatshirt in front of the dog's mouth. Lakota grips the cloth between her teeth and helps me keep the woman afloat.

I look back to see two people download a skiff from the yacht.

* * *

"We got to get Moran and Dee out of her apartment, fast," I tell Vinny as we head toward Dee's place, soaking wet. "I'm sure they have her address."

He nods and starts to say something.

"I'm freezing," Lillian says through chattering teeth, so I don't hear what Vinny was trying to say.

"We all are, Lillian," I snap back. I've about had it with that woman, but still I address her concern. "We'll see if we can scrounge up some dry clothes at Deidre's place, something for us all. But it'll have to be fast."

Coleen looks at me. "What did you say?"

Lillian caught my gaffe, too. She narrows her eyes at me.

"That was confusing, I know, but you'll have to wait a bit before things become, well, understandable. It's a long story." I realize I've outed myself by saying "Deidre's place" instead of saying "my place."

I could try to cover up my mistake, but really, what's the point? I know my response was clear as mud, but they don't say anything more. Given our situation, I suppose the confusion that I cause isn't that important.

I continue to check back but don't see anyone that seems to be following or coming after us. We hustle along but don't run so fast that we attract attention. Luckily, from what Vinny said, we're only about a quarter of a mile from Dee's place.

Then, out of the corner of my eye, I spot two guys emerging from around a corner of an old wooden building situated on the harbor side. They scan the area. When they look our way, they start moving in our direction but hold back a bit. I try not to act as though I've noticed them. I alert Vinny without making a big deal of it so not to upset Coleen and Lillian or tip off our followers.

They might not be the guys from the skiff, but we need to find out. Vinny and I have worked together a long time and have been in other tense situations. We think alike, so pretty much know what the other one will do in most any circumstance without having to say anything. He's had hours in Ketchikan to get to know the place, I only had a brief glance at the city map. I don't know, though, how familiar he is with the area. But knowing Vinny, he's scoped out the place as best he could in the time he had. I give him the nod to take the lead.

Vinny slows a bit. I realize he's doing that so we won't signal the guys following us that we're on to them. We cross the street away from the harbor, timing it so that two tourist buses will pass right after we get across. It will leave the two men on the curb for a moment, waiting for traffic to clear.

We're coming to the town area. I glance around and sure enough, the buses have done the job for us. The guys are still waiting for traffic to clear. I tell Coleen they'll need to follow Vinny, stay alert, go where he goes, do what he says. Coleen nods and tells Lillian. Thankfully, Lillian isn't freaking out on us. We come to a corner. Vinny takes a quick turn and we duck into a café. Our followers couldn't have seen us slip into this place. I know what Vinny is up to. Every restaurant kitchen, by code, must have a door to the outside.

We bust through the kitchen and out the back door before anyone can say a word to us, but the expressions on their faces says it all. I bet some customers get overcooked or burnt eggs because of our pass-through.

We lost them.

Or at least I hope we did.

We travel around for a while and turn here and there until we slip between two buildings and to the door of a hotel called the Gilmore. We go in and head up the stairs to the second floor. Vinny pulls out a key, and we enter an empty guest room.

"Your sister and Moran are in the room next door," Vinny says. "I got them out of Dee's apartment right after I called you."

"Thanks, Vinny. I should have guessed you'd think to do that."

"Coleen and Lillian can stay in this room," Vinny says then adds, "I put both rooms under my name."

I'm about to go next door to see Dee and Moran then think better of it. If I take the time to see them now, which I'd love to do, especially see my sister, I'll waste precious time. Mandy's still on the ship, and I have no idea what's happening to her. I glance out the window of the hotel. I can see the docks are within a stone's throw just across the street, mostly lined with huge tourist ships. I can't locate our ship. It has to be docked farther down the line.

I need to get to her before those guys or someone on the ship does.

CHAPTER THIRTY-SIX

Mandy

Mandy charged out of the galley's bathroom at Britt like a football halfback shooting through the line. She lay Britt flat then flew out of the galley, not without a little pain to her own body, as well. She shook it off and kept moving.

She'd heard the ship maneuver up to the dock, but it would be a while before the passengers would be allowed to disembark. Now that she was out of the galley's bathroom, she had to find another place to hide until she could get off the ship.

But where?

There were passengers in the cafeteria and lounge area, luggage in tow and ready to depart. But it was obvious that many passengers had to be in their cabins, probably doing some last-minute packing. She slowed down her pace not wanting to appear like she was trying to escape. Britt would soon be up off the floor and after her, and Mandy wanted to avoid people noticing her scurrying through and therefore being able to point out where she was headed. She had no idea where to go but kept moving and turning different directions throughout the ship. As she moved along, she checked out and eliminated possible hiding spots that Britt and others would most likely look for her.

Voices drifted out from an opened cabin door ahead. As she got closer, she realized it was Bev's gruff smoker's voice.

Would she help me? Bev might help but Charlie would be in there, too, and Charlie doesn't like Dee. She doesn't like me, either, judging from the last run-in.

But as Mandy passed, she didn't see Charlie in the cabin. She turned around, ducked in, and closed the door, startling Bev.

"Uh, uh…" Bev gathered her composure, cocked her head, and said in an authoritative voice, "Excuse me, may I ask—?"

"I need to hide under your bed, if I could." Mandy realized how bizarre that sounded, even to her. "I can't explain it to you now. People are looking for me, but I know you trust, uh, Dee." She almost said "Kera." "My need to hide is all about her welfare."

Bev squinted at her. "About Deidre's welfare?"

"Yes, Deidre…Really it is…Like I said—"

"Truly my dear, those sentences are desultory."

"I know they sound disjointed, but believe me, they're related. Many lives are at stake."

"Hmm." Bev scowled and pursed her lips, but Mandy could tell she was considering whether to believe her.

A knock on the door.

Bev reached for the handle.

Mandy's heart leapt to her throat. "Please don't open that door," she whispered. "Please."

"Who is it?" Bev asked through the door.

"It's Britt. I'm looking for someone."

Mandy shook her head as she stared into Bev's eyes. She mouthed, "No. Please don't open it."

Bev seemed to be trying to decide what was going on, what to do. Her hand was firmly gripping the doorknob.

"Please open. I need to check if you've seen someone."

Mandy noticed that Bev had two large suitcases on top of the bed. One was most likely hers, and the other had to be Charlie's, so she should be able to fit under the bed. She'd have to hope that Bev wouldn't give her away and would play along. Or her other option was to try another halfback maneuver if Bev opened the door. But even if charging and flattening Britt again gave her an escape a second time, where would she hide once she was out?

Not great options but…
She quickly slid under the bed and was greeted by two empty bourbon bottles.

* * *

Charlie came back to the room seconds after Britt left. She and Bev grabbed their suitcases and left. A moment after they'd closed the door, Bev returned to the room, bent down, and shoved her business card under the bed. "I'd so love to hear about all this sometime," she said. "Good luck." Then she left.

The noise from the passengers leaving the ship died down. Mandy wondered how long she should remain under the bed. She knew the captain and Britt would be out searching, waiting for her to surface. Kera wouldn't board the ship since she expected Mandy to meet up in their designated spot in Ketchikan.

Footsteps came down the hallway and neared Bev's room. The door opened and closed. Then the footsteps moved on.

It must be close to the time when she could get off the ship, since someone had just checked the room. Maybe this would be her best chance to escape. Maybe.

With her ear to the door of Bev's cabin, Mandy tried to determine if anyone might be in that section of the hallway. So far, she hadn't heard anything. She'd been there at the cabin doorway too long as she tried to drum up enough courage to leave. Finally, she took a deep breath and cracked open the door. Seeing no one, she opened it wider, stuck her head out, and checked around.

Nobody in sight.

Her shoes were making too much noise. She removed them and headed to the back of the ship where the open-air deck was located and her yoga class was held, close by the stairwell. She was on the top floor of the ship. From there, she'd need to go down one flight of stairs to the level where the ship's exit was located. She moved slowly, thinking slow must be quieter than fast. She passed one cabin after another, all closed doors. But just ahead, she observed that one cabin door was open. She approached carefully and peeked into it. Empty.

Whew!

She reached the end of the hallway where the open area was and stopped. The staircase she needed to get out was located on the other side of the ship. She had the width of the ship to traverse before getting there. Not that far if you weren't trying to escape undetected. She took a deep breath.

Just as she was ready to step out onto the open deck, she thought she'd heard something. A flapping noise. The wind must have caught hold of something, but she couldn't see what it was.

She stepped out into the open area and stood still. Why had she stopped? Being scared wasn't a good reason. It was no time for paralysis, she warned herself. But her feet weren't getting the message. They were locked in place. She sucked in a deep breath and felt them release, but—

An arm from behind wrapped around her neck, squeezed, and pulled her in.

She summoned latent skills she'd learned from somewhere back in a self-defense training. She allowed herself to be moved into the body behind her, then pushed her elbow into the person's gut, and twisted out of the headlock. Kera had told her that if she'd practiced it enough, it would become automatic. And it was, much to her surprise.

But now what?

In her training, Kera had said the best next thing was to run and get away. But Britt was in front of her and blocking her access to the stairs. The only place she could go was back down the hallway and to another staircase on the rear of the ship. She turned and ran, but Britt was faster and circled around in front of her, again blocking her way. Mandy ran toward the guardrail at the edge of ship, the farthest place she could get from Britt. No place to go from there except into the ocean. She'd seen people in movies run to get away, only to end up being trapped. That's just what she'd done. She turned and faced Britt. She stared at the gun Britt pointed at her head. Mandy couldn't breathe.

Britt smirked. "Well, well, well. I found you, and now you die."

Mandy did have one alternative. If she could convince Britt that someone was behind her and she could climb over the rail fast enough, she could jump into the harbor's deep water. That is, if Britt didn't shoot her dead on her way down.

The odds weren't good, but it was her only chance.

CHAPTER THIRTY-SEVEN

Kera

Mandy hasn't shown up at the visitor's center where we'd planned to meet. She must not have gotten off yet. Lakota and I are waiting for her, of all places, behind a totem pole. I'd read that Ketchikan was full of them, like maybe more totem poles than anywhere else per capita…or something like that. Fortunately, this one is conveniently placed for me to be able to watch the ship and allow me to see when Mandy gets off. Vinny's job is to get ahold of the authorities, whoever they are around here, and let them know what's going on, or more likely convince them about what's happening. Getting them to understand and believe us concerns me since it might take some doing. I'm not big on cops but for the first time, probably ever, I'll be more than happy to have them show up.

On my way over here, Wally rushed by me with his suitcases swinging wildly. I don't think he saw me. As he started to break into a run, I called after him but couldn't get him to stop. He was hell-bent for somewhere. I don't know whether I should be worried. Or grateful that he's alive, because it all worked out okay. I would have chased him down, but I had to make a fast decision. Was it more important to get to Wally or get over here to look for Mandy? Though I sure wish I could have found out how things had gone down, ultimately, it's water under the bridge and nothing I can do about it. I just hope Mandy is safe. I take a deep breath then another.

Passengers have been trickling off the ship but, still, no Mandy. The longer I wait, the more nervous I become. I realize by now the captain knows I've taken off with Coleen and Lillian. Did Mandy get caught? Oh Jesus. Is that why she didn't make it to our spot? Hasn't left the ship yet? My heart pounds, like it's going to blow through my chest.

Lakota barks.

I see a woman approach us. It's not anyone from the ship. I tell Lakota to stop barking. I don't want to attract attention.

"What a beautiful creature he is." The woman reaches for Lakota.

Lakota barks again.

"She doesn't let people near her when she's on duty," I tell the woman. I pet Lakota and tell her it's okay. I wish the woman would just go away.

"What's his name?" The woman's undaunted.

"Her name is Lakota," I say as nicely as I can, emphasizing the proper pronoun for Lakota. "She's a working dog and shouldn't have outside attention right now." In other words, get lost.

"Well, she's one stately, handsome animal."

"Thank you," I say. "She certainly is." I don't let up on my vigilance, not appreciating this interruption.

"I'm sorry," the woman says. "I couldn't tell that your beautiful girl is a working dog. She isn't wearing identifying outerwear that would let me know that." The woman smiles and walks off.

The woman's right. Lakota was with Moran, and she'd removed her vest. Lakota also isn't leashed. When Lakota's tethered, it's mostly for other people's comfort, as well as letting her know she has a task to perform. Off the leash, my pooch follows along wherever I go, always watchful. She'd never leave my side unless, of course, I'd ask her to do something. She's obedient and can perform a boatload of commands. I give her a scratch behind her ear and go back to my full-time watching, my eyes glued on the ship, glancing around periodically, keeping a lookout to make sure those guys who followed us aren't nearby. God damn, the longer I wait here the more terrified I am that Mandy's in trouble.

It has been too long. Still no Mandy. Come to think of it, no Agnes, either. I haven't seen a passenger debark in the last ten minutes. They must all be off by now, because many crew members have left the ship as well. Roni told me that the crew is given a treat of a few hours shore leave when they first arrive to go and have breakfast ashore. Then they return to finish their duties. And it seems most of them have left.

Ah, I spot Britt. I wonder if I should approach her and ask about Mandy. I've got to do something soon. I can't just keep waiting here and worrying myself to death. Talking to Britt should be okay since she's Dee's girlfriend. It's possible she doesn't even know that I took the women and left the ship. Or if she knows, it's likely she would be sympathetic to me, though maybe puzzled by my behavior. Well shit, I have to try something, but I sure can't let her see Lakota.

"Lakota, stay here," I command, giving her a hand signal. "I'll be back, girl."

Britt notices me approaching. She looks surprised to see me then smiles. I'm relieved.

"Glad to see you," she says as I come up to her.

"Yeah." I don't know what else I can say without knowing what she's aware of about me leaving the ship, so I just ask, "Have you seen Mandy?"

"Uh, no. I haven't."

"Huh." Britt's response didn't help me understand what she might know. Damn it.

"When did you last see her?" Britt says.

I skip over that question. "I expected to meet up with her, but she didn't show."

"If you'd like, I'll help you find her," Britt says enthusiastically. "I don't have anything in mind to do other than walk up and down Front Street for some exercise and new scenery, since I've already eaten my breakfast."

"Okay, as long as I'm not keeping you from anything." Given Britt's demeanor and what she's said, or didn't say, I'm guessing she doesn't know anything about my disappearance from the ship. Or she doesn't care and wants to hang with me and hope I will remember her.

"Come on," Britt puts her hand on my shoulder. "She's got to still be somewhere on the ship."

"Okay."

Since I can't really ask Britt anything, my thoughts swirl in my head as I try to determine what my situation might be. Britt didn't mention anything about Lillian or Coleen not being on board this morning. She would know they weren't since she's in charge of the kitchen. It was announced that there would only be bagels, juice, and coffee available this morning, and Agnes could easily handle it. Ah, it hits me. Lillian and Coleen probably wouldn't have been scheduled in the kitchen to work. They'd most likely be doing housekeeping duties. Damn. What am I thinking? By this time, they'd be gone. The captain would've already handed them off to someone else under the guise of sending them to better jobs. Britt would know that. Not seeing them would be expected, so no concern to anyone, let alone Britt.

The captain has to still be on that ship. But where? He and Mick might be in the engine room. I know they're still concerned about the engine. But wouldn't the captain be more worried about the two young women missing? He could be anywhere. I need to stay clear of him and find Mandy. My heart won't stop pounding.

"Let's check my cabin," I say as we enter the ship though I doubt she's there. She might have left me a note. My eyes flit around, hoping I don't see Captain James.

"Yeah," Britt agrees, "she might still be packing her things."

I know that Mandy was ready to get off the ship, fast, with or without her luggage, but even so, she'd packed already. Even if she weren't feeling well, she wouldn't lay down. She'd be getting the hell out. It feels like my mind is on speed.

We go into my cabin. She's not there, and I don't see a note. She's not in the tiny bathroom. I kneel and look under the bed.

"Really?" Britt looks at me like possibly I've lost more than my memory.

"Well, you never know, do you? I guess I'm desperate for places to look."

Britt laughs, but little does she know that it wouldn't be the first time Mandy hid under a bed on this ship. Under these circumstances, it wouldn't have surprised me to find her there.

"Since she's not here," Britt says, "she must be in a public area, somewhere, maybe the lounge or upper deck or boat launch. Someplace like that. She might be saying goodbye to someone. You know how that goes."

"Uh-huh." I know that's not the case.

We go through the lounge and into the dining room. I don't see anyone, let alone Mandy. Then I spot Agnes in the galley. She looks over at me.

"Have you seen Mandy?" I ask.

Agnes's jaws are clenched. She shakes her head, but her eyes say something else. And I can almost smell her fear. Since I'm on the ship, she must wonder what went wrong. The plan was for Agnes to get off the ship ASAP when we docked and get to where we'd all planned to meet up.

I don't understand why she's still here.

Until I see the captain come out of the galley, obviously having used the galley bathroom because he's zipping up his fly.

Britt grabs me from behind and locks my arms against my body, keeping me from moving. I'm about to try and break her hold when I see the captain's gun aimed it at me. And there's no way I can get to my piece in my leg holster without being shot first.

I didn't see this coming, at least not Britt's part. That bitch has been playing me along, and Mandy too. Now I realized why she wanted to keep track of my memory issues.

"I'm really sorry, Deidre," the captain says, "but this has to be the end of the ride for you. I liked you. I really did. I even thought you were a good addition to our crew, but you've turned on me, like Nona did. So now, I'm going to have to get rid of you, too."

He actually looks like this is unpleasant for him. I guess selling women into slavery works for him, but he finds murder distasteful. Everyone has their red line.

"Roni's off the ship, right?" The captain looks at Britt for confirmation.

"Yes, sir. I got her to leave the ship, early, so she wouldn't be around to see anything."

"Good. Keeping this operation from her hasn't been easy. I have to get her a transfer, get someone who's not so pushy and checking on stuff all the time. Jesus, I thought she'd never stop asking me to check my passenger roster."

He looks at Agnes. "Get over there with her." He shoves her toward me. "You're obviously in on this, too. That toilet works just fine, now doesn't it?" He throws a nasty look her way.

Britt lets go of me and pushes me toward Agnes. As we crash together, I grab Agnes to keep her from falling. "Agnes has nothing to do with this," I say to the captain.

"And I suppose your friend Mandy didn't have anything to do with it, either."

I open my mouth to say that neither of them did, but before I can—

"Doesn't really matter, we've already taken care of your friend. She won't be talking to anyone. Ever."

"Mandy?" I hope I didn't understand him correctly.

"Yes, Mandy."

"You...you killed her?" I ask again, desperately wanting a different answer.

"Well, no, I didn't. Britt handled it."

I look at Britt. She smirks and nods. "I thought when I sent you out in the ocean with Mick's skiff—that I fixed up—to look for my 'missing person,' you wouldn't make it back in, but here we are."

Anger rises in me like an eruption of scalding water from a geyser. I can feel it pushing at the top of my head as it tries to burst through. I know what comes next. It will be Iraq. It will be bombs. It will be seeing my old girlfriend Kelly flying into a million pieces. I need to interrupt this flashback scenario. Fast. Or it will be the last time I have it.

Breathe, in and out, breathe, in and out, breathe, in and out...

I reach down as though Lakota is next to me. My fingers push through her fur. The vivid image allows my fingers to feel her fur, her warm skin. It calms me.

Then it occurs to me. Lakota.

I let out an eardrum-piercing whistle, startling everyone and freezing the moment.

The captain's eyes are off me, searching around, so I charge him and knock him over and fall on top of him. I struggle to get the gun out of his hand.

I will kill this bastard then Britt.

Britt tries to pull me off him, but Agnes attacks her. I don't think Agnes can do that much harm, but she at least keeps Britt busy. I pound the captain's hand that holds his gun, finally causing him to drop it. But it skids out of my reach. We both scramble toward it. Unfortunately, his arms are longer than mine.

He's about to grab it again when I hear Lakota barking as she tears toward us. She pounces on the captain, snarling, and grabs onto his arm with her vice-like jaws. She bites down.

"Stop! Stop!" the captain cries out. Lakota ignores him and shakes his arm back and forth in her mouth, like caught prey. The captain is screaming, but he's still in pursuit of the gun that's just out of his reach.

As I try to get up, Britt breaks free from Agnes and jumps on me. I'm able to shake her off and slam her to the floor. With that, she's apparently done with this scrimmage. She jumps up and breaks full speed toward the ship's exit.

I pull my gun out from my leg holster. The captain is stretching out for his free arm. I need to get to his gun and kick it out of his reach... Too late. He's got it and has it pointed at my dog who hasn't let go of his other arm.

Two shots ring out...

* * *

I don't know where I am, but I'm lying on the ground and hear water running, like a river or a stream. My shoulder and arm are in pain. I didn't feel them hurt when I was fighting, though they hurt like hell now. But not as much as my soul. My head is on Agnes's lap. She looks down at me and wipes away my tears.

Mandy is dead.

I can't stop crying. I don't remember how or when I got here, but it doesn't matter. I'm never going to leave this spot. I'm never going to stop crying. Agnes is saying something to me, but I can't understand her words through my pain. The few words that do pop up seem unrelated, with no context for my throbbing heart, no meaning to lessen my misery...

* * *

A dog's tongue slurps my face. I don't feel like I can't move my head, but I can look around. We're outside, somewhere, and I see that Agnes is still here with me.

It's dusk, and it's getting cold. Lakota is stretched out beside me, her face close to mine. She whimpers and licks me again, warm and moist, comforting me. My hand touches her. My fingers move back and forth through her fur.

How long have I been here?

I don't care.

I close my eyes…

* * *

"Deidre, Deidre," Agnes says. She runs her hand over my head and pets my hair. "Deidre, we need to…"

Huh? Oh yeah, she thinks I'm Deidre. Of course she does.

My god. Deidre.

My sister.

Where is she?

Is she okay?

I've got to find her.

* * *

I don't know where Deidre lives, but I do know she's in the hotel. Or was anyway. I've got to find her. I struggle to get up and try to get my head together. I lost Mandy. But I still have my sister…I hope.

I get up, brush myself off, steady myself.

"Come on, Agnes, I've got somebody for you to meet."

CHAPTER THIRTY-EIGHT

Kera

I finally make it to the hotel, but they've left. The clerk has a note for me from Dee. It says that Vinny has taken them to her place and gives me her address. Now I know where to find them and feel okay about their being at Dee's—sort of okay—since Vinny is with them. I continue to assure myself that Vinny knows what he's doing. But I don't know what might have happened after I left to find Mandy. It feels like the air goes out of me every time I think about Mandy.

Agnes, Lakota, and I leave the hotel and make our way to Dee's place. I don't know how much farther I can go. My body feels heavy and I can hardly move. It's like I have a rope around me connected to an anchored ship and I'm forced to try and pull it from its mooring.

Emotionally, I've flatlined.

I'll never be the same again. I've lost my Mandy. If it weren't for Dee, I would drop right here and never get up.

At last, we approach the place where Dee lives. It says on the sign in front, "Mary Bergin's Boarding House."

I knock on the door.

"Why are you knocking?" a gray-haired, portly woman with a ponytail asks as she opens the door and sees me.

"My sister lives here," I tell her.

The woman tilts here head, squints, and gives me a confused look.

"I'm Deidre's twin sister," I clarify, helping the woman make sense of what she's seeing in front of her.

That brings a head-jerk reaction from Agnes. Although she doesn't say anything, I can tell that information's tossing around in her brain.

"I'll be." The woman smiles. "Deidre never told me she had a twin. You sure could have fooled me that you weren't Deidre. Well, I guess you did." She laughs and invites me in, pointing to the stairs. "Your sister's room is on the second floor, third room on the right. It's certainly been busy up there today." She looks down at Lakota. "Beautiful dog you got there."

"Mind if I bring her up with me?" I ask.

"Please do." The woman smiles and steps back for us to enter.

We reach Dee's door. She answers when I knock. "Oh my god, oh my god! We were so worried. What happened to you?"

Before I can explain anything, she spreads her arms and we melt into each other. We hold on tight. Neither of us wants to let go and don't separate until I hear Vinny's voice.

"I was about to go out and look for you," he says. "But I had to wait for the FBI to leave." Vinny gives me a hug. "They're interested in talking to you, too."

"I bet," I mumble. "I left a dead body on the ship."

That gets stunned looks, though no one says anything to me.

"The FBI?" I ask him. I know I'll need to talk to them about what happened on the boat, but not yet. One thing is clear now. I know why everyone is safe, being here with cops all around. "Where are they?"

"Right now," Deidre says, "they're in Mrs. Bergin's stitting room, said they needed to talk and make phone calls."

I hadn't seen any marked cars when I came, but then it occurs to me that the FBI doesn't drive regular cop cars and I did see a large dark van accoss the street.

"Yup." Vinny nods. "They came in a flash when I called them. Apparently, both the Coast Guard and the FBI have been surveilling this group for a while now. They didn't mention anything about someone being dead on the ship, though." He frowns. "Then they wouldn't, would they? They hold information close to their vests."

Vinny looks at me expecting more about the dead body, but I'm not up to it. Moran is now holding me tight and rubbing my back, like she does when I'm upset. I don't feel like telling Vinny or anybody what happened.

I just want to wake up from my nightmare.

"Up until this point," Vinny continues, "the authorities didn't have the goods on them. Looks like they will now, thanks to you and your sister."

"What a terrible thing they were doing," Moran says. "It's hard to believe there are people in the world who'd do such a thing."

I turn to Agnes. "And thanks to Agnes, too." That makes me realize that there are two people missing here. "Where are Lillian and Coleen?"

"Coleen has a cousin here in Ketchikan," Vinny says. "She and Lillian are staying with her and her family until the FBI is done questioning them, which, by the way, you and Dee will have to hang around here for a while too. They want to interview Dee some more and, of course, you."

"I've given them my statement," Dee says, "as much as I know."

Vinny turns to me. "Yeah, Dee got into this whole situation thinking she was helping women get jobs, not knowing what was really going on."

"I can't believe what I was part of." Dee's tears start to flow. "When Nona found out, she was killed, pushed overboard. Oh god. Then they tried to kill me, thinking Nona had told me the truth of what was going on, which of course she did."

"Who pushed you?" I ask.

"I don't remember. I don't recall much of anything about that time, only that I went on a hike and stopped to meditate. Well, more like I tried to figure out what I was going to do. I was so upset about Nona, about people on board basically telling me I was crazy about someone going overboard, along with knowing that I'd been involved in slave trafficking. That's it. That's all I can remember until I woke up from the coma and in the hospital. It's a big dark gap in my memory."

"Was Britt on that hike?" I ask.

"Uh…yes. Yes, she was. At the time, I thought it was odd that she was coming. Normally she didn't go on hikes."

"Were you and she ever involved?" I ask. "Romantically?"

"Heavens no. I mean, she was nice enough, but it was never like that between us. I wasn't involved with anyone, if that's your next question."

I'm convinced it was Britt who did it. I tell her and ask, "Did you ever find out that Britt was part of the ring?"

"No." Dee's looks at me as though I'd told her I was straight. "That's really hard to believe. Good grief, I knew she managed staff and the women as well, but not that she was a part of it, knowingly. Nona was only aware that it was the captain's moneymaking scheme. She thought we were all being duped by just him."

"Well, Britt sure was part of it, and she's out there somewhere. She took off when I was busy dealing with the captain." I didn't say killing the captain but that sparked Vinny's need to know again.

"Back to the body on the ship, you mentioned," Vinny says. "We moved on from that so fast, you didn't finish what you were about to say."

Not only do I feel heavy, like I'd gained two hundred pounds, but my coping abilities are on empty. I'm depleted, and my spirit is nowhere in sight. I know it's weird, probably something my therapist would be concerned about, but killing Captain James seems like a mere blip on the screen of my life in all that's happened this past week. Putting two bullets into him is not even a sweet revenge for me—that would assume it's sweet, which it's not. It's just a period at the end of one week from hell. Nothing is sweet, never will be again, now that Mandy's gone.

I'm running on fumes. Nothing left inside.

But what I say is, "I don't want to talk about it anymore."

"Come here, honey. Why don't you lie down?" Moran, my makeshift mother says. She reads me so well.

I'm about to lie down when the door to the bathroom opens…

And an image of Mandy comes out, toweling her hair dry.

I'm stunned. In fact, I'm convinced that I'm hallucinating or seeing a hologram.

Her image rushes over to me. "I thought I heard you out here. Oh god, I'm so glad you finally got here. I was worried to death."

I reach out. My hand doesn't go through her. She must be real. Maybe.

"Where have you been?" Mandy asks. "I've been so scared that something horrible happened to you. I went to the spot we talked about, but you weren't there. Maybe—"

"You worried! Jesus, I thought you were dead! I thought Britt killed you." Mandy and I hug and hold each other tight. I don't think a hallucination or hologram would feel so warm, although I'm still not totally convinced she's real. But everyone in the room seems to see and hear her, too.

"Well, she tried," she says. "I took a high dive off the ship and swam to shore. No worse than off the high board really. But in college meets, I never had anyone shooting at me when I was performing a dive. That part was frightening, but mostly only as I think about it now." Mandy holds up her hands that are still trembling.

"No other dive has been that important," Moran says, shaking her head. "I don't know what kind of scores you received in college, but I'd have to give her a ten on that one."

Everyone else laughs.

I don't.

I still can't get myself to believe I have her in my arms, breathing. As far as my weary mind knows, I can't be one hundred percent certain that I'm not seeing things, or finally having a good dream instead of a nightmare. And if I am in either of these altered states, let's just call it real. Because I don't want out.

Finally, Dee, Mandy, and I sit down on the edge of the bed and join hands. I have them snugged up close on either side of me. If I could suspend time, I'd do it. Just sit here in this moment and let eternity move on without us...

Bella Books, Inc.

Women. Books. Even Better Together.

P.O. Box 10543
Tallahassee, FL 32302

Phone: 800-729-4992
www.bellabooks.com

CPSIA information can be obtained
at www.ICGtesting.com
Printed in the USA
JSHW011609061219
2843JS00001B/5